GODSPEED,
CEDAR KEY

MICHAEL PRESLEY BOBBITT

APHRODITOIS BOOKS

For Liam, the geometric center of the universe.

CONTENTS

1

THE GRAY

By the time the council voted, 3 to 2, to bring down the Number Four Bridge that separated the island from the mainland, and post round-the-clock sentries, it was clear to just about everyone that life would never go back to the way it was. The only people coming across the bridge anymore were stragglers from nearby Sumner. They came looking for refuge or solace or just a bite to eat. The islanders had listened to their determined mayor in the wake of the escalation and made the kind of preparations that those across the channel had not. For them, the boundaries of the known world now began with the channel and ended with the Waccasassa Bay in the Gulf of Mexico.

Everything beyond that was lost.

It's not easy to destroy a bridge, in the best of times. When everyone gathered in the city park to work out the logistics of how it would be done, it seemed they would have to settle on a long project with sledgehammers and pickaxes.

"That'll take forever," John Mitchell bellowed.

He was a massive man—tall, wide, and loud. For thirty-two years, he ran the water and sewer service on the island, becoming invaluable as the only person who really knew where all the pipes and lines were. If the mayor was the figurehead of island leadership, John Mitchell had been the grizzled sergeant in the literal trenches of the town, keeping the water running and the toilets flushing. That kind of power transcends the ballot box, and the economy with which he used words added emphasis to everything he said.

"I'll sink that joker in half a second if no one objects."

"I'm not picking up a sledgehammer if I don't have to," replied the mayor.

"I know we still got laws. I ain't real clear on which ones still matter and which ones don't, but I don't want to hear nothing about how I came to have a little dynamite."

"How much is a little?" asked the mayor.

"Enough."

Cedar Key is a southern town. It lies at the western terminus of State Road 24 in rural Levy County, an hour's drive from Gainesville and the University of Florida. The town is mostly situated on Way Key, one of a cluster of thirteen barrier islands that comprise the Cedar Keys National Wildlife Preserve. They range in size from 1-acre to 165-acres, beginning just across the Number Four Bridge from the mainland and extending roughly five miles into the Gulf of Mexico. Most of the islands are deserted or never contained any meaningful development.

With a few breaks here and there, for most of the past thirty years someone from the David family had sat in the middle seat on the town council, behind the little typed sign that read *The Mayor*.

Hayes David, its present occupant, was first elected when he was just 23 years old. He had assumed the office almost by ascension from his father Mark, who ran the largest fish house on the island before a statewide ban of commercial net fishing upended a generational way of life and a business that had fed a century of Cedar Key Davids. They were not, particularly, political folk. They had occupied Levy County continuously for eight generations since their earliest forbears sailed from Denmark and built their first makeshift homestead on the lost shore of the Waccasassa. Their foray into governing was a utilitarian answer to the idealism of outsiders whose plans for the island never seemed to include keeping it the way it was.

Hayes had been at the helm for most of the past 20 years, ruling by merit and by fiat on the singular mandate that someone had to stand in the gap between an island lost in time and those that would seek to change it into an amalgam of every other coastal place in Florida. Despite his occasional flash of temper and an aloofness that kept him a step apart and above many of his fellow citizens, Hayes was the implacable wall into which the development plans of yankees and mainlanders would reliably crash. This alone made his perpetual, reluctant, candidacy for an office that paid almost nothing and cost at least a pound of flesh a year, a juggernaut with no meaningful challenge.

Hayes briefly left Cedar Key after high school, as many youngsters often did, but was unable to escape for long the reach of its familial and environmental tendrils. The island had a way of holding folks in place firmer than other towns, its trashy siren call something short of beautiful but no less appealing.

It had called to Augustus Steele, widely regarded as the town's founder, when he purchased the land and remaining buildings that had been ravaged and then deserted after a hurricane in 1845. It called again to David Levy Yulee, a prominent plantation owner and senator, to bring the railroad to the island in 1860, connecting the Gulf of Mexico to the Atlantic Ocean. Until recently, it called still to an armada of pontoon boats and Carolina Skiffs most weekends of the year, and to housewives and retirees seeking the world-famous Tony's clam chowder or a sunset boat tour.

The more famous keys at the southern end of the state bore little resemblance to the one dangling just off the coast of Levy County.

"Sand gnats and mosquitos big as cats," Geoff McCloud would often say, bellied up to the end of the bar at The Steaming Clam on Dock Street.

By his fifth or sixth beer, Geoff could be relied upon to tell anyone who would listen about his family being among the first white people to permanently settle the island.

"But if that sumbitch Thomas don't stop writing all that good stuff about us, we'll be overrun with snowbirds. He needs to write about the sand gnats and the stinking damn mud to keep 'em away."

Tides move in and out of Cedar Key like a revolution. The high tide casts the island in idyllic tropical splendor; the low carries the water hard away, leaving the back bayous and bays a shimmering mudscape that smells like a bait bucket left too long in the sun.

Thomas Buck would get sentimental even about the mud.

"Beautiful, isn't it?" Thomas had said to a lady friend visiting from Gainesville.

He was sharp and well-spoken, once described by the mother of his high school girlfriend, to his dismay, as a *silver-tongued devil*. His comfortable charm and perpetual smirk gave him a boyish quality that was disarming and a weapon at once.

"If you say so. It was nice this morning, but where'd the water go?" she asked.

"Wherever it goes before it comes back," Thomas answered wistfully.

"So, half the time it just looks like this?" she inquired further, her delicate nose turned up like only girls from the city can do.

"Yes. Isn't it perfect? I love Cedar Key because the ugly is right out front where you can see it. I always know where I stand here. And when it is pretty, the pretty's never tacky Miami neon or a Jimmy Buffet song you have to sing along to just because everybody knows the words."

"I love Jimmy Buffet," she said.

"Of course you do."

"Wasting away again in Margaritaville," She sang, atonally but determined.

"Spoiler alert," Thomas interrupted, "There actually was a woman to blame. There always is."

The girl smiled because he was smiling when he said it and they stared at the mud together thinking different things. She imagined she might like to get closer to Thomas. He thought of how Annie never would have smiled at even playful misogyny. For a moment, he missed her disapproval like an aimless former prisoner homesick for the familiar walls of his cell.

"Well," he said to her, trying to fill the silence as he always seemed to want to do, "The great thing about the tide is that if you don't like it, another one is always coming."

"I like that," she replied warmly. Then they kissed because there seemed like nothing else to be done in the moment and Thomas closed his eyes hard the whole time, knowing he would not choose to see her again.

After the meeting in the park, Thomas thought again of kissing the girl by the mud, and of Annie, naturally, and a jumbled array of unrelated topics as he waited with the rest of the town while John worked. The morning dragged into the afternoon until, with little warning, he heard a booming voice cry out, "Fire in the hole!"

In an instant, the only way onto Cedar Key was by boat or swimming, and in the wake of John Mitchell's dynamite the residents were resolved to keep the broken world away by all means at their disposal.

Terry Jay wasn't from Cedar Key and held no special affection for it. He lived in the nearby gulf front community of Crystal River, 58 miles from the island by car and 35 by boat. He looked like the kind of man that made his living wrestling alligators or as an enforcer for the redneck mafia. He was distractingly built for a man of sixty. His Popeye arms and barrel chest had led Thomas to give him the affectionate nickname Grandaddy Bench Press, though most folks called him TJ. Despite his appearance, and his affection for airboats, mud bogs and spearfishing, TJ had made his living as a nuclear engineer, working much of his career at the Duke Energy nuclear power complex just outside of Crystal River.

The nuclear reactor was taken offline in 2009 but its iconic smokestacks were never torn down or imploded. It was water vapor, not smoke, that rose from the twin hyperbolic cooling towers, but even when told this fact people still called them smokestacks. For the better part of a half century, they had been a prominent feature on the horizon for people looking across the water from Cedar Key.

While TJ was ambivalent about Cedar Key, he was wild about one of its native daughters, Samantha Maye, a Marine Corps veteran who had made a career driving heavy equipment in Middle Eastern war zones and a life driving weaker boys to distraction with her acerbic tongue and impossible body. She was as comfortable in a mink coat with a martini as she was in a bikini with a box of cheap wine. She had fluttered in and out of Thomas's embrace but kept him on as a friend and emergency contact when she needed rescue from a drunken golf cart crash or someone to moon her doorbell camera with regularity. Samantha seemed to be everyone's cousin on the island, most notably Hayes', so Thomas took to calling her Cousin most of the time, both as an honorific to the level of deep care he felt for her, and as a way to link himself with the David family he so admired.

It was dumb luck for TJ and, as everyone would come to grimly know, the island, that Cousin had been down with a stomach bug the first week of that crisp February. Normally she would have made her regular pilgrimage to TJ's big house on the water in Crystal River. At 7:11 AM of most mornings over the previous year, she would have just been waking there, her dyed blonde hair draped over TJ's solid frame. Because she was home sick, TJ had been with her on the island when the smokestacks across the bay were enveloped in a microsecond of piercing light, and at least from the perspective of those looking across the bay from Cedar Key, simply vanished. All but a fine mist of ash of their physical form was erased from the earth. In less time than the duration of Cousin's first languid morning stretch, almost everyone TJ knew in his hometown reached chemical equilibrium, erased in a moment from the rolls of living people of the world.

Those slightly further from the plant were gone minutes to hours later, and slower processes of dying began in Cedar Key and everywhere else.

Because the island now housed a bona fide nuclear engineer, it would have, if nothing else, an educated narrator informing the awful scenes to come. While the details of how and why the flash had finally come would not be available to those on the island, TJ would be able to provide some insight into what might happen next.

Anyone following the political crunch of the previous months would have seen the list of probable nuclear targets running almost daily on the news. The NAS Jax and Mayport naval bases to the northeast in Jacksonville and MacDill Air Force base to the south in Tampa were near certain targets, along with the Tyndall and Eglin Air Force bases to the northwest. With so many military installations having more strategic value to an enemy, only something approaching total war, it seemed, would have led to Crystal River's civilian power plant being on the target list. Nevertheless, the smokestacks were conspicuously gone from Cedar Key's southern horizon, replaced with a harrowing wall of gray nothing. Only, as TJ relayed to Hayes in the frenzy of activity in the minutes after the flash, it wasn't nothing at all.

When it came to nuclear energy, the gray was everything.

During a decade's-long cold war, movies about nuclear crisis often showed scientists with Geiger counters and other instruments ominously discussing radiation by reporting the number of *rads* present. The Chernobyl and Three Mile Island incidents placed the topic of nuclear disasters fresh again into the public consciousness of the 1980s. In the intervening decades, however, years of peace and relative prosperity put the nuclear issue out of mind for most people.

This was not the case for TJ, whose daily work life had operated in the shadow of a potential nuclear catastrophe. TJ knew that the proper unit for measuring the absorption of radiation in a unit of mass being irradiated was *the gray*, symbolized as Gy. Technically, the gray was defined as the absorption of one joule of energy per kilogram of matter. Visually and practically, the gray horizon across the Waccasassa Bay from Cedar Key was an expanding wall of heat and death, incongruously light and capricious as the winds on which its fallout would be carried.

Eighty years of high-wire diplomacy and bumbling near-misses had transpired since Hiroshima and Nagasaki—a false alarm of Soviet attack during the Suez Crisis in 1956, Kennedy's showdown with Khrushchev in Cuba, a nuclear bomb accidentally falling out of an American B-36 and landing unexploded in a North Carolina field, the heroic efforts of the accidental watch commander Stanislav Petrov, and countless others—somehow culminating in there being no detonations of nuclear weapons in hostility since the Second World War. But walking such a prolonged tightrope requires only a single misstep to cause ruin.

The specter of such ruin generated a significant amount of scholarship to estimate the probability of a nuclear war. Such endeavors tended to go down intertwining esoteric rabbit holes that focused as much on discrediting competing methodologies of study as they did on making firm conclusions. For want of some number to think about, there seemed to coalesce support for a rough probability of one percent.

Stanford cryptologist and mathematician Martin Hellman, in his paper *On the Probability of Nuclear War*, had cautioned that any discussion of a probability—like an interest rate on a loan— had to be framed within a context of time. He continued this logic by noting that whatever the correct probability of nuclear war turned out to be didn't matter much. Ten percent per year meant we could expect a nuclear holocaust to happen within ten years; one percent per year meant we could expect it to happen within one hundred years. He concluded, "The lower probability per year changes the time frame until we expect civilization to be destroyed, but it does not change the inevitability of the ruin. In either scenario, nuclear war is 100 percent certain to occur."

It seemed ironic and irrelevant that the misstep to ruin would finally come in the form of an unresolved conflict on the Korean peninsula from the middle of the last century. The series of Rube Goldberg events leading to the smokestacks' demise were not individually significant, but in unison and in moments brought more destruction than Genghis or Atilla and the sum of all natural disasters in human history.

Hayes and TJ stood, transfixed, on the floating dock that ran parallel to the outside boat ramp, trying to make sense of what they were seeing across the bay.

"What's the worst case?" Hayes asked with unusual calm for the moment.

"If that's what it looks like, it's hard to imagine much worse."

"People will think the reactor blew, but I know it's not operational anymore."

"This wasn't an internal explosion."

"None of our plans considered there'd be one this close. Why would they hit Crystal River?"

"I was hoping you might know," TJ replied. "My foreign policy knowledge doesn't go much past Citrus County."

"At least tell me something to tell everyone to keep them safe," Hayes insisted.

"Stay inside. Interior rooms away from windows. We're gonna get plenty of grays with the wind coming off the water like it is."

"How bad will it get?" the mayor asked, a hairline crack beginning to open in his calculated resolve.

"Luckily there are still some miles between us and that," TJ said, pointing at the advancing column of smoke.

"Enough miles to matter?"

"Hard to say. Maybe. The heat will dissipate pretty quickly, but we won't be able to see or feel any radiation we get."

They stared together at the featureless bay, resolute in the crush of sounds and movement and panic. The moment for contemplation passed quickly and both men pushed into the fray shouting instructions and trying to help. A scatterplot of people scurried for the cover of homes and shops and Denny Gall's breakfast café on 2nd Street. An unnatural, skin-searing warmth drifted onshore in a slow but determined advance until even Hayes and TJ retreated indoors to the City Hall building.

"How long until it's safe for us to get back out there? People need to know we have a plan and that we're going to work it."

"However long it takes. Look at your arms. You're burned pretty good. So am I," TJ replied.

"I've had worse from a sunburn," Hayes protested.

"No, you haven't. And for no longer than we were out there, this is more tissue damage than I'd expect."

"Christ, the tide," Hayes said as the color drained from his face.

"What about it?"

"It was super low this morning. Almost a blow-out. I bet there were a dozen boats on the clam leases."

TJ said, "There's no cover on those boats. They're in real trouble. Anyone that happened to be looking in the direction of the stacks was almost certainly blinded. Probably just temporarily... but the grays are gonna eat them up."

"Then we have to go get 'em," Hayes said. "Thomas was working this morning out on the Corrigans leases. He's got the one on the far end, the closest to Crystal River."

Hayes headed instantly for the door, but TJ was able to grab the back collar of his jacket before he got there.

"Goddammit, stop. You can't do anything for him right now. Where are the PRDs you had the council buy?"

"In a box in the Chief's office... why?"

"I'll put one on and start monitoring the levels. As soon as it's safe, I'll go with you to look for the clam farmers that don't make it in. But it won't do anyone any good if we get sick. Things are going to get a whole hell of a lot worse."

Before Hayes could respond, there was a flicker in the fluorescent lights above them, a terrifying half second of dark before they came on again.

The town did not get its electricity directly from Duke Energy and it was this fact that had been reason to hope the flicker was a hiccup and not a final gasp. Even stern men like Hayes and TJ, though, felt the jolt in their guts when the lights went dark again with a sudden clap. It was still morning in Cedar Key but the edges of objects in the room blended into a muddled haze that would come to permeate life on the island for the indeterminate future.

The heat outside would not last long. Even as fires burned on horizons around the world, their warmth eventually gave way to the creeping monotone of the skies. The gray set in overhead and all around, determined to keep the sun away from the land and waters.

A backwards retelling of the creation story began in earnest on the Earth—Genesis in reverse.

2

THE TEMPORARY SALVATION OF CLAMS

A s the waiting drug on inside the City Hall building, Hayes paced around the room where the city council meetings were held, worrying about his friends on the water. When he passed an old photo on the wall of mullet boats hauling in their catch, his thoughts drifted to the infuriating, improbable path that led to Cedar Key's rise to clam farming prominence.

In the November General election of 1994, voters in Florida passed a Constitutional amendment to ban the most common type of commercial net fishing statewide and to significantly restrict other forms of net fishing. A single persuasively worded paragraph on a ballot would change Cedar Key and dozens of other coastal communities forever.

Almost overnight, the character of the state's fishing villages metamorphized. The gears of commerce for the watermen and women that made their living on the Atlantic and especially the Gulf of Mexico ground to an abrupt halt. Angry commercial fishermen threw boxes of roofing nails in the water at public boat ramps, a reprisal against the recreational fishing community they viewed as a chief instigator of the net ban. The ban did little to bolster recreational fishing numbers but studies from the University of Florida in subsequent years drew tenuous connections between it and modest increases in the fish population. They relied, generally, on dubious methodology and small sample sizes. Further, they discounted entirely the additional conservation efforts that were implemented around the same time. Reports on the economic and cultural effects of the ban were laughably understated to the extent that the fissure between the working waterfront and the government grew increasingly wider.

In Cedar Key, the David fish house closed for good.

On the front porch of the Gulf front house his family could no longer afford, while a surreal sunset heightened the moment with a dramatic flourish of orange and violet, a seventeen-year-old Hayes David was apoplectic.

"I got 'em dad."

"Got who?"

"The asshole weekenders that did this."

"You been hanging out with those Meade boys again?"

"Anybody that tries to launch a boat at the boat ramps is gonna have flat tires," Hayes said gleefully, his hands perched in triumph on his hips.

"Wipe that grin off your face, you dumb shit."

"I don't understand... dad you said they needed to pay."

"They do. But where'd you get the nails, son?"

"Hardware store."

"The hardware store here on the island... where literally everyone knows you're a David?"

Hayes dropped his hands in defeat.

"Bet you charged them to our account, too."

"Yes, sir."

"Signed your name right there on the ticket without a care in the world."

"Well, I didn't think..."

"That much is obvious," his father interrupted. "Go get them."

"Go get what?"

"Every single nail on those ramps. Get your ass in the water and don't come out until you can bring me two full boxes of roofing nails."

"But that'll take..."

"It'll take however long it takes," the elder David exploded.

"It's almost dark and it's cold out."

"Better hurry then." Mark flashed a sharp glance that told his son another word from him would be one too many.

Luckily for Hayes, the hour and the cold air meant the ramps were empty and there was no one around to witness his defeat. The work was grueling, and the nails poked into his white rubber boots just enough to sting the bottoms of his feet. Well into the dark, on hands and knees, Hayes worked without protest until he had filled the boxes and returned them to his father.

"They won't do me any good. You will be waiting at the front door of the Hardware store when they open tomorrow to return these. Get a receipt and sign for the refund."

"Yes sir."

"Bring me the receipt."

"Yes sir. Dad I'm sorry. I was just so pissed off. They're taking everything from us, and I wanted to do something about it."

"There's plenty we can do without exposing the family to trouble."

"Like what? I'm ready. Say the word and you can count on me."

"The first thing you can do is take a few deep breaths, boy. When there's hard stuff that needs doing, you got to stay calm. Temper and passion work against you, Hayes."

"It's hard to be calm when they're coming for our way of life."

"That's when dead calm is all that'll do."

Hayes sighed long and hard, trying to hear the wisdom of his father's admonition but struggling.

"Here's forty bucks. Cash. Take my truck and drive over to Chiefland and get us two more boxes of them nails. Don't talk to anyone while you're there."

Hayes' face was a carnival ride. "For real?"

"Yes, for real. Now get after it so those ramps aren't safe any longer than they need to be."

The thirty-minute ride to Chiefland passed in a moment for Hayes—his father's son more every day—who was about the Lord's work of island vengeance.

Autumn rolled into a hard winter and many of the commercial fisherman rolled out of town for good. The David family, determined to keep working on the water, did something few people in those parts ever dreamed of stomaching— they let the government help.

The clam farming industry came to Cedar Key by absolute happenstance. In the wake of the net ban, the Harbor Branch Oceanographic Institute utilized state funds to develop two programs to help spur aquaculture as a viable replacement for the lost fishing jobs. On the east coast of Florida, a plan to plant clams in the brackish waters of the Indian River was failing. A plan to develop oyster farming on the west coast was meeting a similar fate. An official from the east coast made the trip across the state to Cedar Key, unwittingly carrying a bag of clams in the back of his truck. When he noticed the clams, rather than letting them die, he threw the bag onto the sand spit in the Gulf waters across from the Beachfront Motel. To everyone's surprise, they grew faster and stronger than anywhere they had been tried on the other coast.

There was then and remains now no hard scientific explanation for why clams grow so well in the waters around Cedar Key. Some claim the strong tidal influence on the estuarine waters wash more nutrients into the area. Others point to an ideal mix of salt and fresh water due to outflows from the nearby Suwannee River. Whatever the cause, clams that take more than two years to grow to maturity in other areas of the country do so in around sixteen months in Cedar Key. With this new discovery, the state made a hard pivot and invested in developing clams in Cedar Key. Displaced net fishermen were awarded grants for clam seed, equipment, and gear, along with two-acre submerged land leases where their clams would eventually grow to maturity and market size.

The David family, with little to lose, made a big bet on clamming. With their experience running a large-scale fish house operation, and a family legacy of work on the water, they grew to become among the most successful clam farmers on the island. Over time, their family work ethic and reputation for reliability led them to prosperity on the water again, eventually landing a contract to supply several hundred grocery store locations in the state with fresh clams weekly.

Smaller clam farmers, too, began making a living on the water again. Before the global economic collapse in the weeks leading up to the flash, the clam industry was responsible for roughly forty million dollars of economic impact to the island each year. As with all farming, there were highs and lows in the almost 30 years since the pilot program that started Cedar Key clam farming on its way, but on balance it would be difficult to characterize the clam industry as anything other than a runaway success for the island.

On the day the universe of existence for Cedar Key residents ended at the demolished bridge, one step in the process of growing clams instantly hamstrung the island's prospects for success as an isolated refuge from a world in ruin. Cedar Key clams were not native to Cedar Key or even Florida. They were the *mercenaria mercenaria* species of the northern quahog clam. For a place so entrenched in the lore of southern culture, the irony was lost on almost no one that it was a damn yankee clam that had brought economic salvation to the island. In short, they did not grow naturally in the waters of the Gulf, and without a complicated artificial spawning process in the lab, a process that never took root on the island, no new clams could be grown in Cedar Key.

When Thomas first arrived on the island, while it was still a place of refuge but not yet a last stand, the lure of clam farming hooked him almost immediately. In his life as a writer, he dreamt often of being the kind of man that made something. Clam farming was his next Quixotic endeavor to produce some tangible thing of value besides stories and money. He wanted to be Hemmingway on the water and Faulkner on the page—fearless battling the sea but with a metaphoric lilt to his writing that was more Yoknapatawpha than Key West.

In his first several months working on the water, he was more Gilligan than anything else, running aground often in the shallow waters leading to the clam leases, overheating his old Johnson outboard, never having the right gear on the boat, and generally killing more baby clams than he planted. During the punishing learning curve of the new clam farmer, one decision stood out as a watershed moment for his eventual success— hiring the Admiral.

Rolf Alvarez III was new to the island as well. After growing up in the keys at the southern end of the state, and retiring after twenty years in the Army, Rolf was generally just puttering around looking for something to do. That was how it was told to Thomas by Rolf's wife Jenny, also a former soldier, now running the Cedar Key post office. Thomas had been characteristically oversharing with Jenny about some piece of mail from the Florida Division of Aquaculture, the state agency that oversaw the clam industry.

"My husband has been wanting to learn about clam farming," she said.

"There's a lot to learn," Thomas replied.

"Well, if you ever need help, he'd love to work on your boat."

"Really?"

"It'd be good for him to do something."

"It's pretty hard work and it doesn't pay that much."

"Not much is more than nothing. Let me give you his number."

It was one of those conversations that people have but never follow up on. Thomas followed up. He needed help and wanted someone who was as green a greenhorn as himself to lessen the embarrassment that was sure to come.

On the day Rolf arrived at the inside boat ramp, He came with a giant bag of gear that seemed more suited for a transatlantic voyage than the five-minute ride to the clam leases. He was fit and short without being diminutive, carrying himself with a military bearing that enhanced his stature. His kind eyes belied a temperament wound up like Charlie Daniel's fiddle poised for a battle with the devil down in Georgia. Thomas may have towered over his new crew member but felt sure a fight with him would end badly for them both. He looked at Rolf's bag skeptically, trying to think of the right thing to say to set the tone for their interaction.

"You have any experience on a clam boat?"

"This will be my first day," Rolf replied without a hint of meekness.

"Well, that's good. This is my third day so we can fuck this up together."

Their laughter diffused the tension of the moment and soon they were passing under the Dock Street Bridge and racing toward the leases. Despite the different cultures of their military service, the two men had an immediate easiness between them. The Gulf would kick their asses with regularity over the coming months and that adversity served to cement their friendship in a way that a regular job never could. Despite growing up in Key West and posturing to the contrary, Rolf seemed to know little about boats or the water. As their time working together went along, Rolf ever talking of getting a boat but never actually getting a boat, Thomas began to mockingly call the retired Army First Sergeant *The Admiral*.

The name, and their friendship, stuck.

While Thomas and Rolf had come to know each other by chance, Thomas's friendship with Mayor Hayes was based on concentrated effort. After attending a city council meeting to learn more about the town and to ask some questions about the renovation of the 140-year house he had recently purchased at the corner of E and 3rd in the historic district, Thomas was overwhelmed with admiration for the skillful efficiency with which Hayes ran the meeting. It was an exhilarating display of unassuming, slow-talking authority—part Matlock, part Jimmy Stewart. It was sheer good fortune for Thomas that Hayes was in the middle of a divorce. Thomas had made a life of boneheaded devotion to women that didn't like him much, and it was on this point that the two men would find meaningful common ground. He left the meeting determined to be the mayor's friend.

A little research revealed another bit of good fortune for Thomas's plan. Jonie, the opinionated, striking woman he had been flirting with the past few weeks—flirting insomuch as he smiled politely while she talked at him and occasionally let him tell her she was pretty—was the woman from whom the mayor was presently separated and was soon to be divorced. As soon as he made this connection, Thomas immediately cut ties with Jonie. In a town as small as Cedar Key, this was all that was required for the mayor to know Thomas's friendship was worth pursuing. Other acquaintances and so-called friends had swooped in almost immediately to cozy up to the beguiling Jonie. Hayes had taken quiet mental note of those for whom loyalty seemed to matter little. With no real reason yet for loyalty, Thomas picked a side all the same. He picked Hayes.

Soon they were adventuring on the mayor's boat and Thomas was picking his brain daily about clam farming. Generous with his time and expertise, the mayor seemed to find a valuable exchange in Thomas's way of approaching the emotional issues most men are conditioned to avoid. Thomas's recent divorce and the disarray it continued to cause in him made it safe for Hayes to talk about the present crumbling of his own life. They were the unlikeliest of friends, the mayor a fastidiously squared-away watermen and vice president of the island bank branch, whose attention to detail and order bordered on the frightening, and Thomas a wild-eyed malcontent for whom only the big ideas seemed to matter and about which he could opine at great length.

"You've got all the adjectives, Thomas," Hayes joked.

"I grew up in a trailer in an orange grove. Words are all I've got," Thomas replied with a smirk.

"Uh huh."

"It's true. Well words and a clam boat. I guess I should have learned something about clams before I bought a boat, especially one that's good for literally nothing else."

"Every clammer has a love-hate relationship with their birddog," said Hayes.

"I get why the motor's up front, so that the back is clear for hauling in clams, but I still don't understand how it doesn't sink with no back on it at all."

Pointing to the stern of his birddog, Hayes began to explain, "You see, the design allows for a large amount of displacement of..."

"Yeah, yeah," interrupted Thomas. "It still looks like it should sink. And it's like riding a wild bull to drive."

"It handles fine once you load it down with clams."

"I don't have any clams yet."

"Well, there's your problem. You should get some clams."

"I spent all my money on the boat."

Hayes deadpanned, "Strange business model, but at least it's a cool boat."

The birddog boat had come to be a quintessential Cedar Key image. The captain piloted the boat perched on the bow, just in front of the motor that operated in a hole cut through the deck. The thrust of the motor would lift the bow and the captain up high, offering a perch from which to see the shallows ahead. The Tremblys, Sheffields, and Lisenbys that comprised the Cedar Key clam fleet were all repurposed mullet boats. Even their mechanical net pullers were redesigned after the net ban and mounted on aluminum towers on the stern. These *power rollers* were used to pull heavy bags of clams off the floor of the Gulf.

Prior to the clam farming industry, clammers in northern states harvested wild clams with metal rakes and tongs. It was back-breaking labor and limited in scope by the natural whims of the ocean. As Thomas was learning in dribs and drabs—mostly from Hayes—farming clams was generally a five-step process, with most farmers only participating in three or four of the steps.

The first step involved spawning clam brood stock in a lab environment. By manipulating water temperature and algae levels, clams could be tricked into spawning nearly microscopic offspring. The second step occurred when these tiny clams grew to one millimeter in size, at which time they could be transferred into *raceways*, which are long, shallow, fiberglass trays in barn-like buildings built over or just beside the water. Here millions of tiny clams could grow in a predator-free environment as pumps sucked nutrient-dense water from the Gulf and cycled it through the trays, over the clams, and back out into the Gulf. Operating a raceway was a painstaking and tedious process, as the raceways needed to be cleaned as often as twice a day to keep mud and other sediment from smothering the tiny, vulnerable clams.

"Running raceways is like having a wife and a girlfriend," Mark David was known to joke, though the claim wasn't based on personal experience as his wife Bette, Hayes's mother, was both the sole object of his affection and unquestionably capable of murder should this ever cease to be the case.

The third step was where most clam farmers began their operation. In this step clams that have been in the raceways for a few months and have grown to around four millimeters are ready to be put into nursery bags and planted in the waters around Cedar Key. Most farmers simply purchase these nursery clams from large seed-growing operations. Twelve thousand nursery clams are placed into each four feet by four feet mesh bag, then these bags are fastened together into belts of five to ten bags each and planted in long rows on the clam leases. The nursery clams would grow undisturbed in this configuration for three to five months before being hauled onto clam boats and taken back ashore.

Step four takes the now much larger clams and breaks them down into grow-out bags of only twelve hundred per bag. These grow-out bags have larger holes in the mesh to allow for more nutrients to reach the clams. The grow-out bags are then assembled again into belts and replanted, where they stay from nine to twelve more months.

Step five uses the power rollers to harvest bags full of market-sized clams to be taken to one of the several wholesalers located on and around the island.

Clam farming is not the most complex of agricultural systems, though it does involve some level of mysticism that continually befuddles researchers seeking to eliminate the variables in the growing process that the Gulf of Mexico is determined to interject. For no discernable reason, some years certain leases produce bumper crops and other years the same lease, planted in the same manner, will kill more clams that it grows to market size. A healthy tolerance for risk and uncertainty is as important a tool to the clam farmer as a good boat and a strong back.

Because there were few hard and fast rules for how to run a successful clam farm, and because the endeavor seemed to attract a certain kind of individualist-minded person, most clammers had their own way of doing things. While Hayes' boat, working dock, and leases were impeccably maintained, Thomas's was a hodgepodge of second-hand gear and haphazard planning. If the mayor's operation was a finely tuned Swiss watch—and it was—Thomas' was a drunk uncle in an El Camino with busted taillights.

Eventually, though, both men reliably grew the most beautiful clams, one satisfied with his calculated efficiency, the other waxing poetic about life on the water.

In a flash of light, the countdown clock began ticking on how long the clams on the leases would last in their grow-out bags before they could be eaten or grew too large and suffocated.

They were, with certainty, the last of their kind.

As southerly winds scythed across the island, atomic peril from the wider world came with them, and one house after another would welcome death across its threshold.

3

RACE FOR SHORE

By early afternoon, TJ's personal radiation detector produced a reading that made leaving the safety of City Hall possible. The island's buildings had sustained no appreciable damage. The air was crisp and cool again. People were beginning to venture out. Hayes and TJ sprinted across 2nd Street toward Hayes' dock on the canal at the end of A Street.

"Maybe they all made it back in," TJ said, his unconvincing optimism making the situation worse.

"Yeah maybe."

TJ untied the lines from the front and back of Hayes' birddog, the Expectancy, whiles Hayes pumped the primer and fired up the motor. The low tide had lingered longer than normal but there was just enough water in the canal for the boat to make it out to the bay. TJ cautioned lower speeds until they could assess the conditions further out on the clam leases. Hayes ignored him, pushing the throttle wide open and the bow of his boat into the wind. To their great surprise, no armada of birddogs appeared before them. There had been eleven total on the leases when the smokestacks fell. Only one boat remained in the distance.

They could not know then what would be apparent in the coming days—the captains and crews of the ten boats that made it home would be the first to succumb to the quiet sickness of the sky. As the heat and smoke overwhelmed the clam leases, they raced for home, exposed on the open decks of their birddogs to the leading edge of the irradiated wind. In hours, the fallout would dissipate to levels that could be temporarily endured, but in those early minutes was as fearsome as the face of God. The returning watermen had varying degrees of severe burns, but all were suffering with acute radiation poisoning. As TJ later relayed his knowledge about the appropriate unit of measuring such a thing, they were eventually simply said to have *the gray*. The life and color of those afflicted were slowly drained away while absorbed units of radiation overwhelmed their inner workings. They would themselves, in time and in whispered tones, come to be known as the grays, a too-clever shorthand for the soon-dead among the living.

As the Expectancy rounded the Dog Island leases and started across the expanse between them and Corrigans, the distinctive navy blue of Thomas's birddog, the Judith Jane, became visible. The normally stoic Hayes was overcome.

Thomas had named his working boat after his mother because she was the hardest working person he had yet encountered in his life. Certainly his penchant for hair-brained schemes and giant dreams had come from his father, but every time he chased one of those dreams down and bent it to his will, Judith Jane's son shone brightly in her image. When Thomas was young, his single mother had taken a job as a day laborer at a central Florida phosphate mine, literally digging ditches with a shovel. When she left the male-dominated industry two decades later, she was a leader of men and had built a comfortable life for them both. It was over fried shrimp and coleslaw at The Big Dock bar that Thomas first mentioned naming his boat after his mother.

"Too many ex-wives' names to pick from, I guess. Your mama is a safe choice," Hayes had joked.

"You're lucky I didn't name it after your mom," Thomas shot back.

"If you did, my dad would have burned your boat up and made you watch him do it."

They both laughed because it was funny, and because it was true. Once while Hayes and Mark were elk hunting in New Mexico, Thomas ran into Cousin and Miss Bette at the Trident Lounge of the old island hotel and accepted an invitation to join them for dinner. From the overhead speaker, George Strait was singing *Amarillo by Morning* and by chance Thomas and Miss Bette sang the chorus out loud together with a kind of sweet harmony that caught the bar off-guard. By that evening, Mark David had heard a third-hand embellished story about Thomas singing and dancing with his wife. He sent word back to the island that he intended to, "Shoot Thomas Buck in the dick," immediately upon his return. Thomas was unsure enough about whether it was meant to be a joke that he had a medieval-looking iron codpiece shipped to him express from the Internet. At the big dinner to welcome the hunters back home to the island, Thomas arrived dramatically wearing the metal codpiece outside his pants. Mr. Mark's cackling laughter was a stay of execution for Thomas and early roots for their surprising friendship.

Hayes thought of that idiotic codpiece and a blur of other stupid Thomas stories as the Expectancy closed fast on the Judith Jane. On their approach, TJ mumbled something dire under his breath.

The normally white fiberglass deck of Thomas's boat was charred black but otherwise intact. The edges of some of the clam bags near the stern were melted together. The gear and built-in dry boxes and controls were all where they should be, but the Judith Jane was without her captain on deck.

"Maybe he rode in on another boat," TJ ventured.

"Why would he do that?" Hayes snapped.

"No, I don't guess he would. No Rolf either."

"Thomas likes to plant by himself if it's less than twenty belts. He was probably here alone."

"Well, that's something."

Hayes tossed a line onto Thomas's boat and hopped over onto it.

"What are you doing?" TJ asked.

"Let's at least pull his boat back home. I can't just leave it here."

"Of course."

There was a heavy silence on the water and between them as Hayes tied a methodical knot in the line and then returned to his own boat. TJ slouched on the gunnel, his head in his hands.

The ride back to the island was slower with the second boat in tow and a building chop further impeded their progress. The Judith Jane bounced and swayed in the wake of the Expectancy so much that the lid of the dry box in the center of Thomas's boat flung open and banged closed with a rhythmic clank.

On the fifth or sixth clank, Thomas sprang from the box, punch-drunk and frantic.

The 2000 model Johnson 90-horsepower outboard is widely regarded as one of the best motors Johnson ever made. Affectionately nicknamed *the looper*, it developed a cult following and a reputation for being bulletproof and reliable. The shape of its cylinder and pistons allows for a loop-charged induction where the mixture of fuel, oil, and air loops down the piston to push out the exhaust gas. This differs from a crossflow system where the mixture enters one side of the cylinder and cross flows straight to the other side. The circular motion of the looper motor creates a more efficient handling of the exhaust, which creates more power. Cross flow motors tend to idle a little better, but when it's time to, "Pour the coals on it," as Mark David would say, nothing beats the looper for throaty 2-stroke power.

Thomas knew almost none of the intricacies of his fabled 90-horse looper. He had bought it from a fellow on the internet for a good price and generally ran it like a rented mule. More astute aficionados of the motor, or even marginally observant ones, would know that this looper had one fatal flaw, waiting always to destroy the internal components of an otherwise stellar piece of machinery—the oil injection nipple. Most 2-stroke motors require mixing 2-cycle oil into the gas tank at every refueling. The advent of automatic oil injection meant a user could fill a separate reservoir with oil and the system would mix the oil and gas together just before it went into the motor. This process made for more consistent idling and mixture ratios, but a failure of this system tended to cause a catastrophic failure to an unlubricated motor. The automatic oil injection of the looper seldom failed, but the connection between the reservoir tank's oil line and the motor failed with spectacular regularity. The critical junction between the motor and its life-sustaining lubrication was a poorly made plastic nipple. Better watermen who ran the motor changed out this factory oversight with a metal part immediately. Thomas never did.

It would be some time later in the day before the exact cause of Thomas's escape from the gray would be discovered. A good portion of the clam fleet lay dying, though they would not know this for days to come. Thomas would be among the grays himself, save for the deus ex machina of a shattered plastic nipple and the relative protection of four fiberglass walls.

Just as he had arrived on his lease, the incineration of the smokestacks and perhaps a thousand people in Crystal River happened in an instant behind his back. The resulting shockwave, carried faster through water than over land, had lifted the stern of the Judith Jane six feet out of the water and slammed it back down hard again, sending Thomas overboard and scrambling his brain and balance. When he regained enough composure to try to climb back on the boat, he noticed the sheen of dark oil covering everything behind the motor. Somewhere between the outside ramp and Corrigan's lease L-721, among the farthest away from Cedar Key, the nipple had failed, leaving the full-throttled motor to run miles with no oil.

After considerable difficulty, Thomas was able to slide his way onto the slippery deck. Still dazed, he closed his eyes for what seemed like no more than a moment. Several precious minutes passed. As he lay motionless, a bewildered fleet of boats were ambling back to life and beginning their fateful race for the shore as the false sun of the flash gave way to the advancing gray heat.

When the skin on the back of his legs began to ache and redden, Thomas awoke and raced for the helm of his birddog. He turned the ignition time and again, desperate to hear the familiar 2-stroke growl of the looper roaring to life. Only a labored chug and a sickening metal-on-metal grinding rang out. The heat bore down on him in a muscular advance. Unable to start his motor, and feeling his skin begin to burn in earnest, Thomas emptied the gear from fiberglass dry box in the center of the boat and crammed himself inside, closing the lid over his head and slipping into the darkness. In the sensory deprivation of the box, memories overtook him.

"What do you mean, all of them?"

"I mean how many do you have in the store?"

"Do you care what gauge? Just acoustic or electric, too?"

"Electric won't do us any good. I'm not picky about the gauge. How many full sets of acoustic guitar strings do you have in stock?"

The kid behind the counter at the music store looked perplexed. He tapped away at his keyboard, then did some math on his phone.

"Looks like... uh... 150."

"That sounds great. I'll take them."

"No kidding? You like, getting ready for a music festival or something?"

"Not exactly," Thomas said. "It just might be a long while before I'm able to buy strings and I'd hate to run out."

"You're never going to run out."

"I hope you're right. I bet it's hard to keep coming to work with everything that's going on."

"It is," the kid said with a halfhearted scowl. "I told my mom I shouldn't have to but she said I'm 18 and she'll kick me out if I quit."

"Better listen to mama, I guess."

"What do you think, sir? Think it will really come to... you know?"

"I sure hope not," Thomas replied. "I've always thought of myself as an optimist... but here I am hoarding guitar strings for the whole island."

"What island?"

"I better get a move on. There's still so much to do. Hey, Matt," he said, glancing at the kid's name tag as he deflected the question, "I really appreciate your help. It's a strange time, friend, and I was glad to spend a little of it with you today."

"Yeah man, let me get these strings for you. I mean let me get literally all of them for you."

They shared an overly enthusiastic laugh together, out of place in the tension of the day, a breaking levee that felt good to them both. Days later, when Thomas' hope was proven unfounded, each man would think back to the interaction, recalling it with fondness.

Guitar strings, candles, books, bullets, and bourbon filled his truck, as Thomas headed west on State Road 24, thinking he would maybe never see Gainesville again. He was twenty-one when he first arrived there. It had seemed to him like a dazzling Babylon twinkling on a hill. Poetry Jams and alternative house parties and a free room in the back of the Presbyterian Student center in exchange for mowing the yard, playing the guitar for Sunday service, and cooking the free Wednesday night spaghetti suppers. It was the softest of landings after his separation from the Navy. Free rent. Free food. An instant community. The seventeen dollars in his wallet when he arrived lasted long enough to get a waiter job, and before he realized it was happening, his roots were down and a new life began. His best buddy from high school, Georgie Pilsner, lived in the back of the Methodist student center just across a narrow side street.

"Goddamn Presbyterians," Georgie would yell, laughing, hanging out of his church window.

"Fucking Methodists," came the reply across 14th street in the shadow of the gothic halls of the university. For most people, the doctrinal distinctions between the two denominations were too subtle to identify. The two friends knew them well and cared not at all. They were living for free in a north Florida Gomorrah, feasting on Presbyterian spaghetti on Wednesdays, Methodist spaghetti on Thursdays, Hara Krishna lunch every weekday near the student union on campus, and the kind of spiritual hedonism found only in a college town. Except in the week or two after student loans disbursed, there was seldom fifty dollars between them. Still, all their mornings broke full of possibility. Nothing of the bad to come was even conceived yet. They were young and smart and stupid and free.

The hour drive from Gainesville to the island is built for reflection. Besides single intersections in the small communities of Archer, Bronson, and Otter Creek, the 50 odd miles from hip-culture inanity to the rural southern ethos of the island comprise blurred stretches of swamp water and slash pines. There was a time when Thomas reveled in how out of place he seemed living in a church across from the campus— buzz-cut, clean-shaven, and fit in a town where pseudo-punk angst and self-destruction was the order of the day. The easy hindsight of the highway made his eventual retreat from the city, tail firmly between his legs, seem inevitable. An honest view, however— one he seldom indulged— revealed a deep well of regret for how the city had seemed to change out from under him.

From the early days reading his poems at the Civic Media Center, a counter-culture library and den of radical activists and other weirdos, to three marriages in 20 years, all wonderful and awful and too brief, to a meteoric rise as a writer in his late 30s, the arc of his life had risen and fallen in the coffee shops, community theaters, and oak-tree canopies of Gainesville. The son he shared with his first wife was now a senior in college, which didn't seem possible to Thomas, whose mind tried to convince him daily that he himself was still a young buck in the fullness of youth.

As he rolled through Otter Creek, his truck seemed to know the way home from there and basically drove itself the last 20 miles. Every minute closer to the Number Four Bridge was a loosening of the grip the rest of the world still held on his self-worth. Soon he would see the scattered mangroves of the back bayou and the wide waters of the open Gulf would shut it all out.

College towns are made for moving on from, someplace quaint to think of in the midst of a real life lived elsewhere. Thomas had hung on too long; the town he had grown to love fell out of love with him, finding increasing fault in his lack of adherence to the evangelical zeitgeist of the day. He believed in people first and principle second, reciting in his head as needed his mantra that *what you stand for is important but who you stand for is everything.*

No one back there would ever make such a stand for him. This was ultimately why he had to leave—to find a place with people worth standing for. To find Cedar Key.

Now that it had finally happened, despite eleventh hour overtures that had been at last some cause for hope, and despite unfavorable winds that meant the island would not escape its share of the awful toll, Thomas rejoined the darkness in the box knowing that his side of the Number Four Bridge was the only claim left worth staking.

Robby Watt, whose 4-stroke Yamaha had fired up as expected, and whose thirty years of experience in the clam industry had polished him into a legendary, squared-away waterman, absorbed fifteen grays of whole-body acute exposure on his run back to the outside boat ramp. Hardened by a life on the water, Robby was barely aware of the burns to his skin and refused any treatment for them. By the next morning, he could keep no food or drink down and by that evening could not muster the strength to stand.

Five grays are enough to kill most people within fourteen days. Robby would last six.

A similar fate befell Hodge Hals, the cantankerous old salt who was said to not like even those he loved, and whose clam dock next to Hayes meant Thomas often had opportunity to meet him by chance. Try as he might, Thomas had been unable to move the elder clammer to anything more than forced half-hearted pleasantries. In just shy of four days, Mr. Hals would be the first of so many islanders to slip into the gray for good.

Tom Solaro, the oldest and wildest of the Solaro boys that were just beginning to take the reins of Solaro Aquafarms, would live for twelve days, though for the last three could not speak or move. The seven-millimeter wetsuit he had been wearing provided some nominal additional protection as his boat, the White Lady, pushed through the teeth of the haunted wind between the leases and the shore.

Mark David's clam shop manager and captain of one of the boats in his fleet, Jonathan Millner, seemed unaffected for the first day and half after the flash. His Amish Unabomber persona belied a kind, thoughtful man with a sneaky sense of humor. Because he was so often quiet to the point of stoicism— a common attribute of the best watermen— when the tide in his guts began to turn, no one noticed until he was found prone beneath a tree in his back yard, never to stand again. The shadowy twilight of his final, tortured week shook Mark David to his core.

Justice Anders, who for a decade had run Bryant Lee's bright yellow 28-foot Lasensby and its crew, was gone in a week. Justice had come to some recent notoriety on the island for refusing to give a tardy crewman from another boat a ride out to the leases to meet his captain and crew. While it was true that Sam Cannen had simply overslept and missed his boat, it was also true than every other captain in the fleet, save for Mr. Hals, would have helped without question, reasoning, correctly, that one day they would find themselves in similar need. Justice had scowled at the late man and cited the cold as reason for his refusal. When Sam, determined to put in his days work, walked and swam his way the two miles out to meet his crew, the story spread across the island at breakneck speed. The resulting bad blood between the two men seemed a sad inconsequence when they died hours apart on opposite sides of the island.

Twenty-seven men and two women from the fleet would be cut down, more or less together, for doing what any sailor's gut would tell them in the face of trouble on the water—heading for shore.

Thomas Buck, black from oil and spared by a cosmic turn of fate and poor seamanship, would suffer no more than moderate burns and a week of abdominal distress.

4

IN ALL KINDS OF WEATHER

C ollege football in Florida is a microcosm of the two-party political system of the nation at large. While technically a person could root for the Hurricanes of the University of Miami or the upstart teams at the state schools in Orlando and Tampa, they did so resigning themselves to the same irrelevance of voting for the Green or Libertarian parties in elections. On this issue, the only choice that mattered, one loaded with cultural implications more immediate and more tribal than any choice for the state's governor or the nation's President, was this: the Florida Gators or the Florida State Seminoles. Attending either school was not a prerequisite for admission into the fandom, but lifelong loyalty to your team and seething disdain for the other was required.

Neither Thomas nor his son Luke had attended the University of Florida, but both were die-hard Gator fans. Thomas' undergraduate studies had been at Florida Southern College, a non-football school in his native Polk County. Luke had ventured to the University of North Florida in Jacksonville and become an Osprey in name only. Like his father, his heart bled Gator orange and blue, especially when it came to the UF/FSU rivalry that simmered throughout the year and then exploded at the meeting of the teams every November.

The Gators played their games at Ben Hill Griffin Stadium on University Avenue in Gainesville, affectionately nicknamed The Swamp. One of Thomas' and Luke's favorite game day traditions at The Swamp was the singing of *We are the Boys from Old Florida* at the end of the third quarter of each game. It was a waltz-time tune played by the Gator Marching band, *The Pride of the Sunshine,* while ninety thousand fans locked arms and swayed, singing:

> *We are the boys from old Florida,*
> *F-L-O-R-I-D-A.*
> *Where the girls are the fairest,*
> *The boys are the squarest*
> *Of any old state down our way. (Hey!)*
> *We are all strong for old Florida*
> *Down where the old Gators play. (Go Gators!)*
> *In all kinds of weather...*
> *We'll all stick together...*
> *For F-L-O-R-I-D-A*

The one minute of compulsory community created in the swaying and singing struck a chord deep within the Buck men and stayed with them long after the games ended.

When traveling away from home, it was never hard to find someone wearing a Gator hat or shirt and Thomas, especially, could not resist the urge for a passing, "Go Gators." When the stranger returned the salutation, for a moment a sublime connection was created between people that might otherwise have diabolically opposed world views. The *Gator Nation,* as it was called by the faithful, rose above the divisive identity politics that had seemed to consume the world in recent years. Republicans and Democrats,

Christians and Atheists, Vegans and Carnivores—all were welcome in the fold, so long as they weren't a damn dirty Seminole.

When Cousin heard about Thomas' ordeal in the dry box, she and her best friend Lara headed immediately to his house with a bag of medicine and food. Lara was a wild-haired pixie devil, whose face melted and reconstituted itself depending on the moment and her mood. She had not cared for Thomas in the beginning, finding his continued devotion to Annie, his last ex-wife, to be a sign of the weakness she abhorred in men. During the month when Thomas and Cousin had indulged a flirtation with each other, she developed a habit of only ever looking at Thomas with a skeptical side eye. By the time Cousin found and fell for TJ, though, Lara had softened toward Thomas and even began to feel something akin to friendship with him.

The ladies arrived at Thomas' house to find Hayes on the front porch reading a handwritten note.

"He's gone," Hayes said.

"What do you mean gone?" Cousin asked. "Where?"

Reading from the note, Hayes said, "Luke was in Gainesville to see his cousin Haden run in a Gator track meet. I've gone to find him and bring him back to the island. The phones are out. I hope to be back before dark."

"I thought he was really sick," Lara said.

"Not as bad as the other captains," Hayes replied. "But he shouldn't be trying to drive."

Cousin said, "If he was conscious, he was going after the boy. They had a plan in place in case things got bad. I hope Luke remembers it."

As the geopolitical tensions escalated in the weeks leading up to the flash, Thomas and Luke had developed a protocol for how to respond to a variety of catastrophes that might result from a world on the brink. The protocols varied based on where Luke found himself when a crisis arose. All of them, however, involved Luke getting home to the island one way or another. If there was to be trouble, they reasoned, then they would face it together.

They had faced dark times before.

Luke was born with a rare birth defect called Transposition of the Great Vessels, where the pulmonary artery and the aorta of the heart develops into two closed loops, instead of the correct design where the two vessels intersected so the one carrying blood and the one carrying oxygen could meet and create oxygenated blood to be delivered throughout the body. In short, Luke was born suffocating and blue. A series of improbable circumstances had led to his doctor recognizing the condition in time to have Luke put on a ventilator, saving his life. An emergency laparoscopic surgery to punch a temporary hole between the chambers of Luke's heart allowed for the mixing of his blood and oxygen until open heart surgery could be performed.

Once again, the Gator Nation delivered.

One of the two people that had pioneered the microscopic laser surgery to reroute Luke's tiny vessels was the head of the pediatric cardiology department at the University of Florida teaching hospital. If Luke had been born anywhere in the world, and time permitted, his best chance for survival would have been a trip to see the surgeon in the Fightin' Gator scrubs, Dr. Robert Knopf.

Luke's surgery was a success, but months of recovery and follow-up led to a fussy baby that seldom slept for more than a half hour at a time.

Thomas would sit up with his boy throughout the long nights, singing to him and telling stories about all the wonders that waited for him in the world.

From these early days on, Luke Buck and his father were close. They had endured the child's fight for life and the turbulence of Thomas' failed marriages together, leaning into each other during periods of upheaval. Thomas bore a heavy cross of guilt for being unable to keep a family together while his son was growing up. He tried to compensate by being omnipresent in the boy's life and activities, coaching his little league baseball team when Luke was younger, and his golf team when, as an eleven year-old sixth grader, Luke made the varsity high school team. The Buck men sidestepped the rivalry and angst often existing between fathers and sons, enjoying one another's company in the uncomplicated way of people who liked the same things—golf, history, collecting old military surplus rifles, fishing, rivers, and most of all, Cedar Key. From the time Luke's car seat could be strapped onto the deck of a boat, he and his father spent as many weekends as possible adventuring on the barrier islands that populate the Waccasassa Bay around the main island of Cedar Key.

When Thomas purchased a beat up twenty-four foot 1976 Aquasport cuddy cabin and outfitted it with an underpowered Mercury Force 120 outboard, he let seven-year-old Luke name the boat. While watching a cable TV marathon of *Star Trek, the Next Generation* together, Luke said, "Our boat's just like the Starship Enterprise, except it looks like an old turd." A recognition of Luke's genius flashed in both of their eyes, and they said in unison, "The Turdship Enterprise." Thomas had traded a Ford Ranger pickup with a slipping transmission and two hundred dollars for the old boat, recently patched up after it fell off the previous owner's trailer and slid a quarter mile down the interstate before coming to a tranquil rest in the grass median. The Turdship was ugly, slow, leaked like a colander, and was the most magnificent vessel to ever sail the seas. Before Thomas' father's death after a pernicious battle with cancer, the three Buck men and the mighty Turdship were fixtures in and around Cedar Key, and it was during this time that Thomas began to dream of how he might one day live on the island.

Crossing the Number Four Bridge in the wrong direction, his insides wanting to leave his body from all available ports, Thomas felt little inclination for reflection, worrying only about what impediments might lie between him and finding his son. Remarkably, the station in Sumner was still open and still had gasoline, the pumps running on a backup diesel generator. Thomas filled his truck's tank and four 5-gallon cans he brought with him from his clam dock. He made it as far as Otter Creek before having to pull over. He tried to make it into the tree line but ended up squatting in the ditch just beyond the shoulder of State Road 24. He would stop again between Bronson and Archer, and once more on the outskirts of Gainesville.

There had been a frenzy in the air in Sumner but otherwise it had felt to him no worse than the familiar period of worry leading up to a hurricane's landfall. By the time he passed under the Interstate-75 overpass, though, and approached the Butler Plaza retail district, the world had changed around him. The traffic lights were out. Stores and gas stations were dark. Everywhere there seemed to be people—smashing windows, kicking in doors, entering and exiting building after building with armloads of everything from food to clothes to seventy-two inch televisions. To his right, a Waffle House that had appeared normal on a first glance was alight with flames on a second. The traffic approaching the intersection of Archer Road and 34th Street was tangled and unmoving. The discordant assault of car horns underscored a scene from an end-of-the-world movie, but

Thomas could not make out the reason why. The only apparent damage in his field of view was being caused by people in real time.

When he still lived in Gainesville, faux-outrage had been the order of the day—activists assaulting a Starbucks to end global warming, affluent white ladies lashing themselves to an inconsequential tree with plastic costume-store chains, and an array of other tone deaf and ineffectual displays of angry public virtue. The growing bedlam before him, however, was something different. It was actual fear and tangible panic, not a manufactured college town paroxysm, that was tearing apart the social order.

Thomas turned his truck away from the intersection, jumped a curb, and raced through the parking lot of Whole Foods and behind the old movie theater. Making his way back onto 34th Street, weaving in and out of both lanes of traffic, across medians, and through a retention pond near the natural history museum, he was able to snake his way through the heart of the university campus. From there he met little resistance on his way through the *professor's ghetto*, over Hogtown Creek and into the entrance of the Shady Oaks subdivision.

For the past few hours, all Thomas could think about was making it to this point. He had not allowed himself to even consider the possibility that Luke had already returned to Jacksonville, or that something had come up to keep him from attending his cousin's track meet at all. As he turned into the nondescript middle-class neighborhood through which he had to pass to get to Luke's grandparents' home, he could no longer quiet his mind. If they hit Crystal River, he knew, then Jacksonville and its naval bases were certain to be leveled, along with maybe a quarter million people, his boy possibly among them. He would go there, of course, and to every corner of the earth required, if Luke were not at the designated meeting place at the end of this road.

At the far end of the Shady Oaks neighborhood, an unassuming little road led past a park into a tucked away enclave of mansions called The Commonwealth. Thomas felt a momentary rush of relief and nostalgia upon seeing the familiar three-story antebellum architecture of the Payne homestead. Luke's grandfather George Payne had come from the humblest of Florida beginnings. When the Vietnam War broke out, he enlisted in the Army and worked his way into an officer's commission. After completing the notoriously rigorous Ranger School, Lieutenant Payne shipped out to southeast Asia, leading a platoon into one firefight after another in the Vietnamese and Cambodian jungles. In this role, killing became as natural and commonplace as brushing your teeth or combing your hair—a thing that had to be done more days than not. Lieutenant Payne believed in the mission and in his country, becoming a squared-away soldier who demanded best effort from his men. While other units in the war had elements of counterculture dissent and heavy drug use, Lieutenant Payne's platoon developed a reputation for icy professionalism. Before his time in-country was over, he would be promoted to Captain.

After the war, George Payne enrolled at the University of Florida and studied Real Estate. The same tenacity and integrity that had distinguished him as a soldier underpinned his success as a real estate developer. After dispensing and avoiding death in the jungle over a period of years, the risks associated with real estate speculation were utterly tolerable to him. He grew to relish his reputation as a *wheeler dealer* that would purchase large tracts of land in isolated rural areas, subdivide them into five and ten acre parcels, then sell them with owner-financing to anyone that could come up with a $299 down payment and a promise to pay $199 a month at elevated but not confiscatory interest rates.

George Payne offered quality land and the blue collar American Dream to long-haul truckers, isolationists, and outdoorsy folks of every ilk—land in the woods away from the encroachment of neighbors and the changing modern world, no credit check required. Over time, he began to specialize in properties with frontage along or access to the various rivers and springs that made north central Florida a hidden ecological gem. Selling the tranquility of the Suwannee and Santa Fe Rivers, and the unrivaled splendor of the largest concentration of first magnitude springs in the world, led to success and a standard of living he could scarcely have imagined growing up in a working class neighborhood in Jacksonville.

The house in The Commonwealth was the culmination of George Payne's hard work. He approached its design and construction with the same tenacity as soldering, and the same fervor he had for raising a family with his stern but beautiful wife Jeanie. She had grown up in Columbus, Georgia and had met the young soldier during his stint at Fort Benning. They married and she dutifully waited stateside while he prosecuted his portion of the war on the other side of the world. Their Commonwealth house approached ten thousand square feet of living area over three stories, with imposing brick walls and stately white columns. It had terrified young Thomas when he arrived for the first time to pick up George's daughter Molly for a date. George and Jeanie had filled the big house with children, all fine people and all devoted to family in a way increasingly out of fashion in the world.

Though he would not admit it out loud, Molly was the apple of George's eye. She was poised, articulate, and striking, her long strawberry-blonde hair draping about her shoulders like the mantle of royalty. Thomas was a mere few weeks out of the Navy, living in the back of a Presbyterian church, and riding a motorcycle. He was everything the wealthy father of a beautiful young daughter should naturally detest. And yet, this had not been the case; George and Thomas liked each other immediately. George was surprised by the younger man's deep grasp of American history, and of course the soldier-lord of the manor had seemed to Thomas the embodiment of everything he ever hoped for his own life.

Thomas and Molly pursued a passionate but volatile courtship and married within a year. A year later, Luke was born. Try as they might to follow the example of marriage and family set by Molly's parents, the young couple drifted apart and divorced with relative amicability before Luke's fourth birthday. The extraordinary thing about the relationship between the Buck and Payne families is that the divorce had almost no effect on it. Thomas never lost his code to the automatic gate at the Commonwealth house, and he retained his standing invitation to all Payne family events. The big house and the big family were a stabilizing influence on Luke, and on Thomas, who never considered giving up either. Even after Thomas remarried, his role in the Payne family continued. When he was hospitalized for the better part of a week with a ruptured appendix, George Payne had sat at his bedside for days on end, reading bible verses, shooting the shit, and talking about his grandson's golf game or the scourge of the expanding federal government.

Such was the weight of memory that clouded Thomas' mind when he approached the big house, momentarily obscuring his perception of the turmoil happening as he approached the driveway. He did not recognize the man with the axe, but when he saw it crashing into the front door, the moment of Thomas' nostalgia was ended. Suddenly there appeared several men around the house, throwing bricks and waving guns. Thomas pulled the 12-gauge from behind his truck seat and leapt from his truck to engage the men. As he did, a weakness in his knees and spinning in his head nearly brought him to the ground. Leaning on the truck for support, he could see the Chamberlain house across the street under a similar attack. The Chamberlains were elderly and infirm, he a retired chemist and professor at the university, she a mother and general doer of good in the community.

They would, at their advanced age and considering their abhorrence for guns, be unable to defend themselves.

Thomas steadied himself, gripped the shotgun firmly, and headed for the man with the axe. As he did, an avalanche of sound roared from the house. From his perspective, a peppering of tightly grouped holes appeared in the door, the axe dropped immediately to the floor of the enormous porch, and the man stumbled backwards and down the front steps, landing flat on his back on the concrete walk. The period between the axe man's final chop at the door and the perfect stillness of his undignified death elapsed before Thomas could raise the shotgun to his shoulder. He turned his attention to the men with bricks and guns, just as they began to fall in quick succession. From around a corner of the house came a stalking Captain Payne, his 74-year-old joints and muscles moving fluid and haunting as a malevolent ghost, the barrel of the familiar M16 now sending .223 rounds downrange toward the men attacking his neighbor's house.

Thomas and his forever father-in-law recognized one another immediately and turned toward the Chamberlain house together. As they did, Haden and Luke burst through the riddled door, matching Ruger 14 rifles from their grandfather's arsenal in their hands. Father and son caught each other's notice, but already the four men were moving as a cohesive force toward an enemy across the street. Their collective firepower, and a family line that held even when return shots began to come their way, was too much for the disorganized marauders to withstand. In less than two full minutes, five dead men were strewn across two yards, several others were running in full retreat from the maelstrom, and four men that loved each other began the short walk across the street to the big house.

Luke said, "What happened to you, dad?"

It was only then that Thomas remembered the ordeal of the heat and oil on the birddog, and realized how he must look to others.

"It's a long story, but I think I'm okay."

"It's good to see you, Thomas," George said.

"It's good to be seen. Thank God Haden had a track meet and Luke was here close to you."

Haden said, "Before my race, the power went out and people start acting crazy. They closed the university. When all the smoke started rolling in, I heard somebody say they thought there was a war."

"What have you heard, George?" Thomas asked.

"Almost nothing. The power went out. Then the smoke came. Right before you got here, men just started attacking the house."

With building worry he could no longer hide, Luke asked emphatically, "Dad, what happened?"

Thomas told them everything he knew—the flash and the fallen smoke-stacks, the busted plastic nipple and his retreat into the dry box, what he saw happening to the shops and restaurants in Butler Plaza, and the revolt happening in his stomach since returning from the clam leases.

Luke hugged his father hard, lingering the extra seconds that parents always want and children seldom deliver. The adrenaline was draining away from them now and the gravity of what they had just experienced together was setting in.

"Should we call the police?" Haden asked.

"I think that ship has sailed," Thomas said. The worry in his voice was impossible to hide. "I'm sorry you had to do this, boys. But it was the right thing."

"It feels weird," Luke said.

"It does for me, too, son."

There would be more to say about the killing, and about a world that seemed to be unravelling around them, but in the present moment words were failing. As the building silence between them became unbearable, George said, "Let's go inside and get you cleaned up, Thomas."

"Yes sir. I could use a bathroom."

5

THE AWFULLEST GOAT

Lida Maria Johnson had grown up a Cedar Key David, tormenting her brother Hayes with the belligerent sass she would hone to a razor's edge in adulthood. Like her mother Bette, she was tall, aggressive, and pretty. She was also dogged, funny, and direct, like her father Mark. She wasn't like her brother at all. While he had settled into Cedar Key life and become too entrenched there to ever consider leaving, Lida Maria had built a life in Tampa with her quiet husband Tyson and their two children Michael and Halley.

Her house was in Tampa, anyway. More weeks than not, Lida Maria found some cause to be on the island. Anytime there was a long weekend or some other reason the kids were out of school, she would take them to visit their grandparents. Her husband often stayed behind. The first time Thomas met the friendly if not effusive Tyson, he said, "Oh wow, you actually exist. I was sure Lida Maria had made you up."

So it was that she and the kids were riding their bicycles together, along the shoreline on 1st Street, when the terrible light across the bay altered the history of their lives forever. It was more than an hour after the smokestacks fell before cell phones on the island stopped receiving a signal. During this hour, Lida Maria called her husband over and over. Every call went directly to voicemail before ringing. She sent text after text with no response. She tried emailing and social media messaging apps but her normally attentive and prompt-replying husband had fallen silent. As the worry and then paranoia set in, she began calling again to hear his voice on the recorded voicemail greeting. During the third such call, reception for phones across the island dropped to zero bars and Cedar Key's contact with the outside world abruptly ended.

When he finished scrubbing the oil and mud from his face, Thomas gulped down a glass of Jeanie's famous sweet tea and reminisced about the several months he and Molly had lived on the third floor when they first married. He thought of Jeanie's chicken and rice, the never ending popsicles in the freezer, the Olympic-sized pool and regulation diving board in the backyard where the Gator dive team would sometimes come to practice, the roof of the garage from which he and his brothers-in-law would leap into the water, Molly's sharp mind and supple ass, and losing to George in the exactly one game of chess they would play before George declared his retirement as the undefeated chess champion of the house. So many of his good memories involved the big house and part of him wanted to stay there forever.

Based on what he had witnessed in the past hour, though, emphasized by the bodies lying just beyond a front door his son and nephew had shot through to kill the man with the axe, Thomas was anxious to get his boy back to the island. He was sure there was more to the story of what was happening in Gainesville, but also sure that every minute he spent trying to figure it out was a lessening of the odds they would make it out of the city.

"You sure we can't talk you into staying?" George asked.

"We've been preparing for this on the island for months," Thomas replied. "Luke and I are part of the plans to deal with... well... whatever this turns out to be. We're meant to be there."

"Haden's mama and most of my kids should be here soon," George said. "We'll take care of each other. I've got an emergency plan, too."

"I know you do," Thomas replied. "But if things get bad here there's room for everyone if you can make it to the island. My home will always be your home, George."

"Same to you, Thomas."

Making sure that Luke couldn't overhear, Thomas leaned in close and whispered, "I don't guess you were able to talk Molly out of her New York trip?"

A sad smile crept across the old soldier's face. "Have you met my daughter? No one could talk her out of anything."

"I'll be praying," Thomas said.

"Me too," George said solemnly. "When Luke pieces together what I think we both know is happening... when he realizes where New York would stand in all of this... hold him close, son."

Thomas choked on his reply. "Of course."

"Take care of my grandson, Thomas."

"Yes sir."

There were hugs all around, tears the men tried to hide, and a lingering at the door that was a hallmark of proper southern goodbyes. As they began to leave in earnest, Thomas suddenly felt a need to say something—anything—to consecrate the events that had transpired at the big house on that day and all the days before.

"Go Gators," was the poetry that came.

In unison, a family replied, "Go Gators."

By taking the back road behind the community college and avoiding most of the town, Thomas and Luke made it out of Gainesville with no additional drama. Parker Road took them past the ball fields, where Luke had shined as a little league second baseman, to its intersection with State Road 24 just short of Archer. A right turn there and it would be straight on until they saw water.

"How you holding up, son?"

"I'm good."

"It's okay to not be good. I don't think I'm good. People aren't meant to do what we had to do."

"Yeah, I get it," Luke replied unconvincingly.

Five years before, Thomas had witnessed a similar battle within his son.

It was late February and spring had been early in North Florida that year. The azaleas were tricked into blooming too soon, and odds were even whether they'd make it through March. Luke was a month into being seventeen then, wild blonde hair and confidence flowing from him like the Spring River in Arkansas where Thomas spent summers with his father as a child.

Thomas failed often at setting the best example for the boy. Luke learned too young to shoot Roman candles into a bonfire pile of old couches drenched in gasoline. They sunk a boat together in the Gulf of Mexico, had by then watched two wives packing their things into moving boxes, and diffused the grief of burying the grandfather after which Luke was named by exploding dry ice bombs in the back field behind the church. Thomas taught him to power slide a golf cart through the flooded fairways of the country club on whose 18th hole they lived until they came to their senses and moved to the actual country. They found a charming house on some field-fenced acreage with a sign near the front gate that read: *The Nevermind Ranch*. As Thomas, Luke and Annie drove down the live oak canopied dirt road for the first time, it felt as though the dream of a settled family was finally appearing before them.

With all that fenced land, Thomas decided that goats would complete the verdant dreamscape of their new life. He had always loved goats. They were affectionate and smart. Like himself and his boy they often sought mischief. They were resourceful problem-solvers, doting parents to their kids, and surprisingly athletic. Baby goats, especially dressed in little goat sweaters, were joyful to watch play together. They cavorted. They gallivanted. They took impossible risks and toyed with the laws of physics like Stephen Hawking on a dirt bike.

Thomas bought the first goats he could find for sale. They were a breed he didn't particularly like—Pygmies—but they had horns and goat faces and as soon as he saw them, he was instantly under their spell. Unfortunately, they turned out to be skittish, insufferable jerks. Once he and Luke got them into the Nevermind Ranch pasture, they were nearly impossible to catch. Good goat farming requires you to put your hands on the goats often— for regular checkups, worming treatments, and socialization. Thomas went weeks without ever touching one. Over time, he developed a system of putting out sweet feed in a bucket and when they stuck their heads in to eat, he could occasionally grab them by the horns. But that was the high-water mark of their relationship and Thomas was left wanting.

Then Mabel changed everything.

Thomas wrote a play called *Trailer Park Elegy* and submitted it to the Broadway Bound Theater Festival in New York City. They wisely rejected the rough script he sent them but did so with a detailed critique on how he could make the play better. He decided the rewrite could best be accomplished by adding a 9-minute monologue delivered to a live goat onstage. It worked. The play went on to widespread critical and financial success. To produce that play, Thomas had to undertake an odyssey to find a suitably personable goat with aspirations for theater stardom. He auditioned goats from all over the county.

And then there was Mabel.

She sprinted across the dirt field of the small dairy farm in neighboring Hawthorne the moment she saw Thomas, nuzzled her big Lamancha goat head against his and whispered in his ear, "Alas poor Yorick, I knew him." Or maybe it was, "Baaahhhh." Doesn't matter. Mabel became the stuff of theater legend, and a beloved member of the Nevermind Ranch family. She fell in love and was soon with child. Five months later she birthed Broadway and Bound, twin brother and sister, into the world. During Mabel's gestation period, Thomas systematically rehomed the other terrible goats, resolving to only keep loveable ones thereafter. That is, all except for Speedracer, the uncatchable, awfullest goat there ever was.

Speedracer was so named because she escaped the fence on her first day at the Nevermind Ranch and was so fast she outran a neighbor on a horse trying to catch her. Thomas thought she was gone for good. No such luck. Three days later she was mysteriously back inside the fence and determined to terrorize all the other goats and never allow a human to lay a finger on her. Three times men came to the farm to catch her under the guise of a free goat. Three times she vanquished the invaders. She continued to mercilessly ram the other goats, hog all the hay and sweet feed, and smirk at Thomas from across the field.

Then those sweet goat babies were born, bright and perfect. Speedracer knew Thomas loved them. She wasted no time ramming them viciously against the fence, flipping them over her horns into the unseasonably warm air, snorting and grinning as she squatted to piss on the straw bed he had made for the new kids. Thomas went after her with a net. He chased her from one edge of the field to the next, bloodied his shins on briars and jagged wire fence, and let his failing as a goat wrangler harden into puerile hatred. She couldn't be caught. Broadway and Bound were in danger and Thomas was out of options. There was only one thing to do.

The thirty-aught-six Springfield is a quintessential American round. It had its genesis in 1906 and rose to prominence in the famed M-1 Garand rifle that our GIs used to defeat the Nazis in World War II. It can propel a 165-grain bullet at 3,010 feet per second to accurately hit targets more than a thousand yards away. It has remained a popular cartridge for more than a century because it represents the upper limit of power that is tolerable to most shooters. In simple terms, it kicks like a mule but hits its target like a runaway train. Thomas' 125-pound son would lean into its recoil without a hint of flinch—all sinew and grit like his grandfather—a stone-cold killer his dad used to hold in the palm of one hand.

Luke was a better marksman than his father, though Thomas would never admit it. He was proud to have trained his boy to be safe and capable with a firearm, a rifle behind his particular blade of American grass. But Luke was also tender-hearted and as he reached out to manhood, Thomas relished the dwindling glimpses of the little boy who used to call him daddy and wouldn't fall asleep until he read him *Word Bird* after bath time.

He was slipping away from him by the day, a heartbreaking slow-motion transition from his boy to a man he hoped continued to love him. Luke chose that day to stake a claim on the manhood his father would delay forever if he could. He would be the one to handle the bad business laid inexorably before them.

The Buck family had only ever killed for food. This would be something different—a liberation for the rest of the animals in the field, an honor-killing reckoning from on high. In her defense, Speedracer didn't make it easy. She knew something was happening and frittered about the field on high alert. It wouldn't be a long shot, but it would take a high level of skill.

When it came to it, Luke crouched down into a supported position, worked the bolt action back smooth and cool, chambered the round, and drew a methodical breath. Then a pause that lingered. Thomas steadied himself for a crashing sound that didn't come. His son was frozen but unwavering, a coiled spring behind the Leupold scope, feeling the weight of death hanging in the moment. And when it seemed at last the boy would lose his nerve, Speedracer squinted at the rifle as a thundering blast tore apart the stillness. Bits of goat exploded across the new greens of an early spring, and it was finished.

"You okay?" Thomas asked.

"It feels weird."

"The price of life is sometimes death," he said, the empty cliche furrowing both their brows.

"Yeah, I get it."

It was a thing they knew we would remember forever—that awful goat in pieces and two men taking turns digging a hole.

Thomas pulled himself from the grasp of memory as they passed the US-19 intersection at Otter Creek. He looked over at Luke, saw the blank expression on his face, and recognized it as the same anguish from the goat field. He turned away quickly but could not stop the emotion from washing over him. Something had been lost when Luke pulled the trigger of the thirty-ought-six that day. There had been a heavy price for his coming of age and he had paid it tenfold again behind his grandfather's door and in the Chamberlain's yard. Thomas searched for the right words to say but none would come. They rode on together in silence.

As they neared Sumner, Thomas caught a passing glance of a fake owl on a pole in someone's garden, stationed there to ward off pests. The wise eyes of the plastic scarecrow transported him to the bottom of Anna Ruby falls again, a ring in his pocket and trepidation in his belly. Annie was standing beside him, too observant and smart to be fooled by a surprise but caught up in the moment all the same. He dropped to his knee and presented the ring to her. Before he began to speak, he saw a flash of sunlight reflecting off her necklace charm, a golden owl with wings tucked in, resting in perfect tranquility along the elegant neckline that had seemed such a treasure for him to discover. There would be heartache lining the finite path ahead for them, but in this moment, with the crashing water and the applause of exuberant strangers, Annie's perfect blue eyes reflecting an endless north Georgia sky, and the boyish smile spreading the width of Thomas' face, there existed only the false but comforting promise of love.

It had been more than three years now since Annie drove down their dirt road for the last time. She and Thomas continued to see each other sporadically, playing house for a few days at a time at her new home near Clearwater. One of them had just been staving off periodic loneliness, while the other, even now as he began to contemplate the proximity of Clearwater to the United States Central Command at MacDill Air Force Base, had continued to believe in the insidious promise at the bottom of a waterfall.

The same awful analysis that had terrified Thomas, when he considered how close Luke lived to the Navy bases in Jacksonville, now turned him inside out.

If they hit Crystal River...

He tried to stop the momentum of the thought but already it was racing toward its unbearable conclusion—if they hit Crystal River, then they certainly hit the US Central Command. If they hit Crystal River, then the great love of his life was gone, and he could no more dream of her return.

The station where Thomas had filled his truck and gas cans a few hours before had no unbroken windows remaining and nothing left on its shelves. The diesel backup generator had been unbolted and carried off. Thomas, too, was unmoored. He pushed the accelerator to the floor and stared straight ahead until the Number Four Bridge mercifully appeared before him.

6

CHICKENS AND THE CHIEF

In the town cemetery near its shore along the back bayou, Hayes and Thomas sat on the tailgate of Hayes' Ford, looking anxiously down the road toward the entrance.

"When is Rolf supposed to get here with the truck?" Thomas asked. "I should have gone with him."

"I should have gone with you to get Luke, but you didn't think to ask me."

"I thought about it," Thomas replied.

"Well then you thought about it wrong. You think I don't care about Luke?"

"That's not fair," Thomas said. "I know you care about him, but there's a whole island of people we both care about that'd be in a world of hurt if you didn't make it back."

"Fine," Hayes said, feeling not fine about it but knowing that Thomas was right.

"Fine," Thomas relented. "I'll keep you in the loop from now on."

"Fine," Hayes repeated, in the asshole tone he only ever used for enemies and close friends. "How's Luke? I can't imagine how hard all that must have been on him."

Thomas hesitated, thinking again of the awful goat and the holes in the door at the big house. "He's not great, but at least he's safe here with us now. It was hard on me, too. I showed up to his grandfather's house and all hell was breaking loose. I can't make sense of why it was happening, though. There was smoke everywhere, but I never did see the cause of it."

"No one there knew anything?"

"No. And here's the thing that really got me—I never saw a single police car or firetruck or even heard a siren. The town was being ripped apart and a guy was trying to chop in my father-in-law's front door with an axe, and no one was coming to help."

"I don't think anyone will be coming, Thomas."

"It didn't even look like Gainesville was hit, but people were acting crazy like it had."

"It won't be long before the crazy makes it here," Hayes said. "We're not ready."

As he continued to scan the empty road between them and the cemetery entrance, Thomas made an attempt at optimism. "We've done a lot already. Whatever comes at us, we'll figure it out. You think Rolf can handle this?"

"Don't worry about Rolf. He's got this. I sent Geoff McCloud with him to help. You shouldn't even be out of bed."

"Besides the diaspora underway in my ass, I feel okay," Thomas said with a pained smirk.

"Do I want to know what a diaspora is?" Hayes asked.

"You don't."

"After everything you've been through, it's crazy you're still making jokes."

"The real joke is that I'm only here because I'm a terrible captain. If Robbie and Mr. Hals and the others don't pull through..."

"Don't do that," Hayes interrupted.

"A ten dollar plastic nipple. That's the difference between me helping you smuggle chickens onto the island today or you watching me die later this week."

"You don't know that," Hayes objected.

"TJ doesn't want to worry you, but he says they don't have long."

Hayes looked away from his friend and sighed. "Nurse Toni said as much to me this morning."

"It'll be pretty hard to look anybody in town in the eye when they find out the idiotic reason I'm fine and those real watermen are gone."

"It won't be like that," Hayes said.

"If my motor would have started, I would have followed them to the ramp. As fast as the Judith Jane is, I would've beaten half of them into the shit that's killing those boys now."

"If you're worried about Mrs. Hals or the other Solaro boys or Sam's little girl, then quit whining and figure out how to make things better. I'm glad you found Luke and got him back here, but that's not enough. You don't have the luxury of feeling sorry for yourself. Not when there's so much work to do."

"I'm not feeling sorry for myself."

"Your motor didn't start, Thomas. That's the only thing we know for sure. Everything else is a crybaby *what if* we can't afford right now."

A smothering silence enveloped the two friends. Only one other time had there even been a hint of discord between them, and then it was momentary and insignificant. Thomas had purchased a forty-three-foot-long houseboat he found sitting abandoned in the back bayou mud and needed Hayes' help to pull it out. When it was built in 1968 it had been a technological wonder, but years of neglect had culminated in its most recent use as a crystal meth lab for Skip Meade and a friend from Sumner nobody else seemed to know. Their enterprise turned sour when the lab exploded and caught the boat on fire. Thomas had discovered it as a burned out shell on a surprisingly solid hull and got it on the cheap. The bayou was so shallow that only the highest of king tides would bring in enough water to float the massive, heavy craft.

The only such tide for weeks came at midnight when Hayes had to be on the clam boat early the next morning—actual midnight, not Cedar Key midnight, which was generally accepted to be 9 PM. Even on New Year's Eve, the countdown to the new year and the quaint ball drop—a ball of Christmas lights dropped over the apartment balcony above Tony's with a fishing pole—began promptly at 8:59 and 50 seconds. For Hayes, actual midnight might as well have been the end of time itself and as such his temper, normally holstered when it came to his eccentric friend, was loaded for bear and at the ready. The quick-draw moment came when Thomas's rechargeable Wal-Mart spotlight flickered to darkness on account of, at least to Hayes, "Thomas not charging the goddamn thing."

Thomas had never heard the mayor curse before. So off put and surprised was he by the reprimand, his normally quick wit failed to produce a rebuttal and he instead folded his hands and sat quietly on the bow of Hayes' boat.

"Well don't pout about it, dang. I'm just tired. I'm never up this late. Let's just get this done," Hayes had said with as much of a conciliatory tone as he could muster.

They were able to laugh about it the next day and often thereafter, but the work the rest of that evening to bring the old Nautaline to deeper water was uncomfortable for them both.

This time, Thomas was thankful for the hard medicine, and it had caused an instant change in his outlook and demeanor. "Yeah, you're right. Now's not the time to pout." He had meant it seriously but they both laughed reflexively at the memory of the dead spotlight and the meth lab houseboat.

"Of all the stuff we've done to prepare, I wouldn't have thought of chickens," Thomas said.

"If we can get them here and keep them alive, they're a renewable resource. Truth be told, I'll feel a lot better when I see Rolf and Geoff rolling down this road. We probably should have gone after the chickens right away. From what I'm hearing, no one has power anywhere off the island either and no one's phones are working. Normally in an emergency I get calls from state representatives or the Governor's office. Not only have I not heard from anyone... I also haven't heard so much as a siren or seen a plane fly by."

"Me either," Thomas said. "The Coast Guard base across the bay in Yankeetown would have had sent all kinds of boats and helicopters if they were..."

Thomas stopped the sentence because its natural conclusion became apparent. The stillness of the afternoon and the quiet road in front of them heightened the unease.

"All the stores are closed or empty," Hayes said. "People are getting desperate. It ain't easy hiding seven hundred chickens for a month, even out in the woods in Sumner."

"Jesus," Thomas replied. "I don't guess I've ever seen seven hundred chickens before."

"It's so many. But if we've done the math right it's probably just enough."

Hayes' worry was prescient. As bad as things seemed on the island in the days following the flash, they were exponentially worse across the bridge and those in Sumner began to increasingly come to the island looking for supplies.

Tensions were at a fever-pitch. The fever spiked at the bank, managed since Hayes' departure by Tabby Lowery, whose delicate features, collection of extravagant four-inch heels, and quiet demeanor belied her previous career in the United States Army. Within hours of the power failing, she faced the first legitimate run on deposits in the island's banking history.

That history began with the construction of the Cedar Key State Bank building, in the neo-classical architectural style, in 1912. It operated in that capacity continuously until 1985 when it merged into the Drummond Community Bank and stayed as such for nearly forty years. The relatively recent conversion to Seaside Bank had been met with some consternation from islanders who had become accustomed to the hometown feel of a community bank. As late as 1990, the checking accounts in Cedar Key didn't even have account numbers. Account holders could pick up a blank check from the bank or the Cedar Key Market and simply write in their name and the amount they wanted to draw. For decades, Leddy Bannon had kept a running ledger of the bank's accounts in a box in her office. Before computer databases and the internet infiltrated the financial industry, Miss Leddy's ledger was the last-word gospel on who had what money in the bank in Cedar Key at any given time. In addition to that role, she also taught Sunday school at the First Baptist Church. This is where Tabby had first learned about banking and would first hear of Miss Leddy's famous ledger.

Despite whispers that Hayes and Tabby had been carrying on together when they both worked at the bank, and that indeed this had been the reason for Hayes' divorce, the rumors were simply untrue. They had, however, started seeing each other romantically after Hayes' resignation and his divorce from Jonie was finalized. Because of her closeness to the mayor, Tabby had an insider's perspective on what many had called his extreme measures to prepare the island to deal with the mounting global crisis. For this reason, she had quietly begun to keep a daily printed backup of every account holder's balance, reasoning that in the event of a crisis that disabled the internet, some manner of order could be maintained when depositors wanted cash.

Tabby's premonition had proved invaluable as a crowd of islanders descended on the bank looking to withdraw their money. She met them in the lobby with her head teller Jonah McShane, in front of the teller stations and adjacent to the desk where she often performed notary services for clammers sending in official paperwork to the Florida Department of Aquaculture. Thomas's first interaction with Tabby had been in such a capacity, finding himself mesmerized with the methodical way she handled each piece of paper with dainty precision before signing her name with a flourish and karate-chopping the hard plastic notary stamp onto each page. For a moment that seemed to go on forever, he had been transfixed by the preternatural violence of the whole endeavor. She had certainly not intended the exchange in the way Thomas perceived it but was likewise not oblivious to the strange, if temporary, dominion it had created over him.

With similar deliberation and command, she now stood on a chair so she could be seen and heard by all the anxious depositors gathered at the bank. The diminutive Jonah, awkward and fidgety on normal days and near frantic now as he faced the building crowd, tried to hold the chair steady, but his shaking hands did more harm than good.

"As you all probably know," Tabby began, "Everything at the bank is run through a computer network. Without power we can't access anyone's accounts."

"I need my money," Dave Warble yelled from the back of the crowd. "I'll go get my generator so you've got electricity."

"The issue is the internet," Tabby replied. "We don't have an off-line accounts system. Everything is on the network."

"When is it supposed to be up again?" A voice shouted from the building crowd.

"I don't think you should be raising your voice at her," Jonah said, his own voice rising in defense of his boss. "She's trying to help you."

"It's okay, Jonah. Everyone's just worried but we'll help them as best we can." Tabby turned her attention back to the crowd, announcing, "We haven't been able to communicate with... well... anyone. But I have a temporary work-around. Because of everything that's been going on, I've started printing a ledger at the end of each day with everyone's account balances. It will take some time, since we'll have to do everything with pencil and paper, but with the guidance of the mayor and the town council, the bank is prepared to have all the cash on hand withdrawn to help you during this emergency."

The boisterous crowd seemed placated for the moment until Tabby relayed a fact to them that seemed unbelievable—the bank vault held only $46,350. Banks usually kept only enough cash on hand to handle their daily transaction needs. Larger banks in Gainesville may typically hold as much as a million dollars in cash, but a small branch like Cedar Key had considerably less in the vault at any given time.

Tabby relayed with a calm authority, "Because of the limited amount of cash on hand, and to ensure that every account holder can access some funds, there will be a withdrawal limit for each account holder. Based on the number of account holders we believe to be on the island, that limit will have to be $400."

There was a unified uproar that seemed to shake the walls of the old bank. Jonah held tight to the back of Tabby's chair. At the most fortuitous of moments, the chief of police pushed his way through the door to the front of the crowd. "Settle down, people," he said with one hand in the air and the other tapping lightly against his sidearm, hinting at force he knew he would not have to use. "Tabby's doing the best she can with what she has to work with. If you can't be orderly, then head on back home. But if $400 will help you then start forming a line and we'll get started."

The line began to form. As word spread across town about the limited funds at the bank, it would eventually stretch out the door and almost to the city park. By mid-afternoon, Seaside Bank was out of money.

By the next day, money would cease to be a useful medium of exchange in Cedar Key.

Chief Jank Edwins had spent much of his law enforcement career as a sergeant and investigator in neighboring Gilchrist County. He landed the chief of police job in Cedar Key after Hayes fired the former chief weeks before his scheduled retirement. The firing drew battle lines seemingly down the geometric center of town, pitting neighbors against neighbors and in some instances family members against one another. The frenzy of the ordeal forced people to decide if they were for Mayor Hayes or Chief Vernon, and the tiny island left little room to hide those allegiances. A social media page called the Cedar Key Rumor Mill had become the virtual town square, providing just enough keyboard anonymity to draw out the worst among people but not enough to keep the animosity on the screen.

Hayes had often said that, "Vernon's the best politician on the island," and so long as he had the ability to let folks go with a warning when it suited him, he was never without a broad swath of support in the community. That his leniency was viewed by some as unequal in its distribution seemed to get lost in the syrupy aw shucks of his outward demeanor.

By most accounts, Vernon was a skilled lawman that cared deeply about Cedar Key, but bad luck pulled the rug out from under his law enforcement career in its eleventh hour. A need arose on the island for police action and for reasons that were never entirely clear or generally agreed upon, Vernon refused to answer the call. Creepy Jim, the manager of the Cedar Lodge, so named for his penchant for offering young women at local bars five hundred dollars to let him lick their buttholes, threatened the owner of the Big Dock bar with a knife because he suspected him of running his wife over with a golf cart. When this aggression cost Creepy Jim a broken arm and caused mayhem on Dock Street on a busy weekend night, calls to 911 came in a flurry. Even though he was the officer on duty for the evening, Vernon's phone was off as he went about the business of enjoying his victory lap to retirement.

While the Rumor Mill would float outrageous theories for why Vernon had been fired, from an imagined personal feud between the chief and the mayor to one or both of the men being connected to organized crime, the truth had been more human resources than Hollywood. The council had simply called a department-heads meeting and discussed the appropriate reprimand for a first responder failing to respond. At that meeting someone asked what everyone felt would happen to an on-call plumber that did not take calls. The answer was simple and unanimous; he would of course be fired. If a tradesman's job was dependent on them doing their job, they eventually reasoned before drafting Vernon's notice of termination, then certainly the same standard should apply to emergency services personnel whose neglect of duty could mean the loss of lives.

It would be two full weeks before the next city council meeting, giving ample time for supporters of the chief to mount something akin to a holy war against the mayor and anyone who dared express support for him. *Save Vernon* flyers went up around town and a few of his well-heeled friends began sporting t-shirts with Vernon's face in a cherubic pose above the bubble-lettered declaration: *I Stand with the Chief.*

As the attacks on Hayes became more virulent and personal, Thomas raced to his defense, going after his detractors with a glib ruthlessness that served to raise the temperature of the whole affair. Since the weapons of war on the Rumor Mill were thoughts and words, the writer Thomas dispatched one unhinged accusation after another with the elegant brutality of a buzzsaw. In this arena, he had no equal on the island, and in defense of a man and a family he had come to love, there was no limit to the bad blood he was willing to engender. That Hayes happened to be on the side of right was of little consequence to Thomas, who continued throwing haymakers until the start of the meeting.

The actual meeting was something of a letdown. Several of the chief's supporters stood to tell a story about some time they had been breaking the law and Vernon let them go. Mark David stood on behalf of his son to a chorus of boos. Prescott Phillips, a minister in his former life, rose to calm the passions of the crowd, trying in vain to remind everyone that aside from this issue most of them were friends. He was convivial and generally well-liked, his Kenny Rogers aesthetic and dulcet voice appreciated by men and women alike. That his gentle admonitions were ignored, and even ridiculed, highlighted the depth of the chasm between the sides of the issue and the room.

When everyone that wanted to speak had spoken, Hayes stood from his chair and said, "I want to start by saying I like Vernon. We attend the Episcopal church together. He was a good chief for a good number of years and the island was lucky to have him. I hope when this is all over Vernon and I can be friends again. The last thing I ever wanted to do was to be faced with this kind of situation so close to his retirement. Still, we had an incident where people were seriously hurt. Folks could have been killed. On that night, Vernon had the watch, and he did not answer the call for help. Call after call after call. I lost a long night of sleep wrestling with what had to be done because I sure don't want to do it. But the citizens of Cedar Key deserve leadership in times of trouble and that leadership has to start with their chief of police."

Hayes sat back down to little fanfare and the council voted to uphold Vernon's termination. Then everyone went home and went back to their lives. Hayes had been right about Veron's important contributions to the island, and was sincere in his admiration for the now former chief. To Vernon's credit, after a short period of animosity and adjustment to a retirement whose benefits had not been affected by the firing, he rejoined an active role in the community, finding new ways to serve his church, his neighbors, and his island.

The council got busy interviewing candidates for replacing Vernon, eventually settling on the outsider Jank Edwins over Vernon's long-time lieutenant Colby Weathering. When, months later, Lieutenant Weathering came to the school where his estranged wife worked as a teacher and FFA advisor and smashed in the windows of her car with a baseball bat, the new chief handled the incident with grace and professionalism, exhibiting the kind of calm impartiality typified by good leadership. The chief replaced Lieutenant Weathering with a ruddy-faced recent academy graduate named Sean Basquiat. After Thomas began calling him Officer Biscuit, however, no one ever called him anything else again.

Chief Edwins was round in shape without seeming especially out of shape, and while he was unlikely to beat a criminal in a foot race, his sneaky intellect and observant nature augmented a developed set of police skills not often seen on a small town force. If someone parked somewhere they should not have parked, the chief would write them a ticket; if they were blonde and leggy and parked somewhere they should not have parked, the chief would still write them a ticket. Fairness paired with a jovial spirit was eventually the winning formula that endeared the new chief to more folks than not.

Thomas liked the new chief so much that he began following many of the tedious rules he had until then delighted in thwarting, though he would never break his penchant for mischief. On his birthday in the year before the smokestacks fell, based on his enjoyment of a television show about a Wyoming sheriff, Thomas was gifted a long leather cowboy duster. Wearing it made him feel like a western law man to the extent that, seeing Chief Edwins at the Jiffy store, Thomas pulled a banana from a basket by the register and tried to draw down on the chief with it like Doc Holiday. In half an instant, Chief Edwins flashed double finger pistols while Thomas fumbled the banana.

"You dead. You dead, Thomas. You tried to draw on the man and I killed you dead. Now don't you forget it." He air-spun his imaginary double six-shooters and holstered them in triumph, laughing as he headed for the door and tipping his hat at the cashier with a slow, "Good day, ma'am."

A relieved smile spread across Hayes' face when the huge U-Haul truck appeared at the cemetery entrance. When it reached the back shore and parked, Rolf and Geoff climbed down from the cab, looking like they had just stumbled out of a bar fight. They were scratched, dirty and disheveled. Clearly, the chickens had gotten the better of them.

"You boys okay?" Thomas asked with a feigned concern that was undermined by an accompanying chuckle.

"Screw you, Mr. Mayor. And screw you, too, Thomas," Rolf said while pointing at the two men who were now openly laughing.

"I never doubted you," Hayes cracked.

"We should have made a better plan for how to get 700 damn chickens out of that little barn and into the truck," Rolf said. "We couldn't keep them in the back of the truck with the door rolled up. For a while, Geoff caught them and I guarded the exit but by the time we got a hundred or so in there they worked together to overpower me and escape. I finally solved it, but I had to break the truck a little."

They all walked to the back of the U-Haul and saw the chicken-sized square hole Rolf had chopped into the roll-up door with an axe.

"Once we had the chicken-slot, both of us could catch them and shove them through the hole," Geoff said pridefully. "But 700 of anything is a lot. If I never see another chicken again, it'll be too soon."

"Unfortunately, we'll all be seeing them plenty," Hayes said. "I think we have the back half of the cemetery fenced off pretty good, but these chickens are a big part of our disaster plan. They're too important to leave unguarded."

"Seriously... chicken guard duty?" Rolf asked.

"I think it'll take two people, and we will need to have guards posted 24/7. If every healthy person helps, we should each only have to do it once a month or so," Hayes said.

"What are we guarding them against?" Geoff asked.

"Thieves, first and foremost, but also just that they aren't getting out of the cemetery or drowning in the backwaters or being carried off by owls and hawks. There's one threat that's too big to risk, though, even with guards," Hayes said in an ominous tone.

Thomas shook his head. "I thought you were kidding about that."

"About what?" Rolf asked.

"The shiftiest little terrorists on the island. Chicken-murdering bandits and smarter than half the clammers in the fleet. Coons!" Hayes said with a weird intensity.

Because of its separation from the mainland, Cedar Key had fewer chicken predators on the island than most places, but raccoons thrived there in abundance. It had become a badge of some honor on the island to raise baby racoons on the bottle and turn them into pets that lived in people's homes. At least a dozen people on the island lived with raccoons and their existence in polite society was taken as a matter of island tradition.

"Even if we're watching these chickens day and night, the coons will sneak in and carry them off right under our noses," Hayes said.

"What do we do about it?" asked Geoff.

"We're gonna start eating raccoons and kill every last one we see," Hayes said.

"You think people are gonna go for that? Tony Hankle posts about his raccoons on the internet every day," Rolf said.

In the instructive tone he had subconsciously honed to a knife's edge during contentious town council meetings, Hayes announced, "Well, there ain't any more Internet and there might never be again. Until I hear otherwise, I'm moving along like we're alone in the world on this island and I suggest you do the same. These chickens can lay enough eggs for just about everyone, and we can get some of the FFA kids at the school to start a breeding program. Eventually we might get to eat a chicken from time to time."

Thomas said, "If it's as bad as it seems, it won't be long before word gets out about this. Two guards aren't gonna cut it when folks across the bridge find out about 700 chickens."

"I know," Hayes replied. "We'll have to deal with that soon enough. For now, let's just keep working the plan."

In normal times, the population of the island hovered around 750. During holidays or on festival weekends, that number could balloon five-fold. While the world had teetered for months on the brink, there had been fewer people on the island every day leading up to the flash. Those whose primary homes were in another state had nearly all left to be near their families and support systems. In total, only 352 people were actually on the island when the smokestacks fell. In two weeks-time, that number would be reduced to 325. In a month, the number of people under the mayor's charge would closely match that of the Spartans in the pass at Thermopylae. Their ordeal to come would be less immediate but just as dire.

"It just feels weird to be putting them in the cemetery," Geoff said.

"It's the only place on the island with enough land to accommodate them," Hayes replied. "And the shape of the cemetery means we can mostly box 'em in on three sides with water. John Mitchell's boy Jimmy and the rest of the city crew just finished fencing up this fourth side and a few gaps. Geoff, open that gate so Rolf can back the truck inside the fence and we can let the birds out."

With the truck safely inside and the gate secured, Thomas unlatched the roll-up door and shoved it open. A Hitchcockian aerial advance ensued almost immediately. There would be precious little cause for laughter in the coming weeks, but Hayes couldn't resist a deep belly laugh when the birds knocked Geoff and Thomas off their feet as they raced for freedom. The rush of sounds, feathers and shit as the two men on the ground covered their heads was a fitting coda to the whole strange affair.

The laughter stopped abruptly with the sound of a wailing siren and the chief's police truck racing past the cemetery. Leaving the U-Haul where it sat, the four men piled into Hayes' truck and headed after the chief. They caught up to him as he was parking in front of the school and running inside.

"Follow the chief!" Hayes yelled.

The four friends made their way inside and raced for the sounds of commotion and yelling coming from the cafeteria. There they found the chief handcuffing two men who were covered in blood and cursing. The school lunch ladies, Bev Wemberly and Esther Whiting, with easily 140 years of life between them, stood nearby, coiled vipers ready to strike again.

"Give me a hand, fellas," said the chief.

"What happened here, Jank?" Hayes asked.

"They were loading up boxes of cafeteria food when we came in for work," Bev said, a righteous fire rising in her voice.

"What kind of low-life steals from children?" Esther added.

"I hit the big one with a soup pot," Bev said, holding up a pot that seemed too heavy for her frail arms to even lift, much less wield as a weapon. "Esther got the other one with a pan."

"I can't believe you're still coming into work, ladies," Hayes said. "The school might be closed for a long time."

"We didn't know what else to do, and I figured someone ought to be here to hold down the fort," Bev explained.

"It's lucky I got here when I did," the chief said, "Or these boys might have been hurt a lot worse."

The two handcuffed men looked down and away, more embarrassed than ashamed.

"That's Lane Meade on the left and the other looks like a Meade but I can't place who he belongs to," Hayes said.

"What's your name, son?" The chief asked.

"I want a lawyer," he said defiantly.

"We still doing lawyers, Chief?" Hayes asked.

"I haven't seen any around lately, have you?"

"Not lately. Maybe they can sort it out at the jail in Bronson... unless you gentlemen want to tell us what happened here."

The two Meades glanced at each other, unsure of themselves.

"I know it's just been a few days," Lane began. "But we're out of everything already and there's no place to get nothing. Bronson and Williston have already been picked clean and the road to Gainesville's blocked just past Highway 27. We figured there wouldn't be any more school so they wouldn't need this stuff."

"So, you thought you could just come take it?" Rolf snapped.

"Talk to me when you've gone two days without eating, asshole," the other Meade said.

"I might be an asshole, but I didn't just get my ass handed to me by a lunch lady," Rolf replied, his quick temper instantly ignited.

Hayes intervened to calm the situation, asking Lane, "What have you been hearing in Sumner?"

"I've heard all kinds of things. Thought it was just Crystal River at first, but my daddy says it's everywhere."

"It's some kind of war," the other Meade added. "And maybe we lost it."

Hayes saw the fear in their faces and recognized it because the lack of any reliable information since the flash had made him feel it, too. As much to mollify himself as the young thieves he declared, "We're not in the business of losing wars. I'm sure we'll hear something soon. It's not time yet to go turning on each other. It won't ever be. I know you know better than stealing from a school."

"What's the plan, Hayes?" the chief asked. "I can't reach anybody at the Sheriff's office or the jail. Should I still try to take them in?"

"Looks like these kids just got in a little over their heads here, and Miss Bev and Miss Esther already whooped 'em pretty good. I don't love the idea of risking you on the road all the way to the jail and burning up all that gas, Chief. Especially when we're not sure if there even is a jail."

Thomas said, "Based on what I saw on the first day, I can't imagine how bad it is now."

"We're not just gonna let them go, are we?" Geoff protested.

Hayes squatted down to look the younger men in the eyes. "If we take you fellas back across the bridge and turn you loose, would you promise to stay away from the island?"

The Meades begrudgingly agreed.

"I need you to tell anyone else that's thinking of coming here to take what belongs to us that this is the only warning there will be. From here on out, it's immediate force." Drawing a Springfield Model 1911 from his belt and pointing it coolly at Lane, Hayes continued, "Tell them the island's armed and the island's closed. You understand?"

They nodded to the mayor.

"I need to hear you say it out loud. Lane?"

"Yes, sir. I understand," he replied.

"Me, too," came the second voice.

Hayes lowered his weapon. "Drive them out past the Dollar Store in Sumner and drop them off and get on back as quick as you can, Chief."

"Yes, sir."

Hayes knew his bargain and their word meant almost nothing. He also knew they would not be the last to come for the island's resources. As Chief Edwins pulled away from the school, the mayor had the first stirrings of a drastic idea he would soon present to the council and the town. The venerable Number Four Bridge, a physical and metaphysical connection between the island and the wider world, had become a liability. Bev and Esther had been lucky with the junior varsity Meades, but if the island's defenses were not hardened in short order, it could not hope to stand against the more ferocious raiders that were sure to come from across the channel. Without the bridge, however, any help that might arrive would also be turned back.

The remaining information the council would need to finalize a decision about the bridge would come at great peril and it would come from the sky.

7

———•———

THE LAST FLIGHT OF CAPTAIN McCOOL

I n the late afternoon hours of 30 January 1968, Marine Corps First
Lieutenant Robert B. McCloud walked the city streets of Hue in
South Vietnam as he had many times over the past several months. The
seventh-generation Cedar Key native was a freshly promoted helicopter
pilot with the Marine Medium Helicopter Squadron-165 (MMH-165).
Prior to this day, his duty in Vietnam had been underwhelming, flying
routine supply and transport missions in his Boeing CH-46 Sea Knight
helicopter, affectionately nicked namedthe *Phrog*. He had become accustomed to regular flights to supply the US Military Assistance Command,
Vietnam (MACV) via Hue's Tay Loc Airfield.

Until 1945, the ancient imperial city of Hue had been the capital of
Vietnam and was still its cultural and historical cradle. For the past 150
years, it had somehow remained untouched by the ravages of war. Col-
onizing French forces in Vietnam were defeated in 1954 at the battle of
Dien Bien Phu, leading to a summit in Geneva between the French and
Vietnamese, along with representatives from the United States and China.
There a cease-fire was negotiated, along with a temporary division of the
country along the 17th parallel. French forces would remain in the South,
and Ho Chi Minh's forces would remain in the North. The city of Hue
lay below the 17th parallel but even as tensions between the communist

leaders in the north and western democratic nations intensified over the next decade, and eventually metastasized into the Vietnam war, Hue had largely remained out of the fray.

At a strategy meeting with Lyndon Johnson in Honolulu in 1966, General William Westmoreland had warned the American president about the significance of Hue. When asked what his next move would be if he were the enemy commander, Westmoreland said without hesitation, "Capture Hue." Explaining that the city was the symbol of a unified Vietnam, he continued, "Taking it would have a profound psychological impact on the Vietnamese in both the North and the South, and in the process the North Vietnamese might seize the two northern provinces as bargaining points in any negotiations."

Two years after this meeting, almost to the day, Lieutenant McCloud had noticed a change in the normal rhythm of the city as he walked along the bank of the Perfume River. Shops were closed much earlier than usual and the one establishment that never closed at all, the local brothel, was boarded up and empty. At a time when the city would normally be preparing to celebrate the Vietnamese new year of Tet with fireworks and ornate decorations, the streets were eerily deserted. The lieutenant developed the sinking feeling in his belly that local residents knew something he did not.

To his historical credit, the Army of the Republic of Vietnam (ARVN) Lieutenant General Ngo Quang Truong suspected an imminent attack on Hue. From his headquarters inside the walled Citadel, a fortified city-within-a-city, he dispatched a reconnaissance platoon and an Australian Army adviser to scout the northern bank of the river, the most likely route for an enemy attack. From the cover of bushes, the scouts waited for evidence of an enemy advance. Though he had leave for the next three days, Lieutenant McCloud's foreboding compelled him to return to the airfield to secure his helicopter.

Shortly before midnight, General Truong's scouts observed a long column of enemy soldiers materializing in the darkness. They were witnessing the 800th, 802nd, and 12th Sapper battalions marching along the riverbank toward the city.

North Vietnamese sappers were the army's *Bo Doi Dac Cong*, roughly translated as *soldiers in special forces*, elite commandoes that were well-supplied, highly trained, and possessed of a reputation as ferocious fighters. In hushed tones, the allied scouts relayed the enemy's approach to General Truong at division headquarters, who immediately dispatched a reconnaissance aircraft from Tay Loc airfield. It returned from the foggy night two hours later reporting nothing unusual. The general remained convinced an attack was eminent. He recalled the scouts to the headquarters within the Citadel and took stock of his defenses, depleted to fractional levels due to most of his soldiers being on leave for the upcoming Tet holiday.

At half past three in the morning on 31 January, a North Vietnamese signal flare illuminated the night sky over Hue. Four sappers dressed in the uniform of the ARVN, having gained access to the city earlier in the evening via a drainage culvert in the southeastern wall of the Citadel, overwhelmed the guards at the closed Chanh Tay Gate, killing them before they could raise an alarm. They used explosives to blow open the gate, allowing the 800th battalion and a portion of the 12th Sapper Battalion to infiltrate the city and head toward the airfield. Simultaneously, thirty sappers scaled the northwestern wall and overpowered the guards at the An Hoa and Hau Gates, opening them to a waiting infantry company. This force headed for General Truong's headquarters.

Through the early morning hours, coordinated enemy infiltrations of the city persisted, meeting little to no meaningful resistance. All but a small section of the airfield where Lieutenant McCloud's helicopter was hangered fell to the enemy, who destroyed every aircraft they encountered. McCloud and a small force of South Vietnamese Hac Bao soldiers and support personnel mounted a determined defense of the hangar and the southeastern end of the airfield.

Fourteen enemy battalions would attack Hue as part of coordinated attacks across South Vietnam that came to be known as the Tet Offensive. While ARVN and American military leaders had for some time expected a country-wide engagement from the enemy, the beginning of the Tet Offensive had still caught them generally by surprise. This surprise was felt more acutely in Hue than anywhere else, where furloughed defense forces and bad weather augmented the trouble for the South Vietnamese and American defenders.

As General Truong became increasingly worried that his headquarters would be overrun, he issued a call for the Hac Bao soldiers to fall back to its defense. Believing this withdrawal would lead to the fall of the remainder of the airfield, Lieutenant McCloud resolved to try to fly his Phrog out of the city. If he could reconnect with his squadron, he reasoned, he would be able to get back into the fight. Despite withering enemy fire and several rounds taken to the body of his aircraft, he managed to lift over the southern wall of the Citadel, hugging the waters of the Perfume River below the tree line for concealment, and escape to the relative safety of his squadron.

McCloud would be debriefed and would get a night's sleep before being pulled back into the hostilities. On 1 February, Army General Tolson had ordered his division's reconnaissance element, the 1st Squadron, 9th Cavalry, to scout positions near the southwest corridor of the city. Enemy fire had brought down one of the Army's UH-1 helicopters, perhaps the chopper most associated in the public consciousness with the Vietnam War, and its crew was holding out against an overwhelming enemy force. It was pure chance that Lieutenant McCloud, tasked with delivering supplies to another nearby unit, noticed the siege of the downed Army crew. With gunships strafing the area in a seemingly indiscriminate manner, McCloud swooped down into the melee and landed, using his sidearm to provide feeble cover fire for the American soldiers racing toward his helicopter. When he pulled his craft up and away from the firefight, the rescued Army men were dumbstruck with the icy precision of the Marine at the controls.

A dazed soldier, seeing double through broken eyeglasses, mistook the single silver bar on Lieutenant McCloud's uniform as a Captain's insignia. Yelling above the wash of the rotors, the soldier asked, "What's your name, sir?"

"McCloud," the lieutenant shouted back.

"Pretty cool flying, Captain," the soldier replied.

"Captain McCool!" Another soldier yelled with the enthusiasm of Lazarus returned to the miracle of life.

Lieutenant McCloud did not correct him. Though he would eventually become a Captain and then a Major and finally retire as a Lieutenant Colonel, tales of the *Fire-flight of Captain McCool*, as it became known, followed him throughout his military service and into civilian life.

The Tet Offensive would eventually end in the sound defeat of North Vietnamese forces across the country and the recapture of Hue by the South. Still, largely due to the bloodbath that was the 33-day Battle of Hue and the grim optics of the entire offensive, public sentiment in the United States turned against further prosecution of the war. At a moment of great triumph, and with the enemy on the ropes, the US would begin an acquiescence into the disquietude of its first significant military defeat. Like so many Vietnam veterans, Captain McCool would spend the rest of his life bitter that their costly achievements during the Tet Offensive, and indeed the entire war itself, would be abandoned on the precipice of victory to appease those on the home front who had not joined them in the fight.

Back home in Cedar Key, with his new son Geoff and wife Melinda Beth, the latter becoming the namesake of the stone crab boat he would use to earn a living for the rest of his life, Robert McCloud settled into a life of relative prosperity but spiritual angst. On nights when the stillness of island life beset him, he would drift with ease but not comfort from the bourbon to the ancient walls of the Citadel and the banks of the Perfume River.

A month went by, shrouded in difficulty and death, since the fall of the smokestacks. During this time Cedar Key slid into a pre-industrial version of itself, with idle leisure replaced by the daily physical toil required to keep the Reaper at bay. The frenetic scurrying of the unprepared had run its course, as had the naive hope that help was coming. In the first few days, before it became clear that gasoline simply could not be purchased anywhere within a tank's drive, many folks had set out from the island to find loved ones or to seek answers and supplies. Those that returned did so with the knowledge that the Meade boys had been telling the truth about the surrounding small towns being picked cleaned. Of those that returned, only Thomas had made it further east than Bronson, and by the second week after the flash the desperation of those across the bridge made crossing it too unsafe for most on the island to attempt.

In normal times, the passing of a month of days would seem to happen in a blur. As the reality of life without electricity and modern conveniences set in, the minutes of each day slowed to a tedious crawl. Front porch bartering replaced the fiat currency economy and the bosom of western abundance and frivolity shriveled to a nub in Cedar Key.

Buelah Hancock was the first of the non-watermen on the island to die. A longtime member of the Cedar Key Water and Sewer Board, Ms. Hancock was quick to pass judgement on and lash out against anyone in her field of view. When questioned, even during a campaign for reelection, about the lack of meaningful improvement in the island's fresh water supply or the Board's inaction to address the existential threat of saltwater intrusion into the shallow aquifer of the area, she would most often choose disdain and personal attacks over dialogue. If there had been a coroner on the island, they would have demurred about the cause of her death to the kind of noncommittal generality often assigned the passing of old, ill-spirited people. But while her death would likely have been put down as natural causes, it was the fear and stress of the unnatural sun across the bay that had simply overwhelmed her bitter heart. In a world where Billy Joel could still be heard from speakers, there might well have been some axiomatic truth in the saying that *only the good die young*, but in the new reality of life on the island and maybe, as far as anyone could tell, anywhere, death was happy to visit anyone and for the most trivial of reasons.

Type 1 Diabetics Sheridan Phillips, Margie Van Landing, Tom Foster, and Bob Corliss held on for varying amounts of time after their unrefrigerated insulin went bad, but none past a week. A half dozen type 2 diabetics began to pass over the coming weeks. A list of ailments that were previously benign if treated with readily available prescriptions began to bear their teeth. An accelerated Darwinism laid siege to the island, despite the best efforts of Hayes, Thomas, Rolf, and TJ to solve the new survival problems that seem to arise daily.

Adding to the practical troubles of the island was an intangible enemy that served as a force multiplier to the despair of daily life—the lack of meaningful information about the wider world. Without some idea of the fate of the nation or even larger nearby cities in Florida, Hayes and other leaders felt handcuffed when making plans for how best to protect the citizenry. Thomas' hour in Gainesville, at the genesis of the unrest there, had generated more questions than answers.

Had the city been attacked, and he simply didn't see where?
If not, where was all the smoke coming from?
Why was there no police presence?

When seventeen chickens were stolen by a marauding pick-up truck plowing through the wire fence that secured the birds in the back half of the cemetery, Hayes had seen enough and reached out to a man he knew would answer the call.

"Of course."

This was the immediate reply from Lt. Colonel McCloud when Hayes first broached the subject. The mayor explained that a reconnaissance flight to scout for signs of life or ruin would be invaluable to the planning of the island's future. As TJ began to lay out all the risks associated with the flight, specifically the possibility and even likelihood of encountering deadly fallout if the larger cities were hit as hard as feared, there grew a twinkle in the old pilot's eye. Despite a family he loved and an island he belonged to, a few decades of catching stone crabs in the relative safety of the Gulf had left him unrecognizable to himself. In his dreams he was never far from the controls of his Sea Knight helicopter and the high walls of the Citadel, though he had not actually flown in more years than he could remember.

"It's been a little while," Colonel McCloud mused.

Hayes said, "No helicopters on the island, but you can fly planes, too, right?"

"Give me a half hour with the manual and I could fly the space shuttle through a thunderstorm."

"Sounds like our guy," said TJ.

"There's a Cessna 172 tied down at the end of the runway now. It doesn't belong to anyone we know," Hayes said.

"Hell no," the Colonel replied. "I'd rather walk than fly that high-winged station wagon. Bob Corliss kept a Piper Archer in his hangar by the runway. I'm sure Mary would be glad for his plane to be put to good use. One time Bob and a couple buddies and I flew that old bird all the way to the Bahamas. We had it so weighed down we could only fill the fuel tanks up halfway or it wouldn't get off the ground. We had to keep landing when we reached a quarter tank and fill it back up to half. Took us all day to make it down there but we had a ball."

"How far could you go on a full tank and still make it back home safe?" Hayes asked.

"Is the Piper full?" TJ interjected.

The Colonel answered, "Except when we were flying heavy, Bob always kept it full. He was a squared away pilot to the end. I'd be shocked it wasn't full of 100 low lead, topped off with oil, and ready to fly. His plane has the Lycoming 360 engine. It burns about 10 gallons an hour. If I don't push it wide open, the 48 gallon tank should give me about five hours of flight time until bone dry. At least 500 nautical miles, maybe 550."

"That's more than I thought," Hayes said. "Is that enough to see what became of Tampa and back up to Jax and over Gainesville on your way home?"

"Plenty," said the Colonel. "I've made that loop many times. I could get a clear view of Orlando and Canaveral, too."

"We'd know so much if we just knew whether or not they were still standing," Hayes said.

The Colonel replied with a forgotten bravado, "Consider it done, Mr. Mayor."

That was the extent of the planning for the mission. Hayes and TJ would pay a visit to Mary Corliss, who as predicted granted the use of her husband's plane with a sense of pride and even something akin to joy. The following day, the seventy-two year old Marine would fly a mission into harm's way once more. This night, he would make love to his wife on the sofa in the living room, extravagantly burning a scented candle and holding her into the small hours of the morning.

On their walk home, Hayes began to feel the weight of what he had asked of the Colonel. "How dangerous will this flight be, TJ?"

"I keep thinking about what had to have happened for Crystal River to be targeted," TJ replied.

"Me, too. If they had a bomb for the power plant, surely they had several for the military bases in Tampa and Jax, at least."

"If that's the case," TJ speculated, "Then there's no telling how much radiation is floating around out there."

Hayes continued the thought TJ was exploring. "So, if the Colonel comes back with the bad news I think we expect he's gonna find…"

"Yeah," TJ said. "I don't see how he won't get hammered with grays."

"It doesn't matter that you told him all this. Once we told him what we needed, nothing would keep him out of that plane."

"That's true, but I think we knew that upfront. And we're just gonna have to find a way to be okay with that, Hayes. If you could fly a plane, I'm sure you would have done it yourself."

"Would I?"

"It doesn't matter. For all we know it's still a war out there. The Colonel knows more about that environment than anyone else on the island. We need the military pilot to fly this mission. He probably needs it, too. The way I see it, if we don't all do the things we know how to do, when they need to be done, what kind of a chance do we stand in the long run?"

"There's a chance he could be fine though, right?"

Unlike his friend Thomas, who would have known the right thing to say in a moment as delicate as this, TJ hesitated. The few beats of punishing silence moved around and through them both until they became unbearable.

Hayes said, "We better get on home and get some rest so we can see the Colonel off in the morning. He's gonna get an early start."

Since the day the smokestacks fell, sunlight was seen on the island with less and less frequency. In normal years, foggy winter days often blanketed Cedar Key in gray but as this March dragged on and spring approached, the lack of color and light began to take a toll on everyone. So it was that dawn and the night it came to replace were nearly indistinguishable to Colonel and Mrs. McCloud as they walked with their adult son Geoff toward the George T. Lewis Airport on Piney Point. At just 2,355 feet long, it was the shortest public runway in Florida and had often been utilized by flight instructors in Gainesville to teach their students short-field take-offs and landings. Every other year or so, an unskilled, usually non-instrument-rated pilot would crash there, most often on take-off. Because the waters of the Gulf and the horizon tended to blend together from the vantage point of the pilot, visual clues would mislead them into believing they were flying toward the water. The natural inclination to continue to pull back on the yoke to gain altitude would eventually increase the wing's angle of attack to such a severe degree that air would cease to flow under and over it, resulting in a stall. The low altitude just after take-off meant there was no real chance to recover.

Colonel McCloud's training meant he would rely on the altimeter in the familiar Piper Archer and would have no trouble taking off from his home airfield. As the McClouds rounded the corner past Mike Carline's house, appearing in their field of view came a sight that took the breath from them. Melinda Beth began to sob, clinging to her husband's arm to stay on her feet. The younger McCloud caught the Colonel's gaze and was swept into a wave admiration for his father and his hometown. Nearly every able-bodied person in Cedar Key was there, lined shoulder to shoulder down both sides of the runway. A thundering cheer spread across the field and even the old Marine indulged a burst of pride and then deep gratitude.

Thomas and Hayes held opposite ends of a giant hand-painted banner that read, "Give 'em Hell, Captain McCool."

Such a scene in a movie would be too sentimental to be believed, but none of the assembled islanders, and certainly not the McClouds, seemed to mind. For the first time in the past awful month, they had reason to feel good about themselves and a reason, however small, for hope.

Captain McCool put the familiar plane through a methodical but short preflight check, then kissed his wife and son. He climbed over the wing and into the cockpit, fired up the Lycoming engine, and taxied to the end of the runway. Though there were no other planes that could hear him, he tuned the radio to the Common Traffic Advisory Frequency of 122.9, pressed the button on the plane's mic and said, "Piper Archer, November 82083, departing Runway 23 for southbound departure."

With an uncharacteristic flourish befitting the moment but not the military man, he added, "Captain McCool, with orders to give 'em hell. Roger that and happy hunting. Godspeed, Cedar Key."

The Archer fired itself into the gray morning sky and was gone.

8

THE NEW WORLD

The forty-eight gallons of fuel in Bob Corliss' airplane could have kept the Colonel aloft for around five hours at normal cruising speeds, perhaps another thirty minutes if he had worked to conserve fuel. When five hours came and went since the dramatic feel-good scene of his departure, anxiety swept through the crowd that had reassembled to see his return. By hour six, most people had gone home. As the sun began to set at the western end of the runway, only Melinda Beth, Geoff, Thomas, and Hayes remained.

The high emotions of the day had settled into bone-weary exhaustion. All the encouraging possible scenarios for the Colonel's absence had been discussed and eventually, though not out loud, dismissed. Thomas persisted in a dogged optimism that relied on the possibility of the Colonel having landed at some other airport, but no one could muster the energy to believe it. A month of skies without even the sound of aircraft overhead had conditioned them out of believing in a world where flying machines were still plausible. The miracle of Captain McCool having slipped the surly bonds of Cedar Key's gravity earlier in the day was the final mystic scene from an old world story.

In the new world, no magic remained.

The McClouds would keep vigil at the runway for most of the next several days, but the unwelcoming sky remained silent and gray.

For Hayes, the missing Colonel was a battle cry. Any doubts he harbored about the right course of action were turned out of himself and replaced with a booming call to action. He would call an emergency meeting of the town council for two days later and spend the interim riding his bicycle door to door encouraging everyone on the island to attend.

In the old world, he had often been teased for riding a bicycle when golf carts were the preferred mode of transportation around the island. In the new world, a top of the line four-wheel-drive pickup truck couldn't be traded for a bicycle with two good tires and a working chain. In the little wooden basket attached above the rear tire was a yellow legal pad and a few pens. He would leave a handwritten notice of the meeting at any home where he couldn't talk directly to the occupant. The decisions that lay ahead would likely split the council, as even trivial matters often did in the past. In addition to wanting the residents to have meaningful input about the plan he intended to present, Hayes felt a need to remind everyone that the government of the town, if not the nation, continued to function.

In times of prosperity, it was a common feature of southern culture to hold government, especially that of faraway state and federal masters, in perpetual contempt. The Cedar Key ethos had always been more Jefferson than Hamilton, and the town leaders were viewed with slightly less disdain than those in Tallahassee and Washington. When society was threatened with actual collapse, however, the essential idea of government transformed from a yoke to be thrown off whenever possible to that of a lighthouse in the storm. Even when severely limited in its ability to provide for the citizenry, the thought of its continuance was a comfort in times of upheaval.

At most council meetings, the mayor could count on reliable opposition from Sally Rosencrantz, a blank page of a woman who asked obvious, rudimentary questions during every proceeding as a way of making sure she appeared in the official record, and Slim Worthman, a bad haircut masquerading as a full human being. Because of his ironclad alliance with Susie Coles, the swing vote often came down to Nanette Hera, a congenial woman whose desire to be liked made her the most pliable of the council members.

Susie Coles was a Tasmanian Devil hiding in angel wings held on with duct tape and superglue. Nothing of consequence happened in Cedar Key without Susie's blessing and, usually, her guidance. Before the smokestacks fell, she ran the welcome center at the Chamber of Commerce, in addition to her work turning the local food bank into a model of efficiency and quadrupling the number of families it fed every week. She was especially enamored of Thomas, whom she called Peter Pan because of his youthful exuberance and unwillingness to grow up. She learned quickly that Thomas had no ability to tell her no when she called looking for help on some project or another. Because of her loving manipulation, Thomas served on the school's advisory council, unloaded the delivery truck at the food bank, planted trees for the city's tree committee, captained a boat for the coastal cleanup days, and dressed up as the Grinch for the annual Christmas parade.

Because of Susie's relentless energy and refusal to accept defeat, the
nearby coastal community of Suwannee— situated where the Suwannee
River has its confluence with the Gulf of Mexico— replaced its aging and
overabundant septic tanks with a state-funded city sewer service. This new
infrastructure dramatically reduced the nutrient outflows into the Gulf,
paving the way for the oyster industry's triumphant return to area and
preventing harmful pollution from reaching Cedar Key. Additionally, in
tandem with Hayes, her advocacy for the clam industry in Cedar Key was
a key reason the working waterfront never gave way to the development
pressures that had squeezed other coastal communities in Florida. Her
partnership with the mayor, and their mutual love for the island, made
them a formidable team, especially when Cedar Key faced the serious issues
that others with less resolve would seek to sidestep.

"I'm worried about Nan," Susie whispered to Hayes as the crowd was
gathering for the emergency council meeting.

"She's smart and understands the situation," Hayes replied.

"Yeah, but she's like a little kitten that gets picked up and dropped.
There's no telling what'll happen when she hits the ground. I'm a beat up
old coon that falls out of trees so often I don't even feel it anymore. But
even I'm feeling the impact of all this shit, Hayes. I don't know if she can
hold up."

"She'll hold," Hayes replied.

"I guess we'll find out."

The emergency meeting had been moved from City Hall to the park
to accommodate the whole town. The council sat at a table in the gazebo
where the Chamber served hot apple cider during the yearly Christmas tree
lighting ceremony. It was often remarked that during the holiday festivities
in the waterfront park, Cedar Key felt like a Hallmark movie. In the last
days of a cold March, against the backdrop of daily funerals, abducted

chickens, and the absent Colonel, it all felt like the setting for a different kind of film.

The assembled islanders formed a semi-circle around the gazebo so they could hear the proceedings. Hayes stood to lead everyone in the Pledge of Allegiance, as he did for every council meeting. The familiar words felt foreign in his mouth as he contemplated the possibility that a pledge was being made to a Republic that no longer stood. Especially given the primary purpose of this meeting—to consider removing the physical connection between the island and the rest of the country—every syllable demanded reconsideration. *One nation, under God, indivisible.* Were they not considering such a division from the nation as the pledge deemed impossible? Where was God's hand in any of this? The Number Four Bridge was not just a tangible connection between Cedar Key and peninsular Florida; it was the link between here and there, us and them, the way the world used to be and the way it would never be again.

As expected, Sally Rosencrantz and Slim Worthman made anemic arguments for the possibility of any arriving help being turned away by a missing bridge. The fear and paralysis evident in their tone rang hollow. The assembled islanders had spent the past month persevering in the face of hardship and death—burying their loved ones in the morning and planting spring vegetables in the afternoon. Every day that passed without word from the wider world solidified the collective realization that the island would rise or fall on its own.

No serious person continued to believe that help was coming.

As Hayes began to rise in rebuttal, Nanette Hera waved him off. Standing to the fullness of her five feet, zero inches, she produced a withering glare at Rosencrantz and Worthman as she walked in front of the council table and onto the gazebo steps to be closer to her fellow citizens.

"My colleagues mean well," she began. "I know they love Cedar Key as much as the rest of us, but you can love a place and still be wrong about how to best protect it. Each day since the smokestacks fell has been a little harder than the day before. I think most of us are about out of what little food we had saved up. I've been learning to sew a mullet net. Linda Richland has converted the grill at Fannie's Cafe into a wood stove and keeps the fires going to cook the fish and crabs so many of you have been busy catching. I see yards plowed into gardens all over town. Prescott Phillips is on that goofy three-wheeled bicycle all day long, delivering food to shut-ins, checking on the infirm, and praying for anybody he can lay his hands on. Several of the houses with wells have converted them to hand pumps and opened them for use by everyone. James Mitchell is working on a plan to get the central water system back up and running. The Chief and his deputies continue their work, as do the men at the firehouse. All around the island, our neighbors are doing what they can, not just for themselves but for others. The world is changing. The world has changed. I wish that none of this had happened, but if we don't change as well to meet the challenges of this new life, we will absolutely die."

Nanette held the crowd in her strengthening grasp like a tent revival preacher calling down the holy spirit.

"We can't save everyone," she continued. "We have come to a circle the wagons moment in our history, and I am resolved that the wagons will begin and end on this side of the Number Four Channel. We cannot defend the island if our enemies can just stroll across the bridge to steal food from our school or plunder our chickens and eventually kill us to take what we have. The bridge must come down."

Hayes and Susie were thunderstruck by a version of their friend they had never witnessed before.

"Are there any public comments before we vote?" Hayes interjected, recognizing that Nanette's newfound statesmanship had reached its zenith. No one stood to speak formally but chants of, "Bring it down," broke out, signaling widespread acceptance of the 3 to 2 vote that was to come.

Hayes announced to the crowd, "Three votes in favor, two opposed. The motion carries. After this meeting adjourns, we'll get started figuring out how to make it happen."

The dissenting council members shrunk into themselves, knowing they had misjudged the temperament of the town. Slim, especially, had felt such a backlash before. When the miserable Pennsylvania transplant Margaret Van Landing began a war against the working waterfront, filing endless formal complaints about the boats and gear that adorned the streets and yards of the island, and threatening litigation against the town, Slim made the mistake of taking her losing side of the argument, daring to suggest that Cedar Key would be better for tourists if it looked more like other coastal towns in the state. Thomas wrote an excoriating rebuttal of the yankee's attacks, implicating Slim as a co-conspirator and existential threat to an island legacy the net ban had tried but failed to extinguish. From then on, Slim could seldom eat a meal out or shop at the market without a waterman stopping to give him a piece of their mind.

Hayes continued, "In addition to new safety measures like removing the bridge, I've prepared a list of proposed new city policies for everyone to think about between now and the next meeting, which I propose for a week from today. That will give you time to reach out to the council members and register your opinions before we vote."

The new policies included allowing any citizen in the outlying areas of the island to petition for an eminent domain action for vacant houses closer to town. Since much of the daily toil of life now revolved around acquiring and transporting water from the wells with hand pumps, and in keeping with the belief that absentee owners were unlikely to return to their island homes, it made sense to consolidate as many of the residents as possible closer to community resources. A successful petition would require a written pledge to keep the property in good condition and to return it to the previous owner should they ever return.

Another initiative traded city resources to help turn any birddog into a sailing or rowing vessel in exchange for clam farmers donating a significant number of their clams to a general fund for distribution to all residents. No individual farmer or family could hope to eat the millions of clams in their grow-out bags before they grew too large and died, but a steady supply of communal clams would go a long way to supplement other food that could be grown or caught. All size and catch limit restrictions were removed for people fishing for sustenance. Green turtles, once a staple food for islanders before over harvesting in the early twentieth century led to their protected status, were back on the acceptable menu.

To involve the citizenry in the functions of city maintenance and pro-tection, Hayes proposed a ten-person citizen deputy program whereby ten randomly drawn citizens would be deputized for a month at a time. During their time as deputies, they would work on city improvement projects, spend time patrolling with the police department, learning firefighter tech-niques at the fire house, and putting in workdays with the public works department that kept the town functioning and presentable.

A round-the-clock chicken guarding program would be formalized to alleviate the strain put on the small number of residents that had fulfilled this role since Rolf and Geoff first brought the birds to the island. A similar rotating guard schedule would be implemented for the shoreline near the Number Four Channel.

Hayes expected only a handful of his initiatives to pass and was shocked when, a week later, all were approved.

By unanimous decree, the constitutional net ban was repealed.

9

BLOOD IN THE WATER

John Mitchell's dynamite implemented the will of the people, and another month passed, a little easier than the last but not without hardship. Something resembling a rhythm of daily life began to take hold. Proficiency with a cast net or hunting bow supplanted bank accounts and stock portfolios as symbols of status. An island that had taken care of its own in the old world better than most places learned from necessity to redouble those efforts.

In a multitude of ways made more evident by the day, it became clear that the survival of anyone on the island was closely tied to the survival of everyone.

Just before dawn on the thirty-second day after the bridge came down, two boats carrying ten armed men, seven of them Meades, quietly paddled past detection by the guards on the island side of the channel and made landfall near the FWC fishing pier adjacent to State Road 24.

By noon, for the first time since February of 1865, Cedar Key would be at war.

Obadiah Meade was born in the military hospital on Depot Key in August of 1842, the same month Colonel William J. Worth, commander of the U.S. Army in Florida during the Second Seminole War, negotiated an agreement there with Seminole leaders to effectively end the war. Two months later, a hurricane would cause such widespread devastation on the tiny island that it was abandoned. Obadiah and his parents relocated across a half mile channel to Way Key.

Later that year, Augustus Steele utilized the Armed Occupation Act of 1842 to purchase Depot Key and its remaining buildings for two hundred and seventy dollars. He renamed the island Atsena Otie, a crude derivation of the Muscogean Indian words for *cedar island*. In 1845, the Cedar Key post office was established on the island with Steele as its first postmaster. A lighthouse constructed on nearby Seahorse Key increased shipping in the area and Atsena Otie saw its trade and population begin to increase as well. In 1861, the Florida Railroad was completed with service from Fernandina Beach on the Atlantic Ocean to Way Key on the Gulf of Mexico. Obadiah's father, James Meade, found employment at the train station.

The Civil War brought devastation and economic hardship to the area. Obadiah enlisted in the 1st Florida Reserves of the Confederate Army, determined to defend his home against the invading Federals. For two years he saw little action, but in February of 1865, twenty-two year old Obadiah found himself mustered with one hundred and twenty men from a variety of Florida units, including cavalry, infantry, and four artillerymen manning a single 12-pounder cannon. The hodgepodge regiment was commanded by Captain J.J. Dickinson, a famed commander of cavalrymen heralded as the Swamp Fox. Just after dawn, the southerners, who were angry at Union forces for damage they had inflicted on civilian property in a recent raid, caught up to the larger enemy force alongside the railroad trestle at the Number Four Channel. In fierce fighting, the Swamp Fox and his men gave hell to the yankees. When the battle ended, the Union forces had sustained losses totaling five killed, seventeen wounded, and three captured. Confederate casualties were limited to six wounded, including Obadiah Meade, who caught a glancing blow from a mini-ball that still managed to tear a five-inch section of his left calf muscle from the bone and land him in the channel. He had to be pulled from the water over which, decades later, the first Number Four Bridge would be built.

Compared to the sound defeat they had suffered at the Battle of Cedar Key three years prior—the event that had incited young Obadiah to en-list—the Battle of Station Four, as it came to be known, was a feather in the cap for southern soldiers and local residents alike. Obadiah would spend several hard months recovering from his battlefield wound but would enjoy a position of honor throughout Cedar Key and the surrounding area for the rest of his life.

The Florida Railroad had sustained extensive damage during the war but eventually returned to service for passengers and freight. The Eberhard Fab Pencil Company built a sawmill on Atsena Otie that was used to make cedar slats for its pencil factory in New York. Based in some part on the reputation he had earned in the service, twenty-six year old Obadiah Meade took a job as a foreman at the sawmill and worked there for the next twenty-eight years. When Henry Plant completed his railroad to Tampa in 1886, it poached shipping from Cedar Key, leading to a significant economic decline in the area and the eventual closing of the Cedar Key line.

On an early September morning, the Great Cedar Key Hurricane of 1896 sent a hundred mile per hour, ten-foot tall wall of water across Atsena Otie, devastating the sawmill and all but a handful of buildings. Four of the surviving homes with the least damage were floated on barges across the channel to Way Key and erected on what is present day 1st Street, just down from the Beachfront Motel. Except for a few people that held on until the early twentieth century, Atsena Otie was abandoned and the town of Cedar Key reconstituted itself across the channel on Way Key.

Obadiah and his wife moved to a clapboard house near the old rail line. They produced a total of eight children, six of which lived to adulthood. When he passed away in 1918 at seventy-two years old, Obadiah had participated in a war between states of his own country, and witnessed the beginning and end of The Great War. He was called a friend by most people that knew him and left behind eighteen grandchildren that would produce forty-one great grandchildren. His roots in Cedar Key spawned what would become one the most prominent families on and around the island.

Before the smokestacks fell, arguments on the Cedar Key Rumor Mill often devolved into a longtime resident dismissing a counter viewpoint by invoking what Thomas came to call the *local rule*. In golf, many courses will post a list of local rules, which are specific rules for that course that operate outside the official rules of golf utilized everywhere. For example, a particular course may have an area of decorative flowers they do not want golfers trampling into in search of a lost ball. To save the flowers, they may invoke a local rule giving a free drop to a golfer whose ball lands in this area rather than a penalty that might normally apply. In Cedar Key, there was only one local rule, and it was straightforward—the locals rule, and newcomers need not have an opinion about anything to do with the island. Less straightforward are the qualifications for being a local. Having attended the Cedar Key School was a good start, but if your grandparents attended the school, even better. Geoff McCloud was nicer than most with his invocation of the local rule, but every time he brought up the seven generations of Cedar Key McClouds that came before him, he was invoking it all the same. The line between legacy and entitlement was as blurred in Cedar Key as the vision of a drunk Meade on Dock Street being thrown out of a bar and yelling, "Do you know who I am?"

Thomas' family could claim a Florida lineage predating statehood, but despite having renovated and moved into a declining historic home on E Street and his participation in numerous community-enhancing endeavors, not least of which was the annual charity event he founded and organized to raise thousands of dollars for the school, The Cedar Key Shark Swim—a half-mile swim across the channel from Way Key to Atsena Otie—he would never be accepted as a local by the mostly do-nothings on the *Rumor Mill* whose last names were Whidden, Hancock, O'Steam, or Meade.

It didn't seem to matter that the so-called real locals were mostly absent from the governance, business, and civic activities of the island, or that the gallantry of Obadiah Meade at the Battle of Station Four was diluted each successive generation until his surname became synonymous with the outlaw underbelly of the area. By the time Abbadon Meade, Jr. was born in the 1970s, no Meades remained on the island of Cedar Key. They had long since retreated across the bridge to cheaper land in Sumner and Otter Creek. In the false hierarchy of locational seniority, the irony of Meades claiming ownership of an island on which no Meades resided was conveniently overlooked.

"If they think a bridge will keep me from an island my family built, they got a shock coming," said Little Don Meade, who was holding court behind a doublewide on four acres of scrub and sugar sand. What money he didn't make from selling skunk weed, meth, and heavily cut coke to junkies on the dirt roads spreading out from State Road 24 in Sumner came from sending his boys to trespass and harvest palmetto berries from other people's land. They could be sold for as much as three dollars a pound to companies that ground them into capsules marketed to cure everything from balding to erectile dysfunction.

The younger Abbadon was dubbed Little Don as a child, well before it could be known that he would tower over Abbadon, Sr. by the time he was twelve years old. When he dropped out of the Cedar Key School at age 16, he was five inches taller than his six-foot father and pushing three hundred pounds. He grew wider with the years and by comparison made John Mitchell seem like a normal-sized man.

While Little Don's rhetoric had the swagger of a warlord, the reality of his situation, and that of most others in Sumner, was dire. Little Don himself had become sickened to the brink of death by the end of the first month after the electricity went out and he exhausted all the gasoline he could barter or steal to run the generator that powered his well. A week of drinking water from the shallow pond in the state preserve near his land—water he had not thought to boil—had turned his gut into a microbial battlefield. A few weeks of boiling the water had breathed some life into him, but the scarce small game and fish his boys could harvest were not enough to keep the desperation at bay. As the hunger pangs reached deeper into him, they were met with a building rage that grew focused on the island his four-greats grandaddy Obadiah had bled to defend. He couldn't understand how five people he didn't vote for could just decide to cut him off from his birthright.

"It's that daddy's boy Hayes David," Little Don announced to his own two sons Jake and James. The JJs, as they were known, were whimpering shadows of the father on whom they relied for everything. Individually they seldom rated mention but as a collective unit could occasionally amount to half a damn at whatever menial task Little Don had set them about.

"He thinks his money and being the mayor means he owns the island," Little Don continued. "That piss ant town council does everything he says. They're shutting us out because Hayes David told them to."

"We can't let him get away with it," one of the JJs replied.

"We gotta get him," said the other.

Little Don's indictment of Hayes was a common refrain about successful people that could be heard in communities everywhere, but the missing Number Four Bridge was not the only barrier between the Sumner Meades and the Cedar Key Davids. Contrary to Little Don's belief, money was not the main reason for this separation. There exists almost everywhere a natural bell curve of achievement. Those at the top and bottom of the curve tend to come from families with a long history of immobility within the curve. Outliers sometimes fall from the top in spectacular fashion, and the American dream is predicated on stories of those at the bottom that claw their way upward, but in the long run, the specific behaviors of success or failure seem to be as hereditary as genetic coding.

Hayes' personal ambition was as strong as anyone's, but there existed always a grounding of this ambition in the sandy soil and middens of the island. His devotion to Cedar Key made his run for mayor at just twenty three years old less absurd than it would have been for anyone else. In unguarded or inebriated moments, even the Meades and others who didn't care for Hayes would still begrudgingly admit the *cocky little shit* did always put Cedar Key first, even if they disagreed about what was Cedar Key and what was not.

Residents in the unincorporated community of Sumner all had Cedar Key addresses. In the old world, most of them made near daily trips to the island for some reason or another—using the boat ramps that provided access to the Gulf, working at one of the restaurants or on a clam boat, mailing a package at Jennifer Alverez's post office, dropping their kids off at the Cedar Key School, or picking up food at the mom and pop grocery store. It had not been lost on Hayes and the rest of the council that these people felt a natural attachment to the island because their lives were intertwined with it. In normal times, most of them were accepted as Cedar Keyers like anyone who lived on the island proper. The peril of the new world, however, elevated simple geography above sociological considerations and a proverbial line in the sand had to be drawn somewhere. As the remnants of the Number Four Bridge settled into that sand at the bottom of the channel, Little Don saw the line as a call to battle.

By the time he reached the decision to send armed men in boats as an opening salvo of a war his lineage and poor circumstances convinced him to wage, his resolve had steeled into a solitary objective—the death of Mayor David.

10

THE SECOND BATTLE OF CEDAR KEY

As the muted light of a gray dawn began to push the darkness from the water, only one of the two guards that would normally be stationed at the channel was at his post. When TJ had a migraine hit him suddenly, only an hour before shift change, his partner had told him to head on home. Weeks of guarding a channel across which no one ever seemed to come had led to a general complacency among the sentries. By comparison, chicken duty was more eventful because at least occasionally an ambitious osprey would need to be shooed away or a runaway hen apprehended with a foot chase. Cold coffee and boredom had led Prescott Phillips to idle daydreaming while Little Don's amphibious force quietly paddled within fifty feet of the guard post and landed undetected around a bend in the shoreline from it.

Father Prescott Phillips, affectionately called Folksy Phillips by Hayes and Thomas due to his penchant for long-spun yarns about nothing of consequence, was in contrast a lion in the pulpit, electrifying the normally staid Episcopal sanctuary with fiery calls for God to answer for the forsaking of his children. Though he had attended seminary in his youth and pastored churches in his life before moving to Cedar Key, his island church had a regular vicar who commuted more than two hours each week from the Clermont area in central Florida. When it became clear that neither Father Jan Mavis, nor anyone else, was likely to return to the island, Prescott had assumed the shepherd's role for the flock at Christ Church on D Street.

A trickle of orange light found a hole in the gray sky above the channel, illuminating a sleepy brown pelican floating on the water. A glint of this light bounced from one of the pelican's sharp blue eyes and back toward Folksy, who would enjoy it warmly for a fraction of a second before all the light in his eyes and life snapped to black. A few feet behind him, the younger of the JJs held a shaking revolver as he watched Folksy slump into the channel and drift away.

Little Don had been explicit in the instructions to his two sons, three cousins, stepbrother, and four Sumner minions that comprised the landing force of small boats in which he himself had been too large to fit—slip past the guards at the channel and head as quickly and quietly as possible to the mayor's house on A street. They had been on the island for less than five minutes and were already off-script. More than any of the awful events that would transpire over the next few hours, the ambush murder of the minister would galvanize the islanders' determination for Old Testament vengeance. "For Folksy," would become an esprit de corps mantra for citizen soldiers working up nerves and turning off old world civilities.

The elder JJ knew immediately that his brother's actions would lead to consequences from their father, but this knowledge only served to lower his inhibitions about further insubordination. Since that dam had already been broken, by the time they passed Maggie and Andy Crofts' house a few hundred yards from the channel, it was he who kicked in the door. With so many houses on the island left abandoned by out of state owners or those that had slipped into the gray, the elder JJ encountered a statistically improbable situation on the other side of the door. Andy had been aboard Robby Watt's boat the morning of the flash and had drifted away the same day as his captain; Maggie died a few weeks later, seemingly for no reason at all. These circumstances would have otherwise worked in favor of the plundering Meade were it not for the following unlikely and ultimately devastating facts: First Sergeant Rolf Alverez, III had moved his family into the Crofts house, the closest to the channel, making it a de facto forward operating base; First Sergeant Rolf Alverez, III had been a perennial US-Army combat fighting champion.

When the older Meade came barreling through the busted door, drunk with adrenaline and power, Rolf brought him to the ground with an elegant movement of hands as though he were conducting a virtuoso string quartet. The contrapuntal fugue of their interaction began with the exposition of the Crofts' old rotary telephone smashing into the bridge of the elder JJs nose in frenetic, staccato eighth notes, followed by melodic, childlike whimpering as Rolf delicately choked the invader into a palliative decrescendo, tiptoeing toward the ignoble coda as death stood to applaud.

Nothing so orchestral awaited the younger JJ who, upon seeing his older brother's body thrown unceremoniously through the front door—bouncing down the front porch steps and into the mud—charged with hysterical lack of forethought toward the waiting Rolf, who calmly shot him through the left eyeball with the Sig Sauer that only ever left his hip for baths, sleeping, and shooting Meades in the face.

A second body tumbling off the porch invited no additional engagement from the landing force, who turned and ran from the doorway across whose threshold Rolf's perdition song continued to ring out.

Rolf raced up to the widow's walk of the old house and could see the remaining armed men moving along State Road 24 toward town. By the time he was able to isolate the largest of the remaining targets, Little Don's stepbrother Jesse, in the scope of the comically overpowered .300 win mag rifle he had purchased for a big game hunt years prior, nearly a quarter mile ranged between them. Even at that distance, the round was a runaway train on its exit through the lumbering Meade's fatty chest.

The landing force was now reduced to seven men whose stake in the endeavor was considerably less than that of their fallen associates. Still, the specter of Little Don's wrath on the other side of the channel bid them to continue. A dead mayor would not balance the loss of two sons and a stepbrother, but no dead mayor would make returning to Sumner completely untenable. Seeing a man's chest explode, which was a description of Jesse Meade's exit wound devoid of hyperbole, scattered the others from the road and into the cover of trees and mangroves. They would continue their fateful advance, but the going would be slower for the remaining two miles between them and town.

Thomas' kidding about the Admiral's lack of boating prowess wasn't based in fact. It's true he never managed to get a working boat of his own on the water, but it was also true that he could run one just fine. The Crofts' 17 foot skiff was still tied to their dock and Rolf had made sure not to let anyone, including himself, pilfer the gas from the tank so that it would be available in an emergency. Rolf made his way down from the window's walk and toward the dock. He fired up the skiff and raced it along the shore toward the guard shack and the gunshot he had heard shortly before the first of the JJs burst through his front door. Well before he reached the shack, he saw the fallen minister face down in the water, a partially exposed oyster bar keeping the body from the pull of the falling tide. Rolf pulled the skiff alongside the bar and with some difficulty was able to drag his friend's body from the water. There would be a time to let the feelings in, but not while armed invaders continued toward town.

Since the landing party was on foot, even now Rolf could beat them there by racing the boat through the back bayou, past Thomas' houseboat, under the low bridge across from the bait shop, and into the channel leading to Hayes' clam dock. He hadn't known that Hayes was the target of the raid, only that Hayes' dock was the quickest way into town. A big high tide meant Rolf could run a direct course through the backwaters without fear of running aground. The tide was so high that even with his own lack of height and the low-slung skiff, he had to duck down passing under the little bridge at close to full throttle.

Luck and the early hour of his arrival at the dock saw the mayor and Thomas there to greet him. The friends often began their days at the dock, which had become an informal command center for the endless list of new tasks required for the island to bridge the gap between the old world and the new. The concern on Rolf's face and the weapons he had piled on the bow of the skiff alerted the men there was trouble even before he pulled alongside Hayes' dock. When he did, the body on the deck came into view, disfigured by the revolver such that Hayes and TJ could not immediately identify it. In the low light of dawn, it took Hayes a few moments to spot the Episcopal Service Cross that Folksy often wore pinned to his collar. It was a five-fold form of the ancient crusader's cross, symbolizing the five wounds of Christ at his crucifixion.

Hayes was gut-punched but steady, his face steeled with resolve even as his hands began to shake in building anger so much that he had to hold them out of view behind his back.

"What happened, Rolf?"

Talking fast but cool, Rolf began to relay the events of the past half hour. "I heard a shot come from down by the channel a little before my door got kicked in. When I was up on the widow's walk I could see the men heading toward town but couldn't see Folksy or TJ back at the guard station. I had spoken to them the night before when they arrived. I only heard one shot, and when I made it down to the shack, I only saw Folksy. I didn't spend long looking, though, cause I wanted to get here as quick as possible."

"How far ahead of them do you think you are?" Thomas asked.

"I hauled ass here, and after I shot the third guy, they got off the road pretty quick. They're on foot and they'll have to cross the little bridge in front of Fannie's to get to town. I think we can beat them there."

Carrying multiple weapons each, they ran as quickly as possible toward Fannie's Café. Along their path, they would pass the Cedar Key Water and Sewer office. John Mitchell saw them coming and met them outside. Thomas relayed a truncated version of the story and tossed him a rifle, a little .22 caliber peashooter. It was semi-automatic, though, and had an extended clip holding 25 rounds.

John said, "Go on ahead. I can't run as fast as you boys. I'll signal the city crew and we'll meet you there," then ran back inside the office and produced a bullhorn and used it to blast three short tones. In less than a minute, his son Jimmy and Jack Custard rounded the corner of C and 3rd, matching Glock model 19s borrowed from the police department in their hands. Three short tones constituted the all-hands alert developed after the smokestacks fell. The alert meant that anyone available was to head toward the sound, armed for trouble. Before James had finished relaying the story, Chief Edwins appeared in his black F-150 police truck, the only vehicle on the island authorized to use gasoline from the 525-gallon above-ground tank the city kept behind the public works building. With him were four of that month's citizen deputies, including Geoff McCloud, Denny Gal, Randal Solaro, and Hayes' mother Miss Bette. Jack and the two Mitchells piled into the back of the truck and all eight headed for Fannie's, arriving nearly simultaneously with Hayes, Thomas, and Rolf, who had been on foot.

Linda Richland came out of the café to see about the commotion. "Best get back inside, Linda," the chief called out. "Armed men coming. They got Folksy... maybe TJ, too."

Linda did go back inside, but reappeared moments later with her grandfather's Winchester over-under shotgun. "Let the motherfuckers come," she said, joining the others.

"Mom, no," Hayes said when he saw Miss Bette climbing out of the truck.

She replied with the calm authority that made her as feared on the island as she was beloved, "You don't get to tell me no, Hayes. I'm here to help."

"Please, Mom. You'll be helping if you go get dad and anyone else you run into on the way. Tell them to come quietly down 6th Street and keep their heads down."

Miss Bette relented, not because she was told but because the plan made sense. She slipped down the side street and started the three block walk home to find her husband Mark.

Jack Custard and Jimmy Mitchell took up positions under the far end of the little bridge, where they could spring out in ambush at an opportune moment. Denny Gall and the older Solano boy Randal took similar positions under the near side. Rolf climbed the outside stairs to Linda's apartment above the café, supporting his rifle on the railing of the little wooden balcony that provided a clear line of sight to the bridge and points beyond. John Mitchell and Geoff McCloud posted themselves up on the back deck of the café, behind one of the few remaining large cedar trees in Cedar Key. Thomas slipped into the mangroves just beyond the bridge, two mismatched handguns in his grasp.

"Clear as far as I can see down 24," Rolf called down from Linda's balcony.

The chief said, "How 'bout it, Hayes? You and me see if we can get on down the road a bit and try to get behind them when they go by? We could box them in toward the café and all these guns."

"I like the plan, but someone needs to be here to direct all the folks my mamma's gonna scare up. If I know her, you'll have the better part of an army here shortly."

"Then why don't you stay here, too? They can't get by us if they're heading toward town."

"We need to know for sure they're still coming," Hayes reasoned. "If they lose their nerve and head back, we won't know, and they'll just get away. And what if they are kicking in other doors between the Crofts house and here?"

"That's fair. Just don't engage until we get 'em hemmed up here at the café. When we open up on them, you hit them from behind and cut off their escape."

Hayes carried his Springfield 1911 in one hand and held a preposterous 14-inch bowie knife from Rolf's cache in his other as he sprinted across the little bridge and into cover alongside the road past it. He worked his way from one protected position to another, eventually reaching the building that had been the David fish house before the net ban. In recent years it had been converted into a vacation rental unit, but Hayes still knew the old building like a childhood home. Like he had done as a boy, he wedged himself between an old antenna pole and the back wall of the building, inching up between the two structures until he could pull himself onto the roof. From the back side of the roof, with eyes looking over the ridgeline, he waited.

At the café, Bette David returned with her husband and a dozen others. Armed with guns and bats and machetes—Joffrey Sleady with a hunting bow—they found positions out of immediate sight and waited. Hayes' temper grew moment upon moment in the stillness, the thought of the faceless body in Rolf's boat overwhelming his trademark calm. Thirty long minutes passed, and they waited still, the tension in the air smothering like

Florida humidity in August. When it seemed as though another minute without action would stop the rotation of the earth, the unbearable waiting was ended.

Down the road from the café, a thundering report tore apart the silence. Then another. A third. Screaming. Footsteps pounding toward the bridge.

Hank Blue was the Mikhail Baryshnikov of the mullet filet. He did a variety of jobs around the David fish house, but cleaning mullet was his calling. With a sharp knife and a box of mullet at his side, Hank could fill three ten-pound bags in the time it took others to fill one, and he did so with a kind of artistic rhythm that transfixed eight year old Hayes. Studying at Hank's side, Hayes absorbed his every motion—the clean cut lines, economy of movement with the blade, the poetic kung-fu required to remove the viscera in a single pass.

Hayes' youth and Mr. Hank's unwillingness to lose his place at the cleaning table meant the upstart spent most of his time *scraping the black* from the fish. Mullet have a black membrane lining the body cavity that will spoil the taste of the fish if not removed. It was lowliest of jobs at the fish house, but Hayes didn't mind. On Mr. Hank's days off, Hayes would sneak to the cleaning table and practice carving mullet from whole fish to fillets. Eventually his skill with the knife would become the talk of the fish house, impressing even his stoic father Mark.

As he grew, Hayes would learn every job in the family business—unloading the boats, processing fish and crabs, running the retail shop, and even driving a refrigerated truck on a seafood delivery route when he got his driver's license. He saved money from this work to buy his own fishing boat and began catching and selling his own fish. The first time Hayes watched a box of mullet from his own boat make its way to Mr. Hank's cleaning table, he knew a life on the water was the only vocation that could ever matter to him. Cedar Key's cultural and economic circle began in the Gulf, routed through the loading docks at the fish house, looped into the wider world and back to the Gulf again. The more Hayes learned about this circle, the more determined he was to occupy points all around it.

If it came from the Gulf and there was a market for it, the Davids had their hands in it. By a wide margin, they bought and sold more mullet than any other fish, but they also traded in shark, Jack Crevalle, trout, blue crabs year round and stone crabs in the winter, offshore fish like grouper and snapper, and the kind of camaraderie absent other ways of making a living. Miss Bette would often cook stew or make her famous smoked mullet dip for the captains arriving with their catch. The coffee brewer ran every minute the doors to the fish house were open, and all were welcome to it.

While the rest of the world was changing rapidly around it, the David fish house was a bulwark, fixed in place and time, and would remain so until the government came for the nets. When they did, the boats stopped coming. The tall tales from the docks were told no more, and Miss Bette's stew pot went empty. The sublime artistry of Mr. Hank would lose its avenue for expression, and he would spend the rest of his life mowing yards and drinking until the cancer that came for him seemed almost a mercy.

Hayes worked himself into a comfortable position on the roof, but the intensity of the ordeal made it impossible for him to relax. The slowness of the passing time and the monochromatic sky cast the scene in a kind of noir fatalism that heightened the nerve endings in Hayes' face and hands. He could feel a wisp of moving air or a change in the barometric pressure so intensely that his body did not feel like his own—a pipe bomb moments before the blast. Just as it began to seem that nothing but stillness could ever happen again, a figure emerged from behind a trailered boat and onto the road.

Then there they all were.

A fifty yard stretch of open road spanned across a small canal near the marina's metal drydock building. One by one, the seven remaining men ran across the span and into cover behind the bait shop or Jiffy Store or, for Little Don's cousin Leon, the back wall of the old David fish house.

Countless momentary decisions are made each day in the background of the human mind and are seldom of much consequence. Cheeseburger or chicken fingers; a walk in the park or reading a book by the river; plain socks or argyle socks or no socks at all. A series of neurons in Leon Meade's brain fired in such a way that he chose to go left instead of right after crossing the canal. In a thousand other simulations of this event, such a choice might have meant almost nothing. On this day, however, choosing left put him directly below and in full sight of Hayes, atop a building his family no longer owned but whose walls still bristled with the stories and moments foundational to the David family legacy.

Millenia past. Civilizations rose and prospered and fell in the seven-tenths of a second between the visage of the beleaguered Meade registering in Hayes' consciousness and when he leapt from the roof toward him. The fantasy of human flight from dreams immemorial overtook the mayor and he wanted to live there forever, suspended in the alternate reality of the moment. He was eight years old and talking salty with the mullet men at the docks. Boats were moored one after the other, their holds swollen again with the bounty of the Gulf. As he floated there, old women were repairing nets again on backyard clotheslines. Wellman Herms' sawmill on 4th and E was running once more. Life that had begun in the depths spread to the shore and through Cedar Key and back again to the waters as the cycle had always been. And he would have lingered there until the fall of man if he could, in the comfortable embrace of memory, had not gravity awakened from its temporary slumber and crashed the two men together on the ground.

There had been no opportunity for Leon Meade to contemplate a response. In his timeline, a clank was heard from above and then a man was falling toward him. He did not remember pulling the trigger of the Ruger and did not feel the blade of Hayes's knife entering his right side and lodging in his liver. His next perception was a feeling of chill deep within himself, the vision of the other man holding the side of his face, and blood that seemed to be everywhere at once. Little streams of it began to flow from each man toward the other, mixing between them in the sand and Timucuan middens that had washed on and off the island's shores for a thousand years. Such a display of human frailty could easily have produced an understanding between the two men, each beginning now to recognize the other—the moment of their mortality outweighing the conflict that had mixed their life together on the ground.

Hayes pulled himself from the shock and pulled his hand away from his face. More than half of his left ear, gruesome but recognizable in shape and design, came with it. He reached back to the side of his face time and again, pulling off little bits and piling them in his other hand with the half ear until nothing but the blood remained. A wave of white hot rage washed over him, so intense that it numbed his senses into the kind of dead calm his father had tried to teach him during the ordeal of the roofing nails on the boat ramp. The other man stared blankly at him, and that could have been the end of their hostilities were it not for the faint whisper that came from him.

"I'm sorry, Hayes."

Feeling the moment of his own greatness flicker, diminished by the other man's perverse civility, Hayes disconnected from the physical world around him once more, recalling the countless nautical knots his father made him tie over and over until they were perfect, the meticulously pressed pants hanging in exact distance from one another in the cedar-lined closet of a house impeccably maintained to the point of discomfort, the deck of his working clam boat that had to look clean enough to eat from, the weight of generational legacy, the need to be better than he needed to be at the bank because he had not gone to college but his colleagues had, and, more than anything else, to keep things in order for an island he loved at the end of the world. His squared-away world had spun always on an axis of order. Of symmetry.

Examining the disorder of the flesh in his hand, contemplating the dissymmetry that would be his face if he were to live, Hayes came back to the middens and the other man and the blood, while the levee holding back the darkness inside him gave way. He came back to the knife in the other man's side and pulled it out slowly. Leon could mount no protest. Already the light was fading in his eyes and the time for his departure was at hand.

Hayes was unpersuaded to mercy.

He plunged the knife back into the man, near his naval, struggling to his feet while using the knife for support. Leon Meade's eternal boat was approaching the far bank of the River Styx or Jordan or wherever it was that men like him traveled in the next life, but he had not reached it yet. He summoned the strength and will to feebly squeeze two more shots from the Ruger into the ground and for a scream that could be heard all the way at the café.

Hayes moved the knife in a sawing motion from the man's naval to his torso, cool and precise as Mr. Hank at the mullet table. He reached into the open cavity of the man and pulled a handful of life from inside him, then another, and another, until there was nothing left to grasp and nothing more to take from him. All of it had lasted maybe twenty seconds, and all of it would last forever.

The shots and the scream sent the remaining invaders racing away from the David fish house and toward the café. Hayes returned to the world of linear time and to leadership and gave chase.

There would be heroism on the little bridge across from Fannie's. Certainly, there was. Just showing up to fight made heroes of them all in some way; but mostly, it was an execution. Rolf waited to fire until he saw one of the men turning back toward Hayes, then put the man down from above. A broadhead arrow from Sleedy's bow got the next man in the gut, but before he could take measure of the injury, a rain of bullets overwhelmed the men from Sumner.

The last movement of the last man moving stopped at last and the Second Battle of Cedar Key was ended.

11

BOATS ON THE ROAD

In the old world, Tony Hankle was one-third owner of the third largest clam wholesale operation on the island. His company, Clamazing Seafood, regularly grew, purchased, and sold more than 50 million clams a year. Tony and his best friend and partner Mack Beecham seemed to handle most of the actual work of the company while their high cheek-boned and effusively smiling third partner, Cristopher Tapper, could be found most often on his half million dollar boat with attriactive younger women.

When Thomas had just signed the papers for his first clam lease, before he had planted the first clam, he found himself eating breakfast at a table at Fannie's next to Tony and Mack. As he was prone to doing, Thomas started talking to the strangers all about his new clam farm enterprise. Tony and Mack politely listened to him opine at great length about the various attributes and virtues of the industry before Tony finally weighed in with, "We're in the business, too."

"Oh, cool," replied Thomas. "Where is your lease?"

"Oh, we have a few," Mack said with a wry smile.

Later, after the three had become friends and Thomas learned that by *a few* Mack meant they were among the largest and most successful farmers and wholesalers in the state, they shared a good laugh at Thomas' expense.

In addition to their work at Clamazing Seafood, Tony and Mack's en-
trepreneurial spirit led them to a variety of side ventures, including land
clearing, construction debris dumpster rentals, and marine salvage operations. For this last endeavor, they constructed a giant barge that was stable
enough to haul heavy equipment like front-end loaders and skid steers.
The barge allowed them to bring equipment to projects on the water that
competitors with less ingenuity had to go without. In the wake of the battle
that had left ten Sumner bodies spread between the Crofts' house and
Fannie's Café, this barge would play a crucial role in the island's response
to the attack.

"I say we just throw them in the channel and let the crabs have them,"
Geoff McCloud said as the hodgepodge island army began to appear from
behind their covered positions. Already the chief and a few others were
thinking logistics, but the moment required something less immediate, a
pause to process the violence they had collectively dispensed—a thing most
of them had only ever seen on television.

Cousin had been one of the dozen people that followed Miss Bette back
to the café and now looked dazed holding her uncle Mark's lever-action
Colt and seeing the carnage on the little bridge.

"What's the trouble, honey?" Mark asked his niece. "You did the right
thing."

"You can do the right thing and still be sad about it, Uncle Mark," she
replied.

"I suppose that's true."

"That's Wes Meade there in the front. We went to school together. I
kissed him in the seventh grade."

Thomas put his arm around his cousin friend and stood quietly with
her for a while. A stillness began to settle back over the scene until Hayes
finally made his way closer to the café. Even from the other side of the little

bridge, the blood covering most of his body was visible. Miss Bette raced for her son, stepping over bodies to meet him on the bridge.

"It looks worse than it is," Hayes said as he put his arm around her and they walked together toward the café.

"It looks pretty bad, son. How did it happen?"

"I guess he shot me when I dove off the roof on him," Hayes replied.

"You dove off a roof? Jesus, son."

"I didn't think it through. It just kind of happened."

"That doesn't sound like you."

"I'm not like me a lot lately."

"Get him in my truck," Chief Edwins called out as Hayes and Miss Bette approached the café.

"We're not done," Hayes protested. "We all know who sent them."

"You're done for today," his father said, staring intently at the place where his son's ear should be while everyone else tried not to look at it. "We better get Nurse Toni to clean this up."

"What?" Hayes asked.

"We better get Nurse Toni to..."

"I'm having trouble hearing you," Hayes interrupted.

Mark began again in a louder tone before seeing the dipshit smile on his son's face while he pointed at the side of his head.

"Oh... you piece of shit."

Hayes hobbled to the chief's truck laughing, a pressure release valve for everyone around.

As far as getting an ear shot off goes, Hayes had been cosmically lucky. Notwithstanding that a few centimeters had meant the difference between his present injury and his brains pouring from him on the ground, the actual wound left little tending besides disinfectant and bandaging. The burn marks from the grazing bullet would take longer to heal than the wound where the connection between his head and ear had been. In a month's time, despite the imbalance in his face that would catch a first glance, there wasn't much particularly unsettling about the injury. The hearing from that earhole was diminished to some degree that was noticeable if testing one side against the other, but overall, he still seemed to hear just fine. If anything, Tabby's fanatical affection for the mayor seemed to only increase after the whole ordeal.

After leaving Nurse Toni, Hayes met the chief and Tony Hankle at his dock, where Thomas, Rolf and a sullen TJ were waiting.

"Sure glad to see you, buddy," Hayes said to TJ.

TJ could not look the mayor in the eye. "I should have been at my post."

"Chief told me about it. You can't do much good with a migraine," Hayes replied. "When I get them, everything starts spinning and I throw up."

"I appreciate you saying that, but if I had been there maybe Folksy might still be with us."

"Or maybe you'd both be dead," Thomas interjected.

"Speaking of... Chief, did we tell Maria yet?" Hayes asked.

"Just before I came here."

Choking on uncharacteristic emotion, Hayes said, "Good. I'll go see her later. Reassure her that there will be a reckoning."

"Looks like we got the ones that did it," Thomas replied.

"But we didn't get the one that sent them. And if we don't, he'll keep sending others."

"I'm in," TJ announced with a conviction that underscored the intensity of the gathering and spoke to a misplaced guilt that vengeance would temper but never quiet.

"Yes," said Hayes. "I think you have some business to handle with Little Don. We all do. For Folksy."

"For Folksy," TJ replied.

The men nodded in agreement and the time for sentiment ended. Tony confirmed that his barge could handle the weight required for the first phase of the plan, and the serious men on the dock moved ahead with the exacting details of the operation that would commence at dawn.

Most of the land on the other side of the channel was impenetrable marsh for hundreds of yards. A notable exception was the forty-acre peninsula jutting out into the bay a half mile or so from the guard station. Leanna Beecham, a striking, tumultuous woman with eyes that conveyed empathy and ruthlessness in equal measure, had turned this spit of high ground into an estate that evoked *Tara* from *Gone with the Wind*. Its winding canopied drive led to a stately manor house set high on what passes for a hill in coastal Florida. Clam money and Leanna's tenacity for perpetual improvement had built her enviable home and had also led her on what was meant to be a month-long spiritual sojourn through the Nile River basin in Egypt. The day before the smokestacks fell, she posted photos on social media of her exploring the site of the lost Lighthouse at Alexandria and the Catacombs of Kom el Shoqafa. No one in Cedar Key had heard from her since. Her peninsula across the channel sat in deserted opulence, having somehow escaped the notice of raiders.

Thomas' friendship with Leanna and his visits to the estate had produced a piece of information critical to the mission on which he and eleven other islanders were about to embark—Leanna had designed and poured an immaculate concrete boat ramp on the leeward side of her peninsula.

As the sun first began to rise over the channel, Hayes pushed the throttle forward on his larger bay boat, The Cogency, until the heavy tow line behind it pulled tight. Tony's barge lurched forward and into a quiet advance through the water, hauling the Chief's F-150 and Thomas' old Dodge Ram, each packed with armed islanders—Thomas, Rolf, TJ, Geoff McCloud, the elder and younger Mitchell, Jack Custard, Mark David, Cousin Samantha, and Leanna's oldest son Ryland. Behind each truck, connected with a heavy tow strap, was one of the two jon boats that had landed earlier in the day on the shore near the guard station. Five dead Sumner men were piled into each.

Morning broke before them as Leanna's boat ramp drew near. Landing the trucks on solid ground, even with the benefit of the wide, grooved, concrete boat ramp, was an ordeal. Hayes deftly maneuvered The Cogency toward the shore, then turned hard parallel to it while cutting the tow line. As hoped, the barge continued its forward progress toward the ramp and up onto it. Attempts to move the first truck, however, pushed the barge back away from the ramp and further into the water. It wasn't until ten islanders went into the shallow water to hold the barge steady that the chief's black Ford could get its front wheels off the barge and onto the ramp. From there, the four-wheel-drive crawled the truck off the ramp and onto solid ground with the jon boat full of bodies dragging behind. The process was repeated for Thomas' Dodge and then the landing was complete.

Ryland had been back to his mother's house many times before the bridge came down, and twice more by boat since then. Leanna kept a

storehouse of provisions in the big house at all times, and Ryland and
his younger brother Lex had relied upon them in the first weeks after the
flash. Ryland, especially, would linger there, sometimes for hours, letting
his mother's presence drift from the photographs on the wall and wrap
around him, hoping to summon her into the physical space of the house by
conjuring childhood memories of their family together again. They were
laughing over homemade brisket at the mahogany dinner table or wrestling
their pet racoon on the massive wraparound couch in the living room, always laughing, every good-natured jab at one another a restatement of the
devotion to family that was fundamental to being a Beecham. Twenty-four
year old Ryland was six-foot-two and bearded, a quiet, rugged waterman
in every way, but being in his mother's house without her made him feel
small and lost.

The line of trucks and funereal boats stopped at the house and Ryland
ran up the tall outside staircase and went inside. A few minutes later he
reemerged with an armload of sealed mason jars containing an assortment
of food his mother had pickled—cucumbers, sausages, okra, eggs. There
had been no discussion about such a pitstop, but the sight of the jars
sent a charge through the convoy. Ryland lowered the Ford's tailgate and
arranged the jars on it, opening the lids and inviting everyone to partake.
The dazzling vinegar and spices felt like the holy spirit rolling through a
congregation of sinners. As they ate the strange breakfast together, they
did so in remembrance of those lost since the smokestacks had fallen—a
pickled sausage for Annie, an egg yolk for the Colonel, okra for the watermen consumed by the gray—a communion of friends before the bad
business that lay ahead of them.

Little Don's compound was located within sight of the one gas station
in Sumner, just down a narrow side road, across from the Cedar Grace
RV Park on Shiloh Road. In addition to the fifty year old doublewide

that was his home, the compound contained a collection of ramshackle outbuildings, pole barns, metal sheds, and a menagerie of broken down vehicles, lawnmowers, and old dogs chained to trees. The owners of the RV park once called the county code enforcement office to complain about the eyesore across the street. The day after Little Don was given a citation, the park's clubhouse and laundry building went up in flames and burned to embers before firemen could arrive.

The convoy of trucks, boats, citizen soldiers, and dead invaders made its way from Leanna's peninsula and onto State Road 24. The boats dragging behind the trucks necessitated a slow pace, but they made steady progress. The sparks and grinding sounds coming from the boats on the road could be seen and heard far and wide. As the ungainly parade began to near the Sumner gas station, ten islanders got out and headed down a side road that would take them the back way to Little Don's compound. When they were safely out of sight, Chief Edwins turned on the siren and lights in his police truck. Thomas laid on the horn of his Dodge as they pulled into the parking lot of the gas station, making the biggest spectacle of themselves possible.

After cutting the boats free, they poured five gallons of precious gasoline onto the bodies in each boat and set them ablaze. As expected, nearly everyone within view of the building pyre or earshot of the siren headed toward the station. Little Don arrived with a 12-gauge under his arm, but the sight of his boys, each placed deliberately on top of the pile in separate boats, struck him lame with grief. From the police truck's intercom, Chief Edwins spoke in a menacing tone, "Father Prescott Phillips, killed by these men, sends his regards. Do not come across the channel again." Then, with a flourish that had not been part of the plan, he recited a verse from the book of Isaiah that Folksy had thundered from the Episcopal pulpit in the days after the flash, "Through the wrath of the lord of hosts is the land darkened, and the people shall be as the fuel of the fire: no man shall spare his brother." Little Don, cajoled to action once more by the indignity of the Chief's reprimand, raised his shotgun to fire but the trucks were already speeding away.

As they did, Little Don made out the familiar yowl of his Walker coonhound Buddy, then saw the flames rising above the trees behind the gas station. The full brutality of the plan conceived on Hayes's dock was unfurling as Little Don made his way back toward the compound as quickly as his mucilaginous body would allow. When he rounded the curve on Shiloh Road just before the RV Park, he knew instantly that his burning sons, stepbrother, cousins, and friends had been the trigger of the trap into which he and all those in tow were now walking. Still, the sight of his burning home and the baying of the dogs and the base rage sickening his brain by the millisecond pushed him forward. An expanding universe of fire spread through the doublewide, barns, and trees of the four-acre Meade homestead, chewing up the wood and the air and the dogs.

When the heat from the fire finally halted Little Don's advance, and he paused to realize he could neither save his home nor even get near it, ten islanders emerged from behind RVs across the road. Only a few of them had ever seen Little Don, but the enormous, shotgun-toting man at the front of the crowd was a dead match for the description Hayes had provided. To that point in the operation, the islanders had comported themselves with an almost unnatural calm, methodically executing the plan they had spent all afternoon studying together. Seeing him, though—knowing it was he that had sent the killers across the channel—ended the calm in a sudden rush of collective rage.

It was finished in seconds.

The rifles stopped firing when every moving thing in front of them lay still—Meades and other Sumner outlaws, but also some who had just come to watch a fire. The islanders had sustained no visible injuries, but the scorched Earth of retribution would come for them, too, individually and as a people. The killing on Shiloh Road proved to be the deterrent it was intended, at least for a time, but its cost would come due, paid in slow installments every remaining still moment of their lives.

Thomas and the chief arrived before the dust had settled on the bodies, then drove their army back to the barge, across the channel, and home.

12

HARD LIVING

When they hit Crystal River, the smokestacks were destroyed in a flash of human derangement. But it wasn't until the ambush in front of Fannie's Café, and the siege at Little Don's compound, that the islanders would fulfill Oppenheimer's grainy, black and white prophesy—becoming death, destroyer of worlds.

On the barge ride back from Leanna's peninsula, they knew the world would not be the same. A few people laughed. A few people cried. Most people were silent. Vishnu, multi-armed and terrible, hovered in the fog above the unwieldy boat, leading the forlorn sailors into the long night ahead.

For Luke, the weeks since the killing at the big house and the Chamberlain's yard had given him time to process the heaviness that was just beginning to settle onto the passengers of the barge. He would sit for hours at the piano alone, playing to quiet the memory of the man with the axe and the gray pallor of his face that blended into the concrete walkway. With the guitar strings his father had stockpiled and the antique but well-tuned piano in the house on E Street, there was, at least, always music, narrating life in the new world when words invariably failed.

On the one hundredth day after the smokestacks fell, smoke blew in from the northeast and blanketed the island in gray upon gray. Life was continuing but had seemed to slow to three-quarters pace. In the old world, a northeast wind and a good low tide was a clam farmer's delight. Wind from that direction would blow the tide out and make even the deeper Corrigans leases easier to work for planting or harvesting clams. These were the same conditions on the day that Thomas was thrown from the Judith Jane by the shockwave from the flash across the bay.

Thomas paddled his kayak toward the spot where the busted nipple and the dry box had spared him while so many of his fellow watermen had fallen. In the coming days, he would make the first trial run on the birddog with the oars he had fashioned from scrap lumber and a pair of disassembled Adirondack chairs. If the oars worked, four people should be able to power the Judith Jane to the leases and back with a bounty of clams for sharing. Today, he would be collecting only a few hundred clams for himself and Luke, and Mr. Paul, the wild-eyed old man that lived in the A-frame house across from his.

Mr. Paul may have been sixty years old or a hundred and ten; no one seemed to know. When Thomas asked Hayes about his elderly neighbor, he had replied, "He was real, real old when I was a kid. He's probably immortal."

Even with the difficulties of life in the new world, from the daily struggle to keep enough food and water in a belly, to maintaining a baseline of hygiene to stave off illness, Mr. Paul seemed remarkably spry. In the detached garage adjacent to the A-frame, he continued the same tinkering on old bicycles and woodworking projects that had occupied his time since the Nixon administration.

Since the ordeal in Sumner, Thomas spent an increasing amount of time on the water alone. The solitude was both a reprieve from the hard business of living in the new world and a quiet crucible in which to punish himself for the events that transpired on Shiloh Road. It was no consolation that he had merely driven a truck and not actually participated in the shooting. That would have maybe been better. All human civilizations were built and sustained by killing, and Thomas more than anyone knew that Cedar Key was no different. But at the little bridge in front of Fannie's, he had hesitated when the firing began. It was true that he eventually joined his neighbors in putting down the threat, feeling sure he had actually killed the Meade that Cousin kissed in the 7th grade, but the three seconds of hesitation haunted him as much as the killing and in the same way that driving the truck and not pulling a trigger in Sumner strangely amplified his guilt. Time on the bay helped some, bourbon helped a little more, but even weeks later the weight of it all had barely let up. He knew from the sullen faces on the barge ride home that his anguish was a shared one, but this was small comfort and did nothing to erase the memory of all the bodies strewn about the one man they had come to kill.

When Thomas had filled the little storage compartment of the kayak with clams, he began to paddle for home. As he approached the western end of Dog Island, he saw Luke's matching kayak beached on the shore. Luke was throwing a cast net, looking joyful for the first time in weeks. There is a popular adage among parents that says you're only as happy as your unhappiest child. Since Luke was his only child, the trajectory of Thomas' contentment with the world around him rose and fell in concert with his son's disposition. For Thomas, the end of the world was bearable; a momentary glint of despair in his son was not.

"Dad!" Luke called excitedly. "Dad they're back."

Thomas pulled his kayak to the shore and sprinted toward Luke.

"Who's back?"

"The white shrimp," Luke replied. "Look at 'em running. They're thick as mosquitos."

In recent years, the annual arrival of white shrimp in the waters around Cedar Key had begun to attract the attention of locals and weekenders alike. At first, they would show up sporadically in cast nets and could sometimes be seen poking about the surface in small schools. For reasons unknown to Thomas, the size of the schools and the numbers in the nets had been growing. Last June, while Luke was home from college for the summer, he and his father had filled a giant cooler with them in a few hours of work.

"I've never seen so many before," Thomas said.

The water in front of the Buck men was alive with movement—flits and ripples and swirls stretching across the bay as far as they could see. Each throw of the net produced so many shrimp that Luke could barely pull it back in. In a moment of inspiration, Thomas drug his kayak closer to the edge of the water near Luke and they began to dump one full net of shrimp after another into its hull. Thousands of white shrimp, nearly translucent and some as long as Luke's hand, piled into the kayak. Their distinctive red antennae extended twice the length of their bodies and they seemed to be glowing from their own internal light source. Luke had to stop throwing the net for fear the kayak would sink from all the weight. In that moment, Dog Island was an estuary cathedral, its tidal sacraments made holier by a dad and his kid laughing to the point of tears and stumbling onto the sandy shore.

The tide was low enough that Luke walked alongside the kayak, its hull laden with a bounty they would share with everyone, and pushed it all the way back to shore, the water never reaching above chest deep.

By the time they made it to shore, a small crowd had gathered at the water's edge in the city park, waiting to see why Luke was walking across the bay instead of paddling. When they noticed the enormous shrimp filling the kayak, a buzz zipped from person to person, and a few headed into town to share the good news.

"Put the word out," Thomas announced. "The white shrimp are back, and Luke found them! Let's make a fire and cook these up for everyone around sunset."

Luke seemed especially proud of himself. Since he was seven years old and could first throw a cast net, he had loved it even more than fishing with a pole, especially the moment just before the net broke the surface on its way back up, when everything was possible. It could be empty or overflowing with anything from shrimp to bait fish to mullet of all sizes. Luke and his father were both looking forward to eating something besides mullet and clams, and for some social time in the park with their neighbors.

The past month had entailed daily physical labor for Thomas and Luke. They dug a latrine and built an outhouse in their back yard, assembled the boxes of solar panels that had been sitting in the guest room for weeks, installed a hand pump on the old well head near the front porch, paddled to Atsena Otie to salvage old bricks from the ruins of the Eberhard Faber sawmill for use in building an outdoor fireplace and hearth for cooking, and plowed the side yard under and planted vegetables for the second time in their life together.

Their first garden had been at the Nevermind Ranch, when the goat population there was at its highest level. With little experience and no real aptitude for or special interest in growing vegetables, Thomas and fifteen year old Luke had nevertheless managed to plant a half-acre with melons, tomatoes, cucumbers, bell squash, field peas, banana and bell peppers, okra, and even a few determined if underwhelming corn stalks. At the pinnacle of the garden's success, when everything seemed to be ripening at once, Thomas stopped to admire the work he and his son had done together.

There in the late afternoon sun, with the soft orange light filtering through a mist of water from the sprinklers and making the half-acre seem like the Elysian Fields, Thomas felt detached from his position in space and time—boundless and eternal—the sum of all his ancestors at once. He didn't even like half the vegetables before him, but the fact that he had planted them felt meaningful in a way that bigger events in his life seldom had. He could not remember, even generally, what any of his three wives' wedding dresses looked like, but for the rest of his life he would never be able to forget the minutest detail of this garden sunset, when he was connected to the earth, and he was the earth, and the sunlight and the water.

The following morning, as they walked to the car to leave for school, Thomas and Luke simultaneously detected movement in their peripheral vision. They turned their heads in unison and saw a biblical plague of escaped goats laying waste to their garden. Like locusts devouring Egyptian crops for a vengeful god, the goats seemed to be eating even the atmosphere of the half-acre, bleating in celebration of their good fortune, their orgy of ruminate excess.

"Whoa," Luke said.

"Yeah," Thomas replied.

On the way to school, they talked about golf and the large Hadron collider and how Commander Riker would be cooler if he didn't play the trombone. They never really talked about the garden again.

News of the shrimp spread quickly across the island, elevating the collective mood. Hayes and Mark David each carried giant metal pots to the park and a large plastic jug of precious fry oil. As they began set up the fire pit that would heat the oil to fry the shrimp, there was a spring in their steps and a lightness of mood that felt almost euphoric. Hayes moved with uncharacteristic speed and excitement.

"Hurry up old man, let's get this show on the road."

"I got a story for you about hurrying," Mark said.

"Oh boy," Hayes deadpanned.

"An old bull and a young bull are standing on a hill, looking over a field of fertile cows," he began.

"Lemme guess, we're the bulls?"

"Just listen, son."

"Yes sir. Old bull and a young bull, checking out the cows."

"You're ruining the story," Mark said.

"What's gonna happen to those cows? Dirty stuff I bet."

"I'll start over," Mark replied, pretending to be annoyed. "An old bull and a young bull are sitting on a hill, looking over a field of fertile cows. The young bull says let's run down there and screw one of those cows."

"I knew it," Hayes said shaking his head.

"The old bull says why don't we walk down there and screw all of them."

"Cool story, dad."

"Well, you ruined it, so..."

They laughed together, both men taking in the moment and enjoying the silliness. Mark David had a core philosophy that served him well through every triumph and setback of his life, and he shared it often. It was simple, direct, and the more you thought about it, the wiser it became:

You only need three things to be happy:
Something to do
Something to look forward to
and
Somebody to love

As Thomas settled into the moral incertitude of life after the killings on Shiloh Road, he thought often of Mr. Mark's advice, assessing the progress of his own life against its tenets. At present, there was certainly plenty to do, and in a general way he could look forward to running his birddog on oar and maybe eventually sail power. He was specifically looking forward to the shrimp fry later that evening, but by any reasonable standard, love had escaped him in the old world and the new.

As late afternoon winded down, people began to trickle into the park. On an island known for year round casual attire, and given the difficulties of life after the flash, it was striking to see most of the folks arriving for the shrimp fry adorned in their Sunday best. Women were wearing make-up and men had combed their hair back or parted to the side. Without needing to be told, they had sensed the importance of the gathering and dressed in enough formality to mark the occasion as such. Luke and James Walcox brought their guitars. Simone Beecham brought a hand drum and her powerful, bluesy voice. Geoff McCloud arrived with the colonel's mandolin and fortified calluses on his hands from weeks of near daily playing since his father had failed to return from the sky.

Shrimp hit the oil, Luke hit the opening riff of *Country Roads* and a park full of islanders sang along with John Denver and each other. It was, of course, a song about the Blue Ridge Mountains and the Shenandoah Valley, places that could hardly be more unlike Cedar Key. No one seemed to mind. Something about the moment would have been spoiled with lyrics about a blown out flip flop, stepping on a pop top, or frozen concoctions to help them hang on. The McCloud mandolin hit a twangy lead-in lick and the island chorus belted with abandon:

Country Roads, Take me Home
To the Place, I Belong...
West Virginia, Mountain Mama, Take Me Home, Country Roads

West Virginia was everything on their side of the Number Four Channel, their mountain mama was the Waccasassa Bay, and they were, there in the park together, home.

Hayes and Mark David fried pot after pot of the shrimp from Luke's kayak until it was empty. Bellies and hearts were full. The music continued into the night and there was dancing—dancing as fellowship, dancing as a break in the monotony of toiling to survive, dancing in defiance of a world set against them. Grizzled old clammers were laughing with yankee transplants they would have spurned in the old world. Older and younger kids swung on the park swings together. The petty feuds that seem to always simmer in small towns may not have been erased along with the smokestacks across the bay, but they were diminished as the night in the park went on. In a moment of flourish, Susie Coles hugged Slim Worthman and complimented his hair. Sally Rosencrantz and Nanette Hera danced a jig together and laughed at themselves.

A big high tide made the little beach at the park's edge inviting enough that several kids and a few adults were night swimming. Now and then, rogue beams of moonlight would escape the sky's penitentiary of gray, shimmer across the water and onto the dancers on the beach. Luke played every song he knew and a few he didn't. The work to stay alive the past hundred days had left most islanders thin and ragged, but in the sporadic moonlight they continued to dance and play and swim.

Adjacent to the park, at the eastern end of the public court, TJ, who had been conspicuously absent from the festivities, was hanging from the basketball rim by the bow line from Hayes's boat, his kind face looking serene and blue while his hard body swayed in the warm breeze. A scrap of notebook paper was pinned to his shirt. In TJ's handwriting, it said:

For Folksy. For Sumner. I'm sorry.

At the park, the islanders began to imagine lives worth living again.

13

—·—

THE TWO FIRES

Way Key is divided into three main sections. The most prominent portion of the island, containing Dock Street and the city offices and shops on 2nd Avenue, along with the historic district and Thomas' house on E Street, begins at the Old Fennimore Mill condos and curves around and up G Street to the Cedar Key School. Past that to the left on Gulf Boulevard is Piney Point, shaped like a backwards Italy, containing the George T. Lewis Airport, and bordered by the Daughtry Bayou on one side and the open Gulf of Mexico on the other. Turning right on Gulf leads to the part of Way Key referred to as *past the cemetery* or *out near the museum,* for the self-evident reason that the homes in this area were past the cemetery or out near the museum.

Lizzy Fraydel lived past the cemetery, out near the museum, in an area of high-end homes along Watson Circle that had views of the backwater marsh on one side and clear blue on the other all the way to Playa Escondida on the eastern coast of Mexico.

Six years before the smokestacks fell, Lizzy, her husband Jack, and their boy Jack, Jr. were enjoying a Cedar Key version of the American dream. Lizzy and Jack had grown up on the island and dated through much of high school. He was a sturdy Italian kid with long arms and big hands, imposing on the basketball court and a capable boat captain by the time he was fifteen years old. She was the picture of 1990 chic—big blonde hair and preppy clothes—her face often in a book and her sharp mind full of reckless teenage hope. They married just after graduation, leaving with Jack's father to begin their new lives near his family in Slidell, Louisiana. From his father, Jack learned to build houses. Lizzy learned, too, honing her skills at various facets of finish carpentry, especially fine detail painting. She was proud of her ability to cut in around the edges of the little windowpanes in French doors or other fenestration, never needing to use the expensive blue tape that slowed a painting job to a crawl. After a few years in the bayou, the economy in Louisiana began flagging, just as the one in southern Missouri was taking off. They moved there and quickly found success building and selling affordable houses on the outskirts of the fast-growing resort town of Branson. They did much of the construction work themselves, subcontracting out only the foundations, drywall, and roofs. A few years later, Jack, Jr. was born, and the high school sweethearts began to hear the same siren call that had beckoned so many to the island—Augustus Steele, David Levy Yulee, a prodigal Hayes David. Now it called the young family back home to the comfortable simplicity of Cedar Key and a life on the water growing clams.

The Fraydels were tenacious workers, inventive, shrewd, and tough. Their clam farm grew to encompass a dozen leases that reliably produced clams in incredible abundance. Years passed, and the size of Lizzy and Jack's home, wealth, and only child grew steadily over time. Jack, Jr. worked at his father's side, becoming a sharp waterman with a mastery of clam farming before he left for college at Florida State University. It was a life in full until Leukemia began a punishing courtship of the family captain, wearing him away in fits and starts over five hard years.

When he died, Lizzy and Jack, Jr. leaned into one another. She ran the business side of the clam operation, and he moved home to fill his father's place on the water. The following year was marked by failures and triumphs that seemed to orbit one another in perfect symmetry, each taking a turn at the fore before yielding to the other in a repeating cycle. Just as triumph seemed poised to break free at last, the gray advanced across the bay and upended their lives once again.

The basketball court was dark enough, even with the fire and occasional moonlight illuminating some of the park, that most people had already left for home when Hayes and Thomas saw TJ at the end of the bow line. In the old world, this ~~sitsssssssddd~~ might have triggered hysteria, even in men such as them, but considering all they had seen and done in recent weeks, a cold resignation hung in the air along with their friend.

It wasn't until they found and read the note TJ had pinned to his shirt that sadness finally broke through.

"Son of a bitch," Hayes said under his breath.

"Let's get him down before Cousin sees him," Thomas said.

With his grandfather's pocketknife, Hayes cut the line while Thomas held TJ's legs, sparing his body the indignity of crashing onto the concrete. They removed the poorly crafted noose, and the note, and carried him off the court together.

There was nothing more to be done with TJ until morning, so Hayes and Thomas laid him in the park's gazebo and covered him with a tablecloth from the shrimp fry before walking home, Hayes just across the street to his post-divorce bungalow, and Thomas the third of a mile down 3rd to its intersection with E Street.

When Thomas passed the market and climbed the little hill that led to his house, he saw a flickering light above the trees that seemed out of place and beautiful at the same time. He was entranced by the unnatural glow, walking past his house and toward the light, failing at first to recognize it as the same hell set loose on Little Don's compound in Sumner. When he saw the misshapen outline of his neighbor's three-story Victorian home, flames caving in a portion of the ornate trim on its western wall, Thomas was pulled from his trance and into the realization of the horror before him.

Becca and JB Cranston were among his favorite friends on the island. She was spritely and attractive, dressed often in a summer dress and Chuck Taylor All-Stars, her round glasses evoking every bit of the bad girl bookworm cliché ubiquitous in popular culture. In the old world, Becca had been a professor of English at a satellite campus of Santa Fe College in nearby Archer. Thomas had delighted in giving guest lectures to her writing students and appearing on the college's writing podcast to discuss his plays that had premiered off-Broadway in New York City and the novel he had written about the island. He referred to JB as Captain Awesome for his work as an officer with the Florida Fish and Wildlife Conservation Commission. In addition to protecting the natural resources of the Gulf and his search and rescue work, JB helped Thomas with logistic support for the Cedar Key Shark Swim. He was also funny, decent, and kind, nothing like the game warden stereotype promulgated in the Polk County swamp culture of his youth.

Becca and JB were deeply in love with one another, but the turbulent events of the past hundred days had put a damper on their romance. Faced with daily existential threats and the grueling physical work of survival, their home, like most homes on the island, had become a sexual wasteland. Carnal pleasures had been pushed so far down the Cranston to-do list that a full hundred days had elapsed since last they sought each other's embrace for anything more than a passing hug. The exuberance of the shrimp fry in the park, and the dancing that had begun in jest and ended with the spouses tangled in a steamy makeshift merengue, had rekindled their desire for one another, building steadily on their walk home, and boiling over into a thrilling if awkward Levy County Lambada, as they ambled up the steep staircase to their bedroom on the second floor. JB lit a fragrant candle that Becca kicked over almost immediately in the crush of pheromones and sweat and sex. By the time their bodies uncoupled, spent and floating in the ether of each other, the vintage lace curtains on either side of the bed had gone up, sending rivers of flame across the wall.

The 130-year old house gave in to the fire so quickly that there was nothing for the lovers to do but escape, waking their daughter Tina and gathering their pets on the way out the door, where Thomas met them in the street, JB naked as the day he was born, his wife and daughter sobbing as the balcony porch of their stately home collapsed into the front yard.

The Cedar Key Volunteer Fire Department is a marvel of efficiency and valor for such a small volunteer force. They arrived on the scene in minutes, but not before the circa 1885 Colonial Revival treasure next door to the Cranston home had joined the fire dance now making its way down both directions of 2nd Street. The northeasterly breeze that had made the shrimp fry so pleasant was amplifying now ahead of a storm front moving in from the mainland, intensifying the flames and hampering efforts to fight them. Fire Chief Bob Roberts directed his firefighters—John and Jamie Mitchell, Fire Boat Captain Lenny Mitchell, Jack Custard—along with the citizen deputies arriving with Chief Edwins and a building crowd of neighbors, to find as many buckets and pots as they could carry and form a chain across the block and a half from 2nd Street to the bay.

The firetruck's tank of water could be replenished from the Gulf using pumps running on the truck's diesel engine. Since no new diesel fuel would be available when the city's existing supply ran dry, however, every additional drop of water that could be marshalled into the fight would help extend the fighting life of the truck. For this effort, an old-fashioned line of buckets would need to be filled by hand and passed from person to person from the bay to the fire.

As the flames climbed higher in the sky, they could be seen all the way past the cemetery, out near the museum. Lizzy and Jack, Jr. rode their bikes toward the fire as quickly as they could, passing a line of their neighbors walking and running to help. Twenty years prior, an electrical short in an auditorium ceiling fan at the Cedar Key School started a fire that spread quickly through the high school. In the middle of the night, people from every corner of the island showed up to help. Their efforts saved the lower school from destruction. Hurricanes, fire, pandemics—whenever the wolves of trouble had gathered at the island's door, they were met with determined, collective resistance.

By the time Lizzy and Jack, Jr. made it to 2nd Street, the bucket line was fifty people strong. They took their place in the line and waited for the first bucket of water to reach them. When it did, it was heavier than Lizzy imagined it would be, but with effort she was able to take it from Denny Gal on her right and pass it to her left. Thomas, charred with soot from the falling balcony minutes earlier, reached to his right and took the bucket from her, noticing, perverse in light of the moment and the task at hand, her face—angular and soft at once, calming— his notice lingering into a probing examination of a stranger he was sure he already knew, if only in archetype, in longing—there holding a bucket in the building wind and advancing heat from the fire.

The next bucket saved him. He took it and passed it to Randal Solaro, looking away from her like shielding his eyes from the sun. The buckets came one after the other and he passed them, head down and cowering, until the fire jumped to a house on 1st Street and sent the bucket line scrambling away.

As the citizen firefighters regrouped in the parking lot of the Island Palace condos at the corner of 1st and the Dock Street Bridge, the Cranston house fell in on itself, a total loss. In the collapse, a sliver of burning wood was lofted into the building wind and began an improbable journey at the edge of physical possibility. It rode an updraft more than a thousand feet into the sky over the bay, swift enough to stoke its ember but gentle enough not to extinguish it. At the pinnacle of its ascent, it paused like Achilles at the gates of Troy, surveying the majesty of the city it was about to destroy.

The sliver's descent was gentle and targeted, landing at the first restaurant building on Dock Street, Dugan's on the Gulf, and nestling against its wood novelty siding, the kind that covered the exterior walls of so many older buildings on the island. Even then, the odds of the little sliver amounting to more than a few minutes of smoke were almost unfathomably long. The wind, though, laid low those odds as it blew across the ember, nurturing it to its fullest potential, playing matchmaker for its union with the old wood siding, desiccated by an arid spring.

Mike Dugan had been an excellent chef and, by most accounts, a real jerk, treating his employees so badly that he faced almost constant staff shortages, feuding with fellow island restauranteurs over perceived but trivial slights, or getting wine soaked and taking to the Rumor Mill for unhinged Internet ranting. Had he not fallen in the first wave of the diabetic die-off after the flash, even his out-sized arrogance would have bowed before the firestorm that began in his restaurant and tore across Dock Street with the speed of Alexander smashing Scythians on the Steppe.

When the flames from Dugan's became visible on 1st Street, fire boat captain Lenny Mitchell asked permission to deploy the jet boat and take a team of firefighters to try to fight them. Chief Roberts took stock of the situation—three houses engulfed and the fire moving in two directions—and made a fateful decision. He would not split his forces for the commercial buildings on Dock Street that had gone mostly unused in previous months. The fire department would keep its resources focused on saving homes and people. The jet boat was still deployed, however, at the inside boat ramp. Lenny Mitchell raced it under the Dock Street bridge and toward the houses on 1st Street where he began spraying its water canon toward the fire. The jet boat was a favorite piece of equipment and a badge of honor for the department. It was a sleek vessel about the size of a Volkswagen Beetle and shaped like a Star Trek shuttle craft. It drew water into its intake ports and used a jet motor to spray the water incredible distances. From the bay, the little boat's water cannon could reach houses all along 1st and some on 2nd.

The bucket brigade reformed into a line running from the Island Palace swimming pool, which was easier to access and slightly closer than the bay, and Aunt Faye's Cottage, just then beginning to catch fire. The cottage was part of a row of four houses with frontage on 1st and the Gulf, directly across from Atsena Otie. In recent years all four had been converted into short-term vacation rentals, but their history was far more interesting. Following the Great Cedar Key Hurricane of 1896 that devastated Atsena Otie, the four cottages were among the few structures on the island to not be substantially destroyed. As the town collectively abandoned the barrier island and focused on Way Key as their new home, the four cottages were floated across the channel on barges and placed on new foundations in their current location. Aunt Faye's Cottage, Reba May's Cottage, Ida Marie's Cottage, and Mary & Randal's Cottage were among the most popular rentals on the island and were treasured by locals for their historical ties to the Cedar Key of their ancestors.

Chief Roberts had a philosophy for firefighting that guided his actions in the historic district that night—never waste resources on a structure that can't be saved. This directive was practical and good firefighting practice, but it would have the heartbreaking consequence of letting the fire destroy one of the island's irreplaceable treasures. Just as Becca Cranston had cleaved to her husband in the Biblical sense, now the fire, in the word's confoundingly opposite meaning, cleaved the Historical Society buildings from the island and its residents.

There were two museums on Cedar Key. The first was the state museum out past the cemetery, whose hokey, handmade dioramas and limited exhibits remained exactly as they first appeared in the out of place Frank Lloyd Wright knock-off structure when it was constructed in 1958. For three dollars, tourists would spend an average of ten minutes passing through the underwhelming, government-run attraction. In contrast, the Historical Society Museum comprised two 19th century buildings at the corner of 2nd and D Streets and were packed wall to wall with artifacts spanning the breadth of Cedar Key's hardscrabble, industrious, and wild history. Thomas knew every exhibit by heart, and though he had spent countless days wandering its halls, he never tired of taking visiting guests on a tour through the museum.

As he and Lizzy, Hayes, Luke, the jet boat, and dozens of their neighbors began to make headway against the fires on 1st Street, Chief Roberts concluded, correctly, that nothing more could be done for the Lutterloh building and the adjoining former residence that housed the museum. As the firefighters fell back to form a defensive line to preserve the library, City

Hall, and homes further down 2nd Street, the history of the islanders' great grandparents turned from solid to ash and smoke, then disappeared into the gray night sky.

The fire's assault on Dock Street was less the Siege of Vicksburg and more immediate capitulation. The old wood buildings could mount no defense and they were given no quarter. The Steaming Clam, where Thomas loved to sit at the bar and order fruity umbrella drinks, collapsed through Mike Carline's ice cream and gift shop, famous for its offensive political tchotchke that delighted half the folks buying an ice cream cone, and enraged the other. The Big Dock Bar and Grill, where Hayes, Thomas and Rolf used to have a standing Friday lunch date, stood one moment, and was gone the next. The Quartermaster Suites above the bric-a-brac tourist trap Willy Nilly Gallery were the last to fall, after the M&L Bar, The Tipsy Manatee, The Dock Street Motel, and the fancy Latitudes restaurant that, even at the height of snowbird season, never seemed to be open but still did a brisk business. When there were no buildings left for the fire to consume, it turned its attention to the dock itself. At a cursory glance, Dock Street appeared to be a part of the main island but most of its buildings and even part of the street were built on a three-acre dock held up by large wooden pilings concreted into the bottom of the Gulf. The little wood sliver's progeny, now a blitzkrieg army of destruction, chewed through the wooden pilings, crashed into the saltwater of the bay, and was gone.

The jet boat's fuel tank had to be refilled multiple times throughout the night. Luke would carry five gallon cans of gasoline back and forth from the city's reserve tank to the edge of 1st Street, then wade them out to the boat so the water cannon could operate continuously. The fire truck consumed sixty gallons of diesel fuel between its main engine and the pumps that pulled water from the bay, a third of the city's total supply.

The bucket brigade kept the buckets of water moving until people fell out from exhaustion at the pace of several an hour.

As the first light of dawn began to push away the night, the fire on 1st street was finally extinguished. On 2nd, west of the fallen museum, the less sacred First Baptist Church building, from whose pulpit judgement was dispensed as liturgy, lay in an ash heap worthy of Job. Pastor Willy's contrived sermons had leaned hard into the pseudo-Calvinist theology of predestination, but he had somehow failed to prepare his congregation for the irony of a brimstone church ablaze in hellfire.

East of the museum on 2nd, Benji Iver's coffee shop, Island Pizza, and Virginia Edmonson's real estate office were gone, along with the Tony's restaurant building, save for the iconic sign extolling their world-famous clam chowder. In the old world, television coverage of a disaster's after-math would normally include some local official looking into the camera with defiant resolve and saying, "We will rebuild." After the long night of fighting the fire, neither Mayor Hayes nor Chief Roberts had any defiance left in them, and no expectation of anything being rebuilt.

Still, despite the terrible losses, the islanders had prevailed.

Lizzy began the bike ride back to her side of the island, and as she passed, Thomas finally worked up the nerve to smile at her, then put his arm around his boy while they walked slowly home together.

14

THE WATER TOWER

In front of the Cedar Key School, in view of passing cars and golf carts, sat a giant concrete shark of indeterminate species, and less than stellar craftsmanship. It had a weird look on its face and its paint seemed to be perpetually faded, but the school's mascot was nonetheless beloved by the islanders. In the recorded history of Cedar Key, there had never been a reported case of an official shark attack. Here and there, you could find a story of someone who stepped on a nurse shark and got an ankle bitten, or a fisherman with a quick bite to his hand by a small black tip or shovel nose as they tried to remove a hook from the shark's mouth, but no islander or weekender had ever sustained a serious injury from a shark in the waters around Cedar Key. This fact, however, is not to say that large, dangerous sharks are absent from those waters.

A shark fishing club had often set up shop along the rocky shore curving in front of the Beachfront Motel on G Street, using a kayak to drag enormous baits on lines from heavy offshore fishing reels out to the deep water of the main channel, halfway between Way Key and Atsena Otie. Seldom did they leave without landing a seven or eight foot bull, tiger, or hammerhead shark. Occasionally but not often, significantly larger sharks would emerge at the end of the line after an hours-long fight, man-eaters in every respect. The fishermen would tag, photograph, and measure the sharks before returning them to the Gulf.

When Thomas was new to town, while having dinner on Dock Street with his new friend Hayes David, he looked across the channel and said, "You ever swam across to Atsena Otie."

"If you're gonna be a local, you have to start pronouncing it right," Hayes said.

"It looks pretty phonetic to me," Thomas replied. "At-Sen-Uh-Oh-Tee."

Hayes shook his head and said, "It's a made up word, cobbled together from some Indian words by the guy that bought it when it was Depot Key."

"Augustus Steele," Thomas said, looking proud of himself.

"Since it isn't a real word, there's no official way to say it, I guess, but everyone I know back to my grandparents called it Senny-Otie"

"There's no way to get from At-Sen-Uh Oh-Tee to Sen-Knee-Oh-Tee."

"Well say it however you want, but you'll just sound like a yankee."

"That's a low blow."

"I know," Hayes said, laughing.

"Ok, fine. Have you ever swam to Senny Otie?"

"I've swam in that channel plenty, but never all the way across. My grandmother used to do it when she was a kid."

"Really? It's a half mile."

"Yeah, and fifty years ago it was a rite of passage for kids."

"I think we should bring back the tradition of swimming across the channel," Thomas said excitedly. "We can make it a charity event to raise money for the school."

"Damn," Hayes said.

"What?"

"Of all the dumb ideas you've had... this one is actually genius. I'm mad I didn't think of it."

Wasting no time, Thomas built a website and announced the event in a press release. Followers of his writing from around the country reacted with frenzied enthusiasm. Excitement spread across the island and onto the mainland. Sales of official Shark Swim t-shirts were brisk, and Thomas began mailing them to folks as far away as Oregon, Maine, and confoundingly, Kuala Lumpur. A handful of locals, the same miserable no-accounts from the Rumor Mill that seemed to oppose anything new or fun, attacked him as a self-promoting villain that was willing to risk lives to get attention. It didn't matter; the voices of negativity were drowned out. Thomas couldn't resist poking fun at his self-loathing critics, mentioning them as often as possible in newspaper, radio, and television interviews about the event, encouraging them to buy lottery tickets because they were, "More likely to get struck by lightning on February 29th while winning the Powerball than they were to get bitten by a shark on the swim."

A few months later, with a shoestring budget and not enough planning, the Inaugural Cedar Key Shark Swim raised several thousand dollars for the school's playground budget. Swimmers aged six to eighty-two set out from the sand spit in front of the Beachfront Motel toward Atsena Otie. Lining the swim course were birddogs from across the clam fleet. The open back ends of the birddogs made it easy for tired swimmers to belly up onto them to take a break or throw in the towel. Thomas' friends from Gainesville came out in force to support their friend and the cause.

Tim Mueller, the first new friend Thomas ever made in Gainesville when he arrived there fresh out of the Navy, was a performance artist, poet, playwright, and all around provocateur who had made numerous public pronouncements about his expected triumph in the swim. Tim was not an athletic man or possessed of an abundance of toughness, and he was not an avid or experienced swimmer. Still, he made social media posts and YouTube videos mocking the paltry half-mile distance and daring sharks to attack him. Of the one hundred and twenty-two people that began the swim, only fifteen quit before reaching the white sand finish line across the channel. The very first to give up, well before a brave teenage girl attempting the swim despite having no arms, was a dejected Tim Mueller, who flopped like a toadfish onto Damien Lott's birddog boat, The Clam Hammer, gasping for air and choking on inglorious defeat.

Thomas' buddy from high school, and across-the-street church rival in Gainesville, Georgie Pilsner, flew down from his new home in Virginia for the event. In recent years, Georgie had started swimming and bike riding in the early morning hours before work, transforming his body into the best shape of his life. This transformation led him to the incredible prediction that he would beat Thomas in the swim, despite his Naval veteran friend's reputation as a fantastic swimmer. For this effort, Georgie arrived at the swim in a sleek neoprene swimsuit with a confident swagger. Thomas wore regular shorts and a button-down Hawaiian shirt. On a cloudless, perfect Saturday, the swimmers entered the water, heard the ready-set-go, and began their furious race across the channel.

Swimmers from the University of Florida were among the racers, but none, surprisingly, finished better than 5th place. Hayes and Thomas, their pride hanging in the balance, battled one another the entire race, Hayes eventually finishing three places behind Thomas, claiming, preposterously, an absurd mishap with one of his fins. Thomas finished solidly inside the top ten, bested only by world-class swimmers that frequented competitive swimming events. From the beautiful banks of the barrier island, the finishers sat in the sand and watched swimmer after swimmer claim their share of the day's glory—middle aged women, children, octogenarians, Lida Maria Johnson wearing a plastic shark fin and a too small swimsuit bottom that had to be constantly picked from her butt, folks with a variety of physical disabilities, a paranoid schizophrenic who saw Nazis in the sun rays reflecting on the water, an Episcopal priest, anarchists, a militant South American eco-terrorist, middle schoolers from the Cedar Key School, a 6-year-old from Gainesville—one after another they finished to the boisterous cheering of those already on the shore. Just before Thomas began to announce the winners over a bullhorn, someone called out, "Wait, there's still somebody out there!"

From behind a birddog, on a commandeered inflatable shark raft, appeared the neoprened and imperial Georgie Pilsner, overheated from his poor choice of swimwear in the eighty-five degree water, refusing to accept defeat, kicking and splashing in a wild final push to avoid the shame that would beleaguer Tim Mueller for the rest of his days. The crowd of long-finished swimmers saw in Georgie a reflection of their own life struggles—the toil and struggle of all mankind, really—and erupted in thundering, unified applause. Georgie, invigorated by the exchange of energy from the shore to the water, transcended the limitations of the moment and doubled his pace, gliding onto the shore in the unexpected triumph and majesty of dead last place. In the face of Georgie Pilsner's magnificent anti-victory, Tim Mueller, legs dangling from The Clam Hammer, wept in envy, pride, and joy.

In the weeks after The Great Fire, a melancholy beset the island, dug into a fortified position, and lingered. Productivity slowed for the various projects and programs on which the council and others had been working. Thomas was working through his stockpile of bourbon at a pace that alarmed his friends. In the old world, he mostly didn't drink at all, even ordering ginger ale on the rocks with a twist of lime to give the appearance of drinking at social gatherings while keeping his wits sharp. In the aftermath of Shiloh Road, he had finally discovered the utility of alcohol. Being gregarious and needing no social lubrication, alcohol in the old world had seemed to him a bad trade; a slowed mind and a sick stomach in exchange for feeling altered made no sense to him. Now, saddled with visions of dead strangers in Sumner and a dead friend hanging from a basketball rim—these events linked forever in fact and in memory— alteration was worth almost any price.

Hayes and Susie Coles privately worried that without some reason for collective hope, the island would end up no better than Sumner or Gainesville. Over smoked mullet and poke salad Luke had found growing wild on the interior of North Key, Hayes and Susie, along with John Mitchell and a haggard-looking Thomas, met to formulate a plan to shake the island from its malaise.

"We just need a win," Hayes said.

"I agree," Susie replied. "But it'll need to be something more than a shrimp fry, I'm afraid."

"Still nothing from the outside world?" Thomas asked. "I know a few folks with hand-crank radios, and I know we use a little gas here and there to fire up generators. Any of that electricity being used to keep reaching out? Have we heard anything?"

"Not a peep," said Hayes. "And we used so much gas and diesel fighting the fire, we can't afford to waste any going forward."

"If I had some help, I think I could have the water supply up and running in another week," John Mitchell said matter-of-factly.

"Really?" Thomas asked excitedly. "Why didn't you say something?"

"I just did," John replied.

Hayes said, "Running water would be a massive win. An absolute game-changer. What can we do to help?"

"A month ago, there wasn't much that would've helped, but two days last week had sun and three so far this week. The gray might finally be letting up. Let's head down to the water tower and I'll walk you through it."

Like most small towns in the south, Cedar Key's skyline was dominated by the city water tower. The bright white tower rose one hundred fifty feet in the air and held three hundred thousand gallons of water. *Cedar Key*, in muted red letters, could be seen from the land and the bay. As John Mitchell explained to the group, the tower was filled from a well using an electric pump. The pump needed to run for about two hours at a time to fill the tank from empty to full. Eighteen months before the smokestacks fell, the city utilized a state grant to install a state of the art hydro-electric turbine as part of the water system, an unusual advancement for a town the size of Cedar Key.

City water systems operate largely on gravity, with the water pressure at faucets generated by the water falling from the elevated height of the tower. In the island's relatively advanced system, a hydro-electric turbine was installed at the bottom of the tower, utilizing the force of the falling water to turn a turbine before it heads down the lines to homes and business. This turbine generates electricity that is then used to power the pump that draws water from the municipal well and pumps it back up into the tower, starting the cycle over again. At a first glance, the Law of Conservation of Energy, expressed in equation form as $K1 + U1 = K2 + U2$, and colloquially as *energy can never be created or destroyed,* would seem to suggest the impossible—the city's tower/turbine system could be an infinite energy machine since the total energy of an isolated system remains constant. In practice, the system is far from isolated, suffering from numerous, expected, inefficiencies that lead to only about seventy to eighty percent of the energy from the turbine being preserved for use in operating the pump. In the old world, electricity from the power grid supplied the additional twenty to thirty percent energy required to keep the cycle running.

In his slow drawl, storyteller manner, John Mitchell relayed the details of how it all worked to his friends. Thomas was especially encouraged.

"So, if we can somehow generate enough electricity to run the pump for two hours at a time we can have running water?"

"Yessir," John replied. "In theory."

"Is it a lot of electricity?" Susie asked.

"I guess it's all relative," John said. "But it's not a whole hell of a lot, considering this big ass tower."

"How do we do it then, John?"

"I reckon this hill is as open to the sun as any spot on the island," John said. "I'd feel good about 50 regular solar panels, the normal kind you'd find on a house, to run the pump. TJ had been helping me work on an interface between the panels and the pump. I think it's finished. We just need to round up some panels."

"I've got two dozen in boxes at my house," Thomas said. "Hadn't been enough sun to fool with until lately. I was just about to try to get them going so I could charge my golf cart batteries, but I'll donate them to the cause."

"Well hang on," Hayes said. "You might not have to. Let's see how many we can find on abandoned houses and see if it's enough. If not, we can make up the shortfall with a few from several people instead of you giving up all of yours."

The water tower sat atop a hill adjacent to the Cedar Key School, on a two-acre fenced parcel that would comfortably hold more than enough panels.

"I'll round up some folks and we'll get started looking," Hayes said.

"I'll grab Luke and we'll help," Thomas added.

"Since we're here," Susie began in the tone that everyone knew meant she had a plan, too, and that no matter what the plan was, the best thing for everyone would be to just agree to it upfront. "I've got it figured that forty-eight school age kids are on the island now. Getting the water running will make the *right now* a lot better, but we need to get these kids back in school so the *later on* is worth having, too."

Thomas recognized that she was talking about the second item on Mark David's recipe for happiness, *something to look forward to*, and not just as it related to the kids. Without a reason for adults in the community to believe the next generation had a future worth looking forward to, they themselves would lose their willingness to do the work required to make anything better. After the success of his Cedar Key Shark Swim, and the thousands of dollars it raised for the school, Thomas was asked to join Susie Coles, Lara Sleedy, Mike Allenby, and a few others on the School Advisory Council (SAC). He didn't enjoy committee work but enjoyed saying no to Susie Coles even less. The SAC committee helped chart the strategic goals of the school and had input on how it should spend state and national grants, as well as charity money from events like the Shark Swim, that made their way to the school. Everyone from the SAC committee was still alive and Thomas felt sure they would help.

"Do we have enough teachers to open the school again?" Hayes asked. "I can only think of three that lived on the island."

"Just one, left," John said, "Paige Landry and Miss Norma passed a few weeks after everything happened. My daughter-in-law worked in the office. I'm sure she would help."

"I agree it's time, Susie. Make it work and let's get it going," Hayes said.

"I'll get started putting together a new group of teachers," she replied.

With marching orders for two missions that would, in tandem, hopefully jump-start the island's morale, the friends set out to round up help. Thomas found Luke in the workshop under their house on E Street. The front of the house was level with the street, atop a small hill on the island, but the sloping of that hill meant the back of the house was just over seven feet above the ground. For roughly half the length of the house, a person could walk around in the crawl space below it. Thomas had turned this area into a workshop with shelves and a work bench on one end and pallets of clam bags on the other. It was an ideal workshop, shielded from the hot sun in the summer but still open enough to allow cool breezes to blow through.

"What are you working on, son?"

"Actually, I think I just finished it—a little trailer to pull behind my bike. Thought I could use it for hauling fish and whatever else. It took forever to figure out how to make a bracket to attach it to the bike... but check it out."

He showed his father the attached trailer, about the size of spread-out clam bag, fixed sturdily to his bicycle with what looked like other bicycle parts.

"Dang. This thing looks legit. Pretty crazy timing, too, since we need it right now."

"Cool, what for?" Luke asked.

Thomas explained the mission, watched the light in his son's eyes brighten at the prospect of running water, and felt confident his reaction would be shared by the whole town if they could find enough solar panels to make it work.

"I know a place," Luke said.

"Whereabouts?"

"That mean-ass lady that died. The one that always filed complaints to the city and came to council meetings to complain about her neighbors. Her house. I don't know her actual name, but you told me about her."

"I don't think we should speak ill of the dead, son."

"You can be dead and still be an asshole."

Thomas tried to suppress his laugh, but it was funny, and then they were laughing together.

"Damn it, Luke," Thomas said rubbing his eyes to try to regain his composure.

"Like, Hitler didn't suddenly stop being Hitler just because he died," Luke said, smirking.

"Alright, alright, that's enough. Margaret Van Landing was her name, and yeah, she sucked. But she wasn't Hitler."

"I think if your name is Van Landing," Luke said in an exaggerated aristocratic voice, "You're required to maintain a certain level of pomposity when dealing with the proletariat."

Thomas, laughing, said, "Pomposity is a solid word. At least you learned something at the university, I guess."

"Well anyway, she lives out near the museum," Luke said. "Most of her roof had solar panels."

"Excellent. Let's see if your new trailer can haul them."

Thomas grabbed his bike and the two Buck men headed out, laughing intermittently still. The trailer rode smooth and straight and was easy to pull. Thomas admired his son's work as they pedaled to the far side of the island together.

Both men were excited to discover the solar panels were still where Luke remembered seeing them. It wasn't until they dismounted their bikes that they realized neither had thought to bring a ladder. Luke saw a large green trash can near the driveway and drug it up the outside stairs to the porch of the stilt house. He positioned it below the roof line, hopped onto it and from there was able to spring up onto the roof with the gymnastic improvisation of youth.

"Let's see it old man," Luke said.

"Son of a bitch," Thomas said under his breath before climbing, awkwardly, onto the trash can. Luke shook his head, certain his dad didn't have it in him. Thomas shook his head, uncertain if he had it in him.

"I'm gonna need to see it, too," came a voice from the house across the street. Thomas turned toward the sound, saw a flash of blonde hair, then froze as time halted across the universe. When it began again it did so at a glacial pace, his embarrassment building eon upon eon—an age at least to recognize her face, a hundred millennium to formulate a phrase.

"Hey there," he said, the world suddenly moving faster than it ever had. "I got this."

She wasn't carrying a bucket this time, but it was definitely her. With no choice now but to act, Thomas leapt from the trash can toward the roof, momentarily landing upon it before slipping and tumbling back down toward the can, breaking his fall by grasping the thin aluminum rain gutter before it and he collapsed together. Instantly, he sprang back to his feet, saw Lizzy trying hard not to laugh, then did the only sensible thing in the moment—throwing his arms wide into the air, snapping his shoulders back and head up as though trying to sell a dismount from the uneven bars to a panel of Olympic judges.

"10, 10, 10!" Lizzy cheered.

"Thank you, thank you," Thomas replied with a sheepish wave.

"Jesus, Dad," Luke said from above. "You good?"

"I'm good."

"Imma get you a ladder," Lizzy called up.

"Much obliged," said Thomas, before heading down to finally meet the bucket lady.

15

OLD SHARKS, NEW TRICKS

June of the year the smokestacks fell was drawing to a close. Since that awful morning in early February, the islanders had faced one disheartening setback after another. It would be something short of the truth to say they had met every challenge with honor and courage. Certainly, their resolve was worthy of praise, but in the crucible of those hard five months, there had been less heroism than self-preservation.

The first five months in the year 1890 found the Cedar Key of that era in the grip of its own prolonged nightmare. On January 2nd of that year, William 'Billy' Cottrell was sworn into office as the town's mayor. Thirty year-old Billy was the son of a state senator and had never held a job before taking office. When sober, he could be affable, benign, and even generous. Unfortunately for the residents of the island, he was seldom sober, and when drunk became belligerent and exceedingly cruel. As a child, he got into the mash and stabbed an old man with his pocketknife. As a young adult, he made his sister a widow by shooting his brother-in-law dead.

As mayor, Billy terrorized the residents of Cedar Key, once holding a group of ladies hostage at gunpoint at the general store and laughing as they screamed in fear. He would force random passersby on the street to headbutt each other and fist fight for his amusement or risked being shot. In April after his election, he forced a man to beat a telegraph operator nearly to death to save the trouble of doing it himself. He would cause the shops of people he didn't like to close by ordering citizens not to shop there. On more than one occasion, he required black men to dress in humiliating costumes and march in a parade down 2nd Street. By May, he was threatening the children of his rivals, killing their dogs, and committing outright murder. The citizens cowered in fear, with none of the island's men willing to stand up to the violent mayor.

One fearless woman, Miss Rose Bell, wrote a letter to the President of the United States, Benjamin Harrison, pleading for his help. She told the President that the men of her town were too timid and weak to act, and that she herself had only braved to write because she had no husband or children left for the mayor to kill in retaliation. The President was so moved by her words that he sent the new US Customs agent in the area, J.H. Pinkerton, to investigate. Mayor Cottrell was enraged by Pinkerton's presence in his town and attempted to threaten and intimidate him as he had so many others. Pinkerton stood his ground. He sent a telegram to the White House confirming the accuracy of Miss Bell's claims and informing the President of the threats made against him by the mayor.

In the only instance in American history of a mayor being deposed by a military coup, President Harrison sent a U.S. Navy warship down the channel between Atsena Otie and Way Key. Its landing force came ashore on the 13th of May with orders to arrest Billy Cottrell. The mayor fled the island, sneaking past his pursuers through the backwaters and into the Suwannee River just up the coast. From there he sailed all the way to Georgia and then made his way to Montgomery, Alabama. He was eventually arrested there but was released on bail while he awaited trial, continuing in the interim to get drunk and threaten people at gunpoint. The Montgomery chief of police, Adolph Gerard, had Cottrell arrested again, but he was somehow granted yet another bail. He swore vengeance against the chief, bragging around town that he intended to kill him on sight. On the basis of this threat, Chief Gerard waited for Cottrell's carriage to arrive for a court appearance on November 5th, then shot him twice when he stepped onto the street.

The mayor's reign of terror was over.

Back in Cedar Key, residents were glad to be liberated from the heel of their tyrant mayor, but with only twenty-five years between Appomattox and a federal warship docking on their island, apprehension among the islanders was high. To his credit, President Harrison was sensitive to the anxiety that would be caused by the federal government intervening in local affairs. Referencing the Cedar Key ordeal, he wrote, "It will always be agreeable to me if the local authorities, acting upon their own sense of duty, maintain the public order in such a way that the officers of the United States shall have no occasion to appeal for the intervention of the General Government, but when this is not done, I shall deem it my duty to use the adequate powers vested in the Executive to make it safe."

As the first Fourth of July in the new world approached, one hundred and fifty days had passed since the island's last contact from any government on the other side of the Number Four Bridge. The public order was being maintained with no expectation that any help, executive or otherwise, was coming.

Susie Coles never faced a murderous mayor, but she embodied the courageous spirit of Rose Bell all the same, facing overwhelming opposition often as she moved through the world. When she came for the septic tanks in the town of Suwannee, judging, correctly, that they were damaging the ecosystem of the lower river and the Gulf into which they outflowed, she was decried as an environmental whacko and faced threats to her safety and family. She stayed the course. The new state-funded sewer system she spearheaded in Suwannee became a front line defense for the oyster and clam industries all along the Big Bend gulf coast.

When a south Florida attorney moved to the island and purchased the marina and the first house to ever sell for a million dollars, Susie refused to be bullied by the big spender. The attorney, angry at a fine for cutting down a large tree without a city permit, came to a city council meeting to complain. He began his remarks by listing all the money he had recently spent on the island—two million for the marina, a million for his main house and a half million for another—imagining such a display of his wealth would bulldoze opposition to his cutting down of the single tree. If the attorney had been the resurrected Christ and had spent a billion dollars on the island, Susie Cole's answer to him would have been the same as it was to the blustering transplant from Naples.

"I don't care how much money you have. I came here with nothing, and I'll leave with nothing, and you'll still pay the fine for cutting down the tree."

To her great delight, for maybe the first time in her life of public service, Susie faced no meaningful opposition to her current mission. To the contrary, everyone she spoke to about her plan, even people with no school-age kids, immediately joined the effort, pledging any help they could possibly offer. As she knocked on door after door, word began to spread so quickly across the island that by the twentieth or so door, she could no longer find anyone who hadn't already heard about the school reopening. Every time she left a house, she would emphasize her goodbye with a spirited, "Go Sharks!" that was always met with the enthusiastic reply, "Go Sharks!" A saying that had been routine in the old world had become a rallying cry for the spirit and soul of the island. It generated joy, excitement, and most of all, hope. With the same solemnity of Thomas' *Go Gators* at the big house door in Gainesville, *Go Sharks* now pushed back against the gray, swollen to gluttony on the island's despair.

Invigorated by the town's enthusiasm, Susie took an inventory of students she believed to be on the island, then set about the painstaking and sometimes sad work of verifying her count. After three days of walking, bike riding, door knocking, and old fashioned investigation work, Susie identified forty-five students living on the island. The kindergarten class was the largest, with eight students. 7th grade had five, but most of the others averaged three. There was a solitary eleventh grader and two seniors.

In the old world, the Cedar Key School employed a total of sixteen teachers, one each for kindergarten through fifth grade, four teachers to teach the various subjects to the middle schoolers, five for the high schoolers, and a P.E. teacher. Susie's scholastic census work confirmed John Mitchell's estimate of there being only one of those sixteen still alive and well on the island—Miss Rebecca Morgan, the third grade teacher. The school's articulate, hard-working librarian, Jonya Bollins, was also still around, along with the two lunchroom ladies that had thwarted the young Meade boys from stealing the school's food, and Jenna Mitchell, the front office secretary.

Lena Custard, whose husband James had sent fifteen rounds into the Sumner men on the little bridge across from Fannie's, and poured the gas on Little Don's compound, had volunteered for many years at the school. She was energetic and bright and had the kind of wholesome face that tried to distract you from how pretty she was until, some day by chance, you saw her in the late afternoon sun by the water on G street, or loading cover netting into a dumpster on a Coastal Cleanup Day, and realized how lucky James had been to squirrel her away for himself. Her son had been in the 9th grade on the day the smokestacks fell. Susie had to do little by way of convincing to get her to agree to teach a combined class of kindergarten and first graders.

Maria Phillips taught Sunday School in her husband Folksy's various congregations during their life together. The same island stillness that haunted Colonel McCloud when he returned to civilian life had set upon Maria in the weeks following her husband's death. For want of something to do, mostly, she volunteered to teach the second and third graders while Miss Rebecca, a trained elementary teacher, moved up from third grade to teach the fourth and fifth graders the more strenuous math and reading skills of those grades.

Jenna Mitchell became the de facto principal of the school, though her duties were more organizational and record keeping than the political and bureaucratic work of principals in the old world. She and Jimmy Mitchell began dating when they were both fresh-faced seniors at the Cedar Key School. In the intervening years, Jimmy had gone bald and weathered into a rugged masculine archetype from a Hemingway novel. Even when Jenna's auburn hair gave way to flecks and streaks of gray, she remained the kind of disarming beauty on which small-town cultures everywhere are built and sustained.

For the middle and high school students, Susie focused on recruiting islanders to teach subjects they knew and that would be useful in the new world. As the school's former librarian, Jonya Bollins was a natural choice to teach literature. For her first lessons, she selected *The Lion the Witch and the Wardrobe* for her sixth, seventh, and eight graders, *The Old Man and the Sea* for the freshmen and sophomores, and *Light in August* for the juniors and seniors, the latter beginning as a painful slog and ending, with her guidance and enthusiasm shepherding the young readers through the beautiful, difficult language, as a thing that changed the students into more probing thinkers. The isolation of Faulkner's rural Mississippi in the early twentieth century became for them an unlikely parallel to life on the island at the end of the world.

Joey Bannon, a husky, abrasive clam farmer that had escaped the gray on the morning the smokestacks fell only by way of having scheduled that day for building clam belts and routine maintenance of his birddog, was asked to utilize the training from his military days to teach basic marksmanship for students in the fourth grade on. He had intensely disliked Thomas at first, feeling he ran his mouth too much about the clam industry, inviting attention from outsiders that might seek to move in on a business that locals were reluctant to share. Over time, Thomas wore him down and the two men eventually developed a kind of *Odd Couple* friendship. When a representative for the clam industry was needed to speak to government officials about a crop insurance program, Joey had hesitantly reached out to his new friend for help.

"You need to handle this shit for us, Thomas... you've got that thing... I can't think of the word, but you're good at this stuff. Dammit, what's the word I'm looking for?"

"The French would call it *Je ne sais quio*."

"No bud, that ain't it," Joey replied flatly. "I just meant you're good at talking to fancy assholes."

"Yeah... yeah that makes more sense," Thomas said sheepishly.

Randy Napa had been the island's auto mechanic when gasoline to power automobiles was still a thing that could be obtained. In the new world, he used his mechanical aptitude to help his neighbors with a variety of projects. As haircuts and shaves became less prevalent on the island, his Rasputin aesthetic grew in acceptance with each passing month. As more of them began to look like him, folks that had written Randy off as a grease monkey in the past began to notice his sharp intellect and kind demeanor. The lines between class lost their focus within days of the flash across the bay, and now, five months on, were almost imperceptible. There is an egalitarian quality in prolonged suffering that undermines privilege and perception in the same way a flood abrogates the banks of a river. With the currency of his practical aptitude enhanced by the harsh realities of the new age, Randy became an obvious, excellent choice to become a teacher at the school. Susie recruited him to teach a class she intended to be called *Practical Engineering* but would come to be known to students and parents alike as *Fixing Stuff with Mr. Randy*.

There had not been a music teacher at the school in the old world. Now, James Walcox and Simone Beacham agreed to alternate weeks teaching guitar at the school, with Luke Buck and Doris Goodland, the organist at Christ Church, alternating weeks instructing the students in music theory and the piano.

Bette David, who for many years owned a quilt shop in the building most recently utilized as Denny Gall's breakfast café, agreed to teach quilting and basic sewing, required for all students. From a book in the library, she would learn the basics of sail making, and teach it as a section in her husband Mark's knot tying and basic seamanship class. Eventually, watermen from across the fleet, including Thomas and Jack Fraydel, Jr., would begin to stop in to help teach the young sailors, even as they themselves learned—with more regularity than they would ever admit—things from Mr. Mark they had not even known they didn't know about boat captaining. The woodshop would be reopened, using hand tools that Franky Kain hadn't used since he was a kid himself, learning carpentry at his grandfather's side. Thomas would teach creative writing and a theater class. History would be taught by a rotating list of history enthusiasts on the island, including Hayes David, who would focus on the history of the island back to the Timucuan Indians he had always so admired. Linda Richland would use her restaurant to teach the old-style island cooking of her grandmother, the original proprietor of Fannie's Café.

With no air conditioning, classroom sessions would begin at 7 AM and let out at 11 AM in the warmer months, after which being inside became too unbearable for students to focus. Afternoon lessons would be reserved for shade trees or sailboats or backyard gardens.

Just as Susie had knocked on the first door of the many that would lead, days later, to a fully staffed school and a groundswell of good feeling across the island, Thomas was making the long walk down the outside stairs of the awful Margaret Van Landing's house and across the street to Lizzy

Fraydel's driveway. She met him there with a ladder and a smile that eased his embarrassment.

"Hi, I'm Thomas. I saw you in the bucket line at the fire."

"I saw you, too. I'm Lizzy. My son Jack, Jr. and I were there together."

"That's my boy Luke up there laughing at me."

"You gave us both a pretty good show."

"I really thought I could make it," Thomas said, looking up at Luke, already unbolting panels from the roof.

"I guess you're here to get my neighbor's solar panels. Do you know how to make them work?"

"Yes... and sort of. We're trying to put together enough to run the main pump that pumps water up into the water tower by the school."

"Wait, really?" Lizzy asked. "There's a chance we might get running water again?"

"More than a chance. I think we're pretty close to making it happen. Well, my friends John Mitchell and TJ were making it happen. Just John, now. TJ passed on."

"I'm sorry," she said. "I know John from the water department. I didn't know TJ but I heard about what happened." There was a kindness in her voice that was comforting and believable.

"With so many people gone now, I know we've all lost someone."

"Doesn't make it any easier though," She said, putting her hand on his shoulder and then not knowing what to do with it next.

"Thanks," Thomas replied, putting his hand on hers and then removing it quickly. "Sorry. I don't know why I did that."

"It's fine," She said. "I'm not sure why I put my hand on your shoulder. I feel like I'm making this weird."

"You're making it a little weird."

"Oh," Lizzy replied, unable to find any other words to add.

"I'm good with weird, since you're letting me use your ladder and all."

"I just didn't want to watch some guy die on a Tuesday morning."

"Awful decent of you," Thomas said, and then they were laughing together.

"Guess you better get up there," Lizzy said.

Thomas joined Luke on the roof, and they worked while Lizzy picked small, tart pears from an undersized tree in her front yard. Luke's cart proved its worth, comfortably hauling five panels at a time. He made multiple trips back and forth to the water tower while his father stayed behind to work and steal glances at the lady across the street.

16

WATER, WATER EVERYWHERE

If Beulah Hancock were still alive, she would have no doubt found some way to take credit for the increased sunshine, and for John Mitchell and TJ's work on the water tower. Though her time on the Cedar Key Water and Sewer Board had been distinguished by a lack of meaningful action to protect or improve the town's water supply, she had nevertheless spent her days preening and strutting about the island as though she were Moses about to strike the rock and call forth clean water from the barren land. John Mitchell's humility about the whole enterprise was consistent with his character.

"This oughta do it," John said, as he attached the last row of solar panels to TJ's interface with the pump. "Who wants to do the honors?"

"It should be you," Hayes said, "And we should get the whole town together for a ceremony. I'll award you the Golden Clam citizenship award. This really is an accomplishment that needs to be recognized in a..."

"Nope," John interrupted, throwing the switch and indulging a self-satisfied grin as the pump motor roared to life and water began its journey to the top of the tower.

"Fair enough," Hayes said, laughing.

Thomas and Susie could not contain their joy, hugging and bouncing and woo-hooing like children.

The fact that the skies were clearing enough for solar panels to be a viable source of power generation—months and not years since the flash across the bay— was good fortune for the islanders. If the theory about the destruction of Crystal River's powerplant portending a global nuclear war was correct, the clear skies were also a rebuke of a popular scientist's famous predictions about the atmospheric effects that would accompany such a calamity.

By 1983, Carl Sagan was a household name in the United States and much of the wider world. Having co-written and hosted the PBS show *Cosmos*, which became the most successful science show in the history of television, and winning the Pulitzer Prize for his 1977 book *The Dragons of Eden*, Sagan had bridged the divide between science and popular culture. His academic credentials were unassailable, but he did not look or act like a traditional scientist. He wore turtlenecks and fashionable suits, grew his hair long, appeared on late night talk shows, and spoke with the dramatic affectation of a profligate storyteller.

Sagan's work in the 1970s included studying atmospheric conditions on Earth and other planets—dust storms on Mars and cloud formations on Venus. In 1980, the paleontologist Luis Alverez and his physicist father Walter Alverez presented research concluding that an asteroid had hit Earth during the Cretaceous Period, the impact of which deposited enough dust, smoke, and debris into the air to blanket the Earth's atmosphere, blocking out the Sun. It was these atmospheric conditions, they hypothesized, that had led to the extinction of land-based dinosaurs. Sagan and his colleagues applied the Alverez findings to their own study of climate change on Earth and how it would be exacerbated by a nuclear war. Using data collected from probes in space, Sagan and his team used early computer models to make a dire conclusion—even a small-scale nuclear war could lead to global temperatures dropping between 15º and 25º Celsius, plunging the world into a *nuclear winter.*

Sagan's findings were published in the December 1983 edition of the journal *Science,* where they would reach scientists in a wide range of fields and influence future research for the next three decades. In this paper, Sagan concluded:

When combined with the prompt destruction from nuclear blast, fires, and fallout, and the later enhancement of solar ultraviolet radiation due to ozone depletion, long-term exposure to cold, dark, and radioactivity could pose a serious threat to human survivors and to other species ... The possibility of the extinction of Homo sapiens cannot be excluded.

Two months before this publication made the dire conclusions that would bring controversy and attention to Sagan's work for the remainder of his life, however, he took unusual action for a scientist—appealing directly to non-scientists in the popular media. He wrote an article for *Parade* magazine that was delivered inside newspapers across the country to more than ten million people. The cover of this edition of the magazine featured an image of the globe shrouded in darkness and snow, along with Sagan's words from the story:

Would Nuclear war be the end of the world? In a major exchange, more than
a billion people would instantly be killed. But the long-term consequences
could be much worse...

Sagan's magazine article created an uproar in the scientific community and caused widespread fear in the popular and political culture of the day. Though a team of scientists had worked with him to reach the conclusions presented in the *Parade* and *Science* articles, the nuclear winter concept began to be associated almost exclusively with Sagan, who would spend the rest of his life defending conclusions drawn largely from—as Sagan himself would admit—computer models with significant limitations. Sagan stayed the course, resolved that protecting humanity from the devastating effects of nuclear holocaust demanded not just scientific rigor but also advocacy.

In subsequent years, the bulk of scientific inquiry began to suggest that Sagan's nuclear winter conclusions were at best greatly overstated and at worse verging on propaganda. A basic set of assumptions had underpinned Sagan's conclusions, the veracity of which would come to be widely disputed by the scientific community. These included the idea that a nuclear blast's mushroom cloud would suck soot and debris into the stratosphere where it would remain for years. In reality, most soot would likely remain in damaged buildings and on the ground, its mass too heavy to be carried into the stratosphere. Further, most nuclear blasts do not produce a mushroom cloud large enough to reach the stratosphere, and even when they do, soot and debris that reaches this height would likely only remain there for a period of weeks rather than the years speculated by Sagan. The concept of nuclear winter softened into what some began to call a *nuclear autumn*, a hypothesized period of significant atmospheric disruption but on a scale insufficient to produce an extinction event.

While his reputation endured some tarnishing for his miscalculations regarding the nuclear winter, Carl Sagan remained a tireless advocate for protecting what he called *the pale blue dot* of Earth, the only home in the cosmos humans had ever known. Even when this advocacy veered toward zealotry, on balance the world was made better by a life's work that blended science and humanism into a graceful partnership.

On December 20th, 1996, a rare bone marrow disease redirected the energy of Carl Sagan's life into the collective stream of atoms and electricity animating everything in the universe. For a scientist, he had been prone to frequent bouts of poetry in his writing and speeches, using it to bridge the gap between the quantifiable and that which was yet to be discovered. Bounding through the cosmos again, returned to the star-stuff of his origins, surely Dr. Sagan would have appreciated the poetry of a receding nuclear autumn, and a water tower powered by sunlight finding its way through the gray.

The new water system wasn't perfect. It relied on golf cart batteries to store the power generated by the sun. These were available in abundance on the island, not just from the individual carts that almost every resident owned, but in a fleet of them from the three rental companies that had catered to weekenders in the old world. With careful maintenance and storage, these batteries could be expected to last for maybe five years before they degraded too much to consistently hold a charge. In the new world,

though, five years away was as hard to conceive as five hundred, so immediate were the needs of the day.

On the positive side, the water tower had been designed to provide water
for more than seven hundred residents and hundreds more most weekends
and holidays. With less than three hundred people remaining on the island,
the pump did not have to run often to replenish the tower, so even with
sunlight limited by normal clouds and rain, or obscured by the remnants
of gray from the day the smokestacks fell, the water fairly reliably flowed
and no need for rationing was necessary. The town's sewer system was too
complex and required too much power to bring back online, but in short
order folks began digging homemade 55-gallon drum septic tanks or, more
often, piping their toilets directly into the holes beneath the outhouses that
had served them the past several months. Showers, tap water, and flushing
toilets felt like the dawn of the Age of Enlightenment, breaking after a
thousand years of primitive night.

In the old world, Cedar Key celebrated holidays with a collective enthusiasm. They reveled in the unapologetic patriotism common in most
small southern towns, going all out for the 4th of July with a golf cart
parade and pro-America assembly in the park. Running water had lifted
the spirits of the town to such an extent that Hayes, Susie, and the other
council members thought a big to-do for the 4th would bring the community together. They got to work planning a buffet of mullet and shrimp,
arranging musicians to play in the park, and putting the word out for a
flag-waving parade through the historic district, along the shoreline on G
and 1st Streets, and up 2nd Street to the park.

Thomas began writing a keynote speech for the mayor, tying the island's fight for survival—in sweeping, elevated prose—to the heroism of
the founding generation's war against the vastly superior British empire.
As much to proselytize himself as others about the necessity and even

virtue of the violence he had helped to dispense, Thomas cast The Second Battle of Cedar Key and the killing on Shiloh Road alongside Saratoga and Yorktown. The water tower was the Liberty Bell and the islanders on Tony Hankle's barge were Washington and his soldiers crossing the Delaware on Christmas in 1776.

Fire Chief Roberts got the town's flags out of storage. In normal times, he would use the station's bucket truck to mount flags and patriotic buntings on the tops of the power poles and building facades throughout town. Fuel was too precious now for such a use, but with the help of volunteer firefighters, citizen deputies, and Officer Biscuit, an extendable aluminum ladder was carried to each pole and the flags were painstakingly installed.

The night of July 3rd, gilded with building excitement for the following day's events and spurred on by clean, good-smelling citizens emerging from long-overdue showers and baths, produced a wave of sexual energy that spread through the town like a white-hot rumor. If the evening's friction and kinetic energy from the widespread fornicating could have been harnessed, the island would have electricity for a hundred years. Chief Roberts was summoned to three separate homes that evening, twice being interrupted during spirited, athletic sex with his wife Lauren, to listen to 80 year old hearts palpitating from little blue pills that had sat undisturbed in bottles for five long months.

Jack Fraydell, Jr. sent his mother Lizzy out of the house so that the beautiful, Rapunzel-haired Solaro girl could join him in a bath heated by water he had brought to a boil on a charcoal grill. By midnight, they would say *I love you* to one another for the first time, and by morning, though they would not know it until her sickness arrived many mornings later, Jack, Jr. and Sierra would be expecting—the first new world baby in Cedar Key.

Lizzy rode her bicycle around the island, imagining that she had passed by Thomas' house by chance, disavowing herself of that imagination on her second pass, then finally stopping on her third. Thomas came out onto the porch as she walked up.

"I was wondering how many times you would ride by before stopping."

"Oh god, you could see that?"

"There's not much to do at night but look out the window," he said, smiling.

"I bet that smirk gets you out of so much trouble," she said.

"Half as much as it gets me into."

"Uh huh."

"Can I help you with something," Thomas asked, leaning into the smirk.

"You could help yourself by inviting me onto that porch swing for a bit."

"Welcome, I'm glad you dropped by."

"I'm pretty sure my son's having sex in my whirlpool tub so I needed to get out of the house."

"Oh wow," Thomas replied.

"The whirlpool part doesn't work without electricity but he heated the water in pots on the damn barbeque grill."

"Yeah that sounds serious. I apologize but I didn't know you were coming so I didn't have a bath drawn."

"Alright, alright, how bout you just come sit by me on the swing."

They sat there together into the small hours of the morning, swinging and talking about their lives, their kids, and the people they had lost. A squall line moved across the island and its sideways rain pushed them indoors. When it became clear the rain was set in, Thomas showed her to the guest bedroom, braved to kiss her lightly on the forehead, and said goodnight.

From then on, with no real discussion about it, they were seldom apart. No waterfalls, no golden owls glistening in the sun, none of the extravagant gestures that passed for romance in the old world but rang hollow in the new. The practicality and need underpinning their connection did not diminish a love that would grow slowly over time, in the sandy soil and salt air of life on an island at the end of the world.

Independence Day broke bright and clear on Cedar Key, the clearest skies since the day the smokestacks fell. The community center parking lot, the designated starting point of the parade, was full of people, flags, and joy more than an hour before the 10 AM starting time. Mark David had been stoking a fire in the city park since just after dawn, readying the coals to cook an enormous bounty of mullet he had netted the day before. Jud Bollins and his crew were rowing their boat back to shore, their traps overflowing with blue crabs. Luke Buck pulled a kayak full of clams and white shrimp onto the sandy shore of the park. Chief Edwins and Deputy Biscuit wore their dress uniforms, as did Fire Chief Roberts and his volunteers.

A bullhorn blast rang out into the morning, and Mayor Hayes and the other council members led the parade on its way. The tide was high and the bay was glassy calm. The mating pair of ospreys that lived in the pine tree next to the Seahorse Corral condos swooped and shrieked as they flew above the assembled islanders. In the channel between the main island and Atsena Otie, dolphins drove schools of fish toward one another, working together to increase their catch. It was a Chamber of Commerce day if ever there was such a thing, despite there being no Chamber or meaningful commerce left on the island.

"Peak Cedar Key," Thomas said, taking it all in.

"I've lived here my whole life," Lizzy said. "And I'm not sure it's ever been so perfect."

Such was the flood of dopamine overwhelming everyone when the parade made its way to the park and the islanders began to fill their plates and bellies with riches from the Gulf. As they sat at picnic tables and on the ground to eat, Luke Buck walked to the steps of the gazebo with the Gibson Hummingbird guitar his grandfather had given him the year he died.

> *O beautiful, for spacious skies*
> *For amber waves of grain*

Luke's powerful voice, out of place in his wiry frame, filled the park with the first two lines of the familiar American refrain. A wall of sound came back toward him as his friends and neighbors joined in:

> *For purple mountain's majesty*
> *Above the fruited plain*
> *America! America!*
> *God shed his grace on thee*
> *And crown thy good with brotherhood*
> *From sea to shining sea*

If the song had ended there, on the mountaintop of blended voices, the entire history of the island might have been different. Luke sang on, though, a verse unknown to most, but in the communion of the heightened moment, one that landed with a thunderclap.

> *O beautiful for patriot dream*
> *That sees beyond the years*
> *Thine alabaster cities gleam*

Undimmed by human tears
America! America!
God shed His grace on thee,
And crown thy good with brotherhood
From sea to shining sea

In another time, perhaps, the sentiment of the old song might have washed over the actual words. Here, though, the solemnity of the moment pushed each syllable hard into the rostrolateral prefrontal cortex of every brain pointed toward Luke Buck and his guitar.

O beautiful for patriot dream. On the wall of the hardware store were photos of every islander who had served the country in uniform. It would be hard to imagine a more patriotic place than Cedar Key.

That sees beyond the years. In the opulence and stability of the old world, the patriot's dream of American exceptionalism extended millennia into the future. Half a year into the new world, no news of America had come from across the channel or anywhere else.

Thine alabasters cities gleam. The mood of the day shifted hard on these eight syllables, as one islander after another was forced to consider a thought most had tried to avoid—there might be no cities left at all. Part of the American mythos rested on the idea of it being an example to the world of ideology-driven abundance. Evoking Christ's Sermon on the Mount, the puritan preacher John Winthrop had preached such a vision of America, saying, "As a city on a hill, the eyes of the world are upon us." Certainly, the adults assembled in the park could recall John F. Kennedy or, more recently, Ronald Regan proclaiming the grandeur of America as *a shining city on the hill.* To even imagine such grandeur now felt impossible, perverse.

Undimmed by human tears. This line was the undoing of the whole affair. So many of the bright lights in the lives of the surviving islanders had dimmed to nothing. Digging a grave or two with a shovel leaves an impression on a person. Digging dozens, week after week, darkens a heart.

America! America! God Shed his grace on thee. These lines were a proclamation of God's favor when they were written but now, echoing the fiery consternation of Folksy in the Christ Church pulpit, they were a rebuke—an admonition from a forsaken people to a negligent God. Where was grace in any of this? Where was God to be found at all?

Luke, too, was changed forever as he sang the final, familiar lines in a mournful lilt, his voice breaking at the preposterous notion that the good had been crowned with anything but sorrow.

When the song was finished, Hayes ascended the steps of the gazebo, unfolded the pages of Thomas' speech, contemplated them for a moment, then folded them back.

"Thank you Luke. And thank you to everyone that helped put this day together, who caught and cooked the food, who knocked on doors to get the word out. It's important that all of us get together like this as often as possible. Not just so we can talk about the plans and projects we have going on, but so we can be reminded of who we are. Of what it means to live on this island. To be a part of this community. To be each other's neighbors and friends. Because it's the 4th of July, I came here with a speech about the history of America. About what it meant to be an American. Trust me when I tell you that Thomas wrote me a barn burner and none of you would have believed for a minute that I had anything to do with it."

Subdued laughter rolled through the crowd, a comforting levity.

"But listening to the words of that last verse that Luke sang so beautifully, I'm left wondering what this day means now, in light of everything we've been through. I prayed hard when the Colonel took off in Bob Corliss' old Piper. Not just for my friend's safety, but because I knew how badly we needed to know what happened out there. Was there still a *there* out there? On the day of the flash, Thomas made it to Gainesville to get his boy, but came back with more questions than answers. For many months now, the silence on the radio, in the skies, and from across the channel makes it hard to believe in much beyond this island. I'm an American. All of us are Americans. I don't know how to even conceive of being anything else. But I'll just level with you; I'm losing faith in big ideas. I'm not sure where I'm going with any of this or what I even mean, except this: whatever comes, we'll face it together, like we've done all this time. Whatever our future holds, our past is still rooted in a revolutionary generation that planted a flag against the tyranny of faraway masters. Those are the people we come from. That's who we are. Even if America is no longer a thing, we are still those people, and I still believe in you."

Hayes stepped down from the steps and returned to his mullet and blue crabs with little fanfare. There were no more songs or speeches. There was nothing left to say.

17

CHICKENS IN A COAL MINE

On the 25th of July, after less than a full month of planning, Jenna Mitchell pulled a knotted rope hanging from a large brass ship's bell mounted next to the front door of the Cedar Key School. The assembled crowd, rivaling the one that had lined the runway for the Colonel's fateful takeoff, erupted in cheers. Forty-five students entered the school to meet their nervous new teachers and resume their formal education. It would take some time to settle into the new curriculum and the new routines, but before long a kind of daily rhythm took hold and the school resumed its place at the center of island life.

The school's new bell had belonged to Linda Richland's late husband Nick. In the last years of his life, Nick Richland had been assembling something akin to a Louisiana-style shrimp boat in the canal adjacent to 3rd Street, two parcels down from Hayes David's clam dock. The boat was an eclectic hodgepodge of parts scavenged from a variety of boat styles. The net effect was a boat that looked old but not historic, useful for something but also nothing in particular. Hayes and Thomas had loved looking at the weird old vessel, and when it was finally trailered and hauled away, they felt a twinge of unexpected sadness, not just at the empty space along the nearby dock, but for the last of Nick, an old-time Cedar Keyer, gone for good as well.

Linda had salvaged the ship's bell before selling the boat, and donated it to the school for its reopening. From her apartment above Fannie's Café, she could hear the five long rings that would signify the start of each new school day. She would stop for several moments each time the bell rang, close her eyes and let the memories in.

July faded away. Five more islanders left for the next life, none for any discernable reason. There had been a compulsion in the old world to classify and categorize every death, a tidy label helping to box in the grief. A thing that could be named could be processed, rationalized. In the new world, when people slipped away so often without warning or provocation, armchair thanatology caused more harm than good.

August was less august than normal. Even in the midafternoons, its heat was a paper-tiger, lacking the teeth of Augusts past. The gray was absent now more days than not, and Thomas began driving his golf cart everywhere, the batteries of which were charged with solar panels mounted on the steep roof of his house. Ryland Beecham turned his mother's peninsula into a kind of hunting lodge from which he and other islanders—most often Luke Buck—could access the Cedar Key Scrub State Preserve, a 5,000-acre tract of scrub pines and palmettos. The hogs, whitetail deer, turkeys, squirrels, and armadillos they harvested from these woods could be traded on the island for just about anything. Carrie Sue Erman and her husband Roy had run a clam bag manufacturing operation in the old world. In the new, they commandeered the 19th century iron salt kettle from the state museum across the street from their home and began using it to boil water from the Gulf to make salt. It was difficult work that yielded a valuable commodity. All across the island, needs developed and were met by a web of interconnected dependency that would make Adam Smith proud. A cynic would call it the free market; a sentimentalist would call it community.

Denny Gall was dry-witted and sneaky funny. Operating a single restaurant is enough to run anyone ragged; in the old world, Denny was the proprietor of two, seldom seeming frazzled at the helm of his successful breakfast café on 2nd Street or the wildly popular Steaming Clam on Dock Street. His workdays often began before sunrise and extended into the late evenings, and he somehow still found time to serve on the board of the Chamber of Commerce and personally spearhead the fundraising and planning for the island's renowned fireworks shows on the 4th of July and New Years Eve. He parlayed his restaurateur success into a marriage with a wife that was half-again too pretty for him. Her allure was enhanced by chronic migraine headaches that required her to wear dark sunglasses often, even into the nighttime. The net effect was that Denny would seem to have a Hollywood starlet on his arm during picnics at the park, PTA meetings, or shopping at the market.

"Why are the chickens acting so weird," Denny asked.

"They are a little off, aren't they," Rolf replied.

Denny and Rolf had drawn chicken guard duty in the cemetery together again. They enjoyed each other's company and both were happy to serve, if a little bored at the slowness of the day. No birds had made a break for it. The ospreys and hawks had so far not braved an aerial assault. The fence was holding.

"They seem spooked."

"I had a cook at the café like that. He was a damn fine cook but he always looked like he thought he was being followed. Not like meth-jumpy but still jumpy."

"I remember that guy," Rolf said. "What happened to him?"

"Come to think of it, maybe it was meth. He died."

"Jesus," Rolf said.

"Well, I don't think our chickens are cranked up but something definitely has them on edge."

The chicken program had been an unmitigated success for the island. Eggs were produced in reliable abundance, and the handful of roosters in the flock meant that a selection of fertilized eggs could be left for mama hens to sit on. Already there were three new generations of chicks, the first of which were only six weeks or so away from egg-laying age. Whenever a chicken seemed to be declining, they were culled from the flock immediately. Its body was raffled off in a chicken lottery on the front steps of City Hall. Michael Johnson, son of Lida Maria and grandson to Mark and Bette David, had worked with his younger sister Hallie to build a clam shell chicken lottery machine. Every islander's name was written on a clam shell and put into a tumbler made from chicken wire and scrap wood. The name on the randomly selected clam shell won the bird. Chicken lottery became the must-see TV of the age and always drew a large crowd. With new chicks arriving regularly, there would eventually be a good supply of male meat birds that could be distributed to households on an orderly schedule, but the drama and excitement of the lottery would make it a perpetual entertainment event.

Denny looked across the expanse of nervous chickens and felt contemplative. "When I had the restaurants, I used to buy and serve a hundred dozen eggs a week, and if you cobbled together the 300 chicken breasts and 600 wings we sold at the Steaming Clam every week, that had to of added up to a few hundred whole chickens."

"Dude, what?" Rolf asked. "It would just be 150 chickens with way too many wings each."

"Huh?"

"You could theoretically have additional wings on a chicken, but I don't think you can have a chicken without two breasts... so it seems like we're dealing with 150 freakshow chickens."

"Oh, I see what you're doing. You're missing the point, Rolf, obviously."

"I ate a bunch of wings at that place over the years. If I'd known they came from Chernobyl, I probably would have had the grouper."

Ignoring Rolf's joke, Denny mused on, "The point is that in all those years, selling all those eggs and chickens, I almost never ate any. I preferred steak and potatoes. Seafood. Now, every time I come down here for guard duty, I'm looking at every bird close, trying to see if there's one lagging behind or looking a little sad so we can cull it for the lottery. I'd trade my Carolina Skiff for one of these skinny ass chickens."

"At least we get eggs on the regular," said Rolf.

"Yeah, I guess that's something. But I'm gonna win that lottery one day and when I do I might eat the feathers and the beak and toenails and everything."

"Whoa," Rolf said, before steering the conversation quickly away from poultry.

The birds continued their anxious frittering here and there, and the two friends finished out their shift without incident.

Eight days prior, seven thousand miles to the east, a tropical wave began its first moments of life just off the western coast of Africa. No Jim Cantore Weather Channel theatrics or cable news hype, just a random sequence of oceanographic and atmospheric events that coalesced into a building energy machine. Convection, circulation, forward progress—the wave began an improbable, tumultuous march across the Atlantic Ocean.

It was a cloudless Tuesday afternoon in Cedar Key, bright and alive, but the chickens knew something the islanders did not.

Hayes and Thomas were checking crab traps along the canal when they saw it, the mystic sorcery of a prior age, coming from Johan Hellden's house. They could have dismissed the information streaming into their eyes were it not for the accompanying sounds— the almost imperceptible electric buzz and the comforting white noise hum of an air conditioner.

"How?" Thomas asked. "That's Mr. Johan's house, right?"

"Yeah," Hayes replied.

"I don't think I've met him."

"He keeps to himself. We bought fish from him before the net ban. My dad has some connection to him through our family in Denmark but I don't know the details. Nice guy."

"I'm gonna knock on his door," Thomas said.

"Absolutely."

Johan answered the door, saw the excited look on their faces, and invited them in. They crossed the threshold of the old man's house, looking wide-eyed as though they were seeing Times Square for the first time.

"Mr. Johan," Hayes said with a smile, "You've got some explaining to do."

"Come in, have a seat."

Thomas introduced himself then asked directly, "What's going on here?"

"I never got used to the heat," Johan said, sheepishly. "I thought I'd settle into it eventually but I just never did. Except for a few weeks in January and February, I always felt like Florida was trying to burn me alive. Sit, please."

Hayes and Thomas sat in sturdy wooden chairs at Johan's kitchen table, taking in the almost unbearable luxury of the cold air flowing into the room. In 1902, John Carrier's invention had revolutionized the world and helped the South to finally shake the yoke of Reconstruction; today, its operation was indistinguishable from sorcery.

Johan said, "It took me twenty years to develop a taste for it, but your sweet tea finally wore me down. Let me make you a glass."

Hayes' eyes lit up. Thomas' heart raced.

"No way," Hayes said.

Johan emerged from the kitchen with two glasses filled with tea and dazzling, ethereal ice cubes. Hayes and Thomas buried their faces in their glasses, unable to speak. The ice was a time machine to a world that was gone forever. And yet, there it was, as real as the wry smile on the nonagenarian's face and the chill air from the mini-split unit mounted high on the living room wall. Shortly, Johan would fill them in on the details of how it was all happening, but for now, the three men drank and laughed and took it all in.

Johan Hellden lived the first thirty years of his life in the coastal village of Farhult, Sweden and the next sixty-five on Cedar key, in a five-room cracker house on a canal running parallel to Whidden Avenue. When the net ban displaced him from the only career he had ever known, Johan retreated from life on the water and settled into retirement. A spartan Nordic lifestyle and miserly spending habits had been imprinted on him in his youth. He was sixty-four when the net ban took effect in 1995. When the smokestacks fell thirty years later, he was still living comfortably on his savings and wanted for little.

When Johan first moved to the island, he had come to escape a place where everything reminded him of Linnéa. He first met the girl that would become his wife when her father caught an eight year old Johan picking apples from the tree in her backyard. He had grabbed the boy up by his collar and drug him across the yard, kicking and panicked. Without hesitation, as though it had been the purpose of her existence, Linnéa leapt onto her father's back shouting, "No Papa, no." Surprised by her boldness, he lost his grip on the boy. Johan sprinted across the yard, down the cobblestone road, and into the cover of the tall grasses along the shore of the Bay of Skälderviken.

For the next twenty years, there were few days when Johan and Linnéa did not meet along that shore. After they were married in the summer of their eighteenth birthdays, Linnéa would walk with her husband before dawn to see him off on the herring trawler where he made their living, and would walk back to the shore to meet him on his return. Their life was simple and unburdened from the cares of the wider world. They had little by way of material possessions and were abundantly rich.

In the summer of 1958, to celebrate their tenth wedding anniversary, Johan and Linnéa drove four kilometers to the neighboring village of Jonstorp for a meal at Tunneberga Gästgifvargård, a new restaurant that had become the talk of the area for its extravagant herring buffet. The couple seldom ate out, preferring the familiar comforts of their home. Across the bay in Denmark, the Danes had a word for such comforts, for the safety and cozy feeling of wellness associated with home. They called it *hygge.* Unlike many Swedes, Johan did not possess the deep-seated mistrust of Danes that had overshadowed relations between the two countries for hundreds of years. On the contrary, he found them cheerful, industrious, and friendly. Another interpretation of hygge, as it relates to people, is the concept of *pleasant everyday togetherness.* Johan liked this description best, and had taken to calling his bride Little Hygge from the earliest days of their marriage.

After eating their fill from a selection of twenty-five different preparations of herring, along with dense sourdough bread and a full bottle of wine between them, Johan and Linnéa walked, as they so often did, along the shore of the bay leading to the North Sea. In the perfect serenity of a moon that shone as bright as day, Linnéa stepped awkwardly across a piece of driftwood. She reached for Johan's hand for stability, missing it by millimeters, then tumbled forward onto the beach. A million replays of the fall would have ended with Linnéa sandy and embarrassed, laughing with her husband. This time, time halted at the pointed edge of an unassuming rock—no bigger than the apples Johan had pilfered from her yard those many years ago—peeking through the sand. The meaning and purpose of Johan's life halted, too, as his Hygge lay still as dawn, a crimson halo forming around her auburn hair as it danced in the edge of the silver water where it met the shore.

For two years, Johan continued to fish the waters of the bay, stopping by Linnéa's grave before dawn each morning as he walked to the boat. The grief seemed to only grow over time. In the few months before his thirtieth birthday, he signed on to a boat crew in Gothenburg, two hours north of Farhult, hoping the change of scenery might help lift the weight of her from his chest. Without his morning conversations in the cemetery, Johan could barely function on the trawler, his mind wandering to their walks by the bay, to their final walk and how close his hand had been to hers as she fell. The silver water. The perfect killing machine of the little rock. The still serenity of her instant repose. She was everywhere at once now, in the North Sea fog and the frigid winds that blew even into summer, in the air and the sand and the water.

He had to leave Sweden for good.

It's true that chickens can fly but they aren't good at it. Roosters are even worse aviators. Their body mass to wing size ratio is all wrong for sustained flight. A rooster's typical version of flying involves them running around and flapping their wings to pick up a little speed. In southeast Asia, the Red Junglefowl rooster is something approaching a competent flier, but the handful of roosters knocking boots with the hens in Cedar Key seldom left the ground for more than a peacocking hop to scare off rivals or impress the ladies.

While Hayes and Thomas crunched ice with the old fisherman, the falling barometric pressure in the Gulf began to agitate the dominant rooster in the cemetery. As his distress grew, he ran in wild zigzags through the flock, flapping and crowing and leaping into the air. His theatrics whipped the rest of the birds into a frenzy of inharmonious chicken bitching. Geoff McCloud shrugged at fellow guardsman Lida Maria Johnson as the alpha cock sprang, wings flapping, onto the top of a fence post, to a low-hanging cedar limb, then up to higher branch after higher branch until, seventy feet up the tree, crazed with berserker abandon, he flung himself into the pale blue sky, aerodynamic as a piano, floating for an impossible moment until the surly bonds of Earth pulled him hard into the ground.

The next biggest rooster screwed a dozen hens in the following twenty minutes, staking a claim as the new leader, before he, too, was overwhelmed with the madness of the approaching storm.

18

— • —

ROWBOAT

Johan's beloved Linnéa was named after a prominent Swedish scientist. Carl Linnaeus was born in the countryside of southern Sweden in 1707. After studying at Uppsala University, he began a life of scientific exploration that would lead to him being regarded as the father of modern taxonomy and one of the founders of modern ecology. He was also a physician and zoologist, and developed a formal system of binomial nomenclature, the modern system of naming organisms. His contributions to the scientific community led to his ennoblement in 1761. In multiple fields of study, the abbreviation *L.* is used to denote that Linnaeus was the authority for a species' name. When he died, the *International Code of Zoological Nomenclature* used his body's remains as the type specimen for Homo sapiens. In Swedish lore, there could hardly be a more esteemed historical figure.

Johan often thought of the great man, and how his bride's inquisitive nature and love for the natural world was befitting her name. Mostly, he marveled at her intellect—a league apart from his own—and had spent much of his younger years trying to learn as much as he could about everything he could so that she might one day find him, if not an equal, at least worth her time.

In the years between the Great War and the Second World War, Sweden had focused on developing an alternative fuel system, fearing that petrol would be limited in future conflicts or crises. The result was the development and refinement of the gasifier or wood gas generator. An international economic crisis in the early 1930s led to a decline in demand for the exportation of Swedish timber products. The government's push for wood gas powered vehicles and electricity generation helped to prop up the nation's timber industry. Germany invaded Poland in September of 1939 when Johan was nine years old. Though Sweden would remain technically neutral throughout the war, hostilities limited the availability of petrol to the extent that the nation had to increasingly rely on wood gas generation.

Johan had helped Linnéa and her father build a wood gas generator for their home, and remained fascinated by the process into his teenage years. The war ended a few months after his fifteenth birthday, and the increase in petrol availability led to the rapid decline in wood gas consumption. As quickly as the technology had exploded across Sweden and much of Europe, it faded from widespread use. Johan, though, would continue to associate gasifiers with the formative time in his life when he was young and facing adversity together with people he loved.

"It's just blind luck you walked by when you did," Johan said. "I only finished building the gasifier earlier today. If you'd come any earlier the ice wouldn't have been frozen yet."

Hayes and Thomas finished every drop of their tea and had eaten every cube of ice when Johan started slowly toward the door.

"Come with me, gentlemen."

Johan walked them to the back yard near the bank of the canal where a primitive, almost steam-punk looking contraption hummed and shook as it powered an eleven thousand kilowatt generator, the kind popular in hurricane-prone areas.

"Is that a trash can?" Thomas asked.

"It is," the old man replied. "This design is a little different than the ones we used to make during the war."

Johan explained the rise and fall of the technology in his home country, and how he had never stopped thinking about gasifiers. The technology was fairly straightforward—wood is burned in a firebox in a low-oxygen environment that prevents combustion, resulting in gases that are then burned at high temperatures in a separate container to produce a substance that can power internal combustion engines.

He told them about Linnéa and Linnaeus, the herring bar at the restaurant and the rock that had changed the trajectory of his life. For a normally breviloquent man, he found himself talking and talking, the memories, the solitude, and the difficulties of the new world loosening his tongue. He explained that he could hardly take credit for the machine before them as it was almost exactly the design of the Federal Emergency Management Administration. In March of 1989, fearing a global energy crisis, FEMA published a paper titled *Construction of a Simplified Wood Gas Generator to Power Internal Combustion Engines in a Petroleum Emergency.* Johan's gasifier looked nearly identical to the one pictured mounted on the front of a tractor in the government's sixty-six page paper.

"Why have I never even heard of this?" Hayes asked.

"Because you never had to," Johan replied. "Europeans have always lived a little closer to the edge than Americans. You've had a fair amount of war in your couple hundred years but we've been at it for another thousand. I always knew I would need to make this thing again one day. I knew it. I'm too old to do the work to keep it running all the time, but I had to know if I could still make one."

The machine had its limitations. It was painstaking to keep operating and produced toxic fumes and deposit buildups that had to be routinely cleaned. But it worked. And it could be replicated with all manner of components.

Thomas said, "Thank you for sharing this with us, Mr. Johan."

"I'm going to get the boys at the city to start work on one right away," Hayes added. "Think you could come help them out?"

"Yes sir, Mr. Mayor. I believe I could."

Hayes and Thomas thanked their host again for the tea, ice, and air conditioning, then started to leave.

Johan called after them, "By the pricking of my thumbs..."

"What's that?" asked Hayes.

Thomas called back to the old man, excitedly, "Something wicked this way comes!"

Johan could tell that Hayes was feeling left out. "One of the witches in Macbeth had a premonition about the would-be king being evil. She could feel it tingling in her thumbs."

"Are you having that premonition about me?" asked Hayes.

Johan chuckled. "Nothing so dire, your excellency. My joints ache when the pressure in the air drops ahead of a storm. They've been on fire all day. Maybe I'm just getting old, or maybe something big is out there. Keep an eye out's all."

Thomas could not help but belabor Johan's analogy, and the old man was happy to indulge a parting couplet from the witches. Thomas asked, *"When shall we three meet again, in thunder, lightning, or in rain?"*

The reply came, *"Fair is foul and foul is fair, hover through the fog and filthy air."*

On their walk back, Hayes and Thomas took the route down G Street along the shore and caught a glimpse of what had been troubling their Swedish friend. In summer, afternoon Florida skies feature dark clouds more often than not. *The Sunshine State* was a clever bit of tourism marketing but every Floridian knew to expect walloping thunderstorms as a part of daily life.

"Whoa," Hayes said.

"There's something in that," Thomas replied. The saying was an inside joke to everyone that had known his father. Northeast Arkansas, where Thomas spent summers with his dad as child, was located in the tenderloin of tornado alley. The elder Buck watched the sky with consternation throughout tornado season, announcing at every small gathering of even light gray clouds, "There's something in that." In a dozen years of summers, the only *something* Thomas ever witnessed was rain and occasional lightning, but his father's preoccupation with weather had imprinted on him such that he himself became a conspiratorial sky watcher.

There at the water's edge with his friend, Thomas witnessed something at last. Out on the reef past Seahorse Key appeared a thick wall of black clouds, piling one upon the other, angry, churning toward the channel leading to the island.

Hayes and Thomas stood, entranced, at the curve in the road across from the Beachfront Motel, at the top of the steps that led into the water and the starting point of the Shark Swim where Georgie Pilsner had found glory in defeat and Tim Mueller had defeated himself. The storm pulled at the light around its leading edge, folding bright life into the darkness. Neither man had ever seen a thing so immense, so menacing. When they could bear it no longer, they turned and ran for town, yelling to everyone they passed to get to the gym at the school. As they raced east along 2nd Street toward the fire house and city hall, Jonah McShane walked calmly west along 1st, pushing the hand trailer holding the ornate wooden rowboat he had purchased from Jeff and Lora Sleedy before the smokestacks fell.

Jonah McShane was weird. By any objective measure, he was an outlier in the social circles of the island. In Portland or the East Village, maybe, he would have been a standard deviation closer to the mean, but in Cedar Key, the faraway look in his eyes, militaristic urgency of his gait, and nervous cadence in his voice kept him isolated from his neighbors. Throughout his life, Thomas had kept a menagerie of misfits and ne'er-do-wells as friends and as such gravitated toward Jonah in his earliest days on the island.

They had met often over breakfast at Fannie's Café, and Jonah's teller job at the bank meant there was occasion for the frequent micro-interactions of small town life that so delighted Thomas. Even Thomas, though, had failed to penetrate Jonah's inner shell, in which he carefully guarded the anxiety and rage that if let out would hurt himself and others. Underlying Jonah's struggle was a common affliction in the malaise of modern living; he lacked a meaningful purpose for his life. A world without war is preferable in most ways to one in conflict, but something wild in the hearts of men is lost to aimless peace. The idle leisure of Pax Romana slowly chewed apart the great empire, just as America had declined, in fits and starts, throughout the relative peace of the nuclear age. The west was long won, the oceans conquered, and the atom split— adventure and valor were possible no longer in jobs at the bank and comfortable breakfasts at a regular table. Jonah was rotting from the inside out, his ears perked to the song of the wild without ever having heard it, almost certain not to recognize it were it ever to come.

The rowboat purchase had been an attempt to break up the monotony of his life. At the time, folks thought the two thousand dollars Jonah paid for the boat was at least a thousand too much. It's true the lacquered wood boat was beautifully built, and its trailer allowed it to be pushed around by hand for easy launching, but that amount of money for a boat without a motor just seemed out of place for Cedar Key. Now, when a motor was a liability—something heavy to be removed before oars or sails could be retrofitted—Jonah's acquisition seemed prescient and wise. The wisdom of the deal, however, did not diminish the sad circumstances surrounding it.

For months, Jonah looked forward to Fridays when Gina Birmingham came into the bank to make the weekly deposit from her gift shop on 2nd Street. The deposits, and her shop, were modest, but she seemed to be scratching out a living selling the jewelry she made by hand, paintings from her artist friends on the island, and other bric-a-brac that served no real purpose but occasionally caught the eye of tourists. She was slightly built, pretty but not exceedingly so, and had a warm, welcoming spirit.

"Beautiful weather today," Jonah said, smiling, as Gina placed the zippered rectangular cash bag on the counter in front of him.

"I know," Gina replied. "I've been stuck inside all week, watching boat after boat pass by on the way to the ramp. I can't remember the last time I was on the water. What's the point of living on an island if you never get to be on the water?"

Jonah said, "You should get a boat."

"I wish," she demurred. "What I need is to find a man with a boat to take me."

As he lay in bed later that evening, Jonah replayed the encounter time and again, wondering if Gina had been flirting with him, imagining a half dozen things he should have said to her—*well maybe I'll get a boat then... a pretty girl like you should have no trouble with that... I'll take you boating, Gina.* Anything would have been better than the five seconds of awkward silence before he pushed the piece of paper and the zippered bag across the counter at the teller window, whimpering, "Here's your deposit receipt."

"Thanks, Jonah," she said. "See you next Friday."

That Jonah first spotted the Sleedy's rowboat on his walk home from work that very Friday, he would later decide, was a kind of cosmic joke. He was careful with his money, living frugally in the downstairs studio apartment of a clam farmer's house on State Road 24. He seldom indulged frivolities aside from the three beers he drank every Saturday with Geoff McCloud at the end of the bar at the Steaming Clam. He had two thousand dollars. It's true he had no experience whatsoever on the water, but it's also true he had always wanted to learn about it, reasoning, reasonably, that island life lived only on land was something of a waste. When the bank opened Saturday morning, he withdrew the cash and paid full price for the boat, pushing it home and launching it immediately in the back bayou. In the creeks and channels away from the bay, he would learn basic seamanship out of sight of more experienced sailors.

For three weeks, most days after work and every weekend day, Jonah rowed the boat, venturing further out into the backwaters as his confidence grew. From the Cedar Key Marina, he purchased two lifejackets, a hand-held marine radio, signal flares, and nautical charts of the Waccasassa Bay. On the third Sunday after his purchase, Jonah pushed the rowboat across town and launched it at the main boat ramp. Though he was surrounded by larger vessels, he rowed past the boat slips and under the Dock Street bridge where Thomas and Rolf had departed on their first birddog ride together. As he cleared the no-wake zone and entered the open water of the bay, as if on cue in a scene from a poorly written melodrama, Cristopher Tapping's forty foot yacht, The Reel Deal, whipped around the front of the fishing pier, its twin 300-hp outboards roaring, narrowly missing the rowboat. Jonah saw only Gina Birmingham, bikinied and laughing, and Cristopher's hand on the small of her back, before the wake from The Real Deal rolled the rowboat over as gently as a sleeping baby.

To his credit, Jonah did not panic under the turbulent water, calmly freeing himself from the underside of the rowboat and popping to the surface in his bright yellow life jacket. With considerable effort, he was able to get his capsized craft to the shore and loaded onto the hand trailer. He pushed the little boat back across town and parked it under the side carport of the clam farmer's house.

There it sat for the next two years.

The storm opened its bosom and pulled in Seahorse Key. Hayes and Thomas no longer needed to sound the alarm; the western horizon was a wall of black and visible to everyone in town. A frenzy of movement spread house to house. A few residents began boarding up windows but most retreated toward the school. Three miles of clear blue and calm now ranged between the islanders and the billowing leviathan. At the pace the storm had been moving for the previous few days, this distance should have been covered in around twelve minutes. A half hour passed. Then another. The storm was halted over the barrier key, ripping it branch from branch.

The light station that had once steered sailors away from the dangers of Seahorse Reef was blown into the Gulf as easily as a dandelion puffball scattered by a child's breath. Trees bent and broke almost instantly. The white sand on the windward beach exploded into nothing and huge chunks of land sloughed off into the water. In an hour of the storm's stationary rotation, a third of the key's land mass had simply vanished.

Two hours passed.

In the gym, the lack of movement and the chilling calm pushed the moment to its crisis.

"I can't just sit here," Rolf said. "I need to do something."

"Like what?" Thomas asked.

"I don't know man... let's go look at it at least."

Thomas said, "I'm in," then headed for the door.

Hayes looked about slyly, making sure he wasn't being watched, then slipped out the door and after his friends. Slinking behind him came Lizzy Fraydel, checking on her man.

"Hey wait up," she said.

"Honey, go back inside. It's not safe out here," replied Thomas.

"You're not my mom," Lizzy replied.

The four friends laughed at themselves, sneaking away from safety to go look at a storm. The laughing stopped abruptly a few blocks later when they reached the shoreline on G Street.

Whenever a hurricane is anywhere in the Gulf, even hundreds of miles away, the low tides around Cedar Key become apocalyptically low. The sand spit in front of the Beachfront Motel expands to create a strip of dry land most of the way between Way and Seahorse Keys. For the past several hours, a desert of smooth sand and muddy bottom had stretched all the way across the bay, with only the main channel still holding water. When the tides move out in such spectacular fashion, they usually return with equal force. While Seahorse Key had been battling the stationary storm, the high tide began to arrive, along with a record storm surge. Both were now pushing water beyond its leeward shore and creeping like a wide slow river toward the crest of its bank. The inexorable push of the water was unhurried but determined, building its strength and gaining weight as it bore down on the watchers. Hayes knew the gentle movement across the dry bay was anything but benign.

"Oh God," He said, pointing at the space between Seahorse and Dead Man's Key as it filled in with the advancing water.

Lizzy said, "I've seen some blow-out lows before, but never dry land all the way to North Key."

"Doesn't look like it'll be dry long," Thomas replied.

"It's coming," Hayes said. "We would have been way better off if the storm hit us head on at full speed. It's just sitting out there churning up the surge, and now the tide's coming with it. We need to get back and warn everyone. The gym may not be high enough. We might need to be on roofs."

"Seriously?" Thomas asked.

"What the hell is that?" Rolf asked, pointing to the channel. "Somebody is out there?"

Jonah McShane was rowing his beautiful wooden boat through the channel, on a focused path toward the storm, a serene look on his face and his insides crazed like the leaping roosters in the cemetery. With every hard pull of the thick wooden oars, his boat blended a little more into the darkness ahead of him. As he moved through the calm channel toward the rough water ahead, certain it was the first meaningful thing he had ever done in his life, Jonah steeled his nerve. He would fight the storm or tame it to his will. At the very least, he would reach inside it to see what all the fuss was about, what any of it had ever been about.

"I think that's Jonah, from the bank," Lizzy said.

Thomas felt his heart sink. Rolf indulged no sentiments, choosing instead to turn and run toward the rowboat.

"Rolf, no!" yelled Hayes.

"He can make it," said Thomas. "Let him go."

Rolf sprinted in a diagonal to the channel, picking a point at which he thought he could intercept Jonah. He was incongruously fast, taking the strides of a longer-legged man and closing the distance between them quickly.

"Jonah, stop!"

"Afternoon, Mr. Rolf. Sorry but I cannot stop, friend. Turn back while you can."

Jonah turned his focus back to the path ahead and resumed his methodical rowing. Rolf yelled again for him to stop but the rowboat moved on. He raced to catch up with it again, grabbing the bow to stop its progress.

"You have to stop, Jonah."

"I won't. Let go of the boat."

Rolf tightened his grip. "I'm sorry, buddy. I can't let you do this."

Jonah pulled the metal pin that held an oar in place, then spun the oar hard into Rolf's stomach, sending him to the ground gasping for air. He was immobilized long enough for Jonah to row a meaningful distance between them. Rolf tried to make it to his feet but fell back hard and closed his eyes. He opened them again to see Hayes, Thomas, and Lizzy dragging him back toward the shore. The water continued to come and was upon them as they climbed from the bay to the street. Still it came. They ran the five blocks back to the school as the storm lurched forward and began to move again.

By the time Jonah stopped rowing, the tempest was everywhere and the water was wild. A life of inconsequence pushed him forward as the storm pulled him in. Disappearing into the maelstrom, his unkempt beard blowing wild about his peaceful face, Jonah took off the bright yellow life jacket and smiled. He was never going back to the bank again. Not ever.

19

LANDFALL

They had been lucky and unlucky at once. It would be difficult for them to feel that way in the moment, scattered as so many of the islanders were in attics and on widow's walks and rooftops. The fact that most of the buildings in the historic district and downtown were still standing was an outcome that could not have been predicted when, after eating its fill of trees, land, and bank tellers, the storm began to advance again on Cedar Key.

For some reason or no reason at all, Hurricane Jonah—as it would come to be called when Rolf and his friends relayed the story of the rowboat—stopped just beyond Piney Point, the westernmost point of Way Key, then turned hard north and ran parallel to the shore until, near Sandra Street where the irredeemable yankee transplant Margaret Van Landing had lived a joyless retirement tattle-telling on her neighbors with formal code violation complaints, it turned hard again toward the museum, demolishing a half mile of houses along Hodges Avenue, before a final pivot toward Sumner and points east.

The water from the surge and the high tide was seven feet up the walls of the Faraway Inn, and most of First and Second Streets were three feet deep. Only the houses at the top of the few hills in town—Thomas' at the corner of E and 3rd, Mark and Bette Davis' a block to the east, and a handful of others—sustained no flooding at all. Due to the storm's erratic pivots, no appreciable wind damage occurred in the town center and historic district, but everything past the cemetery near the museum had taken a direct blow from the dirty side of the hurricane. The walls of Fire Chief Roberts' home stood defiantly, though its roof was in pieces strewn across three blocks. When water started pushing slowly into the gym, the islanders holed up there fled to higher ground. Because the school was on the backside of a hill, the water never made it more than shin deep, but by the time it did no one was left inside. Two and three story houses became popular gathering places for refugees from low-lying streets.

Jack Fraydell, Jr. and the expecting Sierra Solaro sat with Lizzy on Thomas's porch.

"I think the worst of it is over," Lizzy said.

"When do you think we'll know about our house?" Jack asked.

"Soon, I hope."

From around the corner of the old house, Thomas appeared in a kayak. The water made the streets on either side navigable by small boat, even as the house sat mere inches above it, dry as it had ever been. Thomas heard stories about how, even in the hundred year flood, water had never reached its floorboards. He was skeptical until he found a hand-typed, paper driver's license in the sand under the house during its renovation. It was dated February 1955 and the ink was as clear and legible as the day it was typed, three-quarters of a century before. Had any water ever inundated the house, the delicate paper document would surely have been destroyed. Thomas imagined what the lady named on the license might have been like. She was born in 1896, the year of the great hurricane that destroyed Atsena Otie and sent the town of Cedar Key toward its present home on Way Key. She was listed as five foot two inches tall, one hundred and ninety-eight pounds, with gray eyes and gray hair. Her occupation was listed as *housewife*. He imagined the graying portly lady overseeing a happy home, and hoped she had loved the house as much as he did. Surely, he thought, she would be proud of it having weathered another big storm when so many of its neighbors had succumbed.

"I'm meeting with Hayes and Rolf to see if anyone needs help," Thomas said. "His dock is under water but he had a little jon boat tied up he thinks he can get to."

"Will you check on my house if you make it that way?" Lizzy asked.

"Of course."

"Jackson's inside," Jack, Jr. added. "I didn't think they would let me bring him in the gym."

"I'll check on him," Thomas said. Despite his relative disinclination toward dogs, the enormous golden retriever puppy was hard not to like. His oversized paws and dopey face almost outweighed his penchant for jumping up and licking. Still, to Thomas' mind, cats were the superior pet. They required little in the way of daily care besides an automatic feeder, a water dish, and a cat door. Further, they were stingy with their affection in a most appealing way, exhibiting none of the cloying desperation of emotionally needy dogs. Thomas's cat Ford, the unrivaled chief of all the island cats and lord of all it surveyed, was as likely to sink its teeth into your hand as it was to seek affection. His interaction with Ford mirrored that of his marriages such that their union felt comfortably familiar.

In his former life, Thomas had let his guard down when Annie wanted a dog. After months of sidestepping the issue, he reluctantly agreed to look at shelter dogs, and the first one he saw so thoroughly captured his heart he knew he would never love another. Franklin was a beagle-coon hound mix with sad, loving eyes and the disposition of a chronic cannabis user. After a few weeks of living with the dog, Thomas decreed his breed to be the *North American Couch Dog* since Franklin seldom left his sofa of repose for anything but snacks and a once daily walk to smell things other dogs had peed on before adding his own pee to the things. When Annie drove down the Nevermind Ranch dirt road for the last time, Franklin had looked back at Thomas with despair in his eyes while she stared only forward at the road ahead. This memory now overtook Thomas in the kayak and triggered a painful realization—if they hit Crystal River, then Franklin, too, was gone.

Thinking about Franklin, even the best memories of their life together, hurt too much to indulge for long, so Thomas focused on paddling the kayak. Before long, he found a rhythm with the two-sided paddle and began to cut a sleek, fast line through the floodwaters. He thought of Jonah, wild-eyed and determined, and how his skinny friend had used all of his strength to will the little rowboat into the wind and rough waters of the storm. He doubted his own mettle in the face of such adversity, already feeling a sting in his arms from the paddling.

His life before Shiloh Road had featured, often to his own detriment, obscene self-confidence, even in endeavors for which he had no experience or practical aptitude. Now, doubt was as familiar to him as the strangers that had fallen with Little Don, their faces waiting always on the inside of closed eyelids or in the stillness of the night. The men outside the big house in Gainesville, and on the little bridge in front of Fannie's, had stuck with him for a week or two before fading away in the daily hustle of life in the new world. No amount of work or preoccupation had been able to push away the bad business in Sumner. Thomas knew he would have to sort it out soon or else join TJ at the end of a bow line; he was almost out of bourbon.

After a few more minutes of paddling, he was relieved to see the water tower and, amazingly, the solar panels, intact. He had to pull his kayak across the dry ground of the hill on which the tower sat. It would be some time before it would be safe to pump water into people's homes again—every destroyed house's water connection would have to shut off or capped—but the sight of the standing tower was nonetheless a lighthouse to his morale.

As he reentered the water above Whiddon Avenue and began to paddle past the school, Thomas heard a quiet electric hum over his shoulder. Rounding the curve in front of the concrete shark that guarded the school's main entrance came Hayes and Rolf. They were moving with some pace in a fourteen foot jon boat powered by the oversized trolling motor from Hayes' bay boat, The Cogency. The motor was hooked to a pair of batteries Thomas would later learn the mayor had pilfered from his golf cart moments after his departure in the kayak.

"Ahoy there, ya maties!" called Thomas.

"Climb aboard," Rolf said.

Ever practical, Hayes said, "Well hang on. Why don't we tie your boat alongside our boat so you don't have to paddle. But that way you'll still have your kayak if we need more space for folks that need rescuing."

Thomas pulled alongside the jon boat and began to tie off to it. Hayes watched with a pained look on his face, trying his best not to intervene. He endured Thomas' clumsy attempt at two square knots before he could take it no more.

"Let me handle that," Hayes said.

"If you can't tie a knot, tie a lot," Thomas replied, smirking.

Hayes was not amused. "You're a clam boat captain, man. How do you not know how to tie a real knot."

"Yeah, Thomas... how do you not know knots?" Rolf mocked in a stilted tone.

"Dick," Hayes said.

Thomas continued the scene, "Rolf, this is serious. What if Hayes' daddy were to catch him with an unserious knot on this very serious boat?"

Hayes said, "You're both dicks, seriously," before he could no longer forestall his own laughter. The momentary reprieve from the difficulty of the day and the agitation in his mind reminded Thomas of the first time the three of them hung out together. They had met for whiskey on his front porch on a cool autumn night, except Hayes only ever drank Bacardi rum and soda water over ice, so Rolf and Thomas had whiskeys while Hayes drank his pirate wine cooler over ice he brought with him in a plastic bag in the little basket of his electric bicycle.

"I wasn't sure if you'd have ice," Hayes had said, shiftily, as he opened the bag.

"You thought I'd have people over for drinks and not have ice?"

"I don't think the mayor trusts your ice, Thomas."

"It's not like that," Hayes said.

Of course, it was like that and Rolf and Thomas made fun of him about it not just for the duration of that evening but most evenings they were together in the future. Just as the three friends were settling into their libations, they heard music coming from the bottom of the 3rd Street hill.

"Is that coming from the Bed and Breakfast?" Thomas asked.

"Oh yeah," Hayes said. "They're having a wedding."

Without any additional discussion, the three friends, drinks in hand, walked down the hill and into the courtyard of the converted Victorian mansion with the sprawling live oak that predated the American Republic.

"Okay, you be the mayor," Hayes said.

"Fine. Rolf, you're the chief of Police."

"Done. Who's Hayes gonna be?"

"Eccentric playwright," Thomas said.

By night's end, they had danced with the bride, drank their fill at the open bar, met an array of wonderful people, and generally had the time of their lives.

"You're an actual, elected official, Hayes. A real-life mayor," Thomas said, stumbling back up the hill to his house. "You're supposed to be the responsible one."

"I hate being the mayor," he replied. "If anyone else would step up and not run the island into the ground, I'd step aside and feel like I won the lottery."

"I hope they never do," Rolf said. "This place needs you."

"Well, I need more nights like this. Thank you, boys." And there were more nights, and boat trips down the Suwannee in the daytime, parties at the pool at Rolf's new house, and bar fights they tried to start but never could—a carefully curated adolescence that grown men need in their lives.

As they would soon discover, however, the work ahead of them in the aftermath of the storm was an entirely adult affair.

"How bad is it gonna hurt," Sierra asked.

"How bad is what gonna hurt?"

Sierra pointed at her belly as she swung on the swing where Thomas and Lizzy had accidentally fallen in love.

"Oh, the baby," Lizzy replied. "Honestly I didn't feel a thing. I was asking for the epidural before we even got to the hospital. I just remember there being no baby, and then there was a baby. Don't try to brave it like those Gainesville hippies... get the drugs." As the last syllable of the reply was leaving her lips, Lizzy realized that nostalgia had gotten the better of her. "Oh... oh God, Sierra. I'm such a dummy."

The swinging stopped suddenly.

"So, like, real bad? There won't be any drugs, right?"

"No. No I don't suppose there will be. But women have been doing this for thousands of years. Everything's going to be fine."

With some trepidation, Sierra said, "A hundred years ago women died in childbirth all the time."

"That's true, I guess," Lizzy admitted.

"You could maybe work on your encouragement game, lady."

Lizzy buried her head in her hands, but Sierra's laughter let her off the hook.

"I'm kidding... it's good. I had just never seriously thought about being a mom so it's all coming at me pretty fast. I guess I always thought I would one day but... not like this. Not with everything that's going on."

"I'm glad this is happening. I can't believe I'm old enough to be a grandmother, but I think we all need this. Nothing makes things matter like a baby. We'll all have a reason to make the island better because your little one deserves a good place to live."

Sierra smiled and the swinging began again.

"I hadn't thought about it that way. I like that, Lizzy."

"Good. We're gonna have a baby!"

It didn't take long for the laughter in the attached boats to subside. As the three friends moved passed the school's gym heading toward Gulf Boulevard, they saw him, tangled in the mangroves along the canal, maybe ten feet away from where he had explained the inner workings of the machine he so loved. Seven thousand seven hundred and twenty-four miles away from the little village where he was born and where he had met Linnéa, married her, lived a decade in her embrace, and then watched her die, Johan had breathed in the waters of the Gulf at the height of storm and returned to his love at last.

Hayes steered the boats toward the body, pulling alongside it and tying one end of a line to Johan's leg and the other to a sturdy mangrove.

"What are you doing?" Thomas asked.

"We might need the space on the boat for people who are still alive. I'm just making sure Mr. Johan's body doesn't wash away. He deserves a proper burial when the water recedes."

"That's what all this rope is for?" Rolf asked.

"Yeah," replied Hayes. "I have a feeling we're gonna need all of it."

The grim work continued all along Gulf Boulevard. Maria Phillips, whose placid, beautiful face never seemed to age, and whose sublime artistry as a sculptor of glass adorned the walls of homes all over the island, was next for the rope.

"Folksy got his girl back, at least," Thomas said, trying but failing to add some comforting sentiment to the moment.

Budd Carem, *The Mayor of Dock Street*, so named for being omnipresent at the bars there, and for handing out clicky pens to tourists personalized with his catch phrase, *Water with Lime, Absolutely*, sat in the confluence of two water oak branches as though he were an action figure posed there by a giant child, smiling even in death.

Rolf had seen enough death up close, in the Afghan desert and the Croft's house near the channel, to know that it seldom looked as peaceful as most people imagine it will be. So when he saw Joanna Halfcock, twisted into the metal fencing that runs along the front of the cemetery, such that only her head rose above the water, he stopped not only to feel the loss of a friend, but to admire the serenity of her pretty face, expressionless but somehow comforting in its requiescence.

Thomas found no comfort in the sight. Unexpectedly, uncontrollably, he hid his face in his hands and wept. As the tears came fast and heavy, it occurred to him that these were the first tears he had shed since that terrible February morning. Thomas was exceedingly fond of Joanna. She was his favorite bartender at Denny Gal's breakfast café, though she was quick to point out that serving his breakfast at the bar didn't make her an actual bartender. He nevertheless continued to unburden on her all of his life's travails as he ate blueberry French toast with scrambled eggs and bacon. Over time, the fake bartender and the oversharing clam farmer developed a morning routine that weaved its way into the fabric of their lives. He was now, to be sure, crying over his friend, but Thomas was mournful for a great deal more than the kind, funny, hard-working woman tangled in the fence.

In all, seven bodies were wrangled and tied to trees or fences along Gulf Boulevard. When they reached Hodges Avenue, there were no more bodies and barely any trees. A stretch of clear water extended a half mile in front of them.

"Keep going," Thomas said. "Most of the people I know who lived back here made it to the gym, but I need to be able to tell Lizzy about her house."

As they rounded the turn at Watson Circle, headed for Sandra Street, the lack of houses where houses should be and the expanse of water where water should not be heightened the mood, already somber from the bodies and the rope. There was plenty of room in the boats but they had found no one, yet, to fill them.

"This isn't how I imagined this would go," Rolf said. "On TV there are always people on roofs happy to be rescued."

"Lizzy had family in New Orleans when Katrina hit," Thomas replied. "They went to help. She said it wasn't anything like she thought it would be. By the time they got there everything smelled so bad it was hard to breath. There wasn't a whole lot of rescuing there either. Boats everywhere and people who wanted to help... but not much to be done but wait for the water to fall."

"There's your answer," Hayes said, turning the boats towards Lizzy's house. The elegant front porch, southern as a *bless your heart* from a sassy grandmother, was gone. Most of the rest of the house, too, was by then strewn across the backwaters and the Gulf. A solitary dormer teetered impossibly above a perfectly intact staircase. Waterlogged photos of Lizzy's former life somehow still hung on the triangular wall created by the angle of the stairs—the three of them, she and Jack and Jack, Jr., smiling, triumphant still life models of the American dream deferred.

Aside from the poetic beauty of the empty space where the detestable Margaret Van Landing had lived, all would have been sorrow on Sandra Street were it not for Jackson, the lumbering, goofy dog, whose oversized head appeared in the dormer window.

Hayes pulled the boats alongside the partially submerged stairs and Thomas jumped out onto them.

"Be careful," Rolf said.

Thomas felt an eerie strangeness as he began his ascent toward the dormer, testing each tread above before stepping onto it, amazed as he went at the improbable sturdiness of the structure. There was something fantastic about steps rising from water without surrounding walls. Lizzy and Jack had built their house with what she called a *staircase to nothing*—the dramatic balusters and ornate spindles that lined the stairs led only to an enormous second floor attic. There had been some discussion about the eventual finishing of the attic into additional living area, but the grandness of the ground floor proved more space than a family of three would ever need. Before the storm, the attic was a treasure trove of furniture, artwork, keepsakes, do-dads and whatnots—the physical byproducts of a life lived over time. Now, only the stairs remained, with a door at the top that led to a fifty square foot or so area around a single dormer.

Jackson, whimpering and frantic, leapt into Thomas' arms when the door opened, his fifty-two pounds destabilizing the footing of his rescuer, who stumbled back several steps before beginning to topple over. In a last second effort to avoid a crippling fall down the wooden stair treads, Thomas jumped away from them, toward what would have been the elegant dining room adjoining the sprawling kitchen with its rustic island made from reclaimed barn wood, falling eight feet into the water and, improbably, hitting no debris. He popped back to the surface, still holding the dog whose giant paws were wrapped around him in a desperate bear hug.

"Holy shit," Rolf said.

Jackson barked something that probably also meant, "Holy shit," while Hayes pulled the dog into the boat.

The three men and the oversized puppy searched every corner of the outlying portions of the island, eventually rescuing a single person, Rikki

Nucker, the eccentric and affable realtor whose family tree intertwined with that of the Davids and a century of Cedar Key history, but not her adoring husband Dilbert, whom they tied, like so many others, to something sturdy, while Rikki wailed and refused to leave his body.

With cajoling at first and then finally physical coercion, she climbed into the boat and they started back, slower as the power from the batteries began to wane.

20

— · —

MY KINGDOM FOR A COCK

The floodwaters receded in just over a week. Bloated and malformed bodies were retrieved and buried. Destruction beyond the cemetery was so widespread that most of the remaining empty houses and many of the condominium units near the town center were filled with those displaced by the storm. Lizzy moved in with Thomas. Jack, Jr., Sierra, and Jackson settled into the little A-frame across the street, empty for the past month since Mr. Paul passed quietly on his three-wheeled bicycle. He had pulled up to the stop sign at E and 2nd, felt a little rush of tired, leaned his head forward for a moment to let it pass, then transmogrified into pure energy racing through the cosmos. He was seventy-eight or ninety or one hundred and eight years old.

There were chickens, alive and dead, seemingly everywhere. As soon as the immediate danger of the storm and its aftermath passed, nearly every able-bodied person in Cedar Key set out together on a great chicken hunt. The chickens had provided a baseline of nutritional support that was responsible, as much as anything else, for a feeling of well-being among the islanders. The thought of losing daily eggs and the chance for a full bird in the chicken lottery was more than most could bear.

Chickens are remarkably skilled at navigating bad weather. They can pin themselves to the ground such that only the strongest of winds can pry them free. Hurricane Jonah's erratic movement had drawn a red line of doom near the intersection of Gulf and Hodges, sparing the cemetery from the heaviest winds. Still, a handful of gusts approaching one hundred miles per hour had strafed the chicken enclosure, each time snatching a few dozen birds from the sand and rocketing them to heights a chicken would never naturally find itself. Few were able to successfully manage the return flight to earth. A month later, while gathering poke salad on North Key, more than three miles from the cemetery, Luke Buck would find three hens living seemingly happy lives on the outer key.

After two hard days, Hayes called off the official search and compiled a chicken census. Seven hundred chickens had first arrived at the cemetery by U-Haul. The breeding program had increased their population to eight hundred and thirty-seven. By Hayes count, the storm had reduced this number by roughly half, to four hundred and twenty birds. Because of the time it took for the floodwaters to recede, none of the dead chickens could be eaten. They were burned in a giant pyre, along with the rubble from a collapsed house on Andrews Circle, to minimize the threat of some dread avian sickness for which the island would have no medicinal defense.

"There's so many of them," Rolf said, watching the fire.

"Yeah," Hayes replied.

"We'll have to cut back on everyone's egg allotment."

"It's even worse than it looks, Rolf."

"I don't know man... it looks pretty bad."

"When we get back to the cemetery, look close and tell me what you don't see."

Something about Hayes' dire tone sent a ping through Rolf's mind. "Oh no," he said.

"I'm trying to not make a fuss about it so folks don't panic."

"Not even one?" Rolf asked.

"Not one. Chickens are like people. The hens dig in and protect themselves and their babies when trouble comes. The roosters bow up and act
stupid. When the winds came, they were running wild while the hens
hunkered down."

"But no roosters means..."

"Yeah," Hayes replied, staring into the fire. "Keep this between us for
now. Maybe one's stuck out in the marsh or in a collapsed house and will
just wander on back."

"I'll keep looking," Rolf said.

In another week of looking, Rolf had found no roosters and none
had wandered up. In that time, word of the lack of roosters had made
it throughout the town and contributed to a collective dismay among
the islanders. As hope was fading, Lida Maria made a spectacular discovery. While on chicken guard duty, she noticed that something was off
with one of the graves in the cemetery. First Lieutenant W. A. Crawford,
CSA—born April 3, 1840, died February 13th, 1865—was buried in a
partially above-ground sepulcher ironically located beneath a flagpole that
flew an enormous American flag. His was a prominent grave, viewed by
almost everyone who entered the cemetery. A corner of the sepulcher's
concrete lid had collapsed, creating a football-sized opening. When Lida
Maria came closer for a better look, she heard it—a mama hen clucking
calmly inside as she sat on four beautiful eggs. The confederate's tomb had
proved a perfect defense against even the strongest winds from the storm.

Within the hour, news of the expecting hen went as viral as a thing can
go by word of mouth. So many people were coming by to get a glimpse
of Jenny Reb and her eggs that a third chicken guard was needed just
to manage the crowd around Lieutenant Crawford's grave. Against the
backdrop of the storm's destruction, egg-mania overtook the island with
the same fervor of frenzied Catholics making a pilgrimage to see the Virgin

Mary's miraculous appearance on a grilled cheese sandwich at a truck stop diner.

"It's definitely a miracle," said a Methodist.

"We are favored by God," replied an Episcopalian.

"We don't deserve these eggs," observed a Church of Christer.

"Eggs won't save you from hell," judged a Baptist.

Denominational differences aside, nothing could dampen the joyous mood of the islanders. It was hard not to imagine that divine intervention had saved the island from a slow chicken extinction. They needed a win and Jenny Reb had delivered.

Work to clean up from the flood commenced around the island, but no real progress seemed to occur as everyone waited for the eggs to hatch. Hayes and Thomas met Mike Allenby, a University of Florida marine biologist, whose fetching wife Minnie had managed most of the vacation rentals in the old world, at the green three-story university building on 1st Street.

Hayes got straight to the point. "Our chances are pretty good one of them is a rooster, right Mike?"

"No species of chicken has as yet managed to thrive in the ocean, so I'm not sure how much my expertise helps, Hayes."

"Oh... I just thought maybe it all kind of worked the same."

"I wanted to know myself so I found a book about chickens in the library."

Thomas was impressed. "There was a book just about chickens in our little library?"

"You'd be surprised," said Mike. "There's more in there than you think." He retrieved the book from his desk, flipped to a page he had book-marked and read aloud, "In mammals, the familiar XX:YY chromosome sequence determines gender, with females having two X chromosomes and males having an X and a Y. In birds, sex is determined by a ZZ:ZW sex chromosome system. Gonadal development in chickens..."

Thomas interrupted Mike with a deep belly laugh.

"What?"

"It's dumb. I'm sorry."

Mike continued, "Gonadal development in chickens provides insight into sex determination for a wide range of vertebrates. In birds, females are the heterogametic sex, carrying one copy each of the Z and W sex chromosomes. Males are homogametic with a ZZ configuration."

This time it was Hayes who laughed inappropriately.

"Seriously, Mr. Mayor?"

"Sorry," Hayes said, trying to get a handle on the laughter but failing as Thomas joined in.

"Sorry, Mike," said Thomas. "I just wasn't prepared for gonads and homogametic roosters, man."

"Well anyway," Mike began with a feigned sternness befitting a man of science, "I'm not sure any of that means much. The book goes on to say chicken eggs hatch pretty close to 50/50 between males and females."

"That's good news then," said Hayes. "We got four eggs so we should definitely get at least one rooster."

"That's not exactly how probability works. In a large sample size of eggs you would expect about half to be male and half to be female but some statistical probability exists that all four of our eggs will be hens or all four will be cockerels or some other mixture."

Thomas covered his face to hide the smirk.

Mike just shook his head. "How is all this funny? Maybe you've heard... it's the end of the world out there."

"It's either gonna end or it isn't," replied Thomas. "But cockerel is a funny word either way."

The scientist relented with a grin of his own. "I guess it is. So look, no guarantees, but I like our chances to get at least one rooster from our eggs. If we do, that little fella is gonna be the biggest VIP in town."

Six days later, four little beaks began to peck cracks into their eggshells. Word spread across the island and baby chick hysteria ensued. Of the two hundred fifty six-and-a-half people left living on the island, two hundred and seven gathered around Lieutenant Crawford's grave, waiting impatiently for mama and her chicks—a savior rooster hopefully among them—to venture out into the world. When several hours had passed with no exodus from the tomb, it was decided to move the crowd a hundred feet behind its opening to give the new family a little room.

Within minutes, a weary but proud-looking mama poked her head out of the hole, surveyed the outside world with twitchy movements of her chicken head, then sprang out with her little brood in tow. Thunderous applause rang across the cemetery, spooking the chicks but not Jenny Reb, who seemed to soak in the attention like a Broadway understudy thrust into the momentary prominence of a lead role. She preened and strutted about the graveyard stage, the hopes of her adoring fans resting on the strength of her mothering in the weeks to come.

In the wake of the hatchings, a wave of pseudo-science, old wives tales, and other quackery regarding the sex determination of chicks swept across the island. Everyone seemed to have a sure-fire method of determining how many of the chicks were hens and how many were roosters. Sharon Johnson had grown up raising chickens in Hatchbend, near the Suwannee River, and swore by a method of dangling a metal ring from a string over each chick. If the ring moves back and forth, she advised, positing a kind of foolproof chicken magnetism, the chick was male; if it made a circle it was female. Sharon confidently predicted two hens and two roosters. Lina Fines, the ill-tempered but likeable restaurant manager at Denny Gall's breakfast café, began turning the baby chicks upside down, announcing that any chick that just lays there is a woman, while the ones that fight to right themselves were men.

"Seriously?" asked Hannah Greek, the sultry-voiced former musical theater major. "I bet a man came up with that."

When all four of the chicks kicked, squirmed, and shimmied to right themselves, Lina, ignoring Hannah's skepticism, jumped for joy, shouting, "Four roosters! Four roosters!" In her excitement she had forgotten the fourth chick was still in her hands and it went flying seven feet into the air. Samantha Maye's military bearing and fast reflexes proved worthy of the moment as she noticed the little puff of yellow in the sky, dove toward it, and caught it gently just before it hit the ground. At this point, the third chicken guard Geoff McCloud, not normally known for clear-headedness, intervened.

"I think that will be enough for today. Why don't we leave Jenny Reb and her babies alone. We've either got a rooster or we ain't. No sense killing them to find out early."

"Wait," came a voice from the middle of the crowd. "There's only one real way to sex them this young. You gotta palpate the chick's vent to engorge it a little. If you do it right you can see a little chicken pecker in there. No pecker and it's a hen."

Surprisingly, this method is fairly accurate, but requires considerable experience to recognize the chicken pecker because it doesn't look much like a pecker at all. Additionally, a novice can easily disembowel and kill a delicate chick in the effort.

"Oh hell no," Geoff McCloud shouted back at the voice, not because he knew anything about the dangers of the technique, but because the voice had come from John Waser, a noted yankee pervert.

"Visiting hours are closed," Geoff announced. "Go on back home and let's let 'em be."

August slipped away. John Mitchell got the water back on. The mullet kept jumping and the clams were still plentiful. Ryland Beacham and his friends brought a steady supply of game across the channel. No one went hungry. There were no invaders and no more serious storms. Three more island women, including Cousin's forty-nine year old best friend Lara, became pregnant. In the new world, a good week was as noteworthy as a good year in the old. The islanders had strung together six good weeks but the uncertainty of the chicks was a kind of spiritual millstone whose weight pressed heavier with each passing day.

While they waited, Hayes and Thomas conspired to create a distraction. "Bread and Circuses," Thomas said, as they walked from Hayes' dock toward the City Hall building.

"Huh?" Hayes replied.

"At the end of the first century, the Roman poet Juvenal wrote a series of satirical poems decrying the erosion of Roman heroism."

"Uh... What?"

"The great Republic had fallen to the reign of emperors. Romans who had once prided themselves on rugged self-sufficiency now depended on free wheat from the government and seemed to care more about entertainment spectacles than improving themselves or their country."

"I wonder if you can even hear the way you talk sometimes," Hayes said.

"Whatever, man. I thought you would get the reference. Gladiators and shit. I'm not trying to sound smart."

"Uh huh."

"I didn't say anything about how it's written in dactylic hexameter or that the *Roman Satura* genre included Horace and Persius."

"Well you just did."

"You wanna hear my idea or not?"

"Soon as the history lesson is over, I'm all ears."

"Fine," Thomas replied. "Bread and circuses just means a distraction from daily life. I think we need to put something together to distract us while we wait on the first of those chicks to start crowing."

"What do you have in mind?"

With widening eyes and the characteristic pep in his voice that had been absent for weeks, Thomas replied, "The Shark Swim!"

"Dang," Hayes said with shake of his head. "I was mad I didn't think of it the first time and I'm mad I didn't think of it this time either."

"Right? We don't need to raise money for anything this time, on account of money isn't real anymore."

"Was it ever?" asked Hayes with a chuckle.

Thomas replied, "I never really understood how money worked. It's just paper. And they can print it whenever they want."

"We should have never left the Gold Standard."

Thomas steered the conversation back to his big idea. "We should do the Shark Swim just to keep a tradition from the old world alive."

"There's a lot about the way we used to live I'm glad to see gone," Hayes said. "But the swim is exactly what we need. Let's round up Rolf and the boys and go door to door to tell everyone."

First, they stopped by Thomas' house where he produced a copy of *The Farmer's Almanac* from his bookshelf. He scanned the pages and then reported, "The next day with a good low tide in the middle of the day is a week from tomorrow. Let's do it then so the sandbar past the channel is shallow enough for folks to take a break halfway across."

"Perfect," Hayes said with genuine excitement.

"McCloud says we got four older hens he doesn't expect to lay anymore eggs. How about we award a hen to the winner of all four divisions from last year's swim—Male, Female, Over-50, and Under 18."

"Hell yes," replied the mayor.

"But do you think we have enough people in all the categories that can swim?"

"I guess we'll see," Hayes said.

Thomas headed for door. "I'll get started telling everyone I can."

As he walked around town to get the world out, Thomas' thoughts naturally turned to Georgie Pilsner, and how his best friend had so inspired the island with his thrilling last place finish in the inaugural Shark Swim. Georgie's new home in Virginia was close enough to D.C. that not even the unreasonably optimistic Thomas could muster hope that his friend still lived. Maybe Tim Mueller had survived in Gainesville but he knew those odds, too, were long.

In the intervening week, Mike Allenby, pursuant to his relentless nature, continued to learn everything he could about chickens. He determined to interject a measure of scientific rigor into the breeding program so the island could maximize their output of eggs and, eventually, excess meat birds. It was during this period of intense chicken inquiry that he made the terrible discovery. After exhausting all available resources from the city library, Mike sought out Janya Bollins, the former librarian at the school, to see if she knew of any additional resources that might help him. In an afternoon of searching the school's modest library, she found a single book for his consideration—*All About Chickens: For Kids.* The book was light on text and heavy on pictures, but serendipitously contained a page about telling the difference between a rooster and a hen, noting that chicks develop saddle feathers near their bellies sometime around two months of age. For hens, these feathers are wide and oval-shaped. For roosters, they are long, narrow, and pointed.

Armed with this information, Mike made his way to the cemetery carrying the picture book with him as a guide. When he arrived, his reputation as a serious person from the university gave him immediate access to the flock. Geoff McCloud, the former truck driver and barfly— summarily dispossessed of working trucks and open bars in the wake of the fallen smokestacks— had found purpose as a self-appointed bodyguard for Jenny Reb and her brood. He spent so much time with them that the birds seldom ventured more than a few yards from him when he was in the cemetery. They developed a habit of leaping into his lap anytime he sat on the ground, and it was this habit that made it easy for Mike to put his hands on the chicks. He simply sat on the ground next to Geoff and waited.

Mike gently examined the first chick, feeling excited to immediately identify prominent saddle feathers. His excitement waned when they looked nearly identical to the oval-shaped feathers on the hen in the picture book. Mike repeated this process with the second chick, the third, and then the fourth. He couldn't believe what he was seeing. All four chicks had easily identifiable saddle feathers but none, by any reasonable measure, could be called long, narrow, or pointed. They all looked indistinguishable from the dainty hen feathers highlighted on page 14 of *All About Chickens: For Kids*.

Mike knew the improbability of these odds. For every egg, the normal probability of either sex is 50%, and the two possible outcomes are mutually exclusive. Multiplying these two outcomes by the four eggs yields $2 \times 2 \times 2 \times 2 = 16$ possible outcomes of hen to rooster ratios. Only one of these 16 possible outcomes could yield zero roosters. Mike did the math in his head: 1 divided by 16 equals .0625. There had been an almost 94% chance of the four eggs producing at least one rooster. It would take some time before the rest of the island would accept Mike's findings, but 100% of the new chicks were absolutely peckerless hens. The island's future, therefore, was in absolute peril.

The scientist thanked Geoff McCloud, noting that he seemed less interesting while forcibly sober, then walked solemnly away from the cemetery to find Hayes and Thomas.

For the first time since that awful February morning, when the horizon across the bay from Dock Street became an instant irradiated blur, Hayes David buckled. He had been moved to uncharacteristic despair at the sight of the Judith Jane without its captain—his best friend—on deck, and certainly the loss of Folksy and TJ and so many others had wounded him, but not even the haunting moral ambiguity of the killings on Shiloh Road had kept him from the stoicism he believed his role as mayor demanded. Because the island needed a steadfast leader in the tumult of the previous eight months, Hayes had not allowed himself the luxury of human frailty. When Mike Allenby walked into City Hall, however, a sullen look on his face and hesitancy in his voice, the famous David fortitude that had served his forebears on their Atlantic crossing, and his father in the ruinous wake of the net ban, was, for the first time in his life, simply unavailable.

"They're all hens, Hayes."

"What? How?"

"They just are. Every goddamn one of them."

"Are you sure?"

"I am."

Hayes opened his mouth, intending to say, "Thanks for letting me know," but only a low moan emerged—a mournful rattle whose vibration shook apart the equanimity he had spent a lifetime cultivating. Mike sat quietly with his friend, whose dignified sobbing lasted no more than a minute.

He was, after all, a David, and there was still work to be done.

21

THE NEW KING

Knowledge of Mike Allenby's discovery was not made public. Hayes shared it only with Tabby and Thomas, the former because he told her everything each night as they lay in bed before sleep, and the latter hoping his friend would have the words to make sense of it.

On his clam dock, agitated and pacing, Hayes relayed the bad news to Thomas.

"Dang, that sucks," Thomas said.

"Seriously, man?"

"What?"

"That's all you've got? Those four hens were a gut punch. I guess I was looking to be talked off the ledge about it."

Thomas slumped into one of the dock chairs. "Oh, okay, I didn't know. I mean... I'm not sure there's much to be said. We're in real trouble."

"You're terrible at this, Thomas."

"Sorry. Just give me a minute to process it. It hadn't crossed my mind that none of them would be roosters. What even are the odds of that?"

"6.25%."

"Whoa," Thomas replied.

"Mike did the math. Now what are we supposed to do about it?"

Finally, Thomas found his footing. "What we always do. We'll figure it out. Surely there's a rooster somewhere between here and Gainesville. Maybe we could trade for one."

"After what we did in Sumner, I doubt it."

"We did what we had to," Thomas said, the words ringing false to both men.

"Did we?"

"I don't know. But it's done and I know I don't want to talk about it," Thomas said.

"We definitely don't have to talk about it."

"Maybe we don't go that way at all," Thomas said. "It would be a long trip, but we could try sailing or even rowing to Inglis or Yankeetown."

Hayes pushed back. "We took down the bridge to separate us from everything on the other side."

"We took it down to stop an immediate threat, and some good it did us. Those Meade boys didn't have much trouble finding their way across. Ryland and Luke are hunting the scrub on the other side almost every day. The scrub in *Sumner*, Hayes. It's a fantasy to think we can isolate ourselves here forever. Eventually we'll need to find out what's left out there. Maybe roosters."

"Yeah maybe," Hayes said. "But not yet. Right now let's do the swim and let everyone enjoy themselves before we tell them the bad news."

"Fine," replied Thomas. "I think everybody could use a little joy right now... and I can't imagine anything more joyful than beating you across to Senny Otie again this year."

"They'll drag me out of the channel dead before I'll lose again to a damn playwright."

"Your mama won't be happy about that... but I'll say nice things about you at the wake."

Just after dawn, Ryland Beecham and Luke Buck walked quietly together through the western edge of the Cedar Key Scrub on the Sumner side of the Number Four Bridge, rifles in hand, tracking a deer they hoped to kill and roast for the Shark Swim celebration the next day. The young men were close in age, and each had mothers traveling on the day the smokestacks fell who had not been heard from since. They didn't talk often of this dark connection between them, but the awareness of it brought them closer. They were skilled outdoorsmen and worked seamlessly together in the woods. Given the limited number of younger people on the island, their building friendship had begun from necessity but was developing into something on which they both increasingly relied.

"What was it like when you went after the Meades in Sumner?" Luke asked.

"Easy," Ryland replied.

"Really?"

"Yeah not really. The details were easy. Hayes put together a solid plan and it went like we thought. But it didn't feel like I thought it would."

"I tried to go on the raid but my dad wouldn't let me. Not after what happened in Gainesville."

"I heard something about that," Ryland said.

"We had to shoot it out with people that were attacking my grandparent's house. It was mostly just a blur of shooting and people yelling. It was hard to tell if I'd hit anyone… except this one guy that was trying to chop down the front door of the house with an axe."

"Jesus, Luke."

"My cousin and I emptied two magazines from our papa's Ruger 14s through the door. I didn't see him getting hit but I watched him die when we came outside. I'm not sure how I thought it would feel, but it was weird."

Ryland said, "I still have a hard time falling asleep at night."

"Me, too. Think it ever gets better?"

While staring into the distance at nothing in particular, Ryland said, "I'll let you know if it does."

Luke replied, "I know we did the right thing, but it still feels… yeah just weird I guess."

Ryland fidgeted with his rifle and pulled aimlessly at the straps of his camouflage backpack. "We did more than we should've in Sumner, probably. I'd probably still do it again after what they did to Folksy but…" Ryland fumbled for words to finish his thought but none came.

Luke eased the tension when he said, "Well for a couple of killers, we're not having much luck getting a deer."

"We're on a fresh track," Ryland said, pointing at the way ahead.

"Alright, Oprah, If we can stop talking about our feelings maybe we'll do some good."

"Roger that," said Ryland.

As the first rays of sunlight began to filter through the sand pines and myrtle oaks—some of the few varieties of trees than can grow in the sugar sand of the fire-plagued scrub land— Luke heard a rustling in a clump of palmettos fifty yards to the south. He motioned to Ryland, who raised the 3x9 scope on the bolt-action Winchester to his eye, identifying eight antler points rising above the cover. Luke, too, now raised his rifle and waited along with his friend, hoping the animal would reveal enough of itself for a clean shot. They both carefully regulated their breathing as they waited, pushing against the rush of adrenaline to slow their heart rates. The muscles in their forearms began to tighten and ache as a full minute passed. The humid air around them sat heavy and still while the buck was frozen in place. Finally, it took a step, then two more, until it was three-quarters of the way into a clearing.

A movement of fingers toward triggers commenced, slow and smooth, then final, regulated breaths whose careful exhalation would put the shooters' bodies into the perfect quietude required for a professional shot. Before either man could fire, a burst of three quick shots rang out from an indeterminate direction. The animal lurched forward a half step, turning his head hard to one side and then the other, bellowing long and low as it fell. It was dead before it reached the warm dew on the ground, three tightly grouped holes in the center mass just behind its front legs.

Luke and Ryland dropped to the ground, taking cover from whomever had put down the deer, then quickly steadied themselves into defensive firing positions, feeling intuitively that a gun battle was inevitable if they were spotted. As they scanned the range in front of them, sweeping their rifle barrels back and forth across the area near the buck, the serenity of the morning began to return. They held their positions, expecting someone to emerge at any moment to retrieve the deer. A half hour passed in what felt like suspended animation but still no one came.

"How long you think we should wait?" Ryland asked.

"As long as it takes," said Luke. "I'm worried the minute we stand up we're gonna get our faces shot off."

"Maybe they didn't see us at all."

"Yeah maybe not, but I'm not taking the chance."

The waiting was a vice whose grip pushed in on the men with each passing moment. When it seemed as though they could bear it no longer, there was a merciful break in the stillness. Rising from palmettos thirty yards to the right of Luke came a green boonie hat atop an AR-15 rifle barrel.

"I saw you move just after I shot the deer," came a high-pitched voice. "I know you're over there and I don't wanna get shot over a deer. Look, you can have it. Just let me back out of here real slow and we'll forget we ever met."

"We haven't met," Luke said, impulsively.

"What are you doing?" Ryland asked in an elevated whisper.

"I don't know, it just came out."

"Well think of something else to say."

Luke called out, "We don't want your deer. You shot it so it belongs to you."

"That sounds nice," came the voice. "But it also sounds like something somebody would say to get me to stand up so they could shoot me."

"Nobody's shooting anybody," yelled Ryland.

In a slightly calmer tone, the voice said, "There's no reason for us to trust each other. So how do we do this?"

"I was hoping you'd have some ideas," replied Luke.

"I don't... but we can't stay like this all day. It's gonna get hot and the deer will spoil and neither of us will get it."

Luke tried to assure the person below the elevated hat. "We're not taking your deer. Are you alone?"

"I don't think I wanna answer that."

"Well I think you are. That grouping was too tight to come from different shooters. There are two of us. My name is Luke and Ryland is here as well. I'm gonna stand up nice and slow, without my rifle. If you try to shoot me, my buddy is gonna rain hellfire in your direction. He's a real good shot so I promise you don't want that to happen. If you don't shoot me, I'm gonna step out in the open. Then maybe you could come out, too."

"Your buddy could still just shoot me when I came out."

"Goddamn it no one is getting shot," Ryland said, ignoring Luke's plan and walking into the clearing with his hands up.

A few seconds later, the boonie hat lowered and to the surprise of Luke and Ryland—who in the excitement of the moment had not associated the pitch of the voice in the palmettos with what they were about to see—a young woman stood up. Green and brown paint covered her face but could not hide pronounced cheek bones and electric green eyes. Draped about her face and shoulders was more red hair than Luke or Ryland had ever seen before on a single person. It seemed to move in rolling waves of its own volition.

Luke stepped from the clearing, awestruck. "You're a girl," he said.

"Son of a bitch," She deadpanned. "Are you sure?"

Ryland laughed at his friend. "Yeah, Luke, how can you be sure?"

"I mean, obviously you're a girl. I just... I guess I just thought..."

"You thought no way a girl shoots a grouping that tight?"

"That's not what I meant."

"Relax, I'm just twisting your tail. My name's Kinsey. I live just up the road in Sumner."

"I'm Luke. This is Ryland."

"You from the island? You look like islanders."

"What's that supposed to mean?" Ryland asked.

"Yeah," added Luke. "What's an islander look like?"

"Like you're eating a little better than us peasants on this side of the channel. Speaking of, why are you on our side anyway? I thought you wanted to be left alone over there. Isn't that why you blew up the bridge?"

"I think there's more to it than that," replied Luke.

"Is there?"

"Look there's no sense arguing," Ryland interjected. "The point is we don't mean you any harm and if you don't mean to cause any trouble for us, we can just walk out of here our separate ways."

"If that's how you want it, that's how we'll do it," Kinsey replied.

Luke felt differently. "Let us help you drag the deer out, anyway."

"Now that I would like to let you do... if you promise not set my house on fire and kill my dogs and shoot up everything to hell."

A hard silence enveloped everything as Luke and Ryland fumbled for something to say. Ryland's mind was flooded with a scattershot of memories from the raid in Sumner, then turned to his friend Folksy and the attack on the island.

He replied in a sharp tone, a scowl spreading across his face, "If you don't have two boats of armed killers coming for us, I think we could have a deal."

An unbearable tension circumscribed the moment until Luke finally spoke up. "If any of us wanted to kill somebody today all three of us had the opportunity. How about we just leave that other stuff alone and get this deer out of the woods so it doesn't go to waste. You can trust us."

"I don't know if that's true," Kinsey said." But the truth is my family could really use this meat."

"It's settled then. Lead the way."

"This way," Kinsey said, pointing in the direction of State Road 24.

Luke and Ryland each grabbed an antler and the three hunters walked out of the woods together.

A light rain fell on the morning of the Shark Swim, but the water between the main island and Atsena Otie was still relatively calm. Almost everyone on the island was congregated in front of the Beachfront Motel by noon. Four birddogs and three skiffs were anchored in a line along the race course, offering a pitstop for tired swimmers and a barrier for those not able to overpower the light current running through the channel.

Lida Maria wore the plastic shark fin on her head that had been such a hit at the previous year's swim. Several months of a new world diet meant the same swimsuit she had to constantly pick from her butt a year prior now comfortably held in all the goods. Cousin Samantha wore a microscopic hot pink bikini and scuba booties, her sun baked complexion looking more Guadalajara than Cedar Key. A wide assortment of inflatable rafts, pool noodles, lifejackets, and other buoyancy devices adorned those whose swimming skills or age made an unassisted half mile swim infeasible. Hayes and Thomas were all business, sizing each other up and posturing extreme confidence for their expected victories.

As the appointed start time approached, Thomas borrowed Chief Edwin's bullhorn to address the crowd. As he did, seeing his neighbors all gathered together there by the water, he felt a wave of pride wash over him. In spite of months of losses too staggering to reconcile, and the creeping despair of knowing almost nothing still from the outside world, they had come, for tradition and fellowship. They had come to spite a wider world too vain and stupid not to kill itself. They had come for each other.

"Welcome friends! I guess we're gonna swim across this channel again."

Cheers erupted from the crowd.

"When we were raising money for the school, I found it pretty easy to guilt-trip everyone into participating. It would have been hard to avoid me the rest of the year if you hadn't come out to swim or volunteer. But now..."

Thomas choked on his feelings, pausing for a few moments to look across the bay and collect himself.

"But now... well now I guess you're here again because you've made the completely unreasonable decision to persist. I keep thinking it'll get easier. Some things have gotten easier, for sure... every time water comes out of my faucet I want kiss to John Mitchell right on the mouth."

The big man replied from the back of the crowd, "I'd be much obliged if you didn't, Thomas."

"Well thank you again for the water all the same, John. And seriously, thank all of you for being here. Given everything we've lost and how hard we've had to work just to keep living, it's asking a lot of you to swim all the way the hell to Senny Otie for no good reason at all."

"Sharks, sharks, sharks! Sharks, sharks, sharks!" came the reply, as the crowd leaned into the feel-good spirit of the school chant.

"Except there is a good reason after all. Maybe the best reason. We're going to swim this channel because it's what we islanders do. And we're gonna keep our nets full of mullet because that's what we do, too. We'll keep our boats running these waters, even if we have to row them our damn selves, because all of this is what we do. We've lost our museum and so many of our parents and grandparents who knew the old stories... but a whole bunch of them are written down and a whole bunch of you know them by heart. As long as we keep telling them... as long we keep living together in and with the Gulf... as long as we keep swimming to the old island... there's a reason to keep on with the keeping on. But if we ever stop swimming, surely all of us will drown."

"Never!" shouted a fired up Geoff McCloud.

Thomas, full-throated with a fist in the air, boomed, "We will never stop. Never!"

A thundering ovation drowned Thomas out before he could go further. Overcome, he joined the crowd and headed toward the water.

"Everyone that's able, come on down and we'll have an official start."

The emotionally charged islanders worked their way down the old concrete steps that led into the water and gathered around Thomas.

"As many of you know, in last year's race I famously destroyed the mayor, besting him in a feat of swimming excellence that some have called heroic."

A laughing crowd turned to look directly at Hayes. "There were extenuating circumstances," he protested.

"Doesn't that sound just like something a politician would say?" Thomas replied to the delight of the crowd. "Well this year our esteemed mayor seeks to settle the score, but I do not intend to go down without a fight." Thomas raised his arms above his head, then dropped them into a dramatic, exaggerated, bodybuilder pose. "If anyone thinks they can keep up, we'll go on the count of three. One... Two..."

Thomas dove into the water and swam for all his worth, while Hayes and the rest of the swimmers stood waiting for the *Three* that never came.

"Son of a bitch," Hayes said, shaking his head, before diving in to give chase.

A stampede of swimmers and floaters splashed forward, including a young woman known only to Ryland and Luke, with an abundance of red hair tucked neatly into her swimmers cap. She smiled at Luke and he smiled back. The moment was the culmination of a cloak and dagger operation conceived hastily as they were parting in the woods the day before, one

Ryland had been opposed to but still helped to affect. The boys had rowed across the channel again that morning before dawn, then hid her in the workshop under Luke's house until she could blend into the crowd at the swim. The exchange of smiles stopped Luke and Kinsey where they stood.

"Let's go," Ryland called back at them.

When they realized the race was leaving them, finally they turned and joined the swim.

Without swimmers from the University of Florida, triathletes, and other outsiders who swam these kinds of distances regularly, and with Luke and Ryland preoccupied with the girl from Sumner, the competitive race portion of the swim quickly became a three-man heat, Thomas narrowly holding onto a lead he had achieved via trickery, Hayes closing the gap, and Michael Johnson, Lida Maria's eighteen year old son, halfway between the two. Unlike Hayes' phantom broken fin from the prior year's race, Michael actually did have a blow out of the heal strap on his left fin. Not even the advantage of youth could overcome the loss of a fin when both of his challengers, excellent swimmers each, had two. In moments, Thomas and Hayes were a distance ahead of Michael that could not be closed in time.

Further back, the maritime parade of inflatables proceeded at a leisurely pace. Grab-assing and horseplay overtook even the most stoic among them. The light rain increased steadily such that by the time most had made it to the sandbar halfway across and stopped for a rest, they did so in a heavy downpour. Sunlight could still be seen as near as Seahorse Key to the west and Dog Island to the east, but the stretch of bay across which so many islanders were now transiting became a gully washer. The more it rained, the more joyful they all became—kids again in mud puddles when the world was a simpler place.

In the closing hundred yards to the white sand finish, Hayes reached deep for all of his available extra energy, making a frantic final push to pull dead even with his friend and rival. As he did, Thomas was waylaid by God himself when a blinding shaft of sunlight—somehow piercing the rain and haze—overtook him, pulling him into the trap of memory. He and Georgie were living in the churches across the street from one another again, a recovering Pentecostal masquerading as a Presbyterian and a sometimes Methodist adrift in the swamp together, spending student loan money on guitars neither could afford and Thomas could barely even play.

Hayes was racing past him then as Thomas turned back to watch the other swimmers, searching for his old friend in the waves and the rain, seeing only the new world before him. By the time the light faded back into the heavy weather, the race was lost.

"What happened?" Hayes asked as Thomas finally pulled himself onto the shore.

"Just taking it all in, buddy. Hell of a race."

"Rubber match next year?"

Thomas replied, "Count on it. I don't know how much longer we'll be able to hold off your nephew. He was even faster this year than last."

"For as long as we can," Hayes said defiantly.

Just then, Michael finished carrying the broken fin and looking annoyed. Before Hayes or Thomas had opportunity to speak, Michael said, "Did you see that?"

"See what?" asked Hayes.

"There!" Michael said, pointing at the edge of seagrass just beyond the white sand of the beach.

"No way."

Half of his bottom beak had been torn off. One of his wings was missing altogether. His left eye was clouded over and useless, and two broken toes made him wobble as he walked, but the tiniest scraggly-ass rooster any of the three men had ever seen was nevertheless before them, as regal as any noble in the gilded halls of Versailles. He made his way to the shore beside them to watch the other islanders finish the swim.

The winds of a storm had snatched him from his lowly station in the flock; the improbability of fate had made him king.

22

THE GIRL FROM SUMNER

For the next few weeks, Luke and Kinsey met most days on Leanna's peninsula, sometimes with Ryland and his longtime girlfriend Ava, often alone. She was so slightly built that she and Luke could ride comfortably together in the one-person kayak he had used to bring the bounty of white shrimp to the city park. Some days they would paddle it from the morning into the early evening, fishing and gathering clams and whelks, walking on the beaches of the barrier keys, chasing dolphins and sunsets. Even after Ryland offered one of the several kayaks at his mother's estate, so that she could have her own, Kinsey preferred to share with Luke.

While his father's relationship with Lizzy had seemed to comfortably appear one day without much fuss, Luke had not stopped fussing over Kinsey since their first armed encounter in the scrub.

"I could tell she liked me right from the start," Luke mused to Ryland.

"You think because she didn't shoot you it means she's into you?"

"Well, yeah, I guess."

"You might have your bar set a little low, buddy."

"I'm just saying, it's crazy right? There are so few girls on the island I thought I was gonna end up with some forty-year-old granny. And then suddenly a girl just pops up in the woods? It's gotta be fate, man."

"I guess she could have shot us pretty easy."

"Exactly," Luke said.

Kinsey made Luke feel comfortable and frantic at once—when they first held hands under the crooked palm tree on Cedar Point, where his dad's theater friends Tim Mueller and Shane Shamrock had once performed a two-man play to an audience that arrived by boat, it felt as though they had been doing it their whole lives and that his insides might also catch on fire. A few days later, with her head on Luke's chest as they lay on a blanket in the sand, Kinsey confessed she was instantly smitten with the way Luke had taken charge of the standoff in the scrub.

"Really?" Luke asked, excitedly.

"Yes really. There was just something reassuring about your voice. And when you offered to drag the deer out for me, it was all I could do to keep it together. I worried the whole time Ryland might still shoot me, but I knew right off that you never would."

"A gunfight would be a rough start to a romance," Luke joked.

"Is that what we're doing?" Kinsey asked.

"Doing what?"

"Romance."

"Oh," Luke said. "I just thought... I mean I didn't mean to presume, because obviously we haven't known each other very long but... in my defense... I guess I just meant..."

"I think the word you're looking for is *yes.*"

"Yes," he said.

"Yes for me, too," Kinsey replied, closing her eyes and squeezing Luke hard.

"Just like that?" Luke asked. "We're a thing?"

"Just like that, love."

And he did love her; with no reasonable basis for it and not nearly enough experience to know as surely as he did, he loved her. The end of the world had a way of compressing things into the urgency of the moment. With no expectations for the future, circumspection was a luxury they could not afford. Impulsiveness was a quality in Buck men passed from one generation to the next like a dominant gene, so Luke settled quickly into the idea that he and Kinsey would simply be together from then on and would work out the details as needed.

Kinsey knew something that Luke did not, however. So distracted was he by red hair that seemed always to be in his face, his mouth, and on his clothes, and by ruggedness belied by a feminine exterior he found so appealing, Luke had failed to notice how little Kinsey shared about her life in Sumner, how skillfully she sidetracked any inquiry about her family.

Luke had somehow fallen in love with a girl whose last name he had never thought to ask.

Even before they were informed about the certainly of all four chicks being hens, those finishing the Shark Swim had still been overjoyed at the sight of the pitiful rooster calmly watching the race alongside Hayes, Thomas, and Michael. In its sorry state, the rooster made no protest when Geoff McCloud, finishing third from last, picked it up and held it gently, an extension of his chicken bodyguard duties in the cemetery. There was no veterinarian on the island, but with the combined efforts of the biologist Mike Allenby and Nurse Toni at the clinic, some basic medical care was administered to the rooster. For the next few weeks, it lived with Geoff McCloud, who fed him by hand and nursed him back to relative health.

The story of how the rooster had come to be named King Arthur is a silly one. During the renovation of the old house on E Street, Thomas knocked down a wall in the central hallway, eliminating a small bedroom and converting the larger open area into a library and music room. The room contained the physical objects that held sentimental value to him: first editions of several books from Joseph Heller and Kurt Vonnegut, a signed copy of Faulkner's *The Sound and the Fury*, the rookie card—gifted to him from his dying friend Blue— of knuckleball pitcher R.A. Dickey, a collage of photos depicting himself, his father, and Luke each at seventeen years of age—the family resemblance as clear as the water from Spring River in Arkansas—the antique piano on which Luke played the most beautiful music, and, curiously, a ceramic figurine of a little boy named Arthur in an elaborate 19th century sleeping gown, pooping into an oversized teacup.

Thomas had not known when Annie gifted him the figurine that such a thing was called an *El Caganer*, meaning *The Pooper*, or that they were popular in the Catalonia region of Spain and were often placed into nativity scenes. He was delighted to learn that when the local council of Barcelona omitted El Caganer from the city's official nativity, decreeing it to be unsuitable for public display, a near revolt ensued. The citizenry viewed its removal as an attack on their cultural heritage and took to the streets, bending the government to the people's will and reinstating El Caganer to his rightful place on the throne.

Thomas' particular El Caganer Arthur had a strained, squinty look on his face that resembled the goopy-eyed countenance of the little rooster. It wasn't a far leap from Arthur to King Arthur when the rooster's convalescence inspired hope that he would indeed be able to serve the frustrated hens as their once and future king.

When it was decided that King Arthur was as healthy as he would ever be, arrangements were made to introduce him, in a controlled environment, to the hens. Until such time as a new generation of roosters came along, it was too risky to just turn him loose in the cemetery where an enterprising predator might carry him away. An oversized chicken tractor was constructed that allowed twenty hens at a time to live with their sovereign. Every few hours, it could be wheeled by the chicken guards to a new stretch of fresh ground for pecking. Geoff McCloud initially protested his rooster buddy being cloistered in such a way while most the of hens roamed free.

"I just don't like it," Geoff said.

"He was a sneeze away from dropping dead when we found him," Hayes replied. "You did a good job nursing him up, Geoff. He'll be in way better shape in his moveable chicken palace than he was on Senny Otie."

Thomas interjected, "I think he's got a pretty sweet gig. Twenty girls at a time, and they get rotated out for new ones every week or so."

"Fine," said Geoff. "But eventually he'll go free, right?"

"Of course," said Hayes. "He's got the best job in town and he can even screw his way into an early retirement."

Suzy Coles, never one to waste an opportunity for community building, and without a current project to occupy her time, planned a celebration of the rooster's return to health and reunion with the hens.

"We can't have a king without a coronation," she said to the town council.

Hayes put his hand over his mouth to stifle a laugh.

"Oh you hush, Hayes," she said. "I'm being serious."

"Oh trust me, I know you are."

"The purpose of a monarchy is to give the kingdom something that binds them together. A shared heritage."

"It's a rooster," Slim Worthman said, rolling his eyes.

"It's the rooster king," Suzy shot back, "And we're going to have a fucking coronation."

On the day of the coronation, Thomas drove Geoff McCloud and King Arthur to the cemetery in his golf cart. As they turned off Gulf Boulevard and made their way past Lieutenant Crawford's tomb, climbing the little hill leading to the fenced-in chicken area, they saw it—a row of people down each side of the road, dressed to the nines, shouting *long live the king!* There were islanders and hens as far as either man, and certainly much farther than the one-eyed king, could see.

"This is wild," Geoff said, scratching the top of Arthur's head and feeling, by association, that he was somehow royal, too.

"I love it," Thomas replied. "I love this town so very much."

Geoff embraced his role as caretaker of the king and became the gate-keeper to Arthur's palace. He was inundated with questions about the sexual habits of the rooster and his hens, from folks he passed on the street and the dozens each day that stopped by the cemetery to see for themselves. To disseminate information more efficiently, he brought a giant white board and dry erase marker from his father's house and nailed it to a tree in the chicken enclosure. On it was a dated column labeled *The King's Consummations* wherein he placed a mark for each time the rooster mounted a hen and furiously pumped her cloaca. Because Arthur had been the runtiest of all the roosters before the storm, he had never been allowed to fertilize a hen. In the first week he was penned up with twenty hot birds, he nearly killed himself from over-exertion, dehydration, and joy as he serviced his harem from dawn and into the night, even sneaking up behind them as they slept on the roosting pole to give them the fertilizer that would hopefully save the island.

While the rest of the island was preoccupied with the reality show of King Arthur's every movement, Luke and Kinsey continued to be consumed with one another. In the woods and on the water, a playful competitiveness drove them to try to outhunt and outfish each other. A lifetime of experiences were compressed into the month since they first met in the scrub. As September rolled into an unusually cool October, they sat most nights by a fire on the peninsula that had become their home base.

"At some point we're gonna have to spill the beans about us," Thomas said.

"What's the hurry? Everything is perfect just like it is."

"I want my dad to meet you, and Mr. Hayes and the others."

"If it doesn't go like we hope, I'm afraid all this will end."

"Don't be silly," Luke said, talking fast. "Who couldn't like you? You're funny and nice and a badass to top of that. And we're doing okay on the island. We've got running water and eggs every day and there's a little cottage no one's using a block from my dad's house. It was a vacation rental before... they called it the Wabi-Sabi Cottage, which I'm not sure what that's all about but it's nice and looks like something from a story book. It's pretty small but we wouldn't need much room."

"Sweet boy, take a breath," she said, unable to hide a smile that spread the width of her face. "You'd want to live with me?"

"Huh? I mean, obviously. I love you."

The moment froze in place. Clearly, they were in love but neither had braved to say it out loud before. Luke, especially, had been waiting for a big moment to say it for the first time, and was embarrassed to have blurted it out in such an inartful way.

"I'm sorry. I didn't mean for it to go like that."

"Obviously I love you, too," she said.

"You do? Ok, cool. Yeah... good. Shit. I don't know what's wrong with me. You get me all turned around."

"You're perfect," she said, pulling him down onto her on the blanket by the fire, her sweetness morphing into something as wild as the scrub where they met, elemental and destructive as the storm that took Jonah, a power she had not known she possessed until that moment with Luke, who, left with only one reasonable thing to do in the moment, closed his eyes and let it happen, knowing from then on there could be nothing to distract him from the purpose he found there for his life—to face the new world with the boldness required to bend it to his will, to be undistracted from the work to make a life with Kinsey, to do all in his power to make the island a place where she could be safe and happy, where—and this thought surprised him most of all because he had never contemplated such a thing before—they could raise children that looked like her and would be as comfortable in the woods and water as their parents, at home in the measured theory and immeasurable soul of the music he would teach them on his father's piano, feral and refined at once, a start on the next generation of islanders who would hear stories about the wonders of the old world too fantastic to believe, and still too feeble to inspire envy because they lived daily in the supernatural splendor of the Gulf.

As they lay entangled on the blanket, their clothes strewn about, the fire began to wane and a chill moved over them.

"I better tend to this fire before it goes out," Luke said.

"One more minute, before things change," she replied.

"This is how it will be from now on," he said, getting up to gather more wood, too caught up in the dreamscape to recognize the worry in her voice.

"Remember in the woods when I asked if you were gonna burn my house down and kill my dogs?"

"I do. But I would never…"

"I know, I know," she interrupted. "Didn't you wonder why I asked about that specifically?"

Luke replied, "Just cause of what happened in Sumner, and you live there."

"Well, yeah, but not just that."

"Whatever it is, Kinsey, just say it. Whatever it is, it doesn't even matter. It can't matter. Nothing matters ever again except you and me."

"Meade," she said. "My name is Kinsey Meade. I don't know how it took this long for it to come out."

"Oh."

"Yeah."

"That's why you didn't want me to meet your family."

"The thing is," she said, talking as fast as Luke a few moments before, "I'm not even from here. I'm not a part of whatever feud is going on. I was visiting from Atlanta when everything went to hell and I just got stuck here. My family is related somehow to the men you killed, but I don't even know them. And by all accounts they probably had it coming."

"I didn't kill anyone over there," Luke protested.

"The men the islanders killed. I heard about your preacher. It was a bad thing they did. But what happened on Shiloh Road was bad, too, Luke."

"My dad says they had to send a message or the Meades would never stop coming for us."

"That may be true. I'm sure it is true. But there were so many, Luke. Some that didn't have anything to do with any of it. It took three days to bury everyone."

"Did you have to help?"

"I did," she said, looking away.

"That's awful."

"There's nothing for me in Sumner. I was visiting a cousin there and then the world went crazy. She died right after. She was sick before. That's why I came in the first place. When her meds ran out she went so fast, Luke."

"Have you heard anything from your parents back home?"

"Nothing. Nobody seems to hear anything from anywhere. That's the scariest part."

"My mom was in New York. Sometimes I imagine she found a way out or some other possible way she's still alive..."

"Oh Luke..."

"But I know she's gone. There comes a point where hope hurts more than no hope."

"I've been hoping somehow that all of this would just never come up and we could live right here at Ryland's mama's house for the rest of our lives. But I knew it had to."

"I don't care about any of it, Kinsey."

"I don't either, but it doesn't only matter if we care. People are gonna care a lot, on both sides of the channel. I barely know the aunt I've been living with. She's nice enough, I guess, but she's only got one rule, and I keep breaking it."

"What's that?"

"Keep away from the island. Keep away from the islanders."

"Is it still that bad over there? Folks are that set against us?"

"I think it will be for a long time, Luke. I don't know anyone over there that wasn't close to somebody that got killed," Kinsey replied. "The last few times I headed here to meet you, I'm sure I was being followed. I took a crazy path through the scrub and lost them, but if anyone knew I was coming here to see you... "

"What?" Luke asked.

"I can see that blowing up into something, is all. And I'm not so sure when you introduce me as a Meade that we'll get a warm reception on your side of the channel either."

"Then just don't be a Meade anymore. Done. Easy."

"Just like that?"

"Just like that. Why not?"

"If not a Meade, then who would I be?"

"Whoever you want to be, I guess."

Kinsey smiled and shook her head. "Try again, Luke. Who should I be?"

"Mine. You'll be mine."

"Deal," she said, pulling him back onto the blanket.

"What about the fire?" Luke asked.

"We won't need it."

The next morning, Luke and Kinsey held hands as they walked to Leanna's concrete boat ramp and set out to the west—paddling across the channel together.

23

— · —

A Prom to Remember

The end of the world is tough on the school calendar. The year the smokestacks fell, the entire spring semester was lost. In the face of nuclear fallout, gun battles with armed invaders, a catastrophic fire, and a once-a-century hurricane, neither of the two seniors remaining at the Cedar Key School would have ever made an issue about missing their senior prom. Because the island has the smallest public school in the state, it had long been a badge of honor for the community to fill in the gaps in funding and personnel required for their students to receive the highest level of educational experience possible. The school had always functioned as the heartbeat of the island and no one seemed willing to let it slip into arrhythmia over something as trivial as societal collapse. Whether they wanted one or not, Annabelle Douglas and Cado Bollins were getting a prom.

If Luke and Kinsey's romance trended Shakespearean, the on-again off-again rapport between Annabelle and Cado skewed low-budget professional wrestling. Seldom had two people ever been less suited for one another while still choosing to punish themselves with continued interaction. Annabelle was bookish and worldly, less from traveling than spending most of her free time in the library. She wore flowered dresses and pearls, volunteered in the community, and used words on purpose that she knew

Cado did not know. Cado had worked on crab boats since he was ten years old, dressed always as though he had just stepped off a working boat, and spoke with a gravel-voiced affectation evoking Randy *Macho Man* Savage. Thomas occasionally hired Cado for patching holes in clam bags or building clam belts for planting, appreciating the younger man's eccentricities.

"Yeah boss... need to get that paycheck," Cado would say anytime he passed Thomas in town.

"You gotta do some work first, Cado."

"Yeah boss. Say the word and I'll knock that shit out quick. You know I will. I do it all so don't go paying Levi or Bernie for nothing cause I'll work them into the ground, boss."

"10-4 Cado."

Something about the idea of a prom, a thing utterly removed from the trials of survival, began to resonate with the islanders. There was a dehumanizing quality to subsistence living that served as a constant reminder of what the flash across the bay had taken from them. Frivolity is dangerous when there isn't enough to eat, so there could only be a prom for Annabelle and Cado because some measure of stability had begun to return to their lives. The more the folks in town heard about the prom, the more they wanted to help make it happen. At a planning session at the school, Suzy Coles posited a thought that began as mere logistics and morphed into a cause for excitement all around the island.

"Obviously voting for prom king and queen is a moot point, but with just the two seniors and one junior, how will there be a prom court or enough people to make it a real dance?"

"Dang, I guess I hadn't thought of that," replied Principal Mitchell.

Thomas, Mike Allenby and the other members of the School Advisory Council looked around at each other, hoping someone else would speak up. When no one did, Thomas mused out loud, "There's so few of us left, why don't we make the prom open to everyone? Cado and Annabelle are king and queen, and we could all be their loyal prom subjects."

"That's funny," Mike said.

A light twinkled in Suzy's eyes. "I don't think it's funny. I think it's genius."

"You think the kids want a bunch of old people at their prom?" Mike asked.

Thomas was suddenly converted to his own idea. "Annabelle is eighteen going on thirty-five. Most of her friends are grownup and she's better read than all of us. I'd let her do my taxes if the IRS was still a thing. Cado will have to be hog tied and drug into the prom to go at all, so he won't mind if we're all there to make it a big party."

Mike said, "I wouldn't mind a night of dancing with the wife. Maybe somebody's sitting on a reserve of booze somewhere and will spike the punch."

"Now we're talking," Thomas replied, his own store of bourbon exhausted days before.

"I'm gonna just pretend I didn't hear that part," Principal Mitchell said, smiling. "But if we're serious about this, I'm game. I'll just have to run it by the county superintendent to make sure they approve."

An instant burst of gallows laughter filled the room.

Luke and Kinsey's worry about their reception on the island proved to be misplaced, at least initially. The political and homeland security concerns about a Meade girl sitting in Thomas's living room were brushed aside by the simplicity of a father's joy upon seeing his son smiling—the whole-body smile that cannot be elicited with a joke or passing moment of ease—for the first time since his arrival on the island after the ordeal in Gainesville.

"Meade, dad. Like the Sumner Meades."

"I don't care if she's a Sumner Bin-Laden," Thomas replied, noticing the way Kinsey clung to Luke's arm and looked at his boy with an affection so innocent and unmolested that any other reaction would be impossible. "She's a guest in our home. And it seems like she likes you, so she's obviously mentally disturbed and needs our help. We can't turn her away."

"That's not funny, dad."

"It's kind of funny," Kinsey replied.

"I'm being serious. We're gonna be together and I need to know if that's okay with you cause if it's not we'll take our chances across the channel."

The moment of disappointment in his father's eyes was a stinging rebuke.

"Alright, son. Careful. If you can think of a single instance, in the entirety of your brief little stint on Earth, when I haven't had your back... right, wrong, or indifferent, then keep on with your little speech. I'm all ears."

"Dad... I'm sorry. I just..."

"It's fine, Luke. If you'll just slow down a little you'll realize how unnecessary this is."

"I know. Obviously I know. That was shitty of me. I guess I'm worried about what Mr. Hayes and everyone else has to say."

"It doesn't matter, son. The world's so small these days, you gotta take love where you find it."

Kinsey chimed in, "Are you for real, Mr. Buck? Do you really talk like that?"

"You'll get used to it," Luke said. "Sometimes I think he's writing his next play out loud and just trying out dialogue in real life."

"Listen, you little shit. That is not true," Thomas protested, smiling.

"Calm down, big shit. I'm just trying to take love where I find it, like you said."

Thomas let the lightness linger for a moment then shifted the mood back to the business before them. "Let's be serious for a minute. Kinsey, did you come here to kill us?"

"No sir."

"Will anyone in Sumner be coming for you when they realize you're gone?"

"Honestly... maybe. I don't know. If they did it wouldn't be for me, though. All they ever talk about over there is revenge. My name might be enough to rile them up, but I'm barely any more a Sumner Meade than you or Luke."

"Fine," Thomas said. "If Luke believes you, I believe you. Whatever comes from Hayes and the council and anyone else... the three of us will handle it together."

Kinsey smiled because she knew then that both Buck men would make a stand for her in a way that no one across the channel had or ever would.

"Just like that?" she asked, parroting Luke when they first discussed the possibility of romance.

"Just like that," Thomas replied. "Unless you need to fight about it a little to make it seem real."

"I'm good. But when you write this scene into your next play, make me sound cooler than I did in real life."

"You're plenty cool," Thomas replied.

"You're perfect," Luke said, pulling her close to him in a hug that lasted long enough to put the moment on edge, Kinsey pressing back against him in a way that said for him to hold on a moment longer, then another, while Thomas first surveyed the scene with placid contentment, wishing Lizzy was there to see it with him and not working in the community garden on Second Street with Cousin and Lara, then feeling a mix of guilt and nostalgia as the simple expression of love between the young people in his living room made him aware of his own heart's beating—his mitral and tricuspid valves closing with a solid *lub-dub* as predictable as the rhythm of the life with Lizzy that had at last saved him from despondency, but also, fainter, the next *lub-dub,* as hisaorta and pulmonary valves closed a sixteenth-beat askew from the proper meter, just as he and Annie had been so often out of time with one another and yet, in moments too infrequent to sustain a life, still exploded across the cosmos in sweet dissonance together—as every additional moment his son held the girl from Sumner, with the dazzling red hair and porcelain skin that so favored Luke's mother, became a universe unto itself—the energy of creation racing away from the hopelessness of Annie and Franklin on the dirt road and back to the family expanding before him.

When the long embrace was over, Kinsey grabbed Luke's hand and said softly, "Thank you honey. So what now?"

"What's the move, dad? Should we talk to the council? If no one else has claimed the Wabi-Sabi, I think it could be perfect for us."

"I'll go talk to Hayes privately first, then we'll bring it to the council. I'm sure we can work it out."

Hayes' first instinct was of course happiness for his friend's boy because Luke was his friend, too. His next, predictably, was to worry about the political nuance of the thing.

"First," Hayes began, "I trust Luke and I trust you. If you vouch for the girl that's enough for me. Suzy, too, and probably Nan. So if it came to a vote we likely have the numbers. It's gonna get slippery with Worthman and Rosencrantz. Since they were opposed to bringing down the bridge... and took a heaping of ridicule for it... I think it'll be natural for them to look sideways at bringing somebody in when we've worked so hard to keep everybody else out. And her last name just cranks the heat up on the whole deal."

"That makes sense," Thomas replied.

Hayes rubbed his chin as he thought out loud, "Weird to think about it on a town level, but this is an immigration issue."

"That does sound weird."

"When Big John set off that dynamite, we were essentially closing our border. We just never made any rules for crossing it. When those fellas came over and got Folksy, we treated it like an act of war and used it to justify what we did on Shiloh Road."

"Whether what we did over there was right or wrong is a different discussion," Thomas replied, though he had long since passed judgement on the affair and was serving daily a sentence he never expected to end.

"Well it is and it isn't, Thomas. The way I see it, and how I think a lot of folks see it, is that once we blew up the bridge, we were separating ourselves from the mainland as sure as attacking Fort Sumter separated South Carolina from the United States."

"So we seceded from the Union?"

"Don't be dramatic. Besides, there doesn't seem to be much of a union left to secede from. We've definitely been making decisions like the only thing that matters is on our side of the Number Four Channel."

"That can't last forever," Thomas said. "We've been lucky. I know how hard we've worked for what we have, but we're still a few bad breaks away from everything falling apart."

"We're doing fine," Hayes protested, a quick scowl spreading across his face.

"Are we?" Thomas asked. "If that little rooster hadn't wandered up, we'd be somewhere on the mainland now trying to get another one. Luke met Kinsey hunting in the scrub in Sumner. Look, I'm glad we took the bridge down. It was a necessary stop gap. I even believe we had to get Little Don or more islanders were gonna die, but..."

Thomas paused to find the right words—a thing he seldom had to do—because he knew the plan they executed in Sumner had come from his friend.

"But what, Thomas?"

"It wasn't your fault. Maybe it wasn't anybody's fault but Little Don's. None of us had ever been in that position before. We just started firing when we saw him. I don't think anyone consciously decided to kill all those people."

The defensiveness Thomas expected from his friend didn't materialize. Instead, Hayes was reflective in his reply. "I guess that's what I'm getting at. What we did over there was rough, no doubt about it... but it's done. If Folksy's murder wasn't the start of a war, what we did in return surely was. And since nothing's been done to end the war, we got to proceed like it's still on. Especially when it comes to the border."

"I know my son, Hayes. He's impulsive and emotional. Like his dad. Like my dad and his dad, too. He'll leave the island if she can't stay."

"And I guess you'd go with him?"

"What kind of a father would I be if I didn't?"

"It's not gonna come to that," Hayes said. "We've just got to come up with a plan that doesn't put us at risk."

"We can't stay holed up here forever. It was a nice thing to think about, but the demographics don't work long-term."

"It's working for now," Hayes said, indignantly.

"But is it really?"

The question was meant as a provocation, but Hayes had been pushed on the issue enough. He changed the subject abruptly, purposefully. "You going to this prom tonight? I thought I'd take Tabby."

"Lizzy and I were gonna go if you guys went."

"Good," Hayes replied. "Have Luke bring his girl, too. Everyone can get a look at them together and get all the gossip out of their system before we get the council together."

Annabelle Douglas wore her mother's eighteen-year-old white satin prom dress. Wendy Douglas had kept it all these years because it was the dress she was wearing the night Annabelle was conceived. Something about her daughter wearing it now felt strange, given how clearly she remembered it crumpled in the floorboard of Henry Douglas' pickup truck in the back of the cemetery by the water, but prom dresses were as rare now as roosters on the island. She was determined that her daughter would have as magical an evening at the prom as she had, though the thought of Cado getting anywhere near the dress filled her with anxiety.

As expected, Cado Bollins had no intention whatsoever of attending the prom. His stepmother Jonya coerced him into it with threats of violence and extra chores if he ruined prom for Annabelle and everyone else in town. When he arrived at the school's auditorium dressed in jeans and a fishing shirt, but with his hair combed back and carrying wildflowers for Annabelle, a collective sigh of relief swept through the room. When he saw her in the white dress, her auburn hair pinned up and uncovered shoulders moving elegantly as she walked in her mother's heels, Cado abandoned the pretense of not wanting to be there. Suddenly he was focused on wanting to dance with her and lamenting that no one had ever taught him how to dance.

As she often did in her life, Annabelle took charge of the situation, crossing the makeshift dance floor and heading toward Cado at the door. The adults in the room parted like the Red Sea moving aside for Moses. Cado had no time to defend himself; quickly he was drug by his beltloop to the center of the room, pulled close to the girl in the white dress, and was, to his and everyone's surprise, suddenly gliding around the room to Jim Walcox's bluegrass cover of a Taylor Swift Song.

"Dang, girl, slow down I don't even know how to dance."

"And yet, here you are Cado... dancing."

"I feel like everybody's looking at me."

"Mostly they're looking at me," Annabelle said. "I'm the prom queen after all."

"How do you know?"

"Well it's either me or you, honey."

"Aww hell. That makes sense. I'm an idiot."

"You're not," she said, pivoting from assertive to nurturing in the manner of all southern women worth a tinker's damn. "Listen to me, Cado. I won't have you talking yourself down like that. You're plenty smart. We're smart in different ways is all. I know things you don't know and you know plenty I could never wrap my head around."

"Why are you being so nice to me, Annabelle?"

"Cause you're the king, dummy. Now shut up and dance with me."

"You can call me dumb but I can't?"

"See, you get it just fine, honey."

Cado smiled, then dared to spin his girl and dip her like he had seen on television, his heart beating double time because she had twice called him honey.

While the room was focused on the king and queen, Luke and Kinsey arrived quietly with Thomas and Lizzy. If the plan had been to not make a scene, Kinsey's flood of red hair and surprising curves in the borrowed dress was its undoing. As soon as Jim hit the last chord of the song, all eyes shifted from the dance floor toward the young couple by the punch bowl. The good news was that no one knew Kinsey. The bad news was that no one knew Kinsey. The room full of probing eyes made her feel as though she was on trial.

Who is this girl?
Where did she come from?
Who said she was allowed to be here?

Kinsey and Thomas could feel the unsaid questions hurling in their direction. He squeezed her hand and whispered in her ear, "Don't worry. I've got you."

"I hope so," she said. "What do we do now?"

Luke surveyed the room, felt the uneasiness of all assembled, and took decisive action. "Hello, everyone," he announced loudly. "This is my girl Kinsey. She's going to live with me here on the island. If anyone has any objection, step up and say so and we can talk about it."

Several dead moments sat heavy in the room but no one came forward.

"Well alright," Luke announced. "If Mr. Jim will play us another tune, we'll see you on the dance floor."

"That's one way to handle it," Hayes said to Thomas.

"He's always been a talk first, think later kind of guy," Thomas replied.

"Hard to imagine where he could have gotten that from."

"Alright, Mr. Mayor. You gonna keep gibbering or you gonna grab your girl and dance?"

So it was that public sentiment was swayed toward the new couple, who danced for hours until Jim Walcox's fingers ached from playing. When he stopped for breaks, Luke took his place and kept the music going. Eighty-one-year-old Miss Gettie, who was waiting tables at Denny Gal's breakfast cafe on the day of the flash, danced circles around even the students, lost in the joyful reprieve of the prom. As the evening drew to a close, the king and queen took a final spin around the dance floor as Luke played a surprising guitar version of a song from *Phantom of the Opera*, one refrain from it holding particular meaning to him since the standoff in the scrub:

> *Say you'll share with me*
> *One love, one lifetime*

Let me lead you from your solitude.

Luke was singing to Kinsey and every islander one to another—music pushing into and against the night— as the magic Wendy Douglas had hoped for her daughter hung in the air of the school auditorium and followed them all home after.

Rolf and Jenna Alverez's home in the old Croft's house near the channel was a solid two miles from the Cedar Key School. They had become accustomed to walking this distance and back most days of the week, but when the prom ended Thomas and Lizzy offered them a ride home in their golf cart. Jenna's voluminous dress and high heels made her decision to accept an easy one. The four friends laughed together on the short ride, still basking in the joy of the evening. As they passed the Tiki Hut and Low-Key Hideout Motel, they all saw it at once—the sharp orange glow illuminating a billow of smoke reaching toward the heavens.

"Son of a bitch," Thomas said, slamming on the cart's brakes. "Jenna, Lizzy, get out here and run back to the motel and wait out of sight until we get back."

"I'm going with you," Lizzy said.

"Sweetheart... I'm not asking. I know Rolf's carrying but I've only got one gun in the glovebox. If they're waiting for us up there, you won't be any good unarmed."

"You should get the others," Jenny said.

"There's no time," Thomas replied sharply. "Cousin had guard duty tonight with Miss Bette. We have to get to them."

Rolf cast an uncharacteristically stern look toward his wife. "Honey, out."

When they neared the channel, both men were relieved to see that the fire was not from the Croft's house and no ambush seemed to be waiting for them. A pile of logs and branches and been arranged into a bonfire that sent flames thirty feet into the air, but whoever had arranged them was gone.

"Do you hear that?" Rolf asked.

"I don't hear anything."

"It's coming from the guard shack."

"Go!"

As they sprinted the rest of the way from the Croft's house to the channel, Cousin's muffled yelling grew louder. With guns at the ready, Rolf and Thomas burst into the door of the shack, finding Cousin and Miss Bette's hands zip-tied and the two women bound together, back to back, with rope.

"Are you okay?" Thomas asked.

"We're fine," Miss Bette said. "Just get us out of all this."

Rolf cut the thick zip-ties with his pocketknife while Thomas worked at the ropes.

"They were actually pretty nice," Cousin said.

Thomas was incredulous. "How did this happen? They were nice when they tied you up? Where are the rifles?"

"Their faces were covered," Miss Bette said. "So I couldn't see who they were, but one of them called us both by our names. I feel a little embarrassed about how it happened, but we're not real soldiers. We were paying attention and keeping a watch on the water. One second everything was fine and the next there were two men pointing guns at us. It happened so fast we couldn't do anything except hand them our rifles when they asked nicely for them."

"I'm just glad you're okay, Miss Bette," Thomas said. "You could have gotten the same treatment as Folksy."

"Did they say what they were here for... what they wanted?" Rolf asked.

Free of her bindings, Cousin spoke up, "They said they were here to leave a message, not to hurt anyone."

Thomas said, "I've got a cart by the fire. Come with me and we'll drive you home."

"What fire?" Miss Bette asked.

Rolf said, "Follow me."

They had missed it in the excitement of their arrival a few minutes before. Just in front of the fire, hauntingly illuminated against the black sky and still water of the channel, was a makeshift flagpole buried in the ground. At its top hung half of a white bed sheet.

"Is that a surrender flag?" Rolf asked. "Why would they do that? Is that the message they came to send?"

Thomas pulled the cart alongside the pole, then climbed atop its roof so he could reach the flag that was drooping in the still night air. "I don't think so," he replied, as he stretched the flag out, revealing a rudimentary skull and crossbones drawn with a black marker. In red block letters below it was a single word:

OBADIAH

24

SHIP OF THE LINE

Emotions were high at the emergency council meeting. The normally reserved Hayes was understandably worked up because it had been his cousin and mother that were tied up in the guard shack. Worthman and Rosencrantz used the situation, predictably, to rail against the removal of the bridge.

In an arrogant tone laid on extra thick as a retaliation for the public rebuke he had taken for his vote on the bridge, Slim said, "Twice now they've come across the channel to attack us. Some good it did us to blow up our only lifeline to the mainland. I said it then and I'll say it again, you people made a big mistake."

Suzy Coles was having none of it. "Two attacks in all these months. How many more would there have been if they could just walk right over? Like always, Slim, you've missed the point altogether. The bridge is gone. You whining about it now isn't helpful. We need to figure out what all this means and how we should respond."

No one had yet deciphered what the ominous Obadiah flag meant, but all manner of theories were floated. Anne Stephens, the longtime steward of the island's public library, referenced a series of children's books from the 1960s featuring an aspiring young pirate named *Obadiah the Bold* in her suggestion that the flag could be a warning an attack was coming from the sea. When pressed about why she thought attackers would give a warning about their plans, she withdrew her suggestion.

The Baptist minister could not resist an opportunity to predict God's judgement for the island just as the prophet Obadiah had done for the Edomites in the Bible. Recounting a ham-fisted version of the story devoid of historical context or even a reconciliation between it and the new covenant of grace promised through Christ in the New Testament, Pastor Willy assured those assembled for the meeting that God was angry. He quoted from the fourth verse of the first chapter of the Book of Obadiah in a laughably ominous tone, "Though thou exalt thyself as the eagle, and though thou set thy nest among the stars, thence will I bring thee down, saith the Lord."

Had Folksy or Father Mavis been among them, Pastor Willy's brimstone would have met a vigorous theological rebuttal. In their absence, Thomas felt he could not hold his tongue.

"Imagine how mad he must have been at you to burn *your* church down and none of the others."

A hush swept across the room as the pastor struggled to formulate a response.

Thomas, angered by the presumption and smug self-assurance of the churchless pastor, doubled down. "If you'll have us believe that God is behind every bad thing that happens, then he's got some answering to do for a hell of a lot more than a homemade flag."

Before the situation could escalate further, Mark David intervened. "Obadiah Meade," he said gruffly.

Anytime Mr. Mark spoke at a public gathering, especially while mayor before his son Hayes had taken over, even people who might be predisposed to oppose him stopped what they were doing and listened carefully.

"Who's that, dad?" asked Hayes.

"A good man that lived in Cedar Key when most of the town was still over on Senny Otie... the father of the whole Meade line. He took a bullet at the Battle of Station Four. Worked at the sawmill after the war."

"What's all this mean, dad? How do you know so much about it?"

"I caught Little Don breaking into the fish house when he was about Luke's age. Hank was with me. We roughed him up pretty good but did him the favor of not calling the police. He wouldn't have gotten such an ass-whooping if he would have just shut up and took his medicine. But he just kept going on and on about how my family didn't belong on the island any more than his. How his great great, hell I don't remember how many greats, grandpa was a hero in the yankee war. How his birthright meant he had a right to what was mine... what I had worked for. I didn't think much of it at the time. I was pretty worked up about him breaking my window and trying to rob me, and pretty focused on kicking the shit out of him... but it stuck with me so I started digging into it. The Meades used to be a great family on the island."

Hayes asked, "You think the Obadiah flag is the Meades telling us the island belongs to them?"

"Well I don't think it's a little boy pirate and I sure don't think God had anything to do with it."

"It makes sense," Thomas said. "It makes more sense than anything else."

Rolf spoke up from the back, "How many of them could there be left? Between that day on the island and the next day on Shiloh Road, we got a pile of them."

"They're like roaches," Mark said. "Kill all you want and there's always more coming."

Hayes was trying to piece it all together. "But why'd they just tie up Cousin and Mom and not kill them like they did Folksy?"

Mark replied, "Your mama said they called them both by name. If that's true maybe they worried what I'd do to them if they hurt my wife and niece. Or maybe there's some southern decency in 'em after all and they couldn't do it cause they were women."

At a moment when a plausible explanation for the invasion had come to light, when no one was thinking about the girl he had brought across the channel to the island, Luke stood to his feet, his voice faltering a little but not his resolve, and said, "Mr. Mark..."

"Yes sir, Luke... you have something for us?"

Hayes and Thomas looked anxiously at each other, sensing what the boy was about to do.

"Your explanation about Obadiah Meade makes a lot of sense, and maybe that's exactly what this is about... but there might be something else."

"What is it?"

"The girl you all saw me with at the prom last night. The woman I love and that I'm going to marry and make a life with..."

Luke paused to consider how best to say what he had stood to say.

Mark said, "Come on son, out with it."

"Her name is Kinsey, sir. Kinsey Meade."

Audible gasps filled the room. Raised voices and insults brought Thomas and Hayes to their feet, ready to come to Luke's defense.

Mark yelled above the commotion, "Alright that's enough. Pipe down. Luke, get up here."

Luke made his way to the front of the room, stopping just in front of the elder David.

"So you mean to tell me... when my wife and niece were tied up at gunpoint, almost certainly by a damn Meade, that you brought a Meade here to the island?"

"Yes sir. She's not one of them, though. She was down from Atlanta when the smokestacks fell. I told my daddy and Mr. Hayes right away. We were gonna bring it to the council the next day after the prom. She's a good person and I love her and if she isn't welcome here then neither am I."

"That's really what you have to say for yourself?"

"Yes sir, it is."

Mark David looked the boy up and down. To his credit, Luke looked the older man directly in the eyes without shrinking away.

"Come here," Mark said, extending his arm and pulling Luke beside him in a sideways hug. "That was pretty damn brave, Luke. I'm not sure I could have done that. Your daddy fought the Meades beside me in front of Fannie's, and he went after them in Sumner. If you and him say your Meade girl's good, that's plenty for me."

Turning to the crowd, Mark continued, "And if it's not good with any one of you, come see me about it."

A palpable silence lingered until finally Luke said, "If it means anything, she won't be a Meade for long."

"It means plenty, Luke."

Without waiting for approval from the council, but with Hayes' blessing, Luke and Kinsey moved into the Wabi-Sabi Cottage three houses down from Thomas. No decisive action was taken on anything at the emergency council meeting where Luke had stood for Kinsey. She had felt it best not to attend the meeting due to the heightened tension of the island's second invasion. This decision meant she had not witnessed Luke's gallantry on her behalf, but in the coming days and weeks nearly every woman she met that had been at the meeting told her the story with gushing admiration.

Thomas was instrumental in talking Hayes out of an impulsive counterstrike across the channel, noting that their actions on Shiloh Road were taken in response to the death of Folksy and this time no deaths had occurred.

"It was my mama, Thomas."

"I know. And if the roles were reversed I'm not sure any amount of reason could stop me from heading over there to get killed... because they're absolutely waiting for us this time."

"Then why are you lecturing me about the right thing to do?" asked Hayes.

"That's the difference between us. You can be reasoned with. One of us has to be the reasonable one and it sure as hell can't be me."

"That's the most reasonable thing you've ever said."

"Fair enough," Thomas said with a smirk.

The ease with which the two men had ambushed Cousin and Miss Bette made it clear that a pair of guards stationed where the bridge used to be was an insufficient defense against those across the channel that would seek to do the island harm. Hayes became fixated on hardening the island's defenses, instituting, with surprising unanimous consent from the council, a series of programs to make it safer. This included the building of additional guard stations and bulwarks at areas where landing crafts would not be thwarted by thick mangroves or other natural impediments, the outfitting of two golf carts with makeshift rifle turrets to create an armed fast-response unit, and regular military-style training for all able-bodied residents.

The islanders felt safer because they had something to do in support of their own well-being. Nothing unites a people like a common enemy or coalesces a collective identity like shared responsibility, so the net effect of the second invasion had been to improve daily life on the island. Each day an attack from the descendants of Obadiah Meade failed to materialize, the less likely it was to be successful.

Of all the new initiatives, none so occupied the attention of Hayes as the formation of a proper island navy. One thing the island had in abundance, besides clams and sublime sunsets on the western horizon of the Gulf, was boats. In addition to the fleet of birddogs and pleasure crafts in yards across the island, the giant blue metal drydock building at the Cedar Key Marina housed more than two hundred boats of every possible size and type. For their navy to be of much practical use, its boats would have to be propelled by something more reliable than the wind and faster than oars. Toward this end, the elder and younger Mitchell men began replicating Mr. Johan's wood gasifier design in various sizes, while Tony Hankle's barge was put into service hauling wood harvested from Senny Otie. When the sawmill operated during Obadiah Meade's tenure there in the late 1800s, the trees on the barrier key had been nearly eradicated. More than a century and a quarter of regrowth meant an abundance of trees in pine and oak, if not cedar.

For a man that had come of age on the water, it was unsurprising that Hayes David had a near obsession with the history of shipbuilding. From the earliest Egyptian shipbuilders dating back to 3,100 B.C., to the masterful Phoenician shipwrights, to the Spanish Armada, Hayes had a wide ranging base of knowledge that he brought to the task of assembling a navy for the island. Of all the great historical ships, however, his favorite came from the Age of Sail—the British Napoleonic *ship of the line*. The massive size of these vessels projected naval supremacy. In addition to being devastating warships, they also served as floating command centers for the fleet.

Hayes' favorite ship of the line was one of the most famous, the 104-gun HMS Victory. The 227-foot long vessel took six thousand trees to build and was manned by a crew of 821. It was launched into service in 1759 and distinguished itself in naval engagements for the next half century, notably during the first and second Battles of Ushant. While fishing on his first boat, Hayes would often sing British sea shanties while hauling in his nets, his favorite commemorating the Victory:

We'll rant and we'll roar like true British sailors
We'll rant and we'll roar along the salt seas
Until we strike soundings in the channel of Old England
From Ushant to Scilly, it's 35 leagues

One of Hayes' favorite things about his friendship with Thomas was that the two men could talk at length about an incredible array of subjects. He knew without asking that Thomas would know about the HMS Victory and the other great ships like it.

"I want to build a ship of the line, Thomas."

"What... why?"

"So it can been by anyone that might think about coming back across the channel. We could keep a rotating crew on it at all times, constantly patrolling."

"Do we even have the right kind of wood to build a ship, or anyone that knows how to do it? We'd need four times the number of people on the island to crew one of those things."

Hayes laughed. "Oh, hell, not an actual ship of the line. I just mean we need to put together our version of one—the biggest boat possible with what we have to use on hand."

Thomas' eyes lit up, not only at the idea now stirring in his head, but at the story behind it, when he and Hayes were new friends having their first real disagreement.

He said, "The houseboat."

"Whoa," Hayes replied.

"Right? It's perfect."

"The aft deck is plenty big to hold the biggest gasifier we could build."

Thomas asked, "Can you imagine how intimidating it would be for that big boat to be motoring through the channel, day and night, lit up like the old world?"

Little boy excitement overtook the mayor. "We could attach a pontoon barge on either side to make fighting platforms. The ones we use for the fireworks show on the Fourth of July."

"I dig the symbolism, obviously," Thomas said.

Work began almost immediately to convert the houseboat into the flagship vessel of the burgeoning Cedar Key Navy. On the day of the flash, so many of the captains and crews from the clam fleet had been pulled into the gray. Those that remained, like Joey Bannon, were eager to find purpose working on the water again and enthusiastically volunteered for service. It would take, by Hayes' figuring, two or three months for the gasifiers to be built, sufficient wood harvested, and twenty smaller crafts converted into the force of makeshift warships that would support the USS Blue Lang. During this time, the island expected an attack at any moment. Each day that passed before the fleet could set sail ratcheted up the tension for the islanders, and especially Hayes. Surely, he reasoned, the Meades would not have risked the invasion and planting of the Obadiah flag if they weren't planning something heinous. And yet, October drew to a close without incident.

For Halloween, many of the islanders met in the cemetery under a sturdy waxing gibbous moon, a few dressed in makeshift costumes. Because of the limited land area on the island, the cemetery had always functioned as a multi-purpose space. A boardwalk and walking trails skirted its boundary, and its frontage along the back bayou was a popular spot for fishing and picnics. Transplants from other places were taken aback by the amount of living that went on in the resting place of the dead. For the locals, it had just always been that way.

The lack of remaining candy on the island made trick or treating something of a bust, but little trinkets and scavenged toys were assembled from folks all across the island so the youngest islanders had something to look forward to. Seeing the young ones so excited for the tokens that would have been overlooked in the old world was a reminder of how much had changed in just nine months, not everything for the worst. With no video games, television, or Internet, the interconnectivity promised but seldom delivered by the digital age was on garish display in the moonlit graveyard, as the most recent generation of islanders hid, chased, and played among the headstones of their great grandparents.

While most of the town congregated in the cemetery, a small boat from Sumner worked its way through the backwaters behind Scale Key, past the Dog Island clam leases, and toward the muddy beach at the city park. Something about the mood of All Hallow's Eve put Cousin in a mournful state of mind. She had stayed for a short while to watch the children play in the moonlight, but left for a meandering walk that ended with her at the basketball court, staring up at the rim where TJ had breathed his last tortured breaths. She sat quietly on the cold cement, remembering the first moment she had seen him, standing like a thick oak but shivering with sapling nervousness as he waited for her to arrive for their first date. Cousin seldom cursed out loud, faithful to her church upbringing, but the sight of Grandaddy Bench Press in the shirt that was purposely a size too small overtook her. "There's a goddamn man," she thought, imagining even then how it would feel to melt into his massive arms.

They weren't all good memories. When it came to fighting, they approached the endeavor with the same electric hunger as their sex, both events as likely to draw blood as joy. Cousin closed her eyes and let them all in, laughing at how mad she had been when he left her in Key West on a lobster diving trip. When she opened her eyes at last, she saw the small fire burning on the beach and a single figure struggling to attach a bedsheet to a makeshift flagpole. The familiar skull and crossbones flickered in the orange light, above the word Obadiah as before.

Once a Marine, always a Marine was the kind of marketing hoopla that made Navy men like Thomas roll their eyes, but as it related to Samantha Maye the axiom rang true. Without hesitation, she began a tactical stalk toward the figure, sticking to the cover of the trees and shadows.

In moments she was upon him. In a few moments more, he lay incapacitated at her feet.

25

—·—

THE BOY FROM SUMNER

The Great Mobilization, as it would come to be known, began on Cedar Key. Everyone seemed to have some kind of job in the buildup of the island's defenses. Once John and Jimmy Mitchell produced the first working gasifier, after several failed attempts that slowly, through trial and error, taught the men which materials worked well and which ones did not, other folks were sent out across the island to gather components to produce the units needed for the boats in the new navy's fleet.

The flagship would require a larger gasifier to run the enormous boat. Smaller units could be reliably made with repurposed propane tanks of various sizes, but none of the tanks on the island were large enough for use in a unit that would power the USS Blue Lang's 225-horsepower motor and electric generator. For this unit, Luke and Ryland salvaged a metal water cistern from the ruins of the lighthouse on Seahorse Key that had been devastated by Hurricane Jonah. They and five other friends rowed the Judith Jane to the barrier island; even with such a sturdy crew they had considerable difficulty getting the giant tank onto the deck of the birddog.

As they worked on building and installing the unit on the flagship, John Mitchell, a man normally unworried by explosions, began to have concerns about the safety of running such a large, mostly untested gasifier on a boat full of people.

"I'm not saying it won't work," John said to the mayor. "I'm just not willing to say it definitely will, either. I feel pretty good about it being able to make the wood gas... but that stuff is just hydrogen and carbon monoxide and it's flammable as all hell. I'm worried about keeping those pressurized gases inside the unit and not blowing a hole through your boat and crew."

Hayes, normally a cautious man by nature, had since his mother and cousin's ordeal become singularly focused on launching the navy. "It'll either explode or it won't, but we've gotta get the flagship in the channel. I know you'll work it all out."

"We'll do our best, but I'd sure keep everyone off the back deck while this thing is cooking."

"Fair enough," Hayes replied.

Just as Cousin began dragging the unconscious figure through the sand, Officer Biscuit arrived in the park, coming to investigate the fire.

"Who you got there, Cousin?"

"Somebody from Sumner I guess. He was putting up another one of those flags."

"Is it one of the guys that tied you up?"

"No," Cousin replied. "I never saw the faces of the two guys in the guard shack, but they were bigger than this one."

"I'll stay here with him if you want to run down to the station and grab the chief and a few other fellas to help us move him."

"We can handle it," she replied, then started slapping the young man in the face and yelling, "Wake up, you piece of shit! Nap time's over."

In a few moments, he did come to, putting his hands near his face to block the blows and screaming, "Stop, stop! I didn't mean any harm. Stop hitting me!"

Cousin continued to pummel him, and Officer Biscuit looked away for a few more seconds before finally intervening to pull her away.

"I think he's had enough, Samantha Maye."

"I'm sorry. I just... I'm just so pissed off they got the drop on us when we were supposed to be on guard."

"That wasn't me, I swear."

"Pipe down," Officer Biscuit said, pulling him to his feet and cuffing his hands behind his back. "You'll get a chance to tell your story to the council."

"Jesus," Cousin said, catching a better look at his face in the moonlight. "How old are you?"

"Twenty-one."

"No way," she replied.

"Fine... I'm seventeen."

"Friggin' great. I choked a kid out and then beat him up."

"You didn't know," Officer Biscuit said.

"I will never live this down."

As they walked the Sumner boy toward city hall, three more Obadiah flags were being discovered around the island—in front of the Beachfront Motel, beside the concrete shark at the front entrance to the school, and right in the middle of the intersection of State Road 24 and 2nd Street. By the time the mayor, Chief Edwins, and the rest of the council were located and summoned to the emergency meeting, all four of the flags had been gathered up and were waiting at city hall. The oil lamps and candles cast ominous shadows around the meeting hall—the kind of setting where bad things happen quickly. The mood and panic of those assembled added to the foreboding.

"If it's an invasion we need to act now!" Hayes insisted.

The chief replied, "I've got my team and all the citizen deputies on armed patrol as we speak. One of the turret carts was finished this morning. Randal Solaro is manning the rifle while his daddy drives. If they're coming across the channel they'll let us know quick."

Mark David's voice rose above the commotion. "Based on where these flags were planted, it looks like they've given up on the channel and are hitting us from all sides."

"Get him up here," Hayes instructed.

Cousin led the boy to the council table.

Hayes asked sharply, "Why are you here?"

"Why are *you* here?" came the defiant reply.

"String him up," came a shout from the back of the room. The idea swept through the crowd and in the fervor of the moment began to take root as a reasonable course of action. A crabber reached for the boy, pulling at his shirt to free him from Cousin's grasp. Cousin yelled for him to stop but suddenly there were hands coming from every direction, pulling at the boy, pushing Cousin to the side. When she lost her footing and fell hard onto the ground, her uncle Mark drew his revolver from its holster and shoved the barrel hard against the forehead of the closest person grabbing at the boy, taking no notice who it happened to be.

The action in the room abruptly stopped. Mark David holstered his weapon and lifted his niece from the floor. The wild swing of emotion from mob fury to sobering reflection had elapsed in the span of less than thirty seconds, such was the dangerous atmosphere of the night. For another several moments, no one dared to speak. Finally, Hayes intervened.

"Let's start over. What's your name, son?"

"Elijah. But I sure as shit ain't your son."

"What's your last name, Elijah?"

In a provocative tone, he replied, "I think you already know that."

"Come on!" Geoff McCloud shouted. "Another bunch of Meades come here in the cover of night planting flags and we're gonna do nothing about it?"

Hayes snapped, "I didn't say we were gonna do nothing. I'm saying we ain't hanging anybody over a flag."

"We got a war on don't we?" came a question from the crowd.

"Maybe we do," Hayes shouted back. "But we're not gonna act like animals. You're not giving me much to work with here, Elijah. These folks are pretty worked up. What's the deal with the flags and the fires? Are they a signal for a landing party?"

"Why would I tell you if they were?"

"You're not in a position to ask me anything. Who sent you? We know who Obadiah Meade was. Doesn't seem like he was the kind of fella to tie up women at gunpoint."

"That wasn't supposed to happen," Elijah said, looking down.

"What Meade is in charge over there now? Is there an attack coming?"

Meekly, Elijah replied, "I've said all I can. Do whatever you're gonna do to me."

"Alright," Hayes said. "We don't have a jail, so... Chief, lock him up in your office until he's ready to talk."

The chief led Elijah away, who stared blankly forward, pulling hard at his handcuffs while he walked.

Hayes surveyed the faces in the room, noticed the mix of rage and fear, and understood he could not leave the moment hanging without saying something.

"He's just a kid," Hayes began.

"Bullshit, he's a Meade," came an angry reply.

"Okay, he's a Meade. But he ain't a full-grown Meade and just so you know right up front... nothing is going to happen to a kid on my watch, you understand?"

There was a collection of groans around the room, but the adrenaline was ramping down and cooler heads were beginning to prevail. They were not, in fact, animals, and absent the fear associated with a stranger and fires burning in the night, a semblance of civility began to return.

Hayes announced, "We'll keep on alert... let him sleep on things and see if he has anything else to say in the morning."

"What if he doesn't?" Slim Wortham asked.

"We'll all sleep on it, too, and see what the morning brings."

A few hours after everyone had gone home, save for Officer Biscuit who volunteered for the first prisoner watch, Luke Buck walked into the City Hall building.

"Evening, Luke."

"Hey Biscuit... how goes the duty?"

"It goes. Not too much excitement guarding a locked door."

"Lizzy thought it'd be a good idea to bring the kid a blanket and pillow and something to eat."

"Pretty funny hearing you call someone a kid, kiddo."

"That's fair. Anyway, you see any problem with me taking some food in to him?"

"I don't see the harm," Biscuit replied.

"I brought a plate for me, and one for you, too. We could eat with him."

"Well hang on now... I don't know about all this."

"You worried he might overpower us both? He can't be a hundred and twenty pounds. You can lock me in there with him and eat outside by yourself if you'd rather."

"Nah, let's both go on in. He's probably scared to death."

"He didn't sound all that scared in front of everyone."

Something about the way Elijah devoured the plate Lizzy had made for him, nearly chewing into his own fingers as he shoved the food into his mouth, hurt Luke deep. As bad as things had been on the island, he had never felt real hunger for any length of time. By the time they exhausted the stockpile of provisions his father had stored in the workshop under the house, the daily egg rations started coming to augment the always abundant clams, mullet, and crabs. Luke thought about what his life had been like at Elijah' age—playing on the high school golf team, raising goats, so many adventures with his dad. There were difficulties, as in every life, but never hunger. Never displacement from a home or a pseudo-war or death as a daily feature of life. He felt ashamed now, watching Elijah lick the plate clean of every faint indication of food, to have been so angry when he was first paraded to the front of the room just beyond the one where the three of them now sat.

"I already ate some before I came," Luke said. "Why don't you have mine as well."

When Elijah snatched the plate without hesitation, Luke saw only someone who hadn't had enough to eat. He no longer cared about the flags or the fires or why they kept showing up. He would leave those issues to his dad and Mr. Hayes. Elijah, though, once his belly was starting to fill, finally had something to say.

"I swear I didn't come here to hurt anybody."

"I believe you," Luke said.

"This was my only part of it. The flags and all."

"Your part of what?" Biscuit asked.

"You took the island away from us cause we lived on the other side of the channel. We worked the waters around it same as you. What right did you have?"

"Your part of what," Biscuit repeated, trying but failing to hide a voice frantic with fear. "It's not too late to calm things down, Elijah. To stop whatever this is. You just have to tell us what's happening."

"I said I didn't come to hurt anybody. And I ain't saying nothing else. Do whatever you want."

Elijah curled into a ball under the blanket, turned away from the other two men, and fell silent.

Expanded patrols continued throughout the night without incident. The new flags, the fires, and the defiance of the boy from Sumner made sleep impossible for Hayes. After a briefin g from Officer Biscuit on his interaction with Luke and Elijah, he walked the full length of State Road 24 from the town center to the channel, taking in the sounds of the evening and contemplating the best course of action. He worried that, even now, Elijah's failure to return home might be accelerating plans for an attack that his flagship and navy might otherwise deter. There in the narrow crease between the heavens and the Earth, insignificant and eternal at once, Hayes could feel the yoke of responsibility laboring his steps and disquieting his mind. The sight of the silver water in the channel, reflecting the splendor of a moon that would be full in two days' time, sent the mayor's thoughts riding seaward on the waves, wishing for anything but the haunting of these visions and the weight of indecision.

Against the backdrop of all that majesty, Hayes' reflection landed on a pedestrian memory. In a city council meeting from a few years back, longtime island resident Abe Belmont stood before the council to seek a variance to the town's development code. Mr. Abe was well-liked in the community, generous with his time and resources, and loved Cedar Key as much as anyone. His advanced age and a terminal neurological disorder meant time was drifting away to get his affairs in order for his three children. Part of his estate included two adjacent vacant city lots. Try as he might, Mr. Abe could not figure an equitable way to split his assets among the children without the two lots creating an imbalance. The development code called for a minimum buildable lot size of 10,000 square feet. Mr. Abe's two lots totaled 29,955 square feet. The variance he sought from the council on that day was to allow his two lots to be split into three separate buildable lots, one each for his three children. Two of the proposed three lots would meet the minimum lot size requirement, but the third would be just 45 square feet short of the required size—about the size of a large kitchen table.

In most other communities, a variance for such a paltry shortfall would almost certainly be approved. On Cedar Key, where every inch of land was precious, where out of town developers stood just beyond the Number Four Bridge with knives, waiting for a moment of weakness from the council so they could carve the island up for their own desires, 45 square feet may as well have been 45 miles. Despite the sympathetic figure of Mr. Abe, trembling but resolute in his petition to council members that were his friends and neighbors, and despite acquiescence from Worthman and Rosencrantz, his petition was denied in the same 3 to 2 vote that had sealed the fate of the Number Four Bridge. That kitchen table speck of land had haunted Hayes every day since the meeting.

When Mr. Abe died, Hayes of course attended the memorial service with the rest of the island. The disdain in the faces of his children when they caught the mayor's gaze had never stopped hurting. Here, beneath the probing inquisition of the gods as he walked back toward town, he could feel it still. He knew that giving in to his friend, even to such a trivial degree, would open the floodgates for others. In slow drips that built variance upon variance into a deluge, the character of the island would be washed away. The reproach from Mr. Abe's children, the sick feeling in his belly when the old man was moved to anger and then tears at the vote, these were the costs of leadership, and he would pay them again because the right answer then had been clear.

When it came to the boy from Sumner, to the flags and the fires, and whether or not a preemptive strike across the channel was required, there was no clarity to be had, even among the stars and the water.

At the Wabi-Sabi, Luke tossed in bed next to Kinsey, unable to shake the image from his head of Elijah licking the plate.

"You okay, honey?"

"Not really," Luke replied.

"Are you worried about what they'll do to him?"

Luke turned to face his girl. "I'm not worried about Mr. Hayes. But you should have seen how worked up everbody was. If Mr. Mark hadn't pulled his revolver, they might have carried him off to the nearest tree."

"Do you really think it would have gone that far?" Kinsey asked.

"Ten seconds before the shouting started... no, never. These are just regular people, not killers."

"Some of those regular people were on Shiloh Road, Luke."

"That was different," he replied, looking back toward the ceiling.

"Was it?"

"I know these people. They're good people."

"Good people do bad things all the time."

"Jesus, Kinsey, that's bleak."

"I'm sorry," she said, pulling Luke's face back toward her own. "I'm not trying to pass judgement. I've just seen what happens when people get whipped up into a frenzy."

"Mr. Hayes and Mr. Mark put everybody in line."

"I'm glad they were there," Kinsey said.

Luke kissed Kinsey on the forehead, then rolled over on his side and tried to will himself to sleep. Such an endeavor, of course, is futile, and shortly Luke was flat on his back, staring up into the dark, hyper aware of the sound and rhythm of his breathing. Kinsey laid her head on Luke's chest and ran her fingers across his belly. The mystic feminine premonition of all women on Earth overtook her.

"Whatever it is you're thinking about doing..."

"What?" Luke interrupted. "I'm just trying to get to sleep."

"Why don't you just go ahead and do it?"

"Honey, what are you talking about?"

Kinsey rolled her eyes and climbed out of the bed. On her way to the kitchen she said, "Give me a minute to fix some food for his trip."

So excited was he by his girl's willingness to be an accomplice in the plan he had not thought to formulate, Luke had no real strategy for how to deal with Officer Biscuit. As he crept quietly toward the front door of the City Hall building, a sack of smoked mullet and pears from Lizzy's yard under his arm, he could see through the glass door that Biscuit was fast asleep. Luke turned the doorknob so slowly he wasn't sure for some time if it was actually turning. Finally, he heard a gentle metal *click* and the freeing of the latch. He pushed on the door, gentle as a little bird, and stepped stealthily into the room. The wood floorboards of the 19th century building creaked like old bones under his feet.

"Careful, you'll wake up Biscuit," came a whispered voice behind his shoulder.

"Ahhh!" Luke screamed, reflexively and wild, as he leapt into the air, leaving his skin and soul in a puddle on the floor.

Biscuit fell backwards out of his chair, tried but failed to spring up to his feet, then scrambled to his knees, fumbling for his flashlight and shouting, 'Who's there?!"

Hayes clicked on his own light, a handheld spotlight whose rechargeable batteries were kept full by the small array of solar panels mounted atop the roof of his house on A Street. Instantly, the room was bright as day—Luke and Biscuit breathing hard as Hayes belly laughed, a sack of food for Elijah under his arm as well.

As the boy from Sumner paddled into the moonlight, passing Dog Island and turning at Scale Key toward home, the mayor put his arm around his best friend's son, expecting to think of some wisdom to impart. He had arrived at the right decision no faster than Luke, however, and managed only, "Best keep this between us."

"Yes sir, Mr. Hayes."

At last, the right words came to venerate the moment. "From now on, just Hayes is fine."

26

ALAS, POOR YORICK

News of Elijah's release was polarizing. Many of the islanders that had been at the little bridge in front of Fannies, or on Shiloh Road the following day, harbored personal animosity toward the Sumner Meades that made it hard to see the boy behind the name. After a few days, however, passions quieted and work continued to harden the island's defenses. In some measure to counteract the impression that he had been soft on the enemy, Hayes redoubled his efforts to complete and launch the navy. With Tabby always at his side, he worked from dawn to dark for days on end without rest, seldom stopping for breaks or even lunch.

Engineering setbacks besieged the Blue Lang's conversion from houseboat to flagship on a daily basis. The fiberglass hull made attaching the pontoon fighting platforms difficult, but the problem was eventually solved by Ike Osbron. In the old world, Ike worked at Cedar Key Hardware alongside Daniel Kiether and the buxom Miss Brenda, a distractingly attractive older lady who knew more about nuts and bolts than any man in town. Ike's workshop was the stuff of island lore, filled with drill presses, lathes, and a wide selection of specialty tools. His skill as a welder, though, was the first thing folks mentioned when he came up in conversation. For the flagship, Ike welded large metal pipes on each end of the pontoon platforms, onto which heavy lines could be attached and lashed to the superstructure of the houseboat. He also fabricated the brackets that would mount the various components of the wood gasifier to the aft deck, and the mounts for eight rooftop rifles.

All around the island, work progressed as though war was inevitable. Scuttlebutt about the formation of a Sumner army dominated the conversation of the day, though there existed no basis for such a claim beyond wild inferences about the meaning of the Obadiah flags. Thomas did his part, especially as it related to work on his houseboat, and donated his v-hull bay boat to the effort as well, but the mood of the Great Mobilization sat heavy on his heart. Missing was the island's spirit that had been on such comforting display during the reopening of the school, the prom for Annabelle and Cado, singing and dancing at Luke's shrimp fry in the park, or the bucket line that fought the great fire. The work on the navy was progressing, but with an automaton lifelessness whose byproduct, for Thomas at least, was a growing sadness.

There's a goat onstage!
Elijah has a dark secret,
and there's a dead lady on the shelf!
Tickets on sale now for Thomas Buck's,
"Trailer Park Elegy!"

Before the off-Broadway and regional productions of later plays that would bring Thomas some moderate fame as a playwright, this was the radio spot running multiple times a day on Gainesville's local NPR affiliate, advertising his second play. That the main character coincidentally shared a name with the boy from Sumner was responsible for the memories now filling his head. Though later plays would be met with wider acclaim and more financial success, the trailer park play, as he called it, was quietly his favorite story he had ever written, in any medium. In it, trailer park manager Elijah finds a box of ashes in the maintenance shed. The cremated woman had sat unclaimed on a shelf there for twenty years. Elijah becomes obsessed with putting on a citywide memorial service for the dead lady on the shelf. When his research about her reveals a reprehensible life of hatred, bigotry, and even animal abuse, his friends and colleagues urge Elijah to cancel the event, worrying about the effect on his reputation of celebrating a woman who was, by all accounts, truly awful. As a way, subconsciously, of reclaiming his own humanity, lost in a dark event that sent him into relative hiding in the trailer park, Elijah persists in his plan to tell the world about the forgotten lady.

Thomas had been hiding in plain sight, a little more each day since the dark event in Sumner that called his own humanity, and even the most basic perceptions he had about himself, into frequent question. Thinking now of Elijah in the trailer park, feeling a renewed kinship with him, pushed a little of the darkness away. Even these many years later, Thomas could still hear the voice of the NPR announcer in his head. It was so over-the-top melodramatic that it had jolted him in his seat the first time it came out of the speakers in the car radio. Over and over now, he heard it, and as he walked home after a day of work on the Blue Lang he found himself trying to make his voice match the memory in his head.

There's a goat onstage!
There's a goat onstage!
There's a goat onstage!

As he turned onto E Street, he had it fairly mastered, and his thoughts drifted to Mabel, the charismatic goat that had so shined in the play. He felt a twinge of sadness when he realized that no goats lived on the island. From that thought his mind darted to:

I mean, the play could be staged without a real goat. It'd be funny in its own way to have an actor play the goat.

By the time he reached his front porch, with no serious deliberation about it, Thomas had decided. There was a copy of the script on his bookshelf. There was a need on the island for nourishment that food could not provide. Despite, or maybe because of, the run up to a war that may or may not come, he would mount a production of the trailer park play. Most of the collective energy of the island had been required for mere survival in the first months after the flash. Now the growing threat from across the channel—real or imagined—demanded the lion share. A full belly and security are important components of life, but they do not, alone, constitute a life worth living. Thomas might not be able to deliver a live goat onstage, but it was within his power to make art in the face of turmoil.

November, tense and frantic with activity, began one moment and seemed to be gone the next. Most of the smaller boats of the navy were nearing completion, but the Blue Lang's conversion would take, by John Mitchell's figuring, at least two more weeks. Each day that passed without an attack produced conflicting sentiments among the islanders, the first being relief, the second a worry that their lack of preemptive action gave the enemy more time to build their strength. Even the Thanksgiving holiday was muted by the lingering unease caused by the flags and the fires. The more time they had to worry about what it had all meant, the more the fear grew within them. The two major engagements with the Sumner Meades had ended with crushing defeat for those across the channel, but without firing a shot they had executed a successful counterattack with bedsheets and markers.

The more the islanders feared the people from Sumner, the more they hated them, unwittingly continuing the cycle of conflict that has been the most prominent through-line of human history. The natural state of civilization, from the earliest Mesopotamian city-states, by any reasonable estimation, was war. The islanders had far fewer differences with the folks in Sumner than the Uruk Sumerians had with the Elamites or Akkadians, and yet, despite a deeply intertwined culture and separated by only a narrow channel, war seemed to be coming as inexorably as the tides.

In the old world, Minnie Allenby and Cathryn Stevens were partners in Seagull Realty. In the few years before the smokestacks fell, they branched out from island home sales and property management to real estate development, staking their combined fortunes on renovating a handful of the island's dilapidated historic commercial buildings. The Cedar Key Mercantile building was the crown jewel of the project. Utilizing much of the original structure and preserving its design elements, Minne and Cathryn brought the old two-story building back to life, creating three vacation rental units on the second floor and a combined general store and fresh fish market at street level.

The fish market was a tiny boutique operation compared to the old David fish house, but for the first time in the nearly three decades since the net ban, there was a convenient place to buy fresh fish, clams, and crabs in Cedar Key. Utilizing a modified net that was legal but considerably less effective than the gill nets that had been banned, Hayes began catching fresh mullet twice a week for his father Mark to smoke and his mother Bette to turn into her famous smoked mullet dip. Tourists and locals alike began frequenting the new fish market and it grew to sell a respectable amount of the David's catch. It wasn't enough money to support a full business, but the routine of catching fish again that would be sold on the island filled a spiritual hole in the heart of the Davids that clam farming success and affluence had been unable to effect.

The market and the mercantile were cleaned out within days of the flash across the bay, and the building sat mostly empty until Thomas received permission to use it for his new theater. A narrow hallway connected the small fish market to the large open area of the mercantile store. This configuration allowed for a stage and audience area in the storefront and a backstage area in the market. A hodgepodge of discarded and unused chairs were scavenged from around the island and arranged to create a thrust or three-quarter round stage. Thomas had fallen in love with the magic of live theater as a kid. At the first play he ever attended, when the house lights faded to black and he sat in a dark room full of people he mostly did not know, he had felt almost shaky with anticipation about what might happen next.

Shane Shamrock, a frequent theater collaborator with Thomas in adulthood, had said once in an interview that, "The great thing about a play, especially a new play, is that anything might happen."

Because the several mystic seconds before the lights came up were such an integral part of the theater experience for Thomas, it never occurred to him to stage his play without theater lighting. Until he could build a gasifier generator for the theater, his home would have to go without the solar panels and golf cart batteries that had provided him a modicum of modern conveniences. The Cedar Key School had a handful of unused basic stage lights in their auditorium, and Principal Mitchell had been glad to give them to the new theater.

The play could have been staged in the school's auditorium or at the town community center with less effort than converting the mercantile building, but such a decision would have made it feel like a one-time event. After cave drawings and mythmaking, live theater is among the oldest of human art forms, surviving pronouncements of its demise from one century to the next. Thomas knew that with a place for stories to be told, stories would continue to be written. The history of the island and the shared struggles of the human experience there would have a place for elucidation, for public examination. Such a hyperbolic description would warrant a side eye almost anywhere else, but not in the theater.

While continuing to work on the navy, Thomas began to view the production of the play as a subversion of the importance of the Great Mobilization. He was of two minds about it, trusting Hayes' desire to defend the island, while worrying about the implication of such a massive ramp up. He thought of the old saying about everything looking like a nail when the only tool you had was a hammer, concerned that having a navy would make everything look like a war. For this reason, he pressed to have the play ready for opening by the time the Blue Lang and the rest of the fleet was ready for its formal launch.

The off-Broadway productions of his plays had been mounted with only a month of rehearsals, but that was with professional New York actors. Surprisingly, a handful of islanders with some high school or community theater experience had shown up to audition for the play, but the lead role carried so much of the dialogue that he felt sure it could not be mastered in the allotted time. When *Trailer Park Elegy* was first staged in Gainesville, a hurricane began to bear down on the Florida peninsula in the penultimate week of the show's run. As the final week of shows was set to begin, the hurricane had turned such that it seemed certain to affect Gainesville in a serious way. There was time to safely stage one show in the final week, but the lead actor's job required him to leave the state to manage the company's emergency response from the safety of their Georgia office. Rather than cancelling the last show, Thomas stepped in to play the role he had written. With a single rehearsal, the show somehow went on. That experience, and more than a little hubris, led to his decision to play the role of Elijah himself.

With the windows open and crisp December air making the afternoon rehearsal in the mercantile a comfortable affair, Thomas gave notes to his actors.

"The good news is, we seem to almost have the words down. The bad news is that you have the great misfortune of having to be in the play with the guy who wrote the play and wants to hear every syllable that's in the script. So please, please study your scripts at home when you can. We can't dig deep into the characters until we know the script so well that their words are our own. There are some real moments starting to happen, though. When Sarah realizes why Elijah has to have the celebration of life for the lady on the shelf... despite all the horrible things he has learned about who she was... the terrible things she did... so much of Sarah's love for Elijah is conveyed in the tiny smile our lead actress has mastered so perfectly. It's hard for me to stay in character even because it just wrecks me. Outside the theater, Anna used to make your cappuccinos at the Prickly Pear. In here she gets to melt your face off with emotion. When Mario cracks open the beer and takes the long drink because he knows when the drink is over he's going to tell the story of the good woman he lost... everyone in the theater will feel the loss with him. When Sham confesses the crazy shit he knows to the goat, he's seeking absolution for all of our sins. What a thing. And when people realize it's Geoff McCloud in the goat costume, after how weird he's been about the chickens in the cemetery the past few months... the laughter is gonna knock the walls down. There are so many small moments that add up to a making a powerful story. We are making them together, friends."

Thomas knew he was being grandiose, but as he surveyed the faces in the room he knew his actors and crew were as caught up in it as himself. This was the reason why the play, why this play in particular, was necessary for the island. For his own path away from the memories on Shiloh Road. There had been scarce opportunity lately to be caught up in anything but boats, flags and fires. The close-knit community of eccentrics in the trailer park would fit in easily on the island.

So, too, would most of the people in Sumner.

27
— • —

THE FOG OF WAR

In the early morning of December 10th, a day before the scheduled opening of the first theatrical production on the island since the closing of The Pearl Theater in the 1930s, and a week before the day-long festival planned for the launching of the fleet, Suzy Coles walked out her front door on 8th Street on her way to volunteer at the school, a block away. Were it not for the mating pair of ospreys that swooped down into her field of view, then straight upward in aerobatic exuberance, she might not have seen it. One hundred and forty feet up, a thick black line was painted through the center of the faded red *Cedar Key* on the water tower. The letters scrawled above it would craze even the most temperate on the island. If the Obadiah flags were a provocation, the single word burning into Suzy's eyes was an incitement.

"*Sumner*, my ass," she said, turning away from the school and heading straight for City Hall.

Even as Cedar Key's southern horizon was still shifting from blue to blinding white to gray, that awful morning those many months before, the architecture of island life was being shaken at its foundation. Idle leisure would fade quickest. Hope and civility would go more slowly. Everywhere were reminders, subtle and overt, of how different the new world would be, despite most people's efforts not to see them, but the island's response to the graffiti on the water tower was a sign that few could overlook.

Within the half hour, it seemed as though everyone on the island was gathered at the base of the tower.

"Any real damage, John?"

"It doesn't look like it, Hayes. It had to have taken ten times the effort to climb up there and scribble that shit than it would have to take out the pumps or the interface to run them."

"I don't get it," Rolf said. "Why go through all this trouble and not hit our infrastructure when they had the opportunity to hurt us good."

Thomas suddenly felt like Slim Worthman on the wrong side of a heated issue, but he spoke up all the same. "Maybe they don't intend any actual harm."

Hayes' temper, already rising from the indignity of yet another infiltration of the island, turned toward his friend. Thomas steadied himself for a reprimand that did not come. Instead, the mayor turned away, and took in a long, slow breath. He walked to the metal ladder built alongside the tower, the same ladder the vandals had climbed in the night. He climbed up ten or so rungs until he could be seen by all assembled, wrapped a leg around for support and shouted.

"Can everybody hear me?"

"We can hear you," Lida Maria shouted back.

Hayes called out, "The people that climbed this tower will hear all of us soon."

Thundering cheers rang out. Angry cheers. A boiling of the collective blood.

"Effective immediately, next week's festival to launch the fleet is cancelled. Our celebration has been preempted. Every seaworthy boat is to be ready to weigh anchor at noon today, three hours from now."

Ten years before the Great Cedar Key Hurricane of 1896 that destroyed Atsena Otie, a steamship was built in Abbeville, Georgia for hauling lumber and cargo along the Suwannee River in Florida. Named The City of Hawkinsville, the 141-foot long by 30-foot wide two-deck paddle-wheeler had a flat bottom that allowed it to navigate a large section of the river, while being sturdy enough to handle the coastal waters around Cedar Key. For a decade, the City of Hawkinsville carried cedar trees from the river basin to Obadiah Meade's sawmill for milling into slats that would be shipped to a pencil factory on the East River in New York City.

The recent publication of Mark Twain's Huckleberry Finn had helped to romanticize the golden age of riverboating. On the Suwannee, an abundance of red cedar trees in the area and the timber boom of the 1880s created a heyday for steamships and steamship captains. They were the toast of the Suwannee and met with warm welcomes at ports from Branford to Fanning Springs. Even before the death knell of the great storm and the destruction of the sawmill, however, by the mid-1890s a decade of depleting the area of red cedars was drawing the lumber boom to a close. The mood on the river after the hurricane was subdued, but steamships continued to do their work.

By 1910, The City of Hawkinsville was hauling the components of a railroad that would put an end to the Suwannee's usefulness as a thoroughfare for commerce. Its captains during this time had none of the swashbuckling flare of their predecessors, when the river was still wild and vibrant. In the summer of 1922, Jeremiah Currie, the last captain of the Hawkinsville, knew the end was near, not just for his ship but for the legacy of life and work on the river that it had come to represent. After delivering a final load of dry goods to Cedar Key, Captain Currie spent a night in the Island Hotel, enjoyed four whiskeys in its Trident Lounge, then walked to the shore where Luke Buck would land his kayak of white shrimp more than a century later. Drunk enough for the kind of reflection that digs deep into a man, he stared across the placid bay, toward a southern horizon his great grandson would see exploding like a dying star, then closed his eyes and made peace with the end.

The next morning, Captain Currie steamed the City of Hawkinsville up the coast and back into the river, thirty winding miles to Old Town, and sank the no longer profitable ship in a deep stretch of water near the railroad trestle it had helped to construct.

There it continues to sit, remarkably intact in the tea-colored water.

Hayes David's flagship lacked the elegant lines and elaborate riggings of the HMS Victory. The original design of the 1968 Nautaline houseboat was blockish and unwieldy; with the additional fighting platforms, gun mounts, and industrial-sized gasifier on its aft deck, the USS Blue Lang cut an even less auspicious jib. There had been no time for a proper test voyage, and much of the interior command center was incomplete, but the motor reliably started and ran. Mr. Johan's gasifier design, on which the entire

Cedar Key fleet of boats would operate, was remarkably simple. Wood was burned in a firebox until it reached around 1,700 degrees Fahrenheit, whereupon its air supply would be restricted, creating flammable carbon monoxide that would then be cooled, ran through a filter, and pumped directly into a four-stroke outboard motor and an inverter generator supplying abundant electricity to the boat.

In the hours between the mayor's fiery address from the side of the water tower and the mustering of boats near the outside boat ramp, cold air from the mainland slowly blew in from the east. As it interacted with the warmer water in the back bayous and the bay, patchy fog began to develop. In dwindling visibility, the Cedar Key Navy assembled for the first time—twenty-one boats in all, ranging from little 16-foot skiffs to mid-size bay boats, to the hulking Blue Lang at the front of a rudimentary formation. Over the VHF radio, Hayes addressed the fleet for the first time.

"All hands, all hands, this is the Blue Lang... form up in your groups of three, and follow our lead. Abeam Scale Key, fan out to your assigned patrol areas—one group each to Live Oak Key, Gulf Hammock, Cedar Point, Candy Island, and Rattlesnake Key, and two groups with the flagship on the Number Four Channel. Cool and easy, men. You too, Cousin. Make your presence known and give hell to any vessel that's not one of ours."

There was a dichotomy to the scene unfolding in the Waccasassa Bay. A fleet of modern boats, something akin to an actual navy, was indeed moving through the water as a cohesive force, but the spectacle of the wood piled high onto each vessel, and the anachronism of the gasifiers, heightened the unreality of the affair.

On the Blue Lang, Luke, Rolf and Mr. Mark manned rifles on the second floor deck, while Thomas kept wood in the fire box and a general watch on the various systems of a boat he knew inside and out. Hayes steered the lumbering boat along at its top speed of eight knots. At the appointed position, the fleet broke formation and the faster vessels sped away to their assigned patrols. As the flagship and its convoy neared the Number Four channel where the bridge had been, a thick wall of white enveloped the six boats. In moments, they could not see one to the other, even just several feet apart.

"Hold your positions," Hayes announced over the radio.

Jud Bollins, captaining the repurposed stone crab boat Miss Jonya, called back, "Roger."

A smattering of other acknowledgements came across the radio and the convoy began to drop their anchors. Rolf and Thomas worked together to lower the huge bow anchor of the Blue Lang. As they worked, Thomas heard a faint hissing from the stern of the boat, almost imperceptible at first but building as the sounds of the falling anchor faded.

Hayes asked, "You hear that too, Thomas?"

"I'm on it," He replied.

Skirting nimbly along the narrow side walkway, Thomas reached the stern deck, turned toward the sound, then lost his connection with the physical world. In an instant, the rear third of the Blue Lang lay in pieces scattered across the channel and onto the decks of nearby vessels. Water rushed into what had been the living room of the houseboat, submerging the tongue-and-grove wood panel walls Thomas had spent so many hours staining by hand. The heavy craft listed hard to its starboard side, then back to port, slinging Rolf and Mr. Mark into the water, dazed but otherwise unharmed. Luke was thrown hard against the metal railing midship, absorbing the blow with the resiliency of youth. Hayes held firm to the wheel during the initial blast, but was now stumbling across the outside deck calling out for his crew.

"I'm okay," Luke reported.

"Down here!" Hayes' father shouted.

Hayes saw the outline of the two men in the water, but the features of their faces blurred into the heavy fog and smoke from the fire now consuming the walls of his flagship. He had been a captain of boats since he was fourteen years old, and this experience was misinforming his brain, racing even now for a way to save his vessel.

"Mr. Hayes," Luke shouted. "Where's my dad?"

The question shook him into the reality of the moment.

Hayes called over the VHF, "Mayday mayday mayday, Blue Lang abandoning ship. All crew accounted for except Thomas. Repeat, Thomas is missing in the water. All hands on the search."

Luke and Hayes leapt together into the fog, the cool water in the channel hitting them like an electric shock.

"Dad! Dad!"

"Thomas!"

Voices from nearby boats called out for the missing man, while the crew of the Blue Lang swam from the deeper water of the channel toward the shore. In a few dozen yards, they reached the shallows that run along both sides of the channel. Luke was wild with motion, running against the waist deep water, calling through tears for his father and screaming at the others, "Find him, find him... help me, please... goddamn it, help me!"

As he pushed against the water and panic, Luke's thoughts disconnected from the events around him, replaying instead a scene from the pool at the Gainesville Country Club. He was eleven and swimming with his father on a cloudless Monday afternoon. The club was closed on Mondays but the Buck men often snuck in to have the pool to themselves. As Luke climbed the ladder from the water, heading for another try on the diving board at mastering the *flying squirrel* that was his dad's signature dive—a leap above the water with arms reaching back to grab both ankles in a preposterous arch—he had slipped and fallen hard onto the concrete pool deck, dislocating his shoulder in horrific fashion.

There had been no pain in his life, before or after, to compare with the searing hurt now shooting down his arms and legs. Luke was jolted into shock, crying out, "Help me, help me, dad!" Thomas leapt from water, scooping up his boy and sprinting for the parking lot.

"It's okay, son. I'm here."

The pain grew so intense that Luke passed out on the race to the hospital. When he awoke along the way, through some mystery of human physiology Thomas did not understand, a calm had enveloped the boy, who grabbed his father's hand and said with an eerie lucidity, "I know you'll take care of me," before slipping back to sleep.

When the boy in the memory closed his eyes again, Luke reopened his perception to the yelling voices and the fog consuming the light around him in the water.

"It's okay, son. I'm here."

And there his father was, blood-soaked but steady, his face charred black as the day the plastic nipple failed on the Judith Jane and the great experiment of humanity failed around the world.

The Blue Lang was lost.

In the end, no one from Sumner had seen the dazzling lights and imposing armament of the island's flagship. They had not seen its gasifier exploding when a pinhole breach in its chamber sent pressurized gases into the open flames of the firebox. They had seen no boats at all. The opaque wall of fog between Sumner and the bay sent the twenty-boat Schrödinger's navy limping back to the island.

The flags and the fires, Elijah's defiance before the council—these had proven more petulance than portent; no attack ever came. The watches and patrols would continue as a new world necessity, but the Sumner War, such that it had ever been, was over.

On the deck of the Miss Jonya, Hayes stared into the mist, a forlorn captain on another captain's boat. His best friend stepped to his side, looking worse-off than he was.

"Sorry about your boat, Thomas."

"Remember the night we first pulled it out of the mud and you were so shitty about it?"

"I remember you forgot to charge the flashlight."

Hayes and Thomas shared a quiet laugh together as the Miss Jonya passed Dog Island and the outside boat ramp appeared in the distance.

"What do we do now, Thomas?"

"We need to get the big Christmas tree up in the park. I'm not sure how we'll do it without a crane... but we'll figure it out."

"Yeah," the mayor replied. "We should've had it up the day after Thanksgiving. I just got caught up in some stuff."

Thomas nodded. "We all did. You'll have to suspend disbelief a little on why the lead actor is all beat to hell, but I hear they got a play opening tonight."

"You gonna go?" asked the mayor with grin.

"Yeah... I thought I might."

Christmas in the park was beautiful as it had ever been, the frivolity of electric lights on the enormous tree counted as waste by no one on the island. They drank hot cider made from pears whose trees had weathered the terrible hurricane, even when the house ten feet away had been torn apart and swallowed by the surging waters.

They raised their glasses to the Gulf—the great provider and the angry god—and to Folksy and TJ and Jonah, to the clam boat captains and crews that sailed into the long gray night, to the dead on Shiloh Road, to Annie, to departed friends and even to the awful yankee lady—a collective toast for the old world lost and the new one unfolding before them, for an island they belonged to, and even, with quiet trepidation, for a bridge that would one day cross the Number Four Channel again.

— · —

EPILOGUE

On the 15th of February in the second year of the new world, a battered Piper Archer burst through low-hanging clouds, sputtering and wild, missing the water tower by a nose hair and plunging, more or less uncontrolled, into the Daughtry Bayou a hundred yards short and wide of the George T. Lewis Airport runway.

An old man emerged from the wreckage, laughing, and began the short swim for home.

Acknowledgements

My heartfelt thanks to the people of Cedar Key, whose influence can be seen throughout the characters in this book, specifically Heath, Mike, and Beth Davis, Ida Marie Johnston, Sue Colson, Ralph and Jennifer Alfonso, Stephanie May, Tara Judd, Tabitha Lauer, Jeff McLeod, Glenda Richburg, Nancy Sera, Anthony Hinkle, Edwin Jenkins, Becky and BJ Johnston, the Sharps, the Allens, the Stephensons, the Solanos, the Mc-Cains, the Schleedes, the Fradellas, the Gills, the Beckhams, the Custers, the Lindhouts, the Winebrenners, and the crews at Steamers, 2nd Street Cafe, Annie's, and the Island Hotel/Neptune Lounge.

Special thanks to Tonya Fradella for her willingness to read every new page with enthusiasm and encouragement.

My 11th and 12th grade English teacher, Iris Cole, told me I would never amount to anything as a writer and I should find something else to do with my life. When my first play premiered in New York City, I tried to find her but she had done the incredibly ungracious thing of dying before I could prove her wrong. She was aristocratic, elegant, and mean. I loved her. Rest easy, Mrs. Cole.

Without G.M. Palmer, who gave me a copy of Kurt Vonnegut's *Cat's Cradle* in high school, my life as a writer might never have materialized. Without his friendship and sharp editorial eye, this book would never have been finished. Thanks, brother.